Newton Country Day School
Prize for National Honor Society
June 2018

Charlotte Moynihan

Buffalo
Spirits

ELIZABETH

BLACK

Buffalo
Spirits

STORY LINE PRESS

2004

Published by
STORY LINE PRESS
Three Oaks Farm, PO Box 1240
Ashland, OR 97520-0055
www.storylinepress.com

Interior design and photograph by Claudia Carlson
Buffalo art by Stan Herd
Cover graphics by Tim Gillesse
Cover design by Sharon McCann

This book was set in Bembo.

Library of Congress Cataloging-in-Publication Data
Black, Elizabeth, 1946–
Buffalo spirits / Elizabeth Black.
p. cm.
ISBN 1-58654-032-7
1. Women journalists--Fiction. 2. Dodge City (Kan.)--Fiction. 3.
Loss (Psychology)--Fiction. 4. Great Plains--Fiction. I. Title.
PS3602.L27 B84 2003
813'.6--dc22
2003017490

*In memory of
my mother's gardens of green
and my father's fields of gold.*

ACKNOWLEDGMENTS

This book is a work of fiction, but it relied heavily on inspiration from family and friends. I wish to thank my parents—who live forever in my memory—for their love, wisdom and courage. In many ways, this book is homage to them. Add to that, my love and gratitude to my sister and four brothers—whose stories I sometimes borrowed and modified to fit the purposes of this novel. For all the family and friends I grew up with, we didn't know it then, but *place*—our wonderful little town and expanse of prairie—played an important role in who we would become.

My thanks to Lynne Rabinoff for her encouragement and unflagging belief in this project. My appreciation to the William Faulkner Creative Writing Competition for being the first to recognize the promise of *Buffalo Spirits* when they named the book a finalist in their 2002 novel category. And special thanks to Robert McDowell and staff at Story Line Press for picking *Buffalo Spirits* out of many fine manuscripts to receive the 2002 Three Oaks Fiction Award and then see to its publication. Their commitment to excellent poetry and fiction is commendable in an age when commercialism has invaded and diluted literary excellence.

Dozens of other writers whose work and research added to my understanding of the issues facing the Great Plains are acknowledged in further reading in the back of this book.

But most of all, I wish to thank my husband Edwin, a writer of great talent and breadth, who took time out from two of his own books, to read the manuscript in its earliest stages and encourage me to persevere. And special thanks to my daughter, Rachel, whose voice and songwriting continually inspires me. Thanks to both Edwin and Rachel for tolerating and encouraging my absences as I hit the road on solitary trips to spend time in the places so important to the story of *Buffalo Spirits*.

Last but not least, my gratitude to the fictional characters in the novel who, once created, took on a life of their own and led me through an adventure of a lifetime.

Elizabeth Black

CONTENTS

PART ONE

Going Home, 1985

She calls me Gentle Wind. I call her Sunflower.
These are our names for each other, and we speak in a language
that is neither hers nor mine. It is the language of the heart.
I call her Sunflower because when she walks the sunflowers turn
their heads to greet her. She calls me Gentle Wind because
when she feels a soft breeze lift her golden hair
she knows that I walk beside her.

1

The Way Home

GOING HOME IS BETTER than being home.

Something about traversing the ground—physically counting off the miles that lay between Chicago and Western Kansas—was crucial to the process of going home. I was not prepared to be home unless I had traveled the distance, literally. Preferably, on tracks of steel going in a straight line. As the train moved west, the tension spooled out of my body. My mind became blank, cleansed of the details of urban survival and the demands of journalistic ambition. A clock slowly unticking. A wheel slowly unturning. Ready to be at peace on the Great Plains where hours move more slowly than any other place on earth.

In my early days in Chicago, my favorite method of getting home was a train called the Kansas City Chief. It started in Chicago, chugging noisily through old stockyards, past oil refineries, smelly factories and crumbling warehouses, then rudely skirted the dirty backyards of neighborhoods, passing under and through graffiti-smeared train trestles. The Chief then whistled into the Illinois countryside passing through endless cornfields and nondescript small towns. By evening, the train was racing through Iowa, then crossing into Missouri, a state I always slept straight through. Well past midnight, the Chief would pull into Kansas City. I would blink in half wakefulness as unwelcome light and people flowed in and out of the train. We would be stuck for an eternity in the under-roof station in Kansas City assaulted by the glare of artificial light until finally, mercifully, the train would lunge into motion and pass into the cool blinking night of Eastern Kansas countryside, its green beauty and gentle hills hidden by darkness. Then through the last hours of the night until dawn, the mournful train whistle marked small town after small town on the Kansas prairie. By dawn we were lost on the flattest plain in the country, the train finding its way from one outcropping of grain elevators—not really towns—to another, stopping briefly for mailbags but few passengers.

Around breakfast time, when the California-bound passengers were cranky and beginning to demand coffee, we would lurch into Dodge City, slowing past the infamous "Front Street" with its once-wild Long Branch Saloon. The Chief would stop for an instant, hardly enough time for me to drag off my one overpacked suitcase.

By my second or third year in Chicago, I had discovered that for a few dollars more I could reserve a sleeper on the Kansas City Chief and my trips home took on an indulgent air of luxury. Shortly after boarding, I would show up at the dining car for a steak dinner. In the 1970s, there was still tablecloth service with waiters in tuxedo-like uniforms. You were formally seated at tables for six in the order in which you arrived, so dinner became a polite social occasion with random strangers. The fixed-price five-course meal often lasted a leisurely two hours. During these meals I met California's first woman State Supreme Court judge, a novelist whose books would later appear on the bestseller lists and an assortment of other interesting characters, all of whom shared a common bond—fear of flying. Then I "retired" to my berth, secured the pull-down bed, and changed into pajamas.

There is no slumber as good as that in a sleeping compartment of a train. Like being in a woman's womb as she moves about her life-business, you are happily rocked in the fluid—tightly, warmly bound within a secure environment, sounds muffled and undemanding.

The conductor, the same aging, cheerful black man always on duty, knowing I slept soundly on the Kansas City Chief, would wake me an hour out of Hutchinson. That gave me thirty minutes to dress, gather my things, and prepare to disembark. But most of the time, I dozed off again, unwilling to be born. Then I would suddenly hear him call out "Dodge City," and I'd have to get off in my pajamas, clutching a coat around my braless torso, lugging my barely-latched suitcase off the train, rumpled, and totally unprepared for sunlight and wind, a preemie, dispelled harshly before I was ready. I'd barely greet my parents before rushing into the station ladies' room to finish dressing.

Mom would assure me when I re-emerged dressed and combed that nobody had noticed. It was our ritual. Of course no one noticed. No one was ever there. I was always the only one getting off—or on—at that stop. Everyone drives in Kansas. No one takes a train.

I'd climb into the back seat of the Oldsmobile, and Dad would swing out onto the nearly empty highway that passed by Front Street. Mom would be excited, almost like a small child, with words tumbling out in happy profusion. About the time we reached the outskirts of Dodge, she would suddenly say, "Becky, are you hungry." Without waiting for a reply, my father would turn into a roadside cafe.

Two eggs over easy. Hold the bacon.

The cafes were nearly always empty except for one or two tablefuls of retired farmers who had the time to jaw over their coffee because now it was their sons out at dawn. Though dressed for rugged work, there would be none for them. They had earned the uneasy luxury of taking their time getting out to the field to check on what was going on without them. So they tarried over long, slow discussions about the price of wheat, politics and the way it used to be and should be again.

During the hour and a half drive beyond Dodge, while Mom talked and Dad seemed lost in thought, I began to notice something: more and more trailer homes were sprouting up on farmyards. Once trailers functioned to house a hired hand or a son and daughter-in-law who wanted some privacy away from the main farmhouse. But now, often as not, the trailer home became the main farmhouse with the former home standing empty and in disrepair. It was as if the farmer had conceded that it was no longer worth keeping up the dwelling. Furthermore, the mobile home—trailer dwellers prefer the term "mobile home"—could be moved out on a moment's notice, signaling, it seemed to me, that farmers all over the Plains were admitting imminent defeat, knowing their final days on the land were coming to an end. Better to be prepared for flight than fight a battle that could not be won. Each visit, I saw more and more trailers. Little did I know my parents were nearing the day when they would move their possessions into a mobile home parked on the edges of their former existence. I could not have borne it if I had known.

My last visit to Western Kansas before we lost the farm had been a glorious golden November week when Thanksgiving came in the midst of a burst of sunny warmth, as if the prairie didn't know winter was coming. Most of the muted greens of summer had become muted browns. The fields of wheat stubble were still yellow-gold, dotted with straw bales standing in the field. Touches of green struggled to remain. Even in winter, the buffalo grass never quite loses its gray-green sheen, and the winter wheat planted in September was now short, thick, and as kelly green as a summertime city lawn. I was home. Thomas was home. And a plump pheasant rooster was roasting in Mom's oven. Our legendary buffalo herd grazed in the pasture. The horses were restless and excited, sensing they would be ridden hard by Thomas, then groomed and fussed over, as it had been in the days before he left them.

Mom was rushing around absentmindedly, trying to manage every detail of her cooking while talking nonstop. She was not used to cooking large meals since all six of her children had grown up and scattered to the farthest corners of the country.

I would give anything to have one more meal with my parents on the farm and then go for a long walk along the ridge looking for arrowheads. I would give anything to sit under the cottonwoods in the U-bend of the creek and write poetry.

I would be content just to know that the creek and the cottonwoods were still there.

During my shamefully ambitious thirties, when I thought time was too precious to waste crossing the distance, I would fly in to Wichita "International" airport, and drive the last two hundred miles in a rental car, cruising at 80 mph on Highway 50, resenting the little towns with their 25 mph speed limits. But always, at the point that the prairie became flat, totally flat, I'd slow down and the tension would travel out of my neck into my fingertips and then dissipate into the stale, nicotine air of the rental car. That's when I would notice the rental car stench and realize that clear air was waiting to fill my lungs. I'd roll down the window so I could smell the earth and draw a deep, deep breath. And I would remember that going home was as important as being home.

THIS TIME I'M DRIVING HOME, oh, not all the way. I can't bear driving through Illinois, Iowa and Missouri. So I flew into Kansas City, and rented a car so that I could at least drive the entire diagonal length of

Kansas, from the very top corner, to the very bottom. I need the time alone on the road.

I am about to turn forty. A grown-up Rebecca returning to Kansas.

My name is Rebecca, Becky to my family. Becca to my Chicago friends.

There is a ritual to this drive. I take Interstate 35 and pass as quickly as I can through the outer ring of the suburbs of Kansas City—which look just like the suburbs of every other American city. Once I'm well into the countryside, I begin looking for the Lebo Junction exit. It's easy to miss. There I stop for a meal if I'm hungry, or a cup of coffee if I'm not. Lebo Junction is an old-time truck stop—the kind where truckers get preferential seating and free phones, where the waitresses have gravelly voices and know all their customers' names and call even the crustiest trucker "honey." The Lebo truckstop store sells everything from toilet paper to TV sets to western-cut leather jackets. I once bought Bill, my photographer friend and sometimes fiancé, a tan suede western blazer here. He wears it every day. We've never married. One of us is always getting shipped out to some foreign assignment, and then when we're both in Chicago for any length of time we get cold feet. Now we've dropped the fiancé business and think of ourselves as friends for lack of a better word. Both our relationship and his Lebo Junction jacket are worn and patched, yet still comfortable.

So don't feel sorry for me. World-trotting journalist. On the road alone. Rootless, childless. Facing forty.

I also stop in Lebo Junction in honor of a Christmas past, when I was desperately trying to get home in time for our family dinner. A blizzard in Chicago had delayed my flight. The plane was headed for Wichita but forced to land in Kansas City because the Wichita airport was closed and Kansas City was about to shut down as well, due to a blinding fog which had settled over the entire Great Plains. I grabbed the last rental car left at Avis and set out for Western Kansas, knowing I would never make supper let alone dinner. It was already eleven o'clock in the morning and I was eight to ten hours away—with the threat of a blizzard moving in.

I was desperately hungry. Nothing had been open in the airport. I stopped at exit after exit. It was Christmas morning and even the three McDonald's along the way were closed. The fog was so heavy I could barely see two car lengths in front of me. There was no one on the road. It was eerie driving down an empty Interstate. Finally, I saw a highway patrol car on the side of the road. I stopped and asked the officer where I could find a bite to eat.

"Go back seven miles to Lebo Junction. They never close."

"I got off at Lebo. There was nothing there," I countered.

"Trust me. There is a truck stop and it never closes. You just didn't see it in the fog. Go to the right after exiting. I guarantee it's there."

So I turned around and took the exit again. I was already in some sort of parking lot before I could make out the outlines of a building. I was astounded to see maybe thirty trucks and twice that many cars neatly parked in rows. I'd been right here not twenty minutes ago and had seen nothing.

When I entered the restaurant, I was greeted by light and music and noise, a huge Christmas tree near the door, and tables and tables of families. The restaurant was serving turkey and dressing, mashed potatoes and green beans dripping in butter, cranberry sauce and sweet potatoes—all the traditional fare of a country Christmas dinner. People were dressed up. Children were running about. It seemed that everyone in this quadrant of Kansas was in this room having a communal Christmas dinner.

Feeling as if I'd stumbled into a Twilight Zone episode, I ordered the Christmas feast. Actually, it was the only choice on the menu—and I was hungry.

A few moments later, as I nursed a cup of coffee, the waitress came over, bent down speaking low. "Honey, the table over there—the Olson family—would like you to join them. They asked me to come over and talk to you."

Poor Rebecca. Alone in Kansas on Christmas Day.

I thought for an instant about how I had planned to bolt my food in ten minutes and get back on the road. But with an edgy mix of gratefulness and embarrassment, I accepted their offer—what else could one do under the circumstances?

I picked up my coffee cup and introduced myself while they moved chairs making room for me. The Olsons were a fourth-generation ranch family in the Flint Hills. They lifted their cups of hot spiced apple cider to my making it home in time for the day after Christmas. One son-in-law hailed from Dodge City and we compared old dust storm stories. After pecan pie, the Olson family began exchanging gifts. Being so large a clan, they had taken to drawing numbers, a tradition my own huge extended family followed as well. I began to excuse myself with apologies about getting on the road, when the old man of the clan ordered me to sit back down. One of the children, giggling, brought me a hastily-wrapped package. Someone had sneaked out into the restaurant's adjacent store. I unwrapped my gift, one I will treasure forever, a puzzle of an illustrated map of Kansas. I inspected it with unabashed excitement. A dotted line traced the old Santa Fe Trail. Down in my part of the state, along the southern cutoff of the Santa Fe Trail, little icons marked Wagonbed Springs, the Cimarron National Grasslands, and the Dalton Gang Hideout near Meade. A peace pipe drawing located Medicine Lodge, where the infamous treaty was forged which, unbeknownst to the Indian chiefs who planted their reluctant signatures, virtually handed over the Plains Indians' last hunting grounds to the white invaders and banished them forever to the reservation.

Little has changed in Lebo Junction during the last ten years.

Today I'm not hungry so I order coffee and, of course, pecan pie. I look around for the Olsons—I always do, just in case—and, on the way out, I leave a business card with the owner's wife who has been manning the cash register for as long as I've been stopping here. I ask her to give the card to Mr. or Mrs. Olson next time they come in. On the back I have scrawled, *I never celebrate Christmas without thinking of you. Love, Rebecca.*

"Old Man Olson passed on last spring," I'm informed. "And Mrs. Olson has Alzheimer's, poor thing, doesn't even recognize her own kids. But I'll give this to the next Olson to come in. Lord knows there's enough of 'em, sweetie."

Shortly after Lebo Junction, I leave the Interstate for Highway 50 and enter one of the last pristine wonders of the world, the Flint Hills. As far as the eye can see, soft, rolling hills and deep valleys are carpeted by tall grass bending and swaying in a unison chorus directed by the wind. There is little traffic on the road and almost no sign of human habitation or manipulation except for an occasional windmill beside a pond of pooling water in a deep valley, or a graying wood corral near the side of the road. Sparse numbers of cattle graze the rolling hills, oblivious to the road's encroachment upon their lazy existence. They are in no hurry. There is endless grass.

I've seen these hills in all seasons. In spring, the grass is hazy apple green with a profusion of wildflower pastels visible only upon a closer look. Now it's the middle of summer, so the bluestem grass has a slight golden aura. In fall it will turn a brilliant red-bronze. The color of the tall grass prairie varies with the amount of rainfall as well as the seasons. But always it is beautiful beyond description. A view from the air is even more stunning. The hills are soft and rounded so smoothly it looks less like the planet Earth than some exotic planet composed of a soft, springy, dough-like material. (I know what it looks like from the air because once I brought Bill along on one of these drives, and he went nuts with the views, having me stop the car every few yards so he could take photographs. When he ran out of film we backtracked to Emporia to buy more. Then when we stopped for gas in Strong City, he walked into the bar next door and somehow found a farmer with a small plane to take him up to shoot aerial views. Eventually, Bill published the photos in a book. He never made it to Western Kansas with me. He just couldn't leave the Flint Hills.)

NOW I TURN OFF ONTO State Road 150, a shortcut that heads straight west. It's little more than a narrow strip of asphalt laid over the hills, rising and dropping sharply like a roller coaster. I can't resist driving fast, making it as physically exhilarating as it is visually. When I get around to writing a book about the most beautiful roads in the world, this will be one of them. I daydream about building a cabin out here somewhere and just staying forever. Bill said the same thing that trip when I left him here. He said that one day when he had the money saved he was going to buy a ranch here and never leave. I told him if he did that I'd marry him immediately, despite my better judgment. He hasn't done it yet. Bill doesn't know how to save money.

The Flint Hills soon give way to flat farmland interspersed with small meandering streams. Here in the center of the state where rainfall is adequate and sometimes bountiful, all the land is tilled and sectioned off into neat squares of healthy green, with hedgerows of cedars everywhere emphasizing the squareness. Farmhouses—most of them two-story, frame Victorians surrounded by mature trees—possess a look of permanence. This is where my mother grew up, hence I have uncles and aunts and cousins in this part of the state, most of them with thriving dairy farms and Victorian parlors closed off by glass doors.

I should stop at my grandparents' graves, just two miles off the road.

But I don't stop. I want to get to Western Kansas before nightfall. Even though my parents are no longer there. Even though our farm is no longer there.

I'm about to turn forty. And I must get home.

The highway now joins the Arkansas River at Great Bend, so named because the river indeed makes a huge bend here. Everywhere, there are black, rooster-like oil wells pumping, sometimes in clusters. These black mechanical birds peck at the earth, bobbing up and down to the rhythm of the oil they pull from its depths.

From Great Bend, the road slants south and west following alongside the Arkansas River, pronounced, by the way, not Arkan*saw* like the state Arkansas, but like Noah's Ark plus Kansas. *Ark Kansas.* We Kansans are offended by any other pronunciation.

A few miles outside of Great Bend, I sometimes stop at Pawnee Rock—*but not today, I must get home*—where a tiny town clusters at the base of a huge rocky shaft that enigmatically juts out of the Plains. Usually, I climb to the top of the rock and gaze in all directions, remembering the thrill of childhood visits here and the story my father would always tell. Colonel Dodge was traveling from Fort Larned back to Fort Dodge one day in 1871 when he found himself in the middle of a huge herd of buffalo. Wondering how large the herd was and what direction he might ride to avoid them, the colonel climbed to the top of Pawnee Rock. To the horizon in all directions, as far as he could see—at least twenty-five miles wide, my father would guess—Colonel Dodge saw a solid brown mass of buffalo slowly lumbering north. The colonel was stuck there five days waiting for the herd to pass before he could travel on to Fort Dodge. Within ten years, this great southern herd, estimated at about twelve million strong in 1870, would be reduced to one dazed old bull and a few bawling, motherless calves.

Back on the road following the southwest path of the Arkansas River, I suddenly come over the crest of a hill and see in the river valley below the legendary Dodge City. My birthplace. To the left, a large smelly feedlot, packed brown with thousands of fattening cattle covers an entire hillside. Dodge is still an endpoint cattle town. They just aren't driven up the trail from Texas anymore. Slaughterhouses, which locals prefer to call *packing*houses, remain a major industry here. And this massive feedlot on the edge of town was one of the first enterprises to apply assembly-line techniques to beef production. Breeders sell or consign their range-fed cattle to such feedlots where the animals are packed into pens and fed grain around the clock under glaring lights that obliterate the night and confuse their eating patterns. Hormone additives in the feed help the cattle fatten more quickly. With little room or reason for movement, the animals expend minimal energy and gain as much as a hundred pounds, most of it fat, in just a few weeks. That increases the sale price, which is based on weight. The beef people have convinced consumers that more *marbling*—the fancy name for interspersed fat— means better flavor. To the beef industry, more marbling means higher profits. For the consumer it means more heart disease.

Opposite the feedlot, mounted horsemen cut from rusting steel stand silhouetted against the sky, as if wary of approaching Dodge City. But when travelers stop to admire this striking sculpture, they are assailed by a smell so repulsive, it sends them hurrying back into their cars. The amount of urine and manure produced by such a feedlot is staggering. The muck builds up in the pens and invariably seeps down the slope towards the river, despite mandated holding ponds below and bulldozed waste mounds inside the pens, which are periodically removed. Fortunately, since the wind blows mostly out of the west, the city is usually spared the feedlot's stench.

I leave the feedlot and the rusting cowboys behind as I descend into this historic valley. While the old buildings in many prairie towns have been replaced by nondescript, utilitarian steel or cinderblock structures, Dodge City remains filled with decades-old, sandy-red brick houses shaded by large trees, as well as a small central downtown area of two-story brick and stone structures. Built to stay. Solid. That's Dodge City. But it wasn't always solid. And still isn't—entirely. Another part of Dodge has plenty of seedy bars to prove the town is still rough around the edges.

I usually stop at Front Street for a cherry coke at the Long Branch, no longer a saloon but a family tourist attraction. But not today. I want to get home by nightfall. If you come at the right time, you're treated to a noisy, messily choreographed gunfight, with young cowboys leaping and rolling off roofs and falling dead in the street. Today it's hot and lazy, and I see neither tourists nor gunfighters. But there are some old bowlegged cowboys on the street but they're not part of any show. Just old retired guys with big ears holding up their cowboy hats. What is it about old men? Do their ears grow bigger or do their heads shrink to make their ears seem bigger?

My father never wore a cowboy hat. He was a farmer through and through.

I may have been born here, but I am still ninety miles from home. I pass the red brick hospital and cross the bridge over the Arkansas. Somewhere just on the west edge of Dodge City I pass an invisible but powerful line—the one-hundredth meridian. Just an innocent line on the globe—little did the cartographers know they had demarcated the line of no return. Some say the Great Plains begins at the one hundredth meridian. It is at that point that the rainfall generally measures less than twenty inches a year—there isn't much that will grow on so little rainfall. And for that reason, when agriculture first came to the Great Plains, banks would not lend money to farmers west of the one-hundredth meridian nor would insurance companies insure crops or property. If you strayed over that line, you were beyond the help of man and sometimes God.

Fifteen miles outside of Dodge, still heading south and west, it suddenly becomes amazingly flat.

I always forget how flat it is.

Western Kansas is the flattest spot on earth. It's so flat that you don't need Galileo to tell you that the earth is round. You can actually see the horizon bending down out of view in all directions. As a child, I assumed that if a hill dared raise its head, a tornado would quickly flatten it. Because of this flatness, land takes up very little of your view. The sky becomes everything. It is your scenery. It is your entertainment. Rainbows arc across the whole sky, sunsets paint their colors from horizon to horizon. Clouds crowd the sky with shapes that conjure up epic stories for daydreamers on long, lazy afternoons.

Then every evening the thunderheads roll in, angry clouds of enormous towering proportions. When night has fallen, the shows begin.

Lightning rips across the sky in patterns so intricate and spontaneous, you never tire of watching. But rarely do these braggart clouds give out any rain, merely teasing, teasing, teasing the parched land with dazzling devilish glee.

During the early afternoons before the clouds move in, the sky is criss-crossed with the white contrails of jets traversing between New York and Los Angeles. As a little girl I spun elaborate daydreams about the people in those airplanes. As an adult whose work often placed me in those very same air lanes between the coasts, I reversed the spectacle, peering out the window down at the landscape below. Shortly after the pilot would announce we were over Dodge City, I would begin scanning for the Cimarron River. Then the North Fork of the Cimarron, and by finding the place where the Sand Arroyo joins the North Fork, I could actually pinpoint our farm.

For other passengers there was nothing to see—that is, until someone invented circular irrigation. My two bachelor uncles were some of the first farmers to test out these contraptions, huge sprinklers on wheels that followed a slow path, often measuring as much as a mile in diameter, employing water pressure to inch them along. These giant sprinklers were a marvel of engineering, conservation and practicality. Soon nearly all the wheat and milo fields in our area became circular. At first, airline passengers marveled at the crazy round quilt shapes. In the early days, I felt it necessary to explain the circles to my seatmates, whether or not they were interested. Now everyone knows. Sometimes the pilots even explain the patterns as part of their in-flight banter.

In my skywatching youth, between the orderly jet trails of commercial flights, were nonsensical spiraling exhaust trails excreted by hot shot pilots from Air Force bases in Colorado and Utah who played crazy, daredevil games in our skies. They regularly broke the sound barrier, rattling our windows and nerves, with not a thought or backward glance.

It was only fitting that our devils also descended out of those skies: predator tornadoes twisting down without warning to grab some prey, wreak some sadistic havoc, then withdraw anonymously into clouds as if nothing had happened. No remorse, no explanation. We knew they were lurking when clouds turned greenish. Our fathers could predict their approach most of the time. You aren't even surprised—well, in fact, secretly delighted—when a funnel suddenly pokes out and heads for the ground. Touchdown. Now run.

You can learn to read the clouds, but you can't predict the path of a tornado. It will turn and go another direction. It will double back. It will mischievously destroy one house and spare the next. The stories in our county are fantastical: The parsonage of our country church gone. Nothing remained but the piano, sitting exactly where it was, with the hymn book turned to the very page the pastor's wife was playing moments before she ran for the basement. One neighboring farmer picked up and gently let down five miles away buck naked. Cows found dazed ten miles from the field where they had been grazing. Everyone has stories and loves to tell them.

And everyone is always prepared for the next one. We kept oil lamps, books and games in our tornado shelter. Indeed, we spent many a summer evening in our damp cellar, while my father watched the boiling clouds searching for the funnel that would send him down the steps to join the rest of the family, already deep into a game of Monopoly.

The pioneers in Western Kansas learned quickly that the only way to survive the daily threat of tornadoes was to live in underground homes called "dugouts." In the fifties, we still lived in a dugout built by my grandfather. It was embarrassing to be so "old-fashioned," but also a bit romantic.

Two years after the tornado flattened our farm—all but the dugout—my father enigmatically decided to build an above-ground home. Just to let us know who was boss, a tornado hit the new house the day before we were scheduled to move in, clipping off a wing of it and stacking the four walls neatly on top of each other a few feet away. My father persevered and rebuilt, but not without a storm cellar of poured concrete under the new wing.

We were not yet hooked into electricity let alone television and therefore blissfully unaware, but I'm told that the rest of the country was afraid of the atomic bomb during those years. They were building bomb shelters and ducking under school desks during bomb drills. We didn't fear the atomic bomb. We had something far more real and immediate. At our one-room country school, we regularly practiced tornado drills. Our teacher, stopwatch in hand, would time us as we raced for a culvert under the road. All twelve of us—ranging from kindergarten to eighth grade—wiggled into the thirty-inch diameter culvert. We had to run for it a few times for real.

While tornadoes stuck fear in our hearts, it was the dust storms that tried our souls. You could see them rolling in. Huge black, boiling monsters on the horizon. If you saw one coming, you had maybe thirty minutes to get to shelter. Hurricane-force winds drove the fine dust. It would choke and kill you in minutes if you were out in it. Even huddled in our houses in the dark, survival meant tying wet handkerchiefs over our faces to filter the air and protect our lungs.

To this day, every February 19th I remember the worst day of our lives. We didn't see the sun at all that day. At noon it was so black you couldn't even see enough light to tell where the windows were. Even inside the house a thick cloud of fine dust hung in the air. When the storm was over, we had to shovel out dust ten inches deep from the house. There was no sleeping during a dust storm. Survival meant vigilance—you had to constantly wet the kerchiefs. We huddled together, like a bunch of bandits, our eyes peering out over our handkerchiefs. But we were not the bandits. The dust storms were—robbing us blind of our livelihood and sanity. Farm animals died, choked by the dust. Crops were ruined. The cleanup took weeks.

Tornadoes were better. Their capriciousness, their unpredictability was . . . well, predictable. You could run to a shelter, you could flatten yourself to the ground and it would pass over. In seconds, the great roar was gone. But dust storms lasted for hours, sometimes for days, penetrating into your pores, your lungs and souls.

Nevertheless, we survived all of it.

Somewhere in those turbulent fifties of my childhood, there were also some good years when the elements allowed our wheat to grow and reach harvest. I remember July days filled with excitement and joy. My mother and sister and I would pack baskets of food, bountiful dinners and suppers, spreading the food out on folding tables in the middle of vast golden wheat fields. My father and four brothers would climb down off their combines, and in the shade of a truck, we'd feast on fried chicken, potato salad, and corn on the cob, washed down by bucketloads of ice tea. Then we'd finish with cool watermelon, spitting the seeds as far as we could into the wheat stubble.

Afterwards, the menfolk would climb back on the combines and work into the night until they dropped. Long after I'd gone to sleep they'd come in—sometimes I'd wake briefly to their muffled talk while they ate a piece of pie left out on the table for them. They'd snatch a few hours of sleep, only to climb out of their beds a few hours later, grab breakfast and return to the field just as the sun dried off the dew. Then the combines would roar again, bringing in the harvest, quick, quick, quick before thunderstorm, hail or tornadoes could grab it from us. I remember one painful July Third when hailstorms destroyed our "bumper" crop. Hail as big as golf balls—as a child I always wondered what size a golf ball was, having never seen one—pounded the wheat into a mush. My father stood at the window and watched without saying a word. It's the saddest I ever saw him. My mother disappeared into her bedroom for hours and sobbed. I could hear it through the walls.

I'm on the cutoff now, our term for the state highway that heads straight west from Dodge to Odyssey. They're going to have a bumper crop this year. (I've never understood why they call it a "bumper" crop. Does the wheat grow as high as the bumper of the truck? Does it "bump" all the scales when you weigh in at the elevator?) The wheat fields stretch lush and green-gold as far as the eye can see on either side of the road. Not because of rainfall, but because the creeping circular irrigation sprinklers have metered out exactly the right amount of water, delivering it in gentle, simulated rain. I wonder if the women still bring supper to the field.

The nearly ripe grain ripples in the wind. Only if you have grown up on these Plains can you thrill to the lyrics, "amber waves of grain." I turn off on a dirt road and stop the car, get out and wade into a field, luxuriating in the smell, color and texture of nearly ripe wheat against a blue, blue sky.

Walking back to my car I stop and look around in all directions. There is no north or south, no east or west. This is part of my ritual: to just stand and look, as if I am the Little Prince surveying his planet. As always, I am flooded with layers of complicated emotions, which I can only inadequately describe as a sense of relief, of safety, of belonging. But it is more than that. There is an undercurrent I cannot understand.

I take a deep breath. I am back on the Plains. Yet I did not really come here of my own accord. It is as if I have been pulled here from the forests and hills by some irresistible force. My love for these Plains is against my will. Consciously, I hate the Plains and left them as soon as I could. Unconsciously, I love them with the aching of an abandoned woman for her lost lover.

Back on the road in my rental car, I continue going west. I'm near now. The sun is dropping to the horizon. I'm on schedule. I'll be home by dark.

Home? I can't go home. I have no home.

Ten years ago, while I was away covering some event in another part of the globe, and while Thomas was away exploring the canyons of the Southwest, and while my older siblings were engrossed in their careers and children, my father was backed into a terrible corner. Not only was the farm lost to us, but the land itself, the very land itself, was lost.

Why is it that the Acropolis still stands, that wild cats roam free in Rome's ancient coliseum, that the Great Wall of China beckons to the earth's revolving satellites, but no trace is left of my childhood home of twenty-five short years ago?

2

A Prairie Paradise

I HAVEN'T BEEN HERE in ten years. I visited my parents only once after they moved into a trailer court just outside Odyssey. It felt so uncomfortable, I never came home again. When Margaret talked them into moving to Denver to be nearer to her, I flew into Denver frequently to see them. I still couldn't think of them as detached from the land, but at least Colorado was a pleasant destination. When we were children, Dad would load us all into the car and head west. We strained our eyes looking for that first glimpse of the mountains and then when we saw the faint jagged purple outline appear above the prairie we all argued over which one of us had spotted it first.

We took a trip to the Rockies at least once a year, more often after Margaret got married and moved to Denver. In fact, we often ventured much farther west—through the Rockies, across the deserts, all the way to Los Angeles. Other times we piled into the car and headed east to visit relatives, sometimes going as far as Kansas City. As for north, we ventured as far as the South Dakota badlands. But we never, never, ever went south. "Nothing interesting south," my dad would say. Even when we took short Sunday afternoon drives we never went south.

It was strange last night sleeping in a motel in my old hometown, stranger still to have no one to talk to. I know plenty of people here, high school classmates, even some uncles and aunts and cousins, but I don't really want anyone to know I'm here. Fortunately, no one recognizes me. I'm just a stranger from "back East." I want to keep it that way.

I'm parked on the "gravel road"—we continued to call it that long after it was paved. I've come to see the Home Place. But all I see is a faint depression where the valley was. It's been plowed so many times, and probably leveled to make the fields more suitable for irrigation. I can see only one long-dead cottonwood where dozens once circled our dugout. If I didn't have some old photographs in my briefcase, I would think the old Home Place was a childhood fantasy.

It's not, I know it's not.

I grew up in a prairie paradise. Our "Home Place," as our family called it, sat in the middle of a low valley along a small creek fed by underground springs that bubbled up amidst a lush growth of willows—hence, my grandfather, Abraham Kluger, named the site Willow Valley. My great-grandmother Bessie, a tiny but tough lady had driven a buckboard wagon in the 1889 Oklahoma Land Rush and claimed a homestead. My great-grandfather, delayed on a train, didn't make it in time for the pistol start. He joined her later. They raised eight children on the Oklahoma farm. For reasons no one has ever talked about, their eldest son, my grandfather, left Oklahoma to buy a cheap plot of land on the nearly treeless plains of Western Kansas. I say nearly treeless, because our paradise was an oasis of trees—a dense, magical willow woods along the creek, large lazy cottonwoods around the dugout house providing shade—these were indigenous to the land. Then my grandfather planted a grove of cedars. "The cedars of Lebanon," he called them—he was also a preacher and fond of speaking in biblical language. I remember him only as a stern old man with thick white hair. Next to the cedars was a cherry orchard with rows and rows of short cheerful trees that "bore the fruit of his labor"—actually the fruit of my grandmother's labor. My only memory of my grandmother, Emma, who measured a mere 4 feet, 8 inches tall and nearly as wide, was of her perched on a stool in the middle of the orchard pitting cherries which she dropped into a large glass bowl on her lap. She used the bend of a hairpin plucked from her tightly wound bun to dig the pits out of the cherries. She did so with a motion deft and purposeful, without even looking. Her round face beamed in smiles and praise as we unloaded bucket after bucketful into a tin washtub at her feet. I was five years old and proud to be helping pick cherries. I picked from the lowest branches while my older siblings handled the higher ones. My oldest brother, Harry—fifteen and almost grown up—climbed the ladder to reach the very highest branches. I wanted to climb the ladder but I wasn't allowed to.

Some afternoons my grandmother would say, "I'm hungry for catfish." And then she and my older sister, Margaret, would disappear down the path toward the creek, holding their willow branch fishing poles, much taller than either of them, over their shoulders as they headed for the creek. I grew up thinking fishing was something only women did. I don't remember one other thing about my grandmother. She died. And I wasn't allowed to go to her funeral. Grandfather stayed for a time in a room in the old coal shed. But then he wasn't there anymore. He went to California to live with my uncle who worked in an airplane factory. And the farm—all of it—was up to my father to manage.

It was a paradise. The path to the willow woods became well worn by the five pairs of feet belonging to us children. "Stay on the path and you won't get lost," my brothers collectively admonished me. Once I went to the woods by myself and I did get lost. I shouted and cried until one of my brothers came to my rescue. The willow woods seemed so awfully big—like Red Riding Hood's forest. But if I went with my big brothers it was not scary. We would sneak oh so quietly into the willow woods, slither on our bellies; hiding behind the tall grass we called bulrushes—like from the Moses story—so we could watch our mother beaver building the dam across the creek. Sometimes her babies were with her, tumbling about getting into trouble. Once I saw her fell a tree all by herself, gnawing it through, as my brother explained, so that it would fall exactly where she wanted it to—right across the creek so she didn't have to drag it into place. Most of the time, when we sneaked up to watch she would spot us, slap the water loud with her tail and her babies would waddle after her as they ran for cover. Clearly, our beaver family didn't like people watching them when they were at work.

Birds loved our paradise. Meadowlarks heralded the spring sitting on fenceposts, warbling their song. They had bright yellow breasts, sort of like the robins in my first grade reading book, but yellow instead of red. And the bobwhite quail—we seldom saw them but always heard them gently calling out "bobwhite, bobwhite, bobwhite." If you did get to see them, it was usually a whole family, with several fat little wobbling babies following their mother in a straight single file line. There was something about them that is downright human. There were more pesky sparrows in our cottonwoods around the house than you could count. We sometimes heard owls at night but seldom saw them. In the afternoon, hawks circled above, effortlessly riding the wind looking for rabbits.

There were two kinds of rabbits in our paradise: jackrabbits with very long ears and powerful back legs—they looked more like miniature mules than rabbits, and cottontails—plump, little rabbits with fluffy tails that I presumed were made of cotton. Also coyotes. And who knows how many other animals we never saw. At night we would hear the coyotes howl. So scary, it would send shivers up my spine. I never saw a coyote, just heard them. Oh yes, and a big mother bobcat, which my brothers saw numerous times. She was dangerous, we were told, every bit as fierce as a tiger, only smaller. She attacked one of our dogs simply because he was curious about her baby kittens. The dog did not survive the encounter. That mother bobcat was one of the reasons I was not allowed to go to the willow woods alone.

The cottonwoods surrounding the house were my favorite trees. I loved the puffy cotton that floated down in the breeze and made white puddles of fluff in the depressions of the hard-packed dirt ground around the house in the summer. Once my brother Joel and a cousin threw a match into a cotton "puddle" and a flash fire moved along the ground in an instant and nearly burned the barn down.

You could fashion whistles out of the heart-shaped cottonwood leaves by folding them in half, pulling then taut and blowing into the stem side. It was a real art. Different pitches could be created according to the size of the leaves. A smaller leaf made a higher pitch. With five of us plus a few cousins we could make a cottonwood orchestra.

There were five of us, until Thomas came along. Then there were six. Some unspoken rule in our family was that while you were given a grownup name you had to earn it. Your life started with a childish version of that name, which always ended with an ee sound. So it went like this: Margaret was Maggie, Harold was Harry, James was Jimmy, Joel was Joey, Rebecca—that's me—was Becky. When Thomas came along, he was of course, Tommy.

We once had three dogs. One was killed by the bobcat, another encountered a porcupine in the willow woods. While he howled in pain, my father tried to pull out the quills with a pliers. Then Dad said, "He's in just too much pain. I have to do something about it." He had a grim look on his face. They made me go inside. Later we buried Jerome who lay limp in the yard looking like a pincushion. That left my favorite, a collie dog named Butch, who became my constant companion—until the day my little brother was born. Jim taught Butch how to play on the teeter-totter with me. We were the same weight, so it worked out. My mother became very angry when she found out.

"What if he jumps off?" she screamed.

Jim replied confidently that he had trained the dog to jump off only when he was at the top and I was at the bottom. Mother was not convinced. But I teeter-tottered with Butch many more times—when my mother wasn't looking—and he never once jumped off when I was airborne.

The day my little brother was born, which just so happened to also be the Fourth of July, when Daddy was rushing home from the hospital to tell us kids about the new baby, he accidentally ran over Butch in the driveway. No one even noticed when Mom came home the next day with baby Tommy. We were all crying and moping about, still mourning the death of Butch, whom we had ceremoniously buried in the cherry orchard. Three days later we finally noticed our new baby brother.

Had I been sixteen like my older sister, I would not have thought our farm was paradise. We were dirt poor. So poor we did not have electricity or running water and we lived in a dugout built into the side of a hill. Our bathroom was an outhouse up a path twenty yards from the house. I remember how cold it was in winter to stick your bare butt down on the wooden ledge with the hole cut in it. It smelled bad too. I couldn't hold my nose because it took both hands to pull down my panties, hold up my dress and hoist myself up on the seat which was too high for someone my size.

Margaret always had to take me, and kept saying, "Hurry, Hurry, I can't stand here all day." The toilet paper would get soggy on damp days and at night. And of course it was dark. But that's why we always brought a flashlight along.

The source of light in our dugout home after dark was an oil lamp that sat in the middle of our round, oilcloth-covered kitchen table. The oilcloth had yellow and white squares and lots of pink and purple flowers inside the squares, except where the pattern was worn away from scrubbing too hard.

The dugout was built into the side of a little hill, so the earth covered the sides and the roof, but the whole front was ground-level—a kind of walkout basement. A veranda-like porch ran the entire length and in summer we put chairs out on it. Naturally insulated by the earth, the dugout was warm in winter and cool in summer. It faced south so we were protected from the north winter wind. And in the summer, the circle of cottonwoods provided cooling shade. We lived mostly in one long room. At one end, closest to the door was the kitchen cabinet my dad built. It featured a thick butcherblock countertop which he was very proud of. A tub which served as a dishwashing "sink," sat on a lower table against the wall. We carried buckets of water from a hand pump well a few feet from the door. The large oak table with the oil lamp was in the middle of the long room. And at the other end was a couch, with a pretty crocheted blanket draped over it to hide the worn upholstery, but it was always slipping down in disarray from us sitting on it. A piano, the single most important item in our home, was against the far wall. We all gathered around the piano and sang every night while my sister played. I spent many of my pre-school hours plunking out tunes I composed and sang to myself sitting on the round piano stool. You could turn it in circles to crank it up higher or lower. I had to spin it up all the way in order to reach the keys.

The piano sat against the thin wall of the "girl's bedroom" that Margaret and I shared, a room so tiny there was barely room for a bed. If Margaret was playing piano when I went to bed, I could feel the wall next to me vibrate. It put me to sleep. Next to my parent's bedroom was the "boy's room," the mysterious, dark domain of my three big brothers, filled with inventions and contraptions and who knows what. I didn't dare go in there. It might be booby-trapped.

Many evenings, when it was too dark to be anywhere but around the one light source, we all gathered around the table and my dad would read from a book. I was too young to remember anything but the tremble and emotion in his voice when he read *Call of the Wild*. But my brothers say that as he would read, the coyotes outside would start to howl and everyone felt the creeps. It must have been sad, because I remember tears dripping out of Harry's eyes and he would wipe it with the back of his hand like he was just itching his eye, hoping no one noticed. But I noticed.

Dad also read *Robinson Crusoe,* and *Little Women*—and *Little House on the Prairie,* which was about a family just like ours, who even lived in a dugout like ours. Laura was a real girl, a lot like me—I know she was real because my grandmother Sara's older sister went to school with Laura Ingalls—so I knew that maybe I could one day write a book too.

There was some trouble in our paradise. But the trouble cast itself more as adventure than adversity. By the time I was five years old I had survived a rattlesnake bite and a tornado. That's how I know it was a paradise. We were somehow divinely protected within the cocoon of the Home Place.

I can recall like it was yesterday, huddling under my parent's iron bed, clutching the legs as a tornado roared through our farm. I did not even know why I had been ordered to crawl under the bed, but my mother's tone had left no question as to the urgency. My father and three older brothers were somewhere out in the path of the tornado repairing the combine, getting ready for wheat harvest. When it was over, my mother rushed outside. I followed. My father and brothers were standing quiet and dazed surveying the damage. They had survived the tornado by lying flat in a ditch that ran between the row of cedar trees and our cherry orchard.

Just days before, my father had finished building a chicken shed and stocked it with several hundred chickens to augment our struggling wheat-farming enterprise. The new chicken shed was gone, wiped out, as was everything else on the farm—except our dugout home. I shall never forget the sight as I looked up. Thousands of fluffy white feathers fluttered slowly, suspended in the quiet still air.

Noah had a rainbow. We were given chicken feathers. Throughout my life, whenever I have passed safely through a traumatic event, I see the feathers fluttering above me.

AT A FAMILY CHRISTMAS GATHERING two years ago, we were all trying to outdo one another in recounting our earliest memories. Harry claimed to remember something that happened when he was age two.

Not to be outdone, I said I remembered something from my toddler days, perhaps as early as two—being bitten by a rattlesnake—but it must just be a dream because if it were true I'd be dead.

My siblings glanced at each other and urged me to repeat my story—even if it was only a dream. And so I put it into words for the very first time.

Every detail of this dream is so clear, I tell them, I can see it happening as if I'm a third person looking down. I'm in back of a shed—it has a sand drift blown high against the back outside wall. The nearly white sand is in waves and layers, getting higher closer to the back of the shed. I like to play in that sand. But my father says if he ever catches me playing there again I will get a spanking. I don't know why he doesn't want me to be there. It's so much fun to play in the sand. I sit in it. The sand is gritty. It gets in my diaper—I distinctly remember I was wearing either a diaper or training panties, because it was wet, and the sand was sticking to my bottom.

There are tunnel-like holes in the sand. Then I notice a snake lying motionless on the sand. It starts moving, slithering slowly toward me. I am fascinated, but I am not afraid. I want to touch it. So I move closer. I stretch out my hand and I call "kitty, kitty," which makes me break into laughter. It's so funny that I'm calling it kitty since it obviously isn't a kitty. It doesn't look anything like a kitty. I'm laughing and laughing at my joke.

Something happens. The snake jumps at me so quickly, I can't even see it. All I know is that my leg hurts terribly, and I'm running to the house. I'm screaming. I'm crying, but I know I can't tell anyone where I was. Daddy says he'll spank me if I play there. I can't tell anyone.

"That's all I remember," I finish.

"That was no dream." They all say it almost simultaneously, looking at each other. And then I hear all the other versions of this story.

My parents were at church for a whole day of prayer and fasting called to bring healing to a neighbor's child who had been diagnosed with leukemia. That's something our country church did when a matter was really serious. My older brothers were supposed to be looking after me but I slipped away from them. Then, they heard me come screaming across the yard. I showed them my leg. There were two distinct telltale puncture marks. Terrified, they ran with me in their arms up the hill to the church, which was a mere quarter-mile from the Home Place. Everyone at church who saw it agreed it looked like a rattlesnake bite. Yet nothing seemed to be wrong with me. My parents rushed me to the doctor in town who also agreed it looked like a rattlesnake bite.

Though I showed no symptoms, Dr. Brennan sucked the "poison" out anyway. His explanation was that I must have been bitten by a deficient rattlesnake, one that had no poison—a freak of nature. My parents had another explanation, which they drew right from their Bible. It was simply a miracle. There was even a verse in the Bible—something about the servants of the Lord being protected from a viper's poison—so my parents reasoned that because they were fasting and praying that day, the Lord had saved their child from the jaws of a viper. To them, it was as simple as that.

It has occurred to me that there is a third explanation. Perhaps it is I who is the freak of nature, immune to the poison of a rattlesnake. At any rate, I now knew my dream was in fact a memory, not a dream. I never had the dream again.

There are a few other dreams I wish I could get rid of.

3

Golden Hill

AS A CHILD I NEVER clearly understood why we left the Home Place. All I know is that just before Christmas and one week before my big sister's wedding, we moved into an above-ground house a few miles south of the Home Place, a house that was ugly, cold and drafty. I hated it. We were supposed to have moved in by Thanksgiving, but a rare October tornado had damaged a corner of the house—coincidentally where my room was to be—plus it had torn off the utility room which Dad had built onto the back which made the house t-shaped. So he rebuilt it.

I didn't really know that we were moving until Dad backed the '45 Dodge truck up to the door of the dugout and my big brothers started loading it. My Mom, sister and I had been busy sewing dresses for the wedding on the old Singer treadle sewing machine. We weren't quite finished with my flower girl dress, when Dad said, "Pack up your sewing things. You'll have to finish it in the new house."

When I asked my parents why we were moving, they said it was so we could have electricity.

"Why can't we just have electricity here?"

"Old Man Houston won't let us."

That made no sense to me. Why should that crippled old man in his Model A Ford have anything to say about us having or not having electricity?

I did not like Old Man Houston, even though he always brought me candy when he came. He would drive his Model A Ford slowly, very slowly, down the driveway and park near the barn. He'd climb out slowly as if every movement was painful, hobble around to the passenger side of the car leaning heavily on a cane with an elaborately carved ivory handle. Then he'd sit down, with a huge sigh, on the running board and light up a cigar. My dad would come from wherever he had been and he'd stand by the Model A and talk. Even if he was out in the field on his tractor and terribly busy, he would stop the tractor and walk in to talk with the old man. If Dad didn't notice, my Mom, who always became very nervous at the sight of Houston's black car slowly descending the driveway, would send Joel running out to the field to get Dad.

Once Dad was there, I'd slowly sidle my way closer to the car and Old Man Houston would say, "I've got a little something for you, Becky." And he'd toss me a yellow butterscotch candy wrapped in red paper. I would murmur thank you, always feeling very embarrassed, very awkward, very guilty, because I liked the candy, but didn't like the old man. While I was backing away and feeling shy, I would hear Old Man Houston say, "Joseph, that is one pretty girl you have. A very pretty girl." He'd wink at me.

Then he'd add, when he thought I was out of earshot, "But if you don't mind my saying so, your oldest daughter is even prettier."

That's true. There was nobody in the world prettier than my sister with her long, curly, yellow-blond hair falling down halfway to her waist and her bright rosebud lips—Mom let her wear lipstick even though you weren't supposed to, according to our church. She wore pretty dresses too because she was the oldest. When she grew out of them, Mom remade them into dresses to fit me.

If my brother, Joel—the one four years older than me—and I tried to hang around the car, Mom called us in to the house.

"I don't want the children hearing Houston's racing stories," she'd tell my dad.

I could never figure out why a man who drove his car so slow and moved even slower would be telling racing stories. Years later I realized she must have said *racy* stories. I noticed that my two oldest brothers also tried to hang around and hear the old man's stories. That is, if Mom didn't notice and call them in to the house too.

As a seven-year-old, I did not understand that the Home Place so lovingly created by my grandfather did not really belong to us anymore. In the thirties, when my grandfather couldn't make his land payments, Old Man Houston had repossessed the land. Our family, however, did not have to move from our home. We merely became tenant farmers on our former acreage. When the Dust Bowl subsided and my father returned from hauling logs in Washington State, he and my mother, now with three children, moved back to the Home Place and my father decided to buy back the land. A few years later, when the grasshoppers ate most of the crop one year and a hailstorm got it the next, my father got behind on his land payments. For a second time the farm was repossessed, and like his father before him, my dad became a tenant farmer. That meant that you paid one-third of your crop to the landlord, and out of the two-thirds you kept, you paid your own expenses. But since expenses usually ate up the whole two-thirds—if not more, the tenant farmer was lucky if he ever cleared even one dollar. It was no way to "get ahead." I constantly heard my dad talking about getting ahead, something he never seemed to be able to do.

When Rural Electrification came to our part of the world, it took forty dollars—if I remember correctly—to bring electricity lines the quarter mile down from the gravel road to our farmyard. Only the owner of the land could authorize it and pay the money. Old Man Houston didn't think it was necessary. So for the lack of forty dollars, we lit our oil lamps, carried water pails into the house and moved our bowels in an outhouse.

"Can't we just pay the forty dollars?" I remember my brothers asking.

"It's not that simple. We don't own the land," my dad would say.

The new house, if you could call it "new," had electricity. A mere flip of a switch on the wall and a room would be flooded with light. We had a real kitchen with running water. No more hauling in buckets of water and heating it on the stove to take Saturday night baths. No more grabbing a flashlight and running outside in your pajamas when you had to pee at night. But it didn't seem like home. The wind blew snow through every little crevice around the windows. Our dugout had been so much warmer. And there were no trees for shade or shelter. It was just a t-shaped house, lonely and by itself on a windy hill. I cried myself to sleep at night, longing for the Home Place and wishing my big sister hadn't gotten married and left me all alone in this now too-big bed.

Plus, the new house was really ugly. My dad made it out of an old army barracks. The war was over and the government was practically giving away their excess army barracks. My dad bought one—I think he paid twenty-five dollars for it—and hired someone to move it all the way from Garden City. He drew a floor plan and built in rooms—a living and dining room, a kitchen, four bedrooms—two at each end of the house, a bathroom, and then he added a utility room at the back over a tornado shelter. The shelter was concrete—floor, walls and ceiling "all poured in one piece like a bunker," as my dad described it. When we moved in, the walls were barely up with drywall hastily nailed in place. The floor was wide, rough wood planks, which he sanded and we waxed. Such a floor is considered quite chic now, but at the time my mother was embarrassed by it and covered it with an assortment of mismatched throw rugs. Every Saturday afternoon when we wet mopped, the damp wood gave off an earthy, forest-like smell. Combined with the scent of Mom's bread for Sunday baking in the oven, a soothing sense of home was finally emerging.

During the winter, my father taped and sanded the drywall and my brothers painted the walls. I choose lilac paint and Mom sewed white lace curtains for my windows. Then my mother ordered me a lilac and white dotted chenille bedspread and a fluffy, fake fur lilac rug from the Sears catalog. It was the most beautiful room in the world. And I began to like the new place.

My father planted four Chinese elms in front of the house, a honey locust outside the back door and a triple row of trees consisting of poplars, Russian olive trees and cedars south of the house to "break the wind." The government gave windbreaker trees away for free. As I understood it, the government somehow thought you could prevent the wind from blowing if you planted enough "windbreakers." I knew how stupid that was, but nobody is going to tell the government they are wrong as long as they are handing out free trees.

When spring came, I understood why my father had chosen this "new place." Just as he said, it was a lot like the old place, but better. It was still near the Willow Valley neighborhood, just two miles upstream. It had a creek—the same creek that ran through the Home Place—with a swimming hole fed by a bubbling spring. The creek was lined with willows, not so thick as the Home Place woods, but still enough to provide shelter to birds and animals. And in the U-bend of the creek was a congregation of big, old gnarly cottonwoods. "Why oh why didn't you put our house in the middle of those cottonwoods so we could have shade like at the old place?" I asked.

"When the first flood comes you'll know why," said my father.

The new place had a nice level field for wheat just south of the spot my father had chosen to put our house, and to the north and west was pasture land. And this is what really excited my father. "This pasture has never been plowed. It's natural prairie. It has been just like this since the beginning of time!" he would exclaim.

Dad took all us kids out to the pasture to show us the buffalo grass which shoots out new plants by sending out runners, each of which casts down its own roots. The resulting root systems are so dense and hardy that settlers cut the topsoil into squares and used the sod as bricks to build their houses. Dad pointed out the prickly pear cactus, the soap-weed, the sagebrush and the profusion of wild flowers—yellow, white, and pale purple. The pasture was alive, home to all sorts of fowl and bur-rowing creatures as well as butterflies and insects of all sorts. "We'll have cattle again," my father said. "Maybe a horse or two."

On the other side of the pasture was low flat ground between the creek that made a huge U and then another sharp little U. "That bot-tom land will probably get flooded every spring so I'll grow alfalfa there. We'll bale it, stack it on the yard and sell it in the winter," explained my father. Then the land gently sloped up again on the other side of the bottomland, creating another field suitable for growing wheat.

To the west of the house the pasture ended abruptly with a cliff—a kind of bluff that dropped down to the point where two tributaries joined, the Sand Arroyo and the North Fork of the Cimarron. While the Sand Arroyo was usually dry, it was known to flood suddenly when rain storms pounded Eastern Colorado. When it did, our whole "bot-tom land" became one huge brown lake. It happened that first spring. We stood on the top of the ridge and looked out over this vast body of water. Now I was happy Dad put our house on a hill.

But it was the more gentle ridge on the north edge of the pasture overlooking the spring-fed swimming hole that was magic. It was laced with little worn down paths and littered with exquisite Indian artifacts. When we first noticed them, Tommy and I ran like children on a treasure hunt, discovering one arrowhead then another—red ones, gray ones, small and narrow and sharp, others large and gently pointed. And now I understood why my dad had been so excited about this pasture that "had never been plowed since the beginning of time."

"We will never plow this," he would repeat over and over again.

But what really excited my dad was that even though he bought the land from Old Man Houston—there was hardly any choice since the Houston family owned nearly the whole county—he did not take the loan from Old Man Houston. Instead he had arranged an FHA loan from the government.

My father had great faith in the government. "Roosevelt got us out of the Depression," he would lecture. "FDR gave me a job surveying land and I never had to stand in a bread line." I grew up thinking Franklin D. Roosevelt personally intervened to give my dad a job. My father was so grateful to FDR, he switched his membership from the Republican to the Democratic Party, making him about the only Democrat in Homer County.

And now the U.S. Department of Agriculture, through something called the Farm Home Administration, in an effort to save struggling farmers like my father, was making it possible to own a piece of land where we could have electricity if we wanted it. Now Old Man Houston could not take our land away for a third time. And now we could keep all of the harvest. For better or for worse, my father was in control of his own destiny to the extent that the wind, dust, tornadoes, droughts, hailstorms, locust and prairie fires would allow.

And never mind the thunderheads that rumbled and ripped lightning but refused to give out rain. We had a well with an electric pump so we could at least water a small part of the earth ourselves. So my mother planted a huge garden.

The second spring we planted a lawn outside the back door bordered by rows and rows of marigolds and red and orange zinnias. And Mom put in a lilac bush under the kitchen window. (Dad had put a window above the kitchen sink at Mom's request so she "could look outside while she washed dishes.") The lilac bush, when it bloomed, would bring tears to her eyes. It reminded her of the lilacs that grew outside her girlhood home in Eastern Kansas. Our lawn was thick and a kind of green that you didn't see in nature—at least not in Western Kansas. Unlike the buffalo grass, it needed to be mowed. So we bought an old used lawnmower at a farm sale. We put up a croquet set and played games in the evening. At night we kids brought blankets out and spread them out on the soft, too-green grass and slept outside under the stars. We fell asleep to the sound of crickets and coyotes while searching the heavens to see if we could spy Sputnik making its slow journey across the sky. My brothers regularly claimed to spot it, but all I saw was the Milky Way, the big dipper, a billion stars, and every once in a while a shooting star streaking down right toward me which always mercifully disappeared before it hit.

Sleeping outside stopped when two strangers brutally murdered the Clutter farm family who lived a half-hour's drive north of us. But that is another story.

Just a mile and a half south of our new farm, we learned there had been a town called Golden City, which once boasted a population just as big as the town of Odyssey. But when the railroad chose to go through Odyssey instead of Golden City, the town died a natural death. A school and a cemetery and a few crumbling foundations were all that remained. If it had thrived, we would be living on the outskirts of a town. Sometimes when my father was plowing, the turned up soil revealed old tin pots and broken dishes. Once he found some marbles. I began calling our farm Golden Hill. My dad said that was not accurate. We were at least a mile and a half from the old Golden City limits.

The move to Golden Hill had been marked by an important event in our family's life. One week after moving into the unfinished house on Golden Hill, my big sister got married. Margaret's wedding was in the Methodist church in town because it had an organ and stained glass windows. Her piano teacher played *Here Comes the Bride* on the organ and it was very dramatic. I was the nervous flower girl in a blue taffeta dress with hair done up in Shirley Temple curls.

Maggie was a lovely bride. The groom was from Denver—where Maggie had gone to be a secretary. He had a turquoise-blue Oldsmobile with gigantic tail fins, and he looked like a movie star with his greased hair combed back on the sides with a kind of swirl on top. He was really cool. We all loved him. Thomas, who was only two at the time, was too young to be a ringbearer but he ended up being part of the wedding party anyway. Right in the middle of the ceremony, he somehow got away from my mother and ran down the aisle to Maggie. I tried to pull him away, but he grabbed onto Maggie's big bride skirt and wouldn't let go. So as not to spoil the ceremony, the preacher just let him stay there and we pretended to ignore him. Later people said it made them cry. Little Tommy just didn't want to let go of his big sister. We all felt that way.

I've always felt that way about weddings—that they are as sad as they are happy. Beginning a new phase of life always means leaving the old. Like with moving from the old Home Place to the "new home place." No matter how much you gained, you always lost something too. We never did come to call Golden Hill a "Home Place," It didn't seem right because it lacked my silver-haired grandpa's stamp of history. And no matter how much I loved Golden Hill, I always felt it somehow belonged to someone else. It was a home place, but whose? We struggled to make it our own.

The old Home Place soon faded into legend. It had been the protected paradise of my innocent years, the Garden of Eden from which I had been prematurely ejected. But Golden Hill was real. It was both good and bad. The windbreaker was overwhelmed by the wind and the poplars would die in the dust storms, but the elm trees out front were beginning to give shade. The wheat struggled but the flood-fed alfalfa bloomed brilliantly each summer. Mom's garden thrived and gave us corn and beans and leaf lettuce, onions and potatoes and radishes, watermelons and pumpkins—every vegetable under the sun. Cattle roamed the buffalo grass pasture, lowing softly when they marched home single file in the evening. They provided us with milk and meat. The flower garden gave us beauty and pleasure. Chickens roamed the yard, laying eggs where they wished.

Some days the dust storms boiled up purple on the horizon and hit with such ferocity we wondered if we would survive. In the winter, blizzards would swirl with blinding whiteness, creating drifts as high as our house. When the electricity would go off during snowstorms I would sit near the gas stove in the utility room and read books by oil lamp light while eating buttered toast.

Like the elm saplings, I was casting down deep roots on Golden Hill—you had to, just to be able to stand. I ran free on Indian Ridge. I soared and warbled with the meadowlarks. Whether the wind came out of the north or the south, I was becoming as tenacious as the buffalo grass which had clung to the prairie soil since the beginning of time.

4

Gentle Wind

DURING THE DUST STORM fifties, brisk, gritty wind was our daily fare. Whipping you. Harassing you. Stinging you. You learned to clutch your schoolbooks close to your belly and keep your elbows in so the wind had nothing to grab. The wind most days was so strong that you got used to either leaning into it or bracing your back against it as you walked. In fact, on those few occasions when the wind didn't blow, you felt you would fall over backwards, because you had become so used to leaning into the wind.

Kids can adjust to anything. Whether a grimy street in Dublin, an alleyway on the South Side of Chicago or a Western Kansas country schoolyard in the middle of a dust storm, there is always a way to rise above it. That's because children carry a spark inside their souls that can transform their whole world into a fantastical playground.

We hunted buffalo on our schoolyard, and loathed the moment the schoolbell rang to bring us in from the hunt after recess. I'm not sure, but it might have even been my idea when I watched a huge, lopsided tumbleweed blow across the yard one day—I noticed that the loping shape of its journey down the length of the schoolyard looked exactly like a running buffalo. Once I'd pointed that out to the bigger boys, the rest was easy.

We each searched the barbed wire fence that ran along the south side of the schoolyard for a perfect tumbleweed buffalo. It needed to be oblong so it kind of lunged while it rolled, yet round enough that it would tumble as fast as we could run. A good "buffalo" was hard to find, so you didn't want to lose it. Then you had to create a spear, a fairly straight branch from a willow tree about three or four feet long would do. Then you whittled the end to a sharp point, sharp enough that it would stick into the ground when you threw it into the "buffalo," pinning your beast to the ground.

Then on the windiest days—which in 1955 tended to be every day—we would retrieve our buffaloes from the fence where we had stored them, then standing together holding our tumbleweed tightly we would line up at the south fence, spaced about ten feet apart. There was a gentle slope down to the northern boundary of the schoolyard. When the oldest boy shouted 'Go,' we'd release our tumbleweed buffaloes, count to ten to give them a decent head start, then chase after them, spear in hand. Then, if we could keep up, we'd throw the spear into the tumbleweed, pinning it to the ground, or at least wounding the beast so its run was slowed by the spear sticking in it, impeding its tumble down the slope.

On really windy days, buffalo hunting was a challenge, and I lost many a good buffalo, because there was no fence down at the lower north end of the schoolyard, only a gravel road. So if it got away from you, it was pretty much gone forever. We agreed on one rule for the hunt: once the buffalo got to the road, we weren't allowed to run across and retrieve it. I imagine that may have been a teacher-imposed rule, since it would not do to have children darting across the road pursuing tumbleweeds and be hit by a truck.

(Tumbleweeds, by the way, are not indigenous to the American West. It's my family's fault actually. The tumbleweed is a "Russian thistle," the seeds of which were mixed in with the winter wheat my forefathers brought from the steppes of Russia when they immigrated to America and began settling on the prairies. The pesky plant loved the arid High Plains and thrived, soon showing up all over the West. It could survive anything the climate dished out. And before long this wild weed became a symbol of the Wild West and the subject of many a lonely cowboy song.)

At the end of recess, our teacher, who hated to even stick her head out the door when the dust was blowing, would stand on the porch ringing and ringing the hand held bell, screaming for us to come in. We'd stash our prize tumbleweeds on the barbed wire fence and reluctantly file back into the schoolhouse. Dirty and sweaty, we'd stand in line at the water fountain to rinse out our mouths which were gritty with sand. Our eyes would be bloodshot, dust sticking to our eyelashes, our hair tangled and matted with dust. We didn't care. All we could think of was the next recess and hope the wind gusts would get even stronger by 2:30 so the hunt would be more exciting.

On days when the wind was lighter and the tumbleweed buffaloes too slow, we'd opt for Annie Over, a game where we tossed a ball over the school roof with opposing teams on either side—I don't remember the point of the game. Or Kick the Can, my favorite—a Western Kansas variation on the game of tag. All it took was one old tin can on a home base. The person unfortunate enough to be "it" roamed around looking for the others who were hiding. If he saw you, he called your name and ran for the can. If he put his foot on the top of the can and called out your name again, you were "out" which meant you were "it." But if you could get to the can first, you would kick it as far as you could, and while "it" went to retrieve the can and put it back on base, you could run off and hide again. With such a variation of ages playing—from first graders to fourteen year olds, it was necessary to construct elaborate extra rules to make the game more fair for the little kids. Actually, we had to do that for all games. Much of our recess time would be spent debating and negotiating rule adaptations. In that sense, the country schoolyard prepared us for living in the world as much as the classroom did.

In buffalo hunting it was easy to level the playing field, so to speak. Tumbleweeds were selected to be perfectly suited to the size and running speed of each child, and we all helped match each other to the right "buffalo." There was, after all, an endless new supply of tumbleweeds amassing at the south fence every day.

Sometimes our teacher convinced us to play the more universal game of softball. One day our game was interrupted by a huge rattlesnake coiled and ready to strike between first and second base. Johnny hit a home run, cleared first, and saw it just in time. We ran for our teacher, who was eating lunch on the shady side of the schoolhouse. She screamed for us to stand back. Mrs. Shaw ran to her house, a little two-room cottage on the edge of the schoolyard that she shared with her Indian "cowboy" husband. She strapped on a fancy leather gun belt with a six-shooter in it. She always wore cowboy boots and tight fitting, low-cut dresses—she had the most gigantic breasts to ever be teamed with a tiny waist. And now with the gun belt strapped to her hips, she was a formidable sight. I'll never forget her stance, feet wide apart, sideways, stretching, her gun arm out straight—like a real pro from a Cowboy movie—as she aimed and shot the snake right through the head. One shot.

Only one shot. Even the big boys were impressed. The snake writhed wickedly and was soon dead. When it stopped moving, Mrs. Shaw let the eighth grade boys cut off the rattle for a souvenir and we tacked it to the bulletin board. Right then, I knew she would make a great buffalo hunter and wondered why she wouldn't select herself a tumbleweed and join us at recess.

But sometimes even the wind and the thrill of the hunt got old, when the gusts seemed to want to rip your arms out of their sockets, and the blowing sand stung your face so bad that you just wanted it to stop.

Sometimes it did.

I remember those rare spring days when the wind was soothing and constant and gentle. When you could face into the wind and it would draw your hair away from your cheekbones, tickle your hair follicles and make you feel free and longing to burst into song like a meadowlark.

Gentle Wind was the name of an Indian girl—my spirit sister—who first began talking to me when I was eight years old. During the first spring that we lived on Golden Hill, I would walk into the pasture and play on the ridge overlooking the creek. I found her brothers' arrowheads and then her mother's grinding stone. And she began to talk to me. She was bronze colored and wore her hair in a long black braid down her back. Her mother made her wear the braid, and she didn't like it anymore than I liked my ponytail. She much preferred to let her hair blow in the wind. Maybe that's why they called her Gentle Wind. So I would undo her braid, and she would yank the rubber band off my ponytail and we would run together along the ridge. Let it get tangled. We didn't care.

I don't know if she was Cheyenne, Kiowa, Apache or Comanche. We didn't think about such labels and I was unaware then that Indians were anything but Indians. What I knew about them came from the artifacts we found in the pasture and a picturebook about a romance between a beautiful Indian girl and the brave she loved. Her father, the Chief, wanted her to marry another young brave. The lovers would steal away to meet under a full moon. The book had lovely watercolor pictures, and I think their love story ended tragically—like Romeo and Juliet. We didn't have TV, so I had never watched the popular shoot-em-up cowboy and Indian shows of the day. I knew nothing of attacks on wagon trains or scalpings. I didn't know about Indian reservations, or even that there were still some Indians left on earth. I only knew what my spirit sister told me.

Gentle Wind didn't like helping her mother with the chores around the campfire anymore than I liked toiling in my mother's hot kitchen. But I kept telling her that at least she could do her work and be out-side at the same time. I was stuck in a stifling house with far too many brothers to feed and clean up after. In the evenings, Gentle Wind and I sat without talking and stared at the sunset. I composed poems and read them to her.

When my baby brother was old enough to come with me, he would run along with me to the pasture ridge and help me gather buffalo chips and make campfires and find arrowheads. I never told him about Gentle Wind. He was happy to be part of my play. And he seemed to have his own elaborate stories running through his head. I just had to make sure he didn't wander out of my sight. Gentle Wind had two lit-tle brothers so she understood.

When I was eleven, I decided I wanted a doeskin dress like Gentle Wind wore. So I borrowed an old raggedy white t-shirt from my older brother—it came down to my knees. I cut a fringe in the bottom. Then I heated a pot of hot water and threw in lots of old teabags. I stewed the t-shirt in the brew until it turned a soft doeskin brown. Then I threaded red and black wooden beads up the bottom fringe. It was a wonderful dress. As soon as I was home from school, I would change into it and run out to the ridge and stay until the sun went down. I loved the feel of the wooden beads hitting against my legs as I ran.

From another part of the pasture, facing west over the confluence of the North Fork and the Sand Arroyo, atop the cliffs—they seemed so large and dangerous then, even though just a mere drop of five or six feet—you had a perfect view of the sunset. Western Kansas has magnif-icent sunsets. I guess all those dust particles hanging in the air caused the brilliant colors, or so I learned in a science class years later.

Sitting on that ridge, legs dangling, I told Gentle Wind everything. The way I felt my teacher sometimes had it in for me. I cried bitterly when I told her about how Mrs. Shaw banished me to the cloakroom for two hours, and to top it off called me a pantywaist. I had no idea what it meant but knew it was an insult. I didn't understand what I had done to deserve such a label.

I talked to my friend about how thin and weak my grandmother Sara—my mother's mother—was becoming. She had lung cancer. The doctor said it must be all the dust getting into her lungs that had caused her illness. Western Kansas was no place for someone who was coughing as bad as she was. So Grandma Sara went to live with my Aunt Catherine in Eastern Kansas where the air was cleaner. Aunt Catherine cared for her and called us frequently to update Grandma's condition— we now had a telephone. It was a party line, and if you were very quiet and very careful, you could listen in to the neighbor's conversation and learn all their secrets—that is, if your parents weren't home to catch you. The problem was that you knew your neighbors could do the same to you.

I realized I was going to lose my grandmother. She and I were very close, and when she had lived on my uncle's farm five miles away, I had spent many hours in her little frame house with the peeling paint outside and the perfectly ordered parlor inside with all the lace doilies on the furniture. Grandma's house was always so clean, so quiet, so dark, so cool.

One day when I was twelve years old, in the last year of my close friendship with Gentle Wind, as we sat on the cliff watching the sunset, she and I both knew instantly just as the sun slipped below the horizon that my grandmother Sara had died.

I ran home, virtually flying a few inches above the buffalo grass, screaming into the house. "Grandma is dead. Grandma is dead."

"Becky, calm down, what's the matter with you. If Grandma had died, Aunt Catherine would have telephoned us."

Barely were those words out of my mother's mouth when the phone rang.

When my mother stopped sobbing, she told us what Aunt Catherine had said. In the last few weeks, Grandma has been so weak she could barely move her head from the pillow. But tonight, just as the sun was setting, Aunt Catherine says she sat up in bed, and flung her arms wide open. She had the most beautiful smile on her face. She said, "Pappa, Pappa"—that's what she called my grandfather who died before I was born—and then she lay back on the pillow and was gone.

We packed our suitcases with our Sunday best clothes and drove to Eastern Kansas. I spent the most terrifying night of my life trying to sleep in the third story attic bedroom of Aunt Catherine's house. How could they have put me up there alone? My mother didn't seem to care that I was frightened by the terrible thunderstorms and loud rain that seemed to go on all night. Here back East when it thundered it also rained. The rain beat against the window. I don't think I even closed my eyes the whole night. I stole downstairs a few times to knock on my parent's room, but Mom was crying and Dad was trying to comfort her, and they didn't even hear my knocking. Lying on my little bed, stiff with fear, jerking rhythmically with that hiccup-like kind of sob that follows when you have been crying for a long time, I gave up trying to fall asleep. There was a bit of early dawn light at the windows. Then I saw a man standing at the foot of my bed. He had wavy brown hair and a short beard. He had kind eyes that crinkled at the corners. I was not frightened. I did not know him, yet he looked familiar. "Do not cry," he said. "I will be taking care of your grandmother now. She has come to be with me." Then he sat down at the foot of the bed and reached out his hand and placed it on the blanket over my feet. I felt the warmth and pressure of his hand. Then he was gone, and I fell asleep.

THE NEXT MORNING we buried Grandma in the cemetery out behind the church where my grandpa had been the preacher. I stood in the front pew holding my mother's hand, glancing behind me, back up to the balcony where I used to like to sit. When I was a little girl and we visited my aunt and uncle, I would sit in the first row up there and hold onto the balcony railing while the elders preached and preached, preached so long and so sing-song, that I would fall asleep with my hands still tightly clutching the railings. It's a wonder I never fell out of the balcony.

But now I was downstairs. Right up front. And my grandmother was forever departed. Somebody else would probably move into her little house with the white doilies, or they would knock it down.

Back on the ridge a few days later, I told Gentle Wind about the kind man with the crinkly eyes. "Do you think that was my grandpa?" I asked her.

She looked at me as if I were a little stupid. "Don't you know that our ancestors always visit us in the night as we are sleeping?"

"But I was not sleeping. I could not sleep."

"That is why he visited you. So you would sleep."

Gentle Wind seemed to know everything. And when she explained things they made so much sense. She understood how much I missed my grandmother. She had lost so many of her own family—uncles, aunts, even her baby sister. She had survived so many tragic events. Worst of all, her people had lost their precious ridge. It wasn't until many years later, that I understood it was my people—white settlers, that is—who took it away from her.

But please, Gentle Wind, do not blame my father. He was not the first to plow this land. He was not the first to plant the amber waves of grain that vanquished your buffalo and brought bread to America. And my father, just as he tithed ten percent of his crop to his God, he also set aside twenty-five percent—a full quarter—of his land to remain in its native state. So the pasture and your ridge is still and always will be, as long as he lives, a profusion of buffalo grass, wildflowers, soapweed, and prickly pear cactus. It will be habitat for quail, pheasant, rabbits, and all sort of burrowing creatures. Gentle, brown, softly-mooing cattle graze my father's preserve. But Gentle Wind, if you and I dance together, maybe we can bring back the buffalo.

One day, out of the blue, our conversations stopped—just as I moved from self-assured, devil-may-care girlhood into unsettled, self-conscious adolescence.

But I will always feel her when the wind blows a certain way, from a certain direction, with a certain sweetness on its breath. When it does, I know she is taking out her braids so the wind can flow freely through her black, wavy hair.

5

Voice on the Wind

SHE CAME CALLING for me so my spirit spoke to her. She called out
not from sorrow but from joy. A heart filled with too much joy, just as
a heart filled with too much sorrow, must spill some out. Her heart
overflowed. I caught the overflow in my cupped hands. I drank from
her joy and lived once more. She warbled with the meadowlark, she
cooed with the quail. Her eyes were the clear blue of the morning sky.
Her hair, spun from gold, flowed like corn silk in the wind as she ran
along the ridge where my old woman spirit walks with a heavy step.
My child spirit answered her call and ran with her. For very long my
child spirit had slumbered through time, but now awakened, her limbs
moved effortlessly.

My old woman spirit is filled with sorrow from all that I have seen.
But my child spirit still believes she will forever be happy and free as
the pair of eagles who soar above our camp, buoyed by the wisdom of
the heavens and bound by love to the earth.

Our clan came to these summer grounds as our refuge from the dev-
astation of the wagons of white men who followed the big rivers
searching for gold. First only a few came. We had seen white men
before. It's said they come from the other side of the sun. We traded buffalo robes for guns. We should never have traded. We should have hidden and not shown our faces. Some took wives of our people and treated them kindly. They spoke with reverence with our chief. So we were
not afraid in the beginning.

But then came others, many others, sometimes with their white wives and children. They came not to trade but to pass through in search of gold and magic which they believed lay somewhere beyond the next horizon. They were hungry. They were thirsty. They were cold. They did not know how to live on the Plains. Their horses and beasts devoured all our grass. They cut down the trees that once lined our Great River, burning both limbs and trunks to keep warm. The wheels of their wagons cut gashes in the earth and made wide rivers of mud where once there had been life-giving grass. They killed the deer and antelope and frightened away the small animals. The birds were afraid of them. Even the sky was afraid and refused to send down rain.

When I was very young, we wintered along the Great River, keeping warm in the earthen mounds we built where the bluffs protected us from the winter wind. Through the dark months we found warmth in fires, songs and dances. We did not fear the snow or cold winds. We were warm inside our winter homes. And when the spring buds formed on the trees, our clan left for our summer hunting grounds. We journeyed south to a special place on a ridge beside a very small river we called Little Buffalo. A river so small no one else cared about it. It was one day's walk from another river we called Big Buffalo. Only one or two times do I remember our warriors having to defend our hunting ground from other tribes who wished to drive us away.

Few other clans bothered our camp because my father was a wise man. He sat and talked with the leaders of other clans when we lived together in our wintering grounds by the Great River. They drew maps on skins and made agreements. Our little river had thick trees for birds and for hiding. It bubbled water so clear it was pleasant to drink and cured many illnesses. When buffalo and antelope came for the water, we would hide and kill what we needed. When large herds moved through the valley, our warriors—all my brothers and my father's brothers and their sons—made a great kill. So there was plenty, and we did not have to move on with the herds. We could stay at our small river and never be hungry.

After a great kill, we would feast for three days. Then we constructed our willow branch drying platforms and we cut the buffalo meat into strips and lay it on the platform to dry in the hot sun. The sundried buffalo strips would become our winter food.

Because we had plenty and did not need to follow the herds, my mother and her sisters and their daughters planted corn and maize and pumpkins in the low valley below the ridge, which was fed by bubbling springs. We would beg the fathers and brothers to stay at our summer camp until their plantings could be harvested. Men did not like harvesting—or staying too long in one spot—but they stayed anyway. They laughed when the buffalo trampled our mothers' fields. But they did not laugh when it was time to eat our mothers' harvest.

When the endless caravans of white men trampled across our sacred hunting grounds to the north and to the south, they did not know about our little river in between. They only cared about big rivers because their beasts needed so much water and their fires craved so much wood. They did not even know we were here. And that is why we could stay and live quietly as my people had for generations without time.

By the time I was a mother, going to the Great River for winter meant dying. Dying of hunger. Dying of White Man's sicknesses. Dying from White Man's devil potions. Dying from water that turned to mud.

By the time I was a grandmother to many grandchildren, they began killing the buffalo. Bands of noisy white men with huge guns rode out on their horses. They killed the buffalo and left them to rot in the sun. The wind was filled with the stench of death. Their bones littered the landscape, making the skies cry with sorrow as the sun turned them white. Even the vultures were moved to tears. And our children were hungry.

First they came for the buffalo. Then they will come for us. When we are gone, what will they come for? The grass?

So even if the Plains around our little river were swept with wind so cold it would stop a heart, we had to stay in our summer camp all winter. We made earth houses with thick walls, dug into the sides of hills. We buried food in deep holes to keep it away from wolves. We covered ourselves with many buffalo robes. We stored up great mounds of buffalo chips to burn through the long winter to keep warm. Even so, babies froze in the dark, bitter days. Warriors who left the winter caves to look for game often did not come back. I survived to become an old woman, sad and bent with trying so hard to draw breath in a land that was dying from white man's curses.

My heart nearly stopped one cold winter when the snow was piled deep and the wind would not relent. We were running out of food. The buffalo chips were so wet they would not make fire. I refused to eat, so the little ones could have my food. As I lay near death, my waning spirit saw visions. Man using roaring creatures to dig up the earth, destroying the grasses and flowers and homes of the small animals who need to burrow into the earth. They did not understand that the grass and the soil are one and inseparable. They ripped up the plants that cling lovingly to the soil and planted instead other grasses that did not wish to grow on the Plains. So their grasses withered and died and the wind blew dust in their faces. But still they did not understand, even as the dust blackened their skies. They dug under the earth and stole their neighbors' water and used it foolishly until the springs refused to bubble and the little rivers became dry.

When my ridge was saved from destruction, my spirit blessed the men who did not touch it, even though it was out of their forgetfulness not their mercy. Many years passed. White men did not care about my ridge. They seldom walked on it, though their beasts loved the grasses and ate it happily. But when this golden child found our ridge, she was filled with love and songs. The sunflowers turned their heads to look at her as she passed by. She picked up the stones we dropped and put them in her pockets. Then when she was finished playing with them, she returned them to their resting spots.

And when she called out to me, I answered.

Then came the little one holding her hand. I did not talk to him. He found company enough in the spirits of the animals who live on the ridge. They loved him. He did not need to talk with me.

There are many generations of spirits who walk the paths of this ridge, wearing them deep with their restlessness. We watch the golden children as they play their innocent games. We surround and seal them in love so they cannot be harmed. The children do not know that great sorrow sits on this rise. They must not know what happened here. They cannot yet hear the lament in the wind. May they grow like the sunflowers, with light around their heads. May the spirits protect their golden petals from the hot wind to come.

Nadi-ish-dena.

6

Willow Valley

I REMEMBER AN EARLIER visit to this old Home Place before every-thing was totally gone. It was a year after I moved to Chicago and the only time I ever brought a boyfriend home to meet my parents. John was a Chicago neighborhood boy, never before out of the city. He was enamored with the idea of country life and jealous of my rural roots—until he saw Western Kansas. I could see in his eyes how disappointed he was with this lackluster land I had described so lovingly. I could even detect the look of pity in his eyes that he tried to hide over my deprived childhood—I'd never thought of it as deprived. But in the same way, I must admit that when he took me to where he grew up, a northside apartment building beside the El tracks with its grimy back alley and gray painted back porches, I had thought the same about his childhood.

Nevertheless, I bubbled on, driving everywhere in the county, show-ing him one site after another. So inevitably, I came here. It was 1970 and a dirt road lead down to the yard. There was still a ring of large cot-tonwoods surrounding the gentle square depression where the dugout once stood. Across the yard, under the shade trees near the row of cedars were wooden picnic tables. I had been told that the place had been turned into a "community park," though it was private property still owned by the Houston family.

The cherry orchard was long since gone, the springs no longer bub-bled and the creek had dried up, along with the willow woods that had lined its bank. Irrigation had sucked down the water level everywhere so all the little spring-fed streams in the area were gone.

But I could still point out the various spots of interest. Here's where the chicken barn was that the tornado took, the outhouse was here, the well with its hand pump and so on.

But in the middle of my monologue a blue pickup came roaring down the drive and screeched to a halt. Out jumped Bob Houston, known in our community as "Young Houston," grabbing a rifle off the back rack with a smooth, much-practiced motion. Shaking it in the air above his head, coming toward us, he yelled. "What are you doing on my land?" His face was red. He didn't recognize me. All he saw, in his rage, was my orange VW bug with Illinois plates and my boyfriend's long hair and beard.

I was frightened. John was frightened.

I wanted to say, You, Bob Houston, YOU get off MY land. I grew up here. Your father took it away from my grandfather during the dust bowl when he missed his last payment. My dad bought it back, and then you personally took it away from him when he fell behind during the dust storm fifties. You sucked us dry, taking one-third of our crops, which didn't even leave us enough to pay for the seed, and wouldn't even let us run an electric line from the road so we could have a refrigerator. We paid for this land twice. You get off MY land. And furthermore, your grandfather was nothing but a lawless gunslinger—I don't care what the legends say. So just put your gun back in your gunrack and turn your pickup around and GET OFF MY LAND.

I didn't say that. When faced with a gun, I'm gutless. I didn't even tell him what my name was. I just said. "We saw the picnic tables and the shade trees and we thought it was a park."

"You thought wrong," he shouted. "Those picnic tables are for members of the community who clear it with me first. And not for outsiders."

John, always diplomatic, said. "We didn't mean to bother anybody. We'll run into town and see if we can find another place to have our picnic lunch."

"You just do that." He stormed back to his pickup, and sat there, waiting for us to leave. We did. By the time I got into the car, I was shaking and starting to cry. Young Houston waited until we drove out and then followed closely behind us to see if we would actually go back to town. So we turned towards town instead of driving to Golden Hill farm.

"Who was that?" asked John. "Is he from that Houston family you were telling me about."

"Yes."

"The grandson of the famous, legendary gunslinger, George Houston?"

"Yes."

"Still slinging guns, I see."

When we got home, I told my father. I've never seen him so angry.

"The nerve. It's a community picnic ground. Everyone uses it and nobody asks his permission. He granted the use of the driveway and five acres to the county. I'm going to go right over there and tell him he just run my daughter off."

I begged him not to.

My father must have talked to him sometime, because several weeks later I got a letter of apology that read. "Becky, I'm very sorry. I didn't recognize you. I saw your strange VW bug and I just thought it was a couple of those hippies from Back East looking for a place to smoke dope."

I probably should explain the term "Back East" which we always capitalize, both in writing and in the *way* we say it. For us, it stands for any place east of an imaginary north-south line running through the middle of Kansas. So Topeka and Kansas City are already Back East. So is Chicago. And of course New York is really Back East. It doesn't really matter how far east, because Back East is an attitude as well as a geographical designation. It is foreign, it is uppity. It is where people don't know the real values in life.

The term originated in the frontier days to designate where settlers had come "from." Back East was the settled area of the country. Anything west was the frontier. In Western Kansas, even the central and eastern part of our state is "foreign." It is, after all, a land of rainfall and hills and valleys. My mother grew up in the central part of the state, which to the casual eye is flat prairie not very different than Western Kansas, but it was so different to us that we pushed it farther east, referring to it as *Eastern* Kansas rather than Central Kansas. In Central Kansas, they talk about "Back East," meaning everything east of *them*. No doubt St. Louis is considered Back East in Kansas City, a place which we consider to already be very Back East.

The word "back" is itself pregnant with meaning. When I moved to Chicago, my Odyssey friends and neighbors said I moved "back" east, even though I'd never been there before. The term carries the sense of giving up on the frontier and moving "back," a chicken-hearted thing for a settler to do. A true pioneer sticks it out. If on the other hand, you moved to California, you were going "Out West." Pushing the boundaries, moving further to the edge of a frontier. That was far more noble. "Out West" had a ring of adventure and gutsiness. North and south, by the way, were irrelevant—the world and values in general were measured on an east-west continuum. For sure, going Back East was a cowardly act, a virtual rejection of one's humble beginnings.

My own family did not subscribe to these East-West notions, though we used the terms along with our neighbors. We had come, after all, from Russia, the other side of the world. And with a grandfather who moved his family from Canada to South Carolina to Colorado to who knows where else, directions were largely irrelevant. Except that Grandpa Jacob always knew where the center was, the place to return to. Kansas, the very *center* of Kansas, in fact.

I had driven to Chicago in my VW Beetle the summer after college graduation on little more than a whim, and when I decided I was going to stay there, I took the train home to collect a few things and say goodbye to my parents. I spent a week in Odyssey seeing friends, preparing myself to leave the nest of Golden Hill. A neighboring farmer stopped by, a friend of my older brothers, saying he was on his way to Dodge to pick up some repair parts, did I want to come along. It was an odd suggestion, but I said yes. I wanted to say goodbye to Dodge City. One of his first stops was a used furniture and appliance store where he dropped off an old refrigerator. While Bernie haggled with the owner over a price for the fridge, I nosed around in back and discovered an old trunk standing behind a shed, crusted with dried mud as if it had been dragged out of the river. I scratched off some of the dirt to reveal an elaborately-constructed, wooden and steel, canvas-covered trunk. When Bernie came looking for me, he asked, "You want that old trunk?"

"Well, kind of, I don't know what I'd do with it. I'm getting ready to move to Chicago. But it's really unusual."

"I'll git it for you," he said in a burst of good will.

He went to find the owner and brought him back to where I was, still scraping mud off the trunk. "How much you want for it?" asked Bernie.

"Nothing," replied the toothless old man. "It's a piece of junk somebody left here. I'd be happy to get rid of it. Just take it."

"Oh no, I don't want something for nothing," Bernie said, with a touch of bravado, which I assumed was to impress me. Bernie handed the man a five-dollar bill. He took it saying, "I feel like a thief taking money for that junk. But if it'll make you happy, okay."

Not sure if it was a gift or whether he was acting as my bargaining agent, I tried to give Bernie five dollars. "Hell, no, this is my going away gift to you," he said. He loaded the crusted trunk into the back of his pickup. "Becky," he said very seriously, "I want you to clean that thing up and take it with you Back East. And every time you look at it, I want you to remember where you come from."

Back at Golden Hill, Bernie unloaded the trunk onto the porch. Even empty, it was heavy. Over the next few days, using a plastic windshield scrapper and a stiff brush, I removed the caked-on mud, cleaned the canvas, polished the wood slats and oiled the leather straps. When opened, the trunk became a bureau—a kind of old-time secretary, with drawers and lots of little compartments. Years later, an antique dealer I dated tried to buy the trunk off me for $100 and was nonchalantly secretive about his interest in it. When I brought in another antique dealer to appraise my trunk, I discovered it was a Civil War officer's trunk. In rare mint condition, considering all the drawers and compartments were intact, it was worth at least $2,000. I have kept it, and will always keep it. And I have also kept my vow to Bernie, who died young of cancer. I have never, and *will* never, forget where I come from.

To do so, however, requires a vivid memory and an active imagination. The markers most civilizations use to cherish their past are missing from this landscape. I'm back now, eighteen years after my aborted picnic with John and thirty-two years after I originally left it, and I can't even drive onto the yard of the old Home Place. There is no road and it's fenced in. All the cottonwood trees are gone. Not one remains. The land has been plowed and maize is growing in straggly rows. I can't even see an indentation where the creek once ran. The church-yard up the incline—can't even call it a hill now—is home to a trailer house and assorted farm equipment. Rusting junk sits around the crumbling foundation where the church once sat.

Down the road a half-mile is the old Willow Valley school site.

I'm there now. And I'm probably risking some other farmer's ire by getting out of my car. But I want to walk on this ground. The one-room red brick country schoolhouse is gone. It was demolished by a tornado. After so many drills, and so many close calls when we'd run for the culvert, it finally happened, but mercifully when school children were no longer here. The school district had been consolidated five years earlier and the building was sitting empty. Since the demise of the schoolhouse was an act of God not man, I feel no bitterness about its disappearance. Just sadness that not even bricks and mortar last in this hopeless landscape.

"They called it a community building for a while and kept it up, but nobody was using it for anything so there was no point in rebuilding it," my dad reported to me on one trip home. When the tornado leveled the building, the farmer who had taken over the property sold the scattered bricks for a few dollars to someone willing to haul them off. I wish I could have kept a brick for myself. The farmer repaired the teacher's cottage, which had sustained very little damage, and used it for a shed. It still sits there, empty, windows broken, deteriorating. The farmer moved a trailer onto the schoolyard and lived there for a few years. He even kept the playground equipment standing for his children. But now the trailer is gone as well as the swings, teeter-totter and merry-go-round. They either gave up farming or moved to town, I'm guessing.

But the boundaries of the schoolyard are still visible and some rusting farm equipment sits at one corner. At the north side, there is the barbed wire fence that once held our buffalo. The yard is mostly hard dirt with occasional weed outcroppings—I can almost make out the softball field and paths around the bases. Maybe it's my imagination. All that remains of the schoolhouse itself is the foundation, with weeds growing inside. It looks so small now.

I step over and stand at the approximate place where my desk sat when I was nine years old. The schoolroom seemed so big then. I can close my eyes and see every detail: windows along the south side, their wide-slat blinds always dusty, with lows shelves underneath to store our books. Out the windows you can see playground equipment, swings, teeter-totter, a merry-go-round. We are lucky to have them. Some country schools don't have playground equipment. When you enter the school there are two cloakrooms to either side where you hang your coats on hooks and store your galoshes underneath in winter. A bank of shelves in each cloakroom holds our lunch boxes. Then the corridor opens up into the one big room. At the end is the teacher's desk. In back of her the whole wall is a blackboard. And I do mean black, not the sickly green they make chalkboards now. Posted above the blackboard are the letters of the alphabet with the correct cursive form of each letter on a second row underneath. Rows of desks face the teacher, little ones up front graduating to bigger desks in the back rows. They are the kind of desk with a seat attached and a slanted desktop that lifts up to reveal a bin to store pencils, crayons, scissors and workbooks. When the teacher is busy with another grade, the only thing you can do is read or fill out workbooks—endless workbooks. The lights that hang from above have bulbs painted silver on the bottom, I don't know why, and they always seemed to buzz. I can still hear them buzzing. A gigantic gas stove in the back heats the room—inadequately, I might add. Attached to the back of the stove sits a square container, which we fill with water to add moisture to the room. We fight over who gets to refill it. In back, on the right, is a sink. Why if we have running water, don't we have flush toilet bathrooms? Would that be too much to ask?

The toilets are outside at the back end of the schoolyard. A boys' one to the left, a girls' to the right with elaborate blinds in front of each. Behind the boys' blinds we hear they have pissing contests, where they stand in a row and see who can piss the farthest. Boys are so nasty. But thank goodness for our blinds. We girls run behind these tall wood panels to get away from the boys and we huddle to gossip and share secrets. Yes, here's where I learned the facts of life, strangely enough from the preacher's daughter who is two years younger than me. How can a seven-year-old know things like this? She tells me how a baby is made. With the man's thing being stuck into the woman's pee pee hole.

That's impossible, I tell her, how could that even work? And no grownup would do such a thing even if it *were* possible, I tell her. My parents certainly wouldn't.

She demurs. "Maybe, I'm wrong." She adds the other details about how the baby begins growing in the mother's stomach, getting bigger and bigger until it's time to come out. Now all this is sounding pretty scientific. Maybe she's right about part of it. She's just got the beginning wrong.

I ask my older cousin (she's eleven) at church the next Sunday—again, behind the cover of the ladies' outhouse blind, constructed pretty much like the one at school. She confirms that Patty's got it right. It does all start that way. And furthermore, the word for it, she announces to me, is "sex." That's the first time I hear that word.

I spent eight years here on this schoolyard, learning all the things kids are supposed to learn. And I learned them well. When I got to high school, a gigantic consolidated district school in Odyssey with four hundred students, I found that instead of lagging behind the town kids as I'd feared, I was way ahead of them. And I'd never even had homework those first eight years. If a teacher had ever assigned any, she'd have been fired. The parents, after all, were the school board. Kids were needed for farm chores when they got home from school. Everyone understood that.

I wrote a lot of plays. We put on programs for our parents on Halloween, Thanksgiving, Christmas and Valentine's Day. We'd perform songs and several plays for each occasion. I was the official playwright—which meant I got to direct too. I produced creepy Halloween skits that scared the daylights out of everybody, inspiring Christmas tales of poor children who got magical Christmas gifts from unknown, unseen strangers, and mushy, romantic tales for Valentine's Day that nobody wanted to act in.

My best play was about an old lady who went to the moon in a rocketship. She found it just sitting out in her cow pasture and she was curious so she climbed in, and boom, it took off. We made a huge rocketship covered with aluminum foil. It had all sorts of dials that lit up—we used Christmas lights. We even dressed somebody up as a black and white cow and he mooed loudly when the rocket ship took off with a gigantic explosion. We couldn't actually make it take off, but we dropped the rollup curtain down hard during the explosion and the audience got the idea. Boy did they applaud. I think we did that one for Halloween. It doesn't sound like Valentine's Day fare.

The Christmas program would always end with my dad and a few others coming down the aisle and handing out brown paper sacks (back East, they call them "bags") filled with stuff, one sack for every person there. In the sack was an orange, an apple, several walnuts, peanuts, and other nuts still in their shells, a red and white striped candy cane, some foil-wrapped Hershey's kisses and a few hard candies wrapped in colorful paper. That was it. The very same contents each year. And we looked forward to those Christmas sacks all year round. The school board bought them, and they always made sure they had just enough for every man, woman and child.

In some other country schools we heard that one of the fathers would dress up like Santa Claus to hand out the sacks. We didn't do that in Willow Valley. We all knew there was no such thing as Santa Claus. That was a fairy tale they tell city kids who will believe almost anything.

And then a few days later we got the same brown sack with the same exact contents at the Willow Valley church Christmas Eve program. So we were double-blessed during the holidays. The Sunday School teachers wrote and directed the plays for the church programs. There was no room for my improvisational skills or my turns of phrases. These were very scripted and always included the same manger scene and I always got to be an angel. The year when I was seven, I was selected to be Mary. I was so excited. Except I had to provide a baby doll for the manger, and I didn't have a suitable doll. All I had was a homemade Raggedy Ann doll, but that wouldn't do. I cried myself to sleep in my room at night. I knew times were really bad and there was no chance that my parents could buy me a store-bought baby doll. I decided to wrap my Raggedy Ann in so many baby blankets that you couldn't tell what it was.

My grandmother Sara came over just before we left for church while my mother was adjusting my costume which consisted of one of her scarves tied around my waist and another over my head fastened under my chin with a safety pin and flowing over my shoulders. "I have a present for you, my grandmother said, handing me a shoebox tied with a red ribbon.

I figured it was new shoes for tonight. Christmas gifts—those few we got—were always practical. I set the box down.

"No, open it now," she urged.

"It's not Christmas until tomorrow," I demurred.

"No, we'll make an exception tonight."

"No, Mamma," my mother rebuked Grandma, "We're late to church. We have to go. Let her open it in the morning."

"No, *now*," my grandmother said sternly.

I opened the box. Inside, nestled in white tissue paper, was the most beautiful baby doll I'd ever seen. Its face was sweet and its head was made of soft, not hard plastic. Its body was pillow-like stuffed muslin, but the arms and legs were soft molded plastic with real pinkish-colored baby skin. It emitted that new plastic smell. I clutched it to me and said, "It's my baby Jesus. It's my baby Jesus."

I was never so happy as I was that Christmas.

IN MANY WAYS THE Willow Valley church was even more the center of the community than the school. It was a white-painted frame building with a steeple and bell tower even though we didn't have a bell. High arched windows. Plain. No stained glass like the ones in town, but that's okay. It would have been too distracting. That's what everybody said. Inside, all the walls were white plaster. The pews were dark mahogany brown. After church everyone would stand around outside in various little groups gabbing and gabbing, as if no one was hungry enough to go home. Sometimes we ate at the church. You could tell if it was a potluck Sunday, because right in the middle of Sunday School, we'd smell the coffee brewing, wafting up from the basement. It had a special church coffee smell. The food was plentiful. If it was a nice day, the tables would be set outside, covered with white paper with bricks to hold the paper down so it wouldn't blow away. Every lady tried to outdo the next one by putting all sorts of creative things in their Jell-O salads—cottage cheese in lime Jell-O, pineapple rings and maraschino cherries in orange Jell-O, black cherries and walnuts in cherry Jell-O, strawberries and cream cheese squares in strawberry Jell-O, grated carrots and diced celery in lemon Jell-O. Then there were lots of platters of fried chicken, sliced ham, creamy potato salads, and of course, mouth-watering pies—cherry, apple, rhubarb, banana cream.

I get hungry just thinking about it.

Pastors came and went in our Willow Springs church. No one much wanted to stay long for such a small church. They were all boring, too. I was always happy when another one left because then we could go back to Grandpa Isaac's sermons. He was my best friend's grandpa, an old farmer who looked just like Abraham Lincoln, tall—way more than six foot—thin, shaggy gray hair, big ears. He looked just like Abe Lincoln would have looked if he had lived to be ninety years old. Grandpa Isaac told the most wonderful stories—things that happened to him when he was a boy in the olden days. And there were always important lessons to learn from his stories, just like Jesus' parables, only Western Kansas style. Everybody listened, even the children. To this day, whenever I think about God, he looks like Grandpa Isaac.

On Tuesday afternoons there was ladies' sewing circle. All the women gathered and sat around in a circle working on a quilt stretched out between them. The quilts were to be sent to the mission field. Whatever would you do with a quilt in a "field," I used to wonder. Us little ones played and tumbled underneath the quilt. It was like being in an Arabian tent and you could see the light shining through the pretty colored squares.

The ladies mostly talked and gossiped and laughed. They were always laughing, sometimes so hard, tears ran out of their eyes. It took them weeks to finish even one quilt. Annie used to laugh so hard she'd nearly choke. From what we could tell, most of their jokes were about our dads.

Eventually, the men in the church built a parsonage on the southern edge of the churchyard. Maybe that would encourage a pastor to stay a bit longer. It was nicer than any of our houses, with a beautiful little lawn and flowers in front, just like you might see in town.

Missionaries were always coming through giving little programs, showing slides and asking for money. One April evening, my parents couldn't go because Mom had a migraine headache and Dad said he had to stay with her. We kids wanted to go, so my two older brothers and I piled into the pickup and went to church. We never missed a chance to see a missionary slide show. You got to see naked breasts—big ones hanging down, and shiny black naked little children running around, the little boys with their little pissers sticking out, little girls with their crack showing, running free not caring about anything.

The missionaries always explained that nakedness was normal for

Africans in the jungles of the Belgian Congo, especially with little children, plus African women were always nursing, and their breasts needed to be available. These were, after all, heathens. But when they become Christians they start wearing blouses, the missionary wife would usually add. Fortunately, in most of the pictures they hadn't become Christians yet.

The slide shows would always end with a picture of the sunset. And then the missionary would start explaining how there was more work to be done. When you saw the sunset pop up you knew they were about to start some sob story and pass around a collection plate to send them back to the mission field. What field were they talking about? You could see from the pictures there were no fields, just jungle.

This particular April evening, we never got to the sunset picture. Rapt inside the church, lights out while we watched the slide show, we hadn't noticed that a dust storm was coming up. Dust storms are generally visible for a half-hour to an hour ahead as a huge purple mass on the horizon, rolling and roiling, getting closer and closer. When you saw it, you rushed home as fast as you could, secured your animals in their barns, made sure all member of the family were in and accounted for, that all the windows were tightly closed, and rolled wet towels were placed against window sills and bottoms of doorways. After literally sealing yourself in, you got candles and kerosene heaters ready because you would lose power and you drew buckets of water if your well was electric-powered. There was an air of panic as you rushed to be ready while nervously peering out the window as the purple mass grew closer.

This particular April dust storm rolled in from the west, the only side of the church without windows. We didn't know it was coming until it hit. In minutes the electricity was out, the wind howled and whistled at the windows and the church building shuddered with the force of the gusts.

Even the missionaries were frightened. We all prayed together loudly. But then someone said, "We can't stay here. We need to get to the parsonage where there will be food. This could last for many hours, maybe days." But there was zero visibility. If we ventured out, we could be lost in the storm and choked by the dust and perhaps walk in the wrong direction.

But someone's uncle knew what to do. If we all lined up and held hands and walked in the direction of the parsonage—at least when we started from the church door we would know which direction to face—even if we went a little wrong, someone in the line was bound to stumble against the parsonage. So it was planned. The little ones would ride piggyback on a grownup so they could protect their faces and so that the wind would not grab them. I rode on my big brother's back and buried my nose in his collar. I was so afraid. I'd never before been outside in a total blackout dust storm. We marched forward, thirty-some people holding hands tightly. Good thing we marched in a line, because it was the last person on the left flank who bumped into the far corner of the house. In our journey of a hundred yards, we had gone so wrong, we had been heading mostly west and not so much straight south like we thought we were. That's how badly disoriented you could become in the dark with the wind seeming to burst in all directions at once.

We stumbled into the house, and were pulled to safety by the big men. There we huddled and prayed and sang through the dark night hoping the storm would end. In the middle of the next morning the wind subsided, the air cleared, and we dug our pickup out from the dust drifts and drove home. Boy, were our parents happy to see us. They didn't know if we were dead or alive. They'd worried all night fearing that we had headed home when we saw the storm but became lost and overcome by the dust before we could reach home.

The little white church was indeed the center of the Willow Springs community. There were weddings here, funerals too. When a new baby was born, we couldn't wait until the first time the parents would bring it to church. Everyone made a fuss. And the pastor would ask that the baby be brought to the front to receive a blessing and announce its name.

Then we got a new pastor, young, just out of seminary. He preached very exciting sermons. People called him charismatic. Town folk started coming out just to hear him preach. Before we knew it, the church was always full to overflowing. By the time I was about thirteen there were so many new church members driving in from town, that the majority took a vote and decided to move the congregation to town. The plan was to build a new bigger church on the outskirts of Odyssey, abandoning our little white wooden country church. Strangely enough, even the country people seemed to think that was the right thing to do. So a very modern blond-brick church was built in town with a high roof and stained glass windows and turquoise blue carpeting and pews with maroon velvet seats. It was really fancy.

The little white country church building was sold to some congregation just over the border in Oklahoma. I stood and watched the day they pried it from its foundation and hoisted the shuddering church up onto a huge flat truckbed. When they had secured it with cables and ropes, they began moving very, very slowly down the gravel road going south. I watched it go. The truck inching along the road. Going south.

I knew that was the beginning of the end. One year later, they closed the country school in a move called "consolidation." Consolidation meant that my little brother had to ride a bumpy bus for an hour every morning to get to school. Slowly the community was ceasing to exist. Now everything revolved around the town thirteen miles away. Just as the springs had dried up, now Willow Valley also dried up. The dust storms were blowing our way of life right off the face of the earth. The only important thing out in our part of the county was the gravel road that led to town.

A year later, they paved the road so we could get to town quicker.

7

Voice on the Wind II

EVEN AS I WATCH the girl spirits move in harmony along the ridge, my old woman spirit sees visions of horror. This golden child will be banished from the ridge just as I was. The cactus will no longer bloom, the spring will no longer bubble, the wolves will not wail love songs at night. Hills will become valleys. Valleys will become hills. Loud roars will echo across the Plains, the earth will shake, and the wind will turn foul.

When I was a girl I saw the hills, as far as the eye could see, covered with brown as the buffalo herds moved slowly following the bloom of spring. The hills will again be brown with beasts, but they will no longer move like a wide brown river flowing south. They will stand dumb waiting for their death. They will be afraid but yet they will not run.

8

Noise on the Plains

IN THE HOME PLACE DAYS, my three older brothers, all near one another in age, were one blurred entity of big brotherness, even though, in truth, they each were distinctly different from one another. The oldest, Harold, was intellectual and spiritual—he taught me to read. The middle one, Jim, was active and rambunctious—he taught me to ride a bicycle. The younger one, Joel, was inventive and mischievous—he played tricks on me and sometimes games with me. They were, as a group, both my protectors and oppressors. I was envious of their independence and secret "brotherhood." The room they shared was a messy den of activity. I didn't dare go in there. Yet, outside the dugout they formed an umbrella of security over me. My mother always claimed they "spoiled me." By the time the boys turned eleven or twelve, they were out in the fields helping my father. And by the time we moved to Golden Hill they were all in high school. Teenagers are no longer part of the family, or at least not in the same way. Then one by one they left to go to college. By the time I reached thirteen, the "boys" were all away at college. I missed them terribly, and would stand for hours looking out the picture window on the day they were scheduled to return home on a holiday break.

So by the time we were well settled into Golden Hill and the elms were starting to give shade, it was just Tommy and me. Mom called us her "second family." Tommy and I were different from the rest. I can only guess that it was our playground—the pasture—that made us different. There is something unmistakably spiritual about ground that has never been plowed, that has remained essentially untouched through millennia of time. I can't explain it. But I could feel it whenever I walked on that ground. Tommy and I found secret places in our holy ground that we never discussed with anyone. For instance, once the earth gave way beneath our feet at the west end of the ridge and we fell into what seemed like a small cave. When we dug about with our fingers searching for clues, we found all kinds of tools and arrowheads—a grinding stone, large flints that seemed like spearheads to us, an abundance of arrowheads, perfectly shaped as if prepared but never used. We at first believed it to be a bear cave, but then decided it was a hiding place or storage place. The fallen-in place was soon blown full of sand and eventually became a faint indentation in the ridge and we forgot about the mystery that surrounded it.

After I left for college, the teenaged Tommy stilled "played" in the virgin pasture, with all his horses and later his fledgling buffalo herd.

I turned thirteen as the year 1959 was about to become 1960. It was the year that the whole world changed. The Beatles visited America. I graduated from the eighth grade. They paved the gravel road. The church moved to town. The country school closed (Thomas would not get to finish out his childhood under the tutelage of Six Shooter Shaw, and there would be no buffalo hunting during recess). And, a mere half-hour's drive away, the Clutter family was murdered in cold blood.

I will never forget that day—the morning after—when we heard about it, not from a newspaper or TV but from that Western Kansas grapevine which buzzed over the party phone lines across the thirty-five miles. That night, Tommy and I and two of our cousins had slept outside on blankets on the lawn, as we often did on warm nights. The next day my father, who personally knew Herb Clutter, grimly informed Tommy and me that we would never again sleep outside at night. Furthermore, he did something he had never done before. He locked the doors before we went to bed. And he would faithfully lock them every night from that day on. He also took Tommy and me to the rifle cabinet in the utility room closet, took the rifle down, and said that tomorrow he would begin teaching us how to use a gun. But the Clutter incident is not the only thing that drove us inside.

It was the noise.

Not only is Western Kansas the flattest place on earth, it is the quietest—or more precisely once was the quietest place on earth. The quiet was one of the things that is said to have driven pioneer women batty in the early days. I would have loved that pristine quiet. For the hush of the prairies was not the absence of sound. It was the lack of meaningless background noise, allowing the subtle, natural sounds to stand alone in their richness. Scores of sounds periodically break the underlying quiet of the Plains, giving life texture—the warbling of meadowlarks, the nocturnal yelping of coyotes, the wailing and whistling of wind. Then came the sounds of man. Farms were far apart in this sparsely settled flat land. But from five miles away, on a still morning you could hear a farmer shouting to his son, cursing his horse or hammering on his barn roof. The sound waves, no matter how trivial, seemed destined to travel until someone could receive them. One knew the goings on of your neighbors even before the advent of party line phones.

In the ranching days, the bawling of cattle and the shrill whiny of horses broke the silence. With the settling of the land and the development of farming on the Great Plains, the roar of farm machinery in the fields, trains on their tracks and trucks on the road entered the auditory landscape. My favorite mechanical noise was the train whistle. In the middle of the night, freight trains rolled through the Plains carrying out grain and sugar beets and bringing in mailbags and farm equipment. From my earliest childhood days, I remember the plaintive whistle of the trains whose track lay five miles from the Home Place. The train seemed to be crying out in loneliness. It was, after all, a train without people except for the engineer and one or two crew in the locomotive. Each train trailed its obligatory caboose at its rear, but the caboose was nearly always empty.

Once, to celebrate my cousin's sixth birthday, my aunt invited ten children to ride the caboose from Odyssey to the next town. It was the first time I rode on a train. Excited out of our minds, barely able to sit still on the wooden seats, we children were the only riders, except for a conductor in his uniform and one or two moms to keep order. We squealed in delight every time the engineer hit the whistle, and I'm guessing he did so more often than usual that day. The whistle took on a new and different meaning up close as it blasted into our eardrums. It was a different sound altogether—robust and celebratory. I learned then, that it was only the distance between the train and myself that made a train whistle sound lonely.

Over the years of my childhood, when I couldn't sleep at night, or when I was frightened, I was comforted by the wailing whistle and the rushing sound of the train, modified and musicalized by five miles worth of airwaves. It became for me a signal that all was normal in the world. Even when we moved to Golden Hill, now seven miles from the tracks, I could still hear the trains at night, only slightly muffled by the additional two miles.

On the Home Place inside our dugout, especially in winter, with the earth itself forming the walls and ceiling of our dwelling, we had been cocooned like badgers curled up in their underground burrows. All was quiet, except for my father's snoring. But that sound, too, was a signal that all was well in the household. In the summer, with windows open, various night noises drifted in through the screens—cows mooing themselves to sleep, turtle doves cooing, owls hooting, yelping coyotes and our dogs answering their challenge. And finally, the annoying chirping of sparrows in the cottonwoods as dawn began to lighten the sky. But for the most part, in this magical indentation in the prairie that we called the Home Place, there was no noise.

Noise entered my world the day we moved into the house on Golden Hill: the constant insidious hum of electricity. People think electricity is invisible and soundless. It is not. Every appliance, whether the refrigerator or the furnace—virtually every item plugged into a socket—creates a noise. Together they formed a hum that altered my world. Worst of all was the noise of the television, which entered our household when I was fourteen. Its high-pitched background squeal assaulted my ears. No one else seemed to hear it, but when Tommy sneaked out of bed and turned on the television in the middle of the night, even with the volume turned all the way down, the high-pitched hum jolted me upright in my bed.

However, it was the roar of irrigation wells that shattered the prairie's stillness once and for all, ushering in a new and sinister era on the High Plains.

Irrigation was the most exciting thing to come to our county. It was going to change life in Western Kansas. There would never be another dust bowl. Never another drought. Never another crop failure. Farmers would prosper as never before, forever freed from the cycle of nature's cruelty. The whole county was buzzing with excitement. In a period of a few months, every farmer who could afford it, or who could borrow enough from the bank, was putting down irrigation wells.

Two decades earlier there had been another frenzy of well-drilling when a vast natural gas field was found under our area. Those wells, which now dotted our landscape, were small, unimposing and quiet, using the principles of air pressure to bring their bounty to the surface. In contrast, the irrigation wells that began springing up all over the country in the mid-fifties were noisy beyond belief. Their gas-fed motors droned on loudly day and night.

Success was measured by the number of wells a farmer owned. Suddenly our "bottom land," was nearly worthless. You needed flat land to run the irrigation ditches. Trees and creeks, cottonwoods and willows, hills and floodplains made land unsuitable for the miracle of irrigation. Only a small portion of our acreage on Golden Hill was a candidate for irrigating, but not enough to justify the expense of digging a well, buying the equipment and bulldozing the land into the controlled, slightly graded fields necessary for ditch irrigation. If the land was unsuitable so was my father's temperament. He wasn't about to bulldoze and dig ditches, or lug siphoning tubes around day and night. There was already too much to be done. On Sunday mornings, other farmers fell asleep during the sermon, exhausted from the backbreaking work of starting siphoning tubes for each and every furrow in their fields.

Farming could ask for no more of my father's soul than it already possessed. He resisted chemical fertilizer as well. It just wasn't natural. He preferred rotating crops, and giving fields a periodic rest. Farming, for him, was an expression of ancient symbiosis, not an act of taming the earth. And the pasture—he had promised himself and his God that he would never plow up the buffalo grass. It needed to stay and bear witness to the way things were supposed to be on the Plains. And once were.

Irrigation was possible in Western Kansas because of the Ogallala Aquifer, a huge underground reservoir of water so vast and close to the surface it would last forever. The Aquifer was the source of the springs that fed the creeks, the oozing buffalo wallows in low spots, and the occasional artesian wells and springfed lakes that had attracted waterfowl to the prairie since ancient times. The Ogallala Aquifer, often described as an underground lake, was really more of an underlying layer of gravel and rocks that held groundwater like a sponge. It was fed by underground flows of water originating from the snowpeaked Rocky Mountains to our west. The Aquifer, however, was not a renewable source of water, as we would learn after twenty years of wasteful, overzealous irrigation. In the hot, arid Plains, a sizable portion of the water pumped into the ditches was evaporating before it was able to penetrate the soil. No matter. Just pump more. And more, and more.

By 1960, there were two kinds of farmers: irrigation farmers and dryland farmers. My father was the latter. And the term was becoming derogatory—synonymous with "backward." At first it didn't much matter. Willow Valley farmers were slow to adopt irrigation. But then, more and more farmers were coming bleary-eyed to church. More and more shiny new cars were showing up in the parking lot. And less dust was blowing in the wind.

Then just across the road from our house, our neighbor put in a well. The drone was maddening. Gone were summer nights under a quiet, star-studded sky. And when I went out to the ridge, if the irrigation well was pumping, Gentle Wind would not join me. It was no use trying to build a campfire or sit and stare at the sunset. The drone in my ears would not stop. Its pitch and intensity changed with the winds and heaviness of the airwaves, but the irrigation well noise never became music, like the train whistle in the night. And it simply would not stop. Gentle Wind and her whispered secrets were lost to me forever.

To escape the noises that were closing in on me I turned to the radio. When my brothers got a new radio, I inherited the old console, a large, bulky piece of furniture, almost like a juke box. There was barely room for it in my small bedroom, but I squeezed it in between the wall and my bed, and listened to the latest hits coming from a station in Oklahoma City. My favorite song was *The Green Fields of Home* by the Four Freshman. It was an achingly lonely song about how they would give anything to see "the green fields of home once again." Shut in my room late at night, I listened to it and cried, missing home before I had even left it.

THE WELL ACROSS THE ROAD that drove me inside had been a late arrival, joining the roar of all the other wells all over Western Kansas.

Together, the wells pumped and pumped, sucking down the water table. Every year the farmers had to dig the wells deeper, sucking, sucking, sucking down the underground reservoir. The springs that once fed the creek had long since dried up, the last of the swimming hole catfish had died off and the pool turned to mud, then dry-caked earth. Now the creek bed was just crusty dirt. Even the wider, grander Cimarron River was dry, a riverbed of fine sand where once there had been the legendary quicksand lurking just beneath the water's surface that sucked whole wagonloads to their death. Now it was a harmless white sand beach, a place for teenagers to build bonfires, drink beer and lose their virginity. Along our creek and other small tributaries, the willows were thinning. Wild ducks no longer came. The top branches of the cottonwoods were dying.

I was turning thirteen. The landscape of my body was blooming while the landscape of the prairie was shriveling.

I endlessly daydreamed that the next dust trail to come down our road would be my secret love, a bronze-tanned, dark-eyed shy boy, suddenly no longer shy, coming down the drive to pick me up and take me away from all this. Sometimes, on hot summer afternoons, when I saw a dust trail in the distance, I would run to the picture window to look out, praying that the vehicle would slow to turn into our drive. But it never did. It just kept driving by. Too fast. Way too fast. Kicking up such a cloud of dust the identity of the driver of the pickup was completely obscured. He could be it, I'd think to myself. He could be the one. Someday he will slow down and come down the driveway. And take me away from all this.

Then I'd run into my room and close the door and listen to the Four Freshman as they mournfully harmonized:

Once there were valleys where rivers used to run . . .

9

Voices on the Wind III

I WILL STOP TALKING with the girl. Perhaps then she will go away. I do not want her heart to be broken like my heart was broken when they drove my clan south. The treachery of white man's counsel. They had taken all the big rivers and their valleys. But they promised they would not touch our land. We would live in peace forever on our summer hunting grounds. But it was all lies.

My father was wise, but he believed that when leaders speak for their people they speak with honor. That was always so with the tribes with whom we wintered by the Great River. But White Man's promises were lies. They spoke these words at Medicine Lodge and drew the words on paper that the hunting grounds south of the Great River would forever belong to our tribes "as long as water runs and grass grows." But it was lies. Water was running and grass was growing when we were forced to march south on dusty trails with no water. I was too old to walk. I was too weak. I wanted to stay with the children, but they had no mercy on an old woman. I do not wish to be buried in the ground along this trail, I said to my daughter. Instead, leave me to die alone with the spirit of the wind. They granted my wish. As I lay dying, I asked the vultures circling above to take my flesh back to the ridge so my spirit could be with my grandchildren. For that I am grateful.

A time will come for the golden child when the water will not run and the grass will not grow. I do not want to see her heart broken when the brown foam oozes over the ridge and destroys all life. If I stop talking with her perhaps she will tire of the ridge and her clan will seek other ground. Perhaps when the eagles fail to return and the wind blows without stopping and the dust swirls into her nostrils and stings her eyes she will heed the warnings. Perhaps she will wish to go away to the other side of the sun where children rule as kings, where her clear blue eyes can search for new and happier spirits. If I stop talking to her.

10

Odyssey

THE SAME YEAR THEY PAVED the road I began high school and the center of my life became Odyssey. Until then it was simply "town." The four most exciting words in my early memories were *let's go to town.* That's what we did if the sky offered us a soaking rain that was going to last all day. Admittedly, those were rare occasions. At the moment the drizzle gave way to real rain, my father would come into the house, all wet and excited.

"Get in the car. Let's all go to town."

And we did. We would pile into the car, babbling in excitement, little ones sitting on older one's laps to all fit in. In town, we'd take our time going through Duckwall's Dime Store to see what new doodad we could buy—if it didn't cost more than 25 cents. When it was raining Dad was generous, but there were limits.

Last stop was Barney's, the grocery store that took credit, the place we bought any food that didn't grow in our garden. Barney's Grocery had that false front you see in Main Street stores in Westerns. In fact, it looked right out of a movie. Never painted, or at least not in the last twenty-five years, the wooden slats had faded to that nondescript dry gray that looks so good in old black and white photographs. Inside, the shelves held all the staples in small quantities, real pickle barrels where pickles floated in brine, huge blocks of Swiss cheese from which Old Man Barney cut a slab and estimated its weight rather than bother to put it on a scale. Three things made Barney's unique and kept it thriving despite the appearance of a modern supermarket on the outskirts of town. One was the meat. Barney's son was the best butcher in town and his meat was always the freshest. Two, farmers could put their purchases on account all year long, and then pay up the day after wheat harvest. That privilege extended to the farmer's kids, so we knew we could drop in after school for a candy bar or a popsicle and never be embarrassed that we had no coins in our pockets like the town kids who got allowances. And three, Old Man Barney handed out candy to all the children.

The floors at Barney's were wide wooden planks with large cracks in between, kind of like our floor at home except Barney never waxed or oiled his. And the planks were so uneven that it made pushing the cart along rather difficult—plus the floor made scary creaking noises as you walked down the aisles.

After Barney's, we'd finish up with a malted milk or a rootbeer float at the drug store soda fountain. We'd sit on the stools at the counter, slurping up our malteds while my father argued politely with the pharmacist about politics.

But in normal times (as in no rain) we went to town once a week on Saturday night. We would all take our Saturday night baths, put on clean clothes and go to town. Stores stayed open late Saturday night in Odyssey to accommodate the farmers. There would be groups of men jawing on every corner while the womenfolk bought fabric in the dry goods store or did their weekly grocery shopping at Barney's. There was plenty of gabbing among the womenfolk too while they stood in line.

Those of us kids who were old enough to be trusted outside of Mom's sight would first check out Duckwall's, then walk from one end of Main Street to the other, parading in our good clothes. Older boys and girls giggled and sized each other up as they passed on the sidewalk. Most of the townspeople and plenty of the countryfolk as well, went to the movies on Saturday night. The theater opened its doors at 7:30 and the movie started at 8:00. We'd walk by and smell the popcorn. During the summer, the theater was closed, replaced by the Drive-In east of town where Old Odyssey used to be located. But we didn't go to movies. It was against our religion. Before I was born, Mom and Dad used to go every week during the War so they could see the newsreels. I think that was just an excuse. I didn't understand why we couldn't go see movies just because there was no war.

The town's photographer—who doubled as Odyssey's historian—was a cranky but lovable bachelor who lived in a back room behind his studio. Everyone called him Photo Joe. He once told me where the name Odyssey came from. He may have made up this story. But everyone accepted it as truth.

Here's how Photo Joe told it: Two strangers, Englishmen from the sound of their accent, one half crippled, one half deaf, rolled into town on the stagecoach, and looked around at all the drunken cowboys, the rowdy bars, dusty streets, tumbleweeds, and the broken-down stores on Main Street.

"This town is really odd, I'd say," said the half-crippled man to the other.

"What's that?" said the nearly deaf one.

"Odd, I'd say," shouted the other.

"Oh, I see, *Odyssey*. So *that's* the name of this place."

Odyssey was odd indeed. Everyone there was eccentric in some way. No one was normal by the standards that reigned outside our world. But we didn't know that when we were growing up, because we didn't have a TV signal yet. There was Photo Joe who remembered every detail of the town's history but always forgot his film. More than once he interrupted a wedding to say, "Stop everything. I have to go home and get film." He chronicled life in the town, giving his photos to the weekly newspaper for little or no money, relying on school class pictures and special events to somehow keep him in food. There was the 300-pound tax assessor who drove from farm to farm to assess the worth of the place in a special car made for him because he was too big to fit into just any car. He always wore a huge straw hat and the same blue and white polka-dot shirt his sister sewed for him—we wondered if he ever washed it. The bets were maybe once a year. There was the druggist who was always way too happy as he mixed up his concoctions in the back. There was the doctor who delivered the babies in town and was whispered to have fathered most of them as well. There was the judge who ate only fish, and the restaurant that made sure they always had catfish for him, even if their son had to play hookey from school to go fishing at the creek down below the town. There was the one woman who didn't have a kitchen in her home because she hated to cook. She wore gigantic movie star wigs and sunglasses, dark red lipstick drawn way outside the lines of her lips. She plucked her eyebrows out and drew in Lucille Ball arches instead. She and her quiet little husband, owner of the hardware store, ate out in restaurants every night—not an easy feat when there are only two restaurants in town, three if you counted the Dairy Queen.

In short, the town was filled with an amazing and delightful array of oddballs who would have been misfits anywhere but in Odyssey. Here, any and all peculiarities were accepted and loved. To be normal—by outside-of-Odyssey standards—would have been boring.

The town's odd assortment of characters bred a kind of tolerance I haven't seen in any other small town anywhere. There was one man who was a survivor of a Nazi concentration camp. He and his family were sponsored by a rancher north of town who had been one of the American soldiers to liberate his camp. He had a hole in the back of his head, a kind of cavity where no hair grew, as if someone had scooped out part of his brain. He kept his head covered by one of those caps you see in old pictures from Europe where the front sort of bags over the brim. I saw the hole once when the wind blew off his cap. Two Japanese families, also concentration camp survivors who had "lost their land during the war," came to Odyssey and started what my dad called a "truck farm" west of town. They grew all kinds of vegetables to sell to grocery stores in the area. When they first got here, as the story goes (which my father loves to tell), farmers in the area told them they couldn't grow vegetables here, that only wheat worked as a crop in this soil.

"Does your wife have a garden?" the eldest Mr. Takeuchi asked.

"Well, yes."

"What does she grow?"

"Bean, lettuce, carrots, you know, all those kinds of things."

"So how do they grow in her garden if only wheat works in this soil?"

(My father usually followed this story with a short lecture on creative thinking, not jumping to conclusions, or other homilies he drew from the ancient Japanese wisdom of our neighbor.) I had always presumed the Takeuchis had emigrated from Japan. Only years later, did I realize they must have been interned in this country during the war, and that their settling in Kansas was a way to get as far away as possible from their previous California life and the horrors of a national scandal no one ever talked about. The Takeuchis and other families who left bad circumstances and horrific memories to start anew were accepted with open arms in Odyssey. There was little anyone needed to do to blend in in Odyssey, because blending was not the point in this town. It never had been.

Our town had a long and colorful history forged by generations of lovably odd characters. Our first sheriff was Wyatt Earp's cousin, a gun-slinger of legendary prowess. One of the first ranchers was the famous Houston family, with the notorious seven brothers who literally ruled the area as they wished. As with nearly every other town in the west, groups of clever con men known as "town planters" came in, circulat-ed all kinds of wildly exaggerated claims about the rosy prospects for the town in newspapers back East, then voted bonds and gathered funds from unsuspecting out-of-town investors. They also raised taxes from the first few eager residents, supposedly for municipal improvements such as sidewalks and streetlights. Then they pocketed the money and disappeared to ride further west and "plant" another town, destined for ghost town status. But I guess Odyssey just wouldn't fade away. When the town planters skipped out, the founding ranch families, farmers and merchants persevered and built a two-story brick school, a hotel, a bank, and an opera house.

At some point, bonds from a bank in New York City came due. Times were tough at the turn of the century because one of many cyclical droughts had set in. When the Oklahoma territory opened up, disenchanted adventurers headed south. Odyssey's population dwindled from 2,000 to barely 100. The town fell behind on both the principal and interest on various old bonds plus a municipal mortgage. Here the story gets murky and old-timers argue fiercely about exactly what hap-pened. The most interesting of the stories says that two New York lawyers representing the bondholders rode into town to collect on the debt one day in 1908. The only way to collect was to foreclose on the whole town. Before the lawyers could transact their business, city offi-cials locked the lawyers in jail along with any other stranger in town, then in three days time they moved the whole town across the river to a paid-for quarter section two miles from the original townsite. The Homer County museum has lots of old photos documenting the move.

They cut the hotel into three sections, moving it on flat wagons drawn by mules. The opera house was also cut into sections. Only the school stayed on the old property, being brick and mortar and therefore impossible to move. They named the new site New Odyssey, which is its legal name to this day.

This version has found its way into two history books, but Old Man Houston said that story is nonsense. "We didn't lock up the lawyers, Odyssey didn't even have a jail at the time, and if we did, we would've had to move it too. What happened, is our mayor escorted them to Dodge where they were not *de*tained, but *enter*tained with free liquor, and free access to any and all of the ladies at Dodge's best brothel. When they returned to Odyssey a few days later it was gone. Nothing to repossess but some foundations and manure piles."

Others claim it took three weeks to move the town, and that the lawyers from back East went to Denver, escorted by the mayor of Odyssey who entertained them even more lavishly than the Dodge story claims. In any case, the town was moved and did skip out on its debt, which, in the prevailing view, served those New Yorkers right.

Odyssey has continued to find creative solutions to any and all problems, with a population of feisty oddballs who won't give up. Unlike the other towns in the area, most residents stayed during the dustbowl thirties, subsisting any way they could. The old-timers say they stayed because they "were too poor to leave." Too stubborn is more like it, my grandfather included.

It's not like that anymore. The liquor shop now sells fine French wines. I see joggers on the outskirts of town. Odyssey now has a golf course, for God's sake! And on the south edge of town, you can find two-story houses arranged in cul-de-sacs. There's a bed and breakfast with an indoor swimming pool. Women employees wear business suits at the bank. They've elected a woman mayor. Teenagers go home after school to watch MTV instead of dragging Main for hours.

Now an oddball would stick out.

MY TEENAGE YEARS are a blur—I remember little more than a few high points, and a fair share of low points. These were agonizing years of trying to fit in with the town girls, and never quite making it. I remember pajama parties where the girls talked about makeup and boys and I was silent and listened. All I had in my mind to talk about were the plots and characters of the novels I consumed liked food. I had read nearly every novel in the public library and craved more.

After school, sometimes I stayed to drag Main with my older cousin, Caroline. She reposed at the wheel reenacting a small-town ritual. You would start at one end of Main Street, about where the hospital was— by this time the town had two doctors and a hospital—then drive the whole length of Main all the way to the gas station which was one block before Main Street intersected the state highway. At that point you would maneuver a wide U-turn, and drive back to the northern end at the hospital where you would again U-turn—the nonchalance with which you accomplished the U, one handed, was a mark of your cool—and then you'd head back down Main. This would all be one smooth never-stopping motion, unless you caught the red light at the one stoplight that marked the exact middle of Main. The challenge was to find the precise rhythm that made it possible to never catch the red. It was a slow ritual because at each block the street dipped to create flood drainage and if you went through a dip too fast, the bottom of your car hit. So dragging Main was decidedly not racing. *That* kind of dragging took place on the highway just outside of town where the pep club had installed the big cement Letter O (for Odyssey). And that was not the kind of dragging I liked. Along the way as you cruised up and down Main, you waved and shouted at every other car of teenagers dragging Main. There could be twenty or more, creating a revolving parade that flowed like a river. Never stopping. Until about 6:00 when everyone went home for supper.

Sometimes we took a break from the dragging to go to the drug-store and sit in one of the booths or on a stool at the soda fountain and have a coke or a rootbeer float.

After passing Driver's Ed in my Freshman year, I earned my own driver's license. On those few days when I missed the bus and was allowed to drive to school in the family car, it was understood I would come right home afterward in case my parents needed the car. Wasting gaso-line with unnecessary miles was out of the question, so dragging Main was not an option for me. But I could take the family car into town on Saturday afternoons for the weekly grocery shopping. This delighted my mother, who hated grocery buying. Actually, my eagerness to help out with this family chore had more to do with the Homer County Library than with Barney's grocery store. The library was always my first stop. I would rush in to check the new arrivals shelf. Having read my way through every historical novel in their small collection, I hungered for more. Often the librarian had put away a new book for me: she already knew what I liked. Other times I browsed through the history section, searching for a glimpse into other times and places.

On my way home from one such Saturday afternoon forage, I noticed the skies darkening as Old Man Barney's grandson helped me carry a half dozen loaded grocery sacks to the car. "You better hurry home," Barney urged me as he stood on the front steps in his blood-spattered butcher apron watching the skies.

I drove as fast as I could. But three miles from home, the clouds let loose above me, dumping a fury of hailstones. The noise of the hail hitting the windshield and top of the car was in itself terrifying. More than that, knowing that the roof of our Oldsmobile was getting pockmarked, I felt overwhelming guilt, as if the storm were my fault—as if I alone had somehow brought on the storm by tarrying too long at the library. Should I stop? Should I continue down the road? In my panic, I left the gravel road and chose the shortcut, thinking I could reach home faster. The ungraded, deeply-rutted shortcut followed the creek, then made a sharp S-turn before it dipped down through the creek bed and up an incline about a mile from our farm. Water was already spilling through the crossing. I slowed and plunged through it, frightened stiff and realizing what a dumb decision it was to take this road. I made it through the rushing brown water, which must have been up to the top of my tires. Filled with relief that the car had not stalled in the water, nor had the current swept me away, I offered a quick prayer thanking God for sparing me from my stupidity. I was only a mile from home.

Then suddenly it became totally quiet. Not a breath of wind, not a drop of water from the dark, threatening sky. Not a sound. Terror struck me. I knew what that stillness meant even before I saw it. A dark brown, churning funnel was heading straight for me.

I was nowhere near our poured-in-one-piece concrete tornado shelter. I was in a car—the worst possible place to be—with a tornado headed toward me. I stopped, bolted from the car, not even slamming the door behind me, and ran in the opposite direction of the tornado, as if I could somehow outrun it.

Then someone was holding my hand, clutching me, pulling me as I ran. I could only see her bronze hand, gripping me so tightly it hurt. "Down! Face down!" she screamed. We hit the ground. She pushed me down hard, her hand flat on the small of my back. "Become one with the earth," she yelled. I flattened myself into the mud, my breasts hurting from the weight of my body pressed to the ground. I turned my head sideways to see her. Her raven dark hair was flying about her face in the wind.

"No, no," she screamed. "Do not look at me, do not look up. Close your eyes, press them into the earth. If you look at them, they will take you."

"Who will take me?" I shouted.

"The buffalo spirits."

I *think* that is what she said. But I cannot be sure, for just then the loudest roar I have ever heard screamed around my body. I felt the wind take my legs, nearly, almost, pulling, lifting me into the air. I hung onto her hand, gripping for my life. My face was plastered into the mud and grass so deeply I could not breathe.

Then it was quiet again. Totally, completely, quiet.

I lifted my head from the mud. "The buffalo spirits?" I asked.

But there was no one there. I wiped the dirt from my eyes with the back of my right hand and looked again. I was gripping, with my left hand, not a warm brown hand, but the stalk of a sunflower. Its leaves, its golden petals, its fuzzy brown head had been stripped off by the tornado that had passed over us, but the stalk remained rooted to the earth. And I remained, holding onto to it, because I had become, in that moment, as she told me I must, one with the earth.

I rose to my knees, then staggered into an upright stance, shaky, barely able to stand. I was covered with mud and bits of grass. The car was nowhere to be seen. It had simply vanished. Rain began to gently, silently fall around me. And I sat back down in the ditch with the naked sunflower stalks and I cried bitterly. Not out of relief that I had survived the second tornado of my life. But because I knew that I would never see her again.

Slowly, still dazed, I walked the last mile home. I had no injuries except for fingernail scratches on my wrist. Shortly after I walked in, a neighbor called to say he'd found our turquoise and white Oldsmobile upside-down in his maize field, smashed as if in a head-on collision. Insurance paid for a new car: a light turquoise Oldsmobile minus the old one's tailfins which were by now *passé*.

I don't talk much about the incident because my brother Jim, home from college to help with harvest preparation, teased me unmercifully about it. He had not once, but twice, rolled the pickup on that S-curve, driving too fast with nothing in the back to weigh it down. Mom and Dad had been relieved that he walked away from the accident without a scratch the first time, but livid when he rolled the pickup a second time. "Boy, are you clever, Becky," he said after I walked in mud-covered and told the family about my encounter with the tornado. "Why didn't I think of that when I smashed the pickup. What a great story."

ONCE I BEGAN high school in Odyssey, instead of looking forward to summers, I dreaded them: long, hot days helping Mom in her garden or cooking for the harvest crew or doing laundry—my mother took in laundry from several bachelors in town to earn extra "pocket change." We didn't have a dryer. So guess who hung the wash out on the line? I daydreamed my way through hot mornings as I struggled with the wet sheets that flapped loudly around me in the brisk wind, blinded both by the noon sun directly overhead and the whiteness of the sheets. By one or two in the afternoon, it was too hot to be out. Even the men-folk took a two-hour respite from the sun and wind after eating the noon meal. We didn't have air conditioning. Instead, noisy fans blew the hot air around the house for some modest daytime relief. Living in a desert clime, we knew that by evening when the thunderheads rolled in from the west, it would cool down. Sweet-smelling, cool air would waft in the open windows as we slept, and by dawn it would be so chilly, I'd need two blankets to stay warm.

Then the heat would start all over again by nine the next morning.

I wasn't needed out in the fields. There were enough boys in the family to handle the farm work. I envied my brothers, imagining how much more fun it would be to be out on a tractor or driving truck during harvest. When I offered, my father would say, "Mom needs you more." And that was the beginning and end of any discussion. During these long, lonely summers of endless housework, I had neither the time nor the transportation to go into town. That meant being away from my new Odyssey friends, who once I was out of sight, did not think to include me in their activities anyway—going to the swimming pool, dragging Main, hanging out at the Dairy Queen—whatever it was they did to laze their way through carefree summers they'd later pine for after school started. I was out of the tenuous social loop that school afforded. In summer, I was invisible.

And so I counted the days until the yellow school bus would again drive onto the yard to take me to Odyssey so I could be with my town friends again. Soon, I'd be back in the loop again, invited to slumber parties, wiener roasts—and sometimes, when I would just accidentally miss the bus, hanging out at the soda fountain after school. (Before I "missed the bus," I always made sure my cousin would agree to take me home later so my parents didn't have to drive the thirteen miles to pick me up.)

Despite the resumption of activities with town kids in September, I still always knew I was really just a country kid. Something apart. Something a little different. For one thing, I didn't speak with a Southern drawl—many of the town kid's fathers worked for the oil and gas fields and were transplants from Texas or Oklahoma. In our home we didn't even quite speak like Kansans, since my German-accented parents had not absorbed the Kansas twang or the expressions of the cowboy stock who had settled Homer County. The truth was, even in those years after Gentle Wind left me, I felt more comfortable sitting on my ridge watching the sunset than trying to be like the others.

Yet I did indeed come of age in the early sixties, a very special decade. I cried uncontrollably for three days when Kennedy was shot. I screamed when Beatles songs came on the radio while we dragged Main. I got up early and teased my hair into a beehive of tangled protein and hair spray that was virtually impervious to the wind gusts as I raced to the schoolbus on blustery November mornings. Like all the other girls, I wore plaid pleated skirts with matching sweaters. The sweaters fit very tight over our stiff, generously padded bras. For a while I had worn black and white saddle oxfords with thick white bobby socks. But by the time I turned sixteen, sheer stockings was considered proper. In the era before pantyhose, stockings necessitated a garter belt with those fasteners that made welts on your thighs after a long day at school. The fifties were barely over. And a certain sense of formality and conformity still ruled, even in Odyssey.

That's why everyone gawked one late-April Friday when I and two of my friends—the gutsiest girls in the class—showed up to school in denim jeans and huge, shapeless gray sweatshirts. We were promptly called into the principal's office and told that we must never again come to school dressed like that. They would have sent us home on the spot, but two of us were country girls who lived far from town. By the next Friday, everyone was wearing jeans and sweatshirts, and there were too many of us to send home.

Here's how it happened. Charlotte heard from her cousin in Kansas City about this new sloppy look becoming popular back East, but no one here sold blue jeans for girls, and certainly not sweatshirts. So after school that Thursday, we went to Capp's, a store that sold workclothes and shoes for farmers. We found the smallest size of men's Levi's we could. Then we bought the largest size sweatshirts we could find. The clerk, a very fashionable, thin woman who looked like a model from a magazine, kept looking at us queerly. Who are you buying these for, she kept asking. Our brothers. Then why were we trying on the jeans? Just for fun, we replied. She nearly refused to sell us the merchandise. When we finally walked out with our purchases, we were doubling up in laughter before we even reached the dimestore.

Actually denim jeans were not new to me. I had worn them throughout my grade school years. Ordered in quantity from the Sears catalog, they comprised my entire school wardrobe. Lined with red plaid flannel to protect my thin legs from the winter wind, they felt wonderful against my skin. But whatever denim jeans were in those years, they were certainly never a fashion statement.

A year after our blue jeans rebellion, Capp's opened a boutique for teenage girls in the back of the workclothes store, which Mrs. Capp stocked with beautiful dresses in sizes 3, 5, 7, and 9. She also offered trendy "sportswear." Eventually, Mrs. Capp would even sell Levi's for girls. Whenever Mrs. Capp got back from one of her buying trips to Dallas, my mom let me go in and pick out one dress. Size 5. By that time, *Seventeen* was being sold in the drugstore's magazine rack, so I knew just what styles were in. Each year, I looked a little less like a country girl and more like a girl from Dallas or Denver.

But in my pasture, with Tommy at my side, I lived another life. I hungered to know more about life on this ridge. Who were the people who once lived here? The summer before I left for college, I began to hunt up everything I could find in the Odyssey library on Plains Indians. But the more I read, the more I realized that no one knew much of anything. One day, an old man, stooped and nearly crippled, overheard me asking questions. He knew more than the books. And he told me that our part of the country had been the center of much history. The Spanish explorer Coronado may have come through here on his way to Quivera looking for the famed cities of gold in 1541. He and his men probably stopped for water at the Lower Springs on the Cimarron River—the place we now call Wagonbed Springs.

"I once found a Spanish sword overlooking the North Fork south of town. I gave it to the Smithsonian Museum in Washington, D.C. I wish I'd kept it," he told me. "Then later at the same spot, I found a gold French coin from the early 1700s. So we know French traders came through here too."

He told me what books to check out that might help me in my search, but warned me that historians themselves were often "wildly inaccurate," especially when it came to identifying just what Indian tribes roamed this part of the country. He said historians had overlooked much of the history of our area because they "didn't think our particular part of the country was of any importance."

I never asked the old man his name. He promised me he'd be in the library the next Saturday afternoon if I had further questions. That next Saturday he didn't come.

I asked my father who the man was. "Oh, that must have been Saul Houston. He was Old Man Houston's cousin. I believe he was educated at Harvard. They brought him in to run the bank back in the forties, so he lived here for a while, but then he went back East at some point. He must be here for a visit."

According to my father, people didn't much like Saul Houston. Some said it was because he'd been educated back East and that Harvard had planted queer notions in his head. "That's not really true," my dad said. "Saul had those notions in his head long before he ever got to Harvard." One of Houston's notions that didn't go over well around Odyssey was that the Great Plains was never meant to be farmed. It should have been left to the Indians and buffalo, he'd said. The land supported millions of buffalo then. Now we were lucky if we could keep a few scrawny cattle alive through a winter. More people lived on the Plains then, than do now, he claimed. And they didn't have to burn oil or pump water out of the ground or apply fertilizer to make grass grow on the Plains. Such pessimistic notions did not make Houston a particularly generous banker to the farmers of Homer County.

Sure enough, we read about him in the *Odyssey News* the next week. He had come from Kansas City to visit relatives but while here had suffered a massive stroke and passed away in the Odyssey hospital. The story told how he had been studying history at Harvard but was called back to Kansas during the war to run the Odyssey Bank. The story also said he had donated many important Indian artifacts to the Smithsonian in Washington D.C., most of which he found on the Houston ranch south of town.

11

Our People

WHITE MEN ALWAYS wished to know the name of our people. When we said, *Our People,* they said, Yes, what is the name of your people?

That is our name—*Our People*, we insisted. They did not understand.

Many seasons ago, too long to count, they called us Padouca. Later, the French traders called us Ga-ta-ka. The Spanish traders called us Katanka.

The English called us Plains Apache. But we are not Apache. Apaches are warlike. We are peace loving. We tried to explain that we do not speak the same language as the Apache so therefore we could not be Apache. Apache means "the enemy." Apache are, in fact, our enemy.

Then they called us Kiowa. We lived with Kiowa in our Winter Grounds, and sometimes our braves take Kiowa wives. But we are not Kiowa. Yet they became confused and called us Kiowa-Apache.

Eventually, when they asked us if we were Kiowa-Apache we just said yes. There was no use in explaining that our name was simply, Our People. In our language "our people" is *Nadi-ish-dena*. It is musical to say, like the song of a bird at dusk who soothes her young in the nest into restful slumber. Nadi-ish-dena. *Nadi-ish-dena*. It is a beautiful name for a beautiful people. We are *Nadi-ish-dena*.

• • •

NOW, AS MY SPIRIT wanders for days without end, I see that white men still puzzle over our clan. They wonder who we were, and how long we lived on this ridge. Before the children came to play in our spirit camp, a grown man, tall and bent, would sometimes walk the ridge. One day he found my father's sword. He saw the hilt sticking out of the dust after the wind had blown sand for days. He was filled with excitement and wonder. He brought other men to the ridge and showed them where he had found the sword. He kept shouting, "Coronado, Coronado. Coronado was here."

The sword had been passed to my father from his father, who had passed it from his father. It was a cherished treasure for many generations. It was a Spanish sword, but it was not left on this hill by a Spaniard. Nor by someone called Coronado. It was brought here many generations ago by a brave from our clan who escaped from a Spanish slave master who called himself a Man of God. He was a cruel master who enslaved our people, forcing the women to plant, and cook and clean for him, and the men to build grand dwellings for him near the great trading center the Spanish called Santa Fe. He wanted his house to become exactly like his home in faraway Spain. If he wanted his home to look like Spain, why did he not return to his own land?

But we are a cunning people, and we love freedom more than anything else. So our clansman escaped in the night. But first our ancestor quietly took the sword from his master as he slept. So quiet was our clansman, that his master did not wake even though it lay beside his ear.

My father said the sword was to remind us that we are slaves to no one. The *Nadi-ish-dena* are proud and free. Slave to no one.

The stooped white man would walk the ridge after every storm hoping that the wind would reveal another sword or perhaps some other treasure. One bitter morning, he found the treasure of my heart, a French gold coin that I once wore around my neck. He was even more excited and again brought other men to the ridge.

The French were here. The French were here, he shouted into the wind. He would have danced in joy if his bent legs had permitted it. It was indeed a gold coin from a noble Frenchman. But the Frenchman was never here. He was on his way to visit us but he became ill and asked his scout to bring us to him. So we packed up our camp and moved ten days east to meet him, to honor the Frenchman who had come so far to bring gifts and greetings from his people. The French were near. But not here. Until the Terrible Day no white man ever intruded on our secret summer grounds beside the Little Buffalo River.

The gold coin was given to me by my grandmother, who received it from her grandmother. Five grandmothers ago, it was given as a wedding gift to the most beautiful maiden to ever have been born into the *Nadi-ish-dena.* Her name was Merry Eyes. One day I will tell you her story. A story we call "The Grandmother's Story."

12

The Grandmother's Story

BECAUSE YOU ASK ME, I will tell you the grandmother's story now. This story was told for six generations. I told my granddaughters. But they did not live to become grandmothers and pass on the story. So it stopped with me.

This is the story my grandmother's grandmother tells about her journey to the other side of the sun. When I tell the story, I usually make it short so the grandchildren will not fall asleep. But because you wish to hear the whole story, I will let her spirit tell as much as she wishes.

MY NAME IS Merry Eyes. The first white man I ever saw was a big chief from a land called France. To reach us, he sailed for many cycles of the moon across a great lake, then through many forests and up many rivers until he came to the place in the East where the tall grasses grow. He marched for many days across the Plains. Braves who lived by a great river—not our Great River, but another one even larger called the Missouri River—journeyed with him to guide him and hunt game for his party. They were joined by Osage braves once they entered the tall-grass prairies. Their party sent out scouts to meet my father and the other chiefs to tell them of the Frenchman's peaceful intentions. He marches with a flag of red and blue that he holds high in the wind to show that he comes in peace, said the Osage scout. He brings a message and many gifts from the King of the Whole World who lives on the other side of the sun. (In truth, the Frenchman said he came from the other side of the *world,* but the Missouri scout who turned his strange language into our own words, did not understand how a world can have two sides when everyone knows the world is one entity with no beginning, no end and no sides, so the scout said "sun," and so it was thereafter repeated as such by all.)

But during his march, the Frenchman became very ill of a great fever. He could not complete the journey. The wind was very hot and the French chief was not accustomed to such heat and unrelenting sunshine, and his fever grew worse. So our medicine man went along with the scouts back to the French chief's camp, bringing special herbs and healing spirits.

Because our clan wished to honor the French chief and was afraid that if he came all the way to our land he would die, my father decided we would travel to meet him. So we packed our belongings just as we did when we were following the buffalo herds. All the women, all the children, the dogs, everything—we set out on a journey east to a neighboring people's wintering grounds, where they have large lodges. It seemed strange to go to a winter place in the heat of the summer. There was great excitement.

As we drew near, with hundreds of people—for many other clans joined us as we made our journey—we heard word that the herbs and incantations of our medicine men had healed the French chief's fever.

When we reached the camp of the Frenchmen, there was great rejoicing, many speeches, much smoking of the calumet pipe, dancing, and feasting. We prepared great quantities of roasted venison and pumpkins and bread made of ground corn. When they said they could eat no more, we offered sweet red berries. The great French chief was beautiful to look at and enchanting to listen to. He spoke with words that were music. His coat was red as blood, with ornaments of gold. His hat was adorned with silver and feathers, almost as beautiful as the festival robes our chiefs wear. His eyes were kind and his laugh was hearty and could be heard around the whole camp.

I was just at the age of becoming a woman. I am told I was very beautiful, but I was shy. I was afraid to come close but I watched the festivities with stolen glances as I served the roasted venison to the French chief, his soldiers and his Missouri slaves. When I came with a great basket of berries, the Frenchman looked into my eyes and smiled. He said something in his strange tongue. His Missouri man slave repeated it in our language. He says you are a very beautiful maiden and that you must be a princess.

"I am the daughter of the Padouca chief," I replied, speaking through the Missouri slave.

The French chief instructed his slave to tell me, "I will praise your beauty most respectfully when I speak with your father. He is a very wise man. We have few men as wise as the Great Padouca Chief in our land."

I was filled with joy to hear his high regard for my father.

As I watched the Frenchman and his party, I saw that his slaves seemed to love their master. His servants were well treated. Not as our enemies treat their slaves. For very long, our enemies, the Foxes, have stolen our people for slaves and treated them harshly. This is the reason for the many wars between us. And I have heard fearful stories of how the Spanish masters from Santa Fe take slaves from the southern Padouca clans and make them work for many hours without rest. This chief's slaves obeyed his commands with joy. And they rested and feasted as if they were not slaves.

Ever since I was a little child I saw visions. I always dreamed of going to the stars. Of seeing great wonders and mysteries. The next day, I asked my father if I could be a slave in the camp of the Frenchman.

He was angry that I should ask such a question. "You cannot be a slave. You are a princess." he replied. But he softened when he saw my downcast face. "The French chief travels with a young, motherless son. Perhaps he needs a wife." That was all that my father said, as he left my mother's tent. My mother began to cry, but I was filled with excitement.

The next day my father came to me and spoke. He was proud but his heart was also heavy. "The French chief thanks me, he says you are very beautiful and that he is very honored, but he says he cannot marry you. He has a wife, far away in the land that he comes from and in that land a man is allowed to have only one wife. I told him that in our land, a chief may have as many wives as he desires. He laughed and said that French chiefs also have many wives, but the holy men in his land do not approve, so the extra wives are considered slaves but are given many gifts and much love and are treated better than a wife.

"So, if you wish, you may join and travel with his party on their adventures, and perhaps to the other side of the sun where he wishes to return many moons from now. He has promised to honor you as a princess and protect you from harm. He will treat you as a daughter, but when you are older, if you wish it, you will become his slave-wife. If he dies before then, you will become the bride of his son. If at any time, you chose to return to your people, he will have his trustworthy servants escort you back to our clan."

I said, "Father, I wish to go with him. But I am old enough to become a wife now. I am no longer a child. In your camp I am a child, but in the Frenchman's camp I wish to be honored as a wife."

My mother wailed for many days as I prepared my belongings and my body to go with the Frenchman. Our shamans said prayers and incantations. They danced with the spirits and blessed my journey. And the old women of our clan told me the mysteries of life.

The French chief stayed for many days to conclude the peace agreements between the seven tribes of the Plains. When they concluded their talks, all the chiefs smoked the calumet pipe and sealed promises to the Frenchman's King of the Whole World that they would stop all wars amongst themselves and refuse to trade with the Spanish or the English.

It was difficult for our chiefs to promise an end to all war between the Plains tribes, though their hearts desired it. So many quarrels break out now that the tribes have horses and our warriors wish to show off their skills. But it was easy to promise not to trade with the Spanish whom we secretly called Dogs, or the English whom we secretly called Vultures. In turn, the French chief said his soldiers would protect us and bring us many gifts and trade our fur pelts and buffalo robes for their axes and weapons and fine red cloth and beads of many colors. The French said we were allowed to steal horses from the Spanish because they had stolen so many of us as slaves to labor in their fields in the South. But we must be very clever about it, as secret as foxes.

The French do not need to tell us how to be clever. We live by our cleverness, but also by our good hearts. We wish no ill. We wish to be left alone to move with the herds of buffalo and sing songs around our fires at night. And we wish for White Man to visit us in friendship but not to dwell in our land. My father says that as sojourners in our land they may honor us with gifts as we will honor them with feasting. The French chief said they have a land that is vast and rich. They do not need our hills and valleys, our Plains and our rivers, except to pass through as respectful guests. My father believes that the words of the French chief are from his heart and truly represent his King of the World. Otherwise, their king would not have sent so many gifts.

And that is why he is giving me as a gift to the Frenchman. I am the seal, the proof of the agreement between them.

I am a willing gift because I believe it is my destiny. It was in the stars before I was born. But my mother weeps without stopping. I wish I could comfort her heart. She is not a dreamer and she does not understand destiny.

When the agreements were concluded, the Frenchman asked for representatives of the seven tribes to go with him to the other side of the sun to meet the Great King of the Whole World. He chose chiefs from each of the seven tribes. A princess from the Missouri, who had been given to him as a slave-bride like myself, and I were also part of the party. I said goodbye to all that I loved—my father and mother, my brothers and sisters, all my family, the birds, the sky, the grass and flowers, the wind, all the precious spirits of our land, and we left the Land of the Padoucas.

We marched across the tallgrass Plains, we traveled by boat down a wide brown river that White Man calls the Mississippi, and arrived in New Orleans, a large village with many Frenchmen and many different tribes of Indians—that's the word they use for us, Indies or Indians. It is a word in their language which has no meaning for us. We are a people of many names, from many lands. They do not understand that. New Orleans is noisy and dirty and I am afraid, but the French chief is my protector. And Hazel, his Missouri slave-wife has become my sister and true friend. She explains everything to me, and she has given me beautiful white woman gowns to wear, she says to impress the King of the World who we are going to see. She also instructs me on how to please our Frenchman husband.

To get to the Frenchman's land, we must go in a very, very large ship over a very, very large lake—but bigger than any lake—with waves so big they may swallow us. The French use the wind to make us move upon the waters. Above the boat are great white flags called sails which catch the wind. We begin our journey on the Great Waters. But after one day we come back to the shore and stop at another village. While we are sleeping in a camp on the land, the ship sinks to the bottom of the Great Water with all our belongings in it. All the gifts our chiefs brought to give the King of the World are lost. We are wailing all day long. We are afraid.

The French chief does not understand that the spirits are angry. He procures another ship and insists we resume our journey the very next day. We are all afraid. For days we are lost on the Great Waters. I am so sick I cannot eat. I can barely move. I pray for the spirits to take me back home. I cry every night. The French chief does not visit my bed. He too is sick, his fever returns and we fear he will die. Our chiefs give him herbs and ask for help from the Spirit of Healing. For many moons we travel, lost in water so vast it is as if we have left the world behind forever.

When we finally arrive in the Frenchmen's land, we are greeted by many people in fine clothes and with horses and carriages as beautifully dressed as themselves. I cannot begin to explain to you about the Land of France. It does not seem real. The dirt is real, the grass, the flowers, the trees—all of it is real, but it does not grow as the spirits intend, but as man intends. They eat fowl that cannot fly away, flesh of beasts which do not roam free. And their gardens grow far more than pumpkins and corn. They live in great lodges made of stone. Everything is different, and now I know that New Orleans was built to remind the Frenchmen of France.

But the biggest surprise is the King of All the World. He is but a child, and an impetuous boy who would not even be allowed to speak around our tribal campfire. He is excited about our visit, and never ceases asking questions about us, which my master patiently answers. He loves us as a child loves a toy. The French are a very strange people. In our land, a chief, even the chief of a small clan must be an old and wise man. In France, a child can be King. Everyone bows to this child and runs to satisfy his every whim. He can cry or scream or demand impossible things and no one thinks that is strange.

This Boy King, almost of the age when our braves become men, lives in the largest lodge in all the world. One room of his lodge is larger than ten lodges of the Cahoya who build the great dwellings in Santa Fe. The walls of his lodge are filled with images of people who are not real. If you touch them, they are flat and lifeless on the wall, yet their eyes seem to follow you as you walk away. The French sleep in great, soft beds filled with goose feathers and covered with many robes of beautiful colors. Their women wear gowns so big they cannot walk. Their powder-white hair is piled so high on top of their heads that they have trouble holding up their heads as they walk. They put red color on their cheeks and lips and talk and laugh in very strange ways. They do not seem to be wise. Even the oldest people behave as children. I wonder if my father would have given his promises to my husband if he had known that their King of the World was but a spoiled child.

The King's lodge is surrounded by many green pastures and flowers of every color and kind, and trees which grow in lines, like soldiers marching. And their paths are covered with many little stones which hurt your feet and make a crunching sound as you walk. Here, you could not be like a fox and surprise anyone for the sound of the little stones tells the whole world you are coming. The Great Lodge is surrounded by forests, dark and deep and filled with deer and strange birds that do not fly. They are as pheasants, but larger, and make an ugly sound like a sick baby crying. When these birds wish to impress their mates, they fan out their tail feathers which are purple and green and glisten in the sunlight. And then these ugly birds become the most beautiful creatures in all the world, dressed and proud as the Frenchmen themselves. They strut about much as does the Boy King.

The Boy King suddenly decides he wishes to become a hunter like the Indies. So he instructs the chiefs to teach him the art of hunting with a bow and arrow. They strip to their loin clothes and paint their bodies because the Boy King wants them to look like they would as hunters in our land. Then the Boy King does the same thing, throwing off his clothes and painting his body. He runs with them, shouting in joy as they hunt the birds. Our chiefs do not want to kill the ugly birds. They cannot fly, so they are too easy to kill. It is against what the spirits teach our people, but they must do what the Boy King demands. So they kill one peacock after another. The field is littered with their dead. And before one afternoon is gone, all the birds in the King's forest are dead.

Our chiefs lament the loss. The Boy King says, "Oh, do not fret, I will have more birds brought into the forest tomorrow."

When we awaken the next morning, the forests around the Great Lodge are filled with peacocks but they are crying for their dead brothers. The French do not hear or understand their cries. They do not know that all life is connected by the spirits who govern the world.

We are urged to feast all day long, until I feel I will be sick forever. We are taken to large lodges filled with people who sit on soft chairs to watch other people sing and dance. How can one not join a dance or sing a song, but merely watch? Then they ask our chiefs to do a war dance for them, and the whole crowd makes a great roar of approval. We are beginning to feel very foolish and very homesick. The French are not such grand people. They are silly like children, and we all want to go home. I am sorry I asked my father to send me with the Frenchman, who has forgotten all about me, now that he is back in his own land with his French wife and young daughter. His daughter is beautiful. I try to caress her golden curls, but his white wife becomes angry and snatches the child away from me as if I am trying to harm her baby. I cry most of the time. The King's servants see me crying and they try to console me. They are French, but because they are slaves they are wise, and they understand that I cry to go home.

And now my belly is getting too large to hide, even beneath the French skirts.

Just when I decide I will pray that the lake take me into its watery depths, my master comes to my bed to talk with me in the middle of the night. He kisses me and holds me and pleads for me to stop crying.

"I love you and I wish that we could go across the waters and journey together to your father's clan and live there on the Plains where I could watch our baby run in the grass. I do not like France as much as I like the New World. Because I made peace amongst your warring tribes, the King has bestowed great honors on me and given me a royal title and a great lodge with land and servants. My French wife and daughter deserve my time and devotion. They have lived alone in hardship while I made my journey to the New World."

"You are to marry my servant Dubois," he tells me. "He will take care of you. I have charged him with accompanying you and the chiefs back to your home. You may serve him and live with him at Fort

Orleans where he will be the chief, or you may go back to your father's clan. It will be your choice."

"I cannot go back to my father," I say. "That would bring dishonor on his name. If I do not say why I have returned, he will believe I was not a good wife or that I brought shame upon you. If I tell him that you sent me away he will think you are a liar and that you do not honor your agreements. And war will come again to our Plains."

For one last night I lie in my master's arms. In the morning Dubois and a carriage and many soldiers comes to escort us to the Great Waters. We are given many gifts—gold and silver, fine clothes and beads in many colors. The Boy King sends many peacocks in cages as a gift for my father. On the ship for many moons I am sick nearly to death. The peacocks in their cages cry for home and we cannot rest.

When we arrive in the noisy city of light they call New Orleans, we rest for one moon and there my baby is born. She is beautiful. The servants of Dubois take care of me and dote on the baby. Dubois gives the baby his name, but he never comes to my bed in the night. Yet he is kind and calls me wife.

When I am strong enough, we set out up the Great Mississippi River. At the end of long days on the river, we alight from our boats, and eat venison and sing songs around our campfires at the river's edge. When we near the Missouri River, an enemy clan of the Missouri attack us as we make camp. Dubois is killed. My baby and I and the Plains chiefs are spared. But the Missouri warriors take me as a slave.

My grandchildren, your eyes grow heavy. You do not wish to hear of my many days of sorrow as a slave. But, like a bunch of pelts, eventually I was traded. A French trader who wore clothing of skins as we do, took pity of this poor lost princess. I did finally return to my father's teepee a few moons before he died, together with my daughter who was now nearly the age I was when I left my home to sail to France. When he asked why I had returned I told the truth. My "husband" had been killed. My father mourned for the French chief, thinking the Frenchman with whom he smoked the calumet was fallen in battle. I did not explain that it was not he who was ambushed and killed on the banks of the Missouri River.

One day a fine young brave, the son of the chief from a neighboring clan, saw my daughter when we came to our wintering grounds, and he wished to marry her. His father and my father talked and made an agreement. It was decided that this young brave would come to live with us and when he was older if he proved himself worthy, he would become the chief. For I have no brothers. They have all been killed in battle. The peace the Frenchman tried to make lasted only a short time. There was no one to carry on my great father's wise ways except my daughter and one day, we hope, her son.

Soon my daughter has a son. I have a grandson. I am so proud. And before long, I have many grandchildren. My daughter's husband becomes chief of our small tribe. And we live in peace because our summer hunting camp is beside a little river that no one cares about. We call it Little Buffalo, because the buffalo come to wallow in the mud of our valley which is flooded each spring. And because many animals drink of our springs, we have all the meat we need. When I was a slave on the Missouri River, I learned to plant corn and maize, pumpkins and beans. So I teach the other women how to grow wonderful things in the rich earth of our valley. I will grow old here on the ridge that overlooks our Little Buffalo River that no one cares about except our clan.

The land on the other side of the sun, for all its riches, is not so beautiful as one sunset on our Plains. All their peacocks are not as beautiful as one golden eagle in flight. Our land is holy and blessed. And my spirit will forever be happy that I could return to my true home. My grandson will become chief of our people. And his son after that. And we will live here forever, as long as the grass grows beneath our feet and as long as the water flows from our springs.

We are *Nadi-ish-dena.*

13

Nomads & Settlers

AFTER LEAVING THE Willow Springs school site, I couldn't make myself drive the extra three miles. I intended to. I hugged the side of the road as semi-trucks—at least a half dozen of them—going the other way, passed by me on the road lumbering toward their destination. I turned around and headed back to Odyssey. And somewhere along the highway south of town, I passed a patch of ground left in its virgin state, so rare to find now. Dotted with sagebrush and soapweed, its pristine beauty was so breathtaking, I stopped and walked in, startling jackrabbits, quail and pheasant. One beautiful ring-necked cock took flight a few feet from where I stood, so near I could see his iridescent green, blue and rust plumage shimmering and flashing in the afternoon sun. The sudden whirring and rustling of his escape sounded the alarm to other pheasants who also took flight. It was a hauntingly familiar sound from my childhood.

So as not to disturb other inhabitants of this patch of prairie, I cut over to the edge of the pasture and walked back to my car on a dirt trail marked by fresh tractor tread. To my left was a maize field, a hybrid grain crop commonly grown to feed cattle. The fresh seedlings, which at this early stage looked like corn plants, stood in straight-as-an-arrow, neat rows separated by deep furrows. To my right was virgin prairie. The contrast was stark, as startlingly different as the two cultures who have battled for the Great Plains. The history of this land is marked by the struggle between nomads and settlers. My family, my own history, is defined by that very struggle. Two human impulses always at war with themselves.

Nomadic hunter and gatherer. Settler, tiller and caretaker of the soil. Which am I? What do I come from? What is at the core of my soul?

I know the answer. I am by nature a hunter-gatherer. My mother was a tiller of the soil who tended a magnificent garden, but I do not even grow herbs in window boxes on my patio as many of my city friends do.

All children must contribute to farm life. And I did—but as a gatherer of eggs, or a picker of mulberries. As a gatherer of eggs I was just as good at finding our chickens' nests as they were at scouting out new locations to hide them from me. Missing a location meant the mother hen could create a nest and hatch babies. Once in a while I looked the other way. As a picker of mulberries I was less than efficient, eating more than I carried home in my pail, with purple-blue stains all over my face and hands to reveal my indulgence. In my mother's garden my contribution was picking green beans. I also made myself useful picking off tomato worms—fat, green squishy creatures that attached themselves to the stems of tomato plants and were almost invisible because they were the exact color of the stems. It took a trained eye to detect them and determined fingers to pull them off the plants because their suction-cup legs so thoroughly wedded them to their host. I saved them in jars and let my mother dispose of them.

Since the pasture was my natural habitat, I gleaned from it those things that were useful. The sweet, wonderful fruit of the prickly-pear cactus and the roots of soapweed, our name for yucca. My mother never wanted to use the roots to make soap as the Indians did, but I assured her if ever we couldn't afford soap I would make some for her.

My brother Thomas was also a hunter-gatherer. He of course drove tractor and helped with farming activities as had my older brothers, but that was out of necessity, not love. The moment he could, he was in the pasture with his horses and, later, the buffalo herd.

I am also a hunter-gatherer in my profession. I hunt down sources, I gather news. I skillfully find what's out there, extracting the necessary nutrients needed to ply my trade.

In his dreams, my father was also a hunter-gatherer, even though he came from a family of settlers. He may have tilled the soil but his heart was not in it. Every chance he got, he loaded us kids into the car and we'd strike out for trips west. We saw the Royal Gorge, Grand Canyon, Hoover Dam, Carlsbad Caverns—every possible interesting point between Kansas and California.

When he married my mother in 1933, they first lived in a one-room cabin-like structure on the Home Place. It was a tough year and an even tougher decade. Although I remember Grandma Kluger as a smiling, bubbly presence, I've heard otherwise. Even Aunt Selma concedes that Grandma made things difficult for her daughter-in-laws, none of whom could ever measure up to her exacting standards of domestic efficiency or frugality. I've heard of a certain battle over a butcher knife. Apparently my mother and father paid five dollars for a good quality butcher knife when an adequate one could have been purchased for two dollars. Grandma Emma gave them hell for it and never let it go. To this day, whenever my father sharpens that butcher knife, he lectures about getting what you pay for. "Always buy quality," he says, brandishing the butcher knife. "See this knife? It's lasted thirty years and is as good as the day I bought it."

Whether it was to escape from Grandma or the Dust Bowl, my father and mother with their new baby girl, Margaret, struck out for the logging country of the Pacific Northwest, as far from the blowing dust as they could get. They were smart not to go to California, where all the Okies headed. My two older brothers were born in a two-room mountain cabin in the woods of Washington State within view of magnificent Mount Baker. I've seen pictures. My dad hauled logs and my mother ran after three toddlers, picked blackberries and made a home for her family. How anyone could leave that beautiful place I will never understand. But eventually, I'm not sure why, they came back to Western Kansas to take over the Home Place. My father had been designated as the son who was supposed to take over the family farm. It was a fate he accepted. It was as if no matter what, Western Kansas is where destiny had placed him and he could not disobey.

There is no question that my paternal grandfather was a settler. Proof of that is the magnificent Willow Valley Home Place he planted in the middle of a desert. But my maternal grandfather was a nomad. Grandfather Jacob, who died before I was born, was a writer, artist, teacher and minister. A product of his times and heritage, he played at farming, the expected profession, but he was a college-educated man of letters as well as an accomplished painter. He left behind both manuscripts and oil paintings. When I first found his self-portrait hidden away in Aunt Catherine's attic, I looked into his eyes and knew that I am from him. He gave me his love of the written word while Thomas received his passion for brush strokes on canvas. I have my grandfather's well-worn books of poetry, most of them printed in the 1880s and 1890s, wonderful leather-bound volumes filled with his pencil notations in the margins, as to the hidden meanings in the lines.

Jacob moved across the West, homesteading, but letting his sons, most of whom genuinely loved farming, turn the sod and till the soil, while he taught in whatever country school was nearby or preached in whatever church that needed him.

When the ugliness of the World War I backlash against German-speaking immigrants began, he packed up his whole family and moved to the northwoods of Canada, where he taught English to Eskimo children.

For a time, he moved the family to a mountain hollow in South Carolina where he established a church and an orphanage—both integrated, a concept unheard of at the turn of the century. My mother loves to tell the stories of how he narrowly escaped being lynched by a gang of white vigilantes for allowing black and white children to attend school together and live as equals in the same house.

My mother remembers a tunnel that their "colored" friends dug under the house so Grandpa could escape into the woods when the vigilantes came knocking. She also remembers crosses being burned in their front yard. I've seen pictures of the orphanage, a large, three-story white frame Victorian house with a wide veranda, always filled with happy-looking children of all ages and hues mugging for the camera.

When he grew tired of fighting his battles in the South, Jacob moved the family back to Kansas from whence they had come, adopting "Aunt Betty," a black teenager to whom the family had become attached.

Back in Kansas, my Grandpa's color blindness did not go down well either. In one particular hotel where the family stopped in Topeka, the desk clerk informed my Grandpa that Aunt Betty would have to sleep outside in the wagon. Coloreds were not allowed in. So Grandpa dug out bedrolls and had the whole family—all twelve of them—sleep outside on the steps of the hotel in protest. My Grandfather—how I wish I could have met him—was a protester long before I became one.

I'm so sorry Grandpa died before I could learn to know him. I also wish I could have known Aunt Betty but she died of a congenital heart problem with she was only eighteen.

By the time my mother was a teenager, they were back in Kansas and Grandpa had a church to pastor on the banks of the Cottonwood River. He sent my mother to a high school boarding school so she would have an education and become a teacher. Besides being a teacher, she wanted to write children's books. As far as I know, she never got around to committing any of her children's tales to paper, though she entertained us with them each night at bedtime. That's why I know about the adventures of my mother's parents because my mother loved to repeat the tales, adding embellishments as she went along, as if perfecting them for the books she intended to write.

But I know much less about my father's family because he seldom speaks of them. I do know that my white-haired grandfather Abraham, patriarch and founding father of the Willow Valley community, and his efficient helpmate, my grandmother Emma, were settlers not wanderers. Of that I am sure. If my father inherited a bit of wanderlust, I'm betting it came from his grandmother Bessie, the woman who rode a buckboard in the Oklahoma Land Rush of April 22, 1889.

What I know about great-grandmother Bessie comes from Selma, my father's oldest sister. Selma considers herself the historian of the family, and is old enough to remember the Oklahoma days. My father has always warned me to take Aunt Selma's stories with a grain of salt because she tends to exaggerate. But I've always preferred to take her stories unsalted. They are spice enough.

The original Kluger homestead bordered the Indian Lands in central Oklahoma. It was good farmland, and they did well. The Quakers had been placed in charge of Indian affairs in the Oklahoma Territories in the 1870s after a corrupt and fraud-ridden Bureau of Indian Affairs had miserably failed in its mission to justly administer the Indian Territories. President Ulysses S. Grant became convinced that a religious group, especially one with the patience of the Quakers, might do a better job. The mission of the Bureau, as the U.S. Government saw it, was to convince the Red Man to give up his hunter-gatherer ways and learn to farm the land, or at a minimum, to raise cattle and sheep, send their children to school, learn the English language, and live in houses—in short, become "civilized." Many nineteenth-century Americans, shouldering their White Man's Burden, also felt it their duty to convince these heathens to adopt Christianity.

The enlightened Quakers believed education was the key. They convinced Great-Grandmother Bessie to volunteer to teach cooking and sewing to reservation women. Bessie, a woman who had not hesitated to drive a buckboard with a team of mules in the Oklahoma Land Rush in the midst of snarling, cursing men, was more than thrilled to take on the challenge. Her efficient and sometimes annoying daughter-in-law—my grandmother, Emma—had taken over most of the housekeeping duties of the extended Kluger family household and Bessie needed some way to make herself feel useful.

Aunt Selma remembers her grandmother Bessie marching about complaining loudly about the stupidity of the Bureau. "I should teach them to cook? They've been cooking for thousands of years. The very idea! And sew? I should teach them to sew? Have you seen their beautiful beaded leather dresses? I should teach them to sew? The very idea!"

Bessie was immediately at home amongst the native women, but clearly more interested in learning their crafts than teaching them hers. So Bessie learned to tan hide, dry strips of beef in the sun, weave cloth, and construct elaborate beadwork. "Her ladies learned, . . .well," here Aunt Selma laughs loudly, "the Indian ladies learned mostly to laugh at Grandma Bessie's jokes."

At any rate, my great-grandfather began to strongly disapprove of Bessie's work on the reservation, and the notions she was bringing home. She was virtually consumed by her work with the Indians. But then Bessie fell ill and had to stop going to see her women at the reservation. The Indians sorely missed Bessie, and to Great-Grandfather's consternation, came to the farm looking for Bessie, bringing herbs and "pagan remedies."

"Grandfather would not open the door to let them in," recalls Aunt Selma, who was nine years old at the time. "Once the women came back with a medicine man. 'A witch doctor,' Grandpa called him. Another time, they came with a young girl who they said carried the spirit of healing. He decided he'd had enough. He called the Quaker administrators and asked that the natives be prevented from bothering the family.

"I don't know what Grandma Bessie's ailment was," continues Aunt Selma. "She wept loudly, she rocked back and forth, she fell into trances, she did not dress or comb her hair, and in her eyes was the look of a wild animal. She constantly asked about the children. Said the children were crying. She would clap her hands over her ears, desperate to shut out the noises she was hearing. 'Go feed the children,' she would beg. Grandfather kept her locked in the upstairs bedroom. Only he and my mother—your grandmother Emma—were allowed to go into the room," recalls Aunt Selma. "Now we would recognize Bessie's condition as some kind of mental illness, but then the family felt she was possessed by evil spirits. My grandfather was convinced the Indian women—especially one old woman she was particularly close to—had put an evil spell on her. The entire church called days of prayer and fasting to bring about Bessie's healing. And even though Great-Grandfather hated Catholics, he sought out a priest from a nearby town at one point and pleaded with him to perform an exorcism.

"Who knows? Perhaps it was some illness she picked up on the Indian reservation. But most likely it was a brain tumor. As a child," remembers Aunt Selma, "I wondered if perhaps it was the sad stories the Indian women told her. She always said, 'theirs was a terrible burden, a hard lot in life.'

"After a few months, Grandma Bessie died in her upstairs room in some kind of convulsive seizure, and a sense of relief flooded over our whole household. I remember Mama walking around in a daze repeating to us children that Grandma Bessie had gone on to her reward in heaven and that we should praise God that her torment on earth was over."

When Aunt Selma told me this story, I wondered aloud whether living next to the Indian reservation had anything to do with Grandpa leaving Oklahoma to settle in Kansas. "Oh heavens no," said Aunt Selma. "Your grandpa never blamed the Indians for his mother's death. It was not the curses of the Red Man that drove Grandpa out of Oklahoma. It was the ignorance and cruelty of white men that made Grandpa seek greener pastures." Then came Aunt Selma's long cascading Kluger-woman laugh, "Or should I say browner pastures!" Aunt Selma never liked Western Kansas. She left for California as soon as she turned eighteen.

That's the most anyone ever told me about how Grandpa Kluger came to settle a piece of the Houston ranch on the North Fork of the Cimarron. But settle he did. And settler he was.

I AM A NOMAD. My various apartments in Chicago have been little more than refueling and repacking stations. I'm always ready to hop a train or plane and be off to somewhere else. I am as comfortable picking my way through a casbah in Egypt or a mountain trail in Alaska as negotiating a snowy Chicago avenue.

I can reduce all that's important to me to a backpack.

Joel, my brother just older than me, is a nomad who teaches modern agricultural techniques to Third World tribes to enable them to stay and survive on their land. So what does that make him? A nomad teaching other nomads to become settlers? He volunteered for the Peace Corps out of college and has roamed from Central America to Southeast Asia, living and working in cultures on the brink of extinction. He stays in touch through long letters that Mom cherishes and stores in a special shoebox. Thomas is also a nomad, the purest one in our family. His home is obviously wherever he parks the '45 Dodge flatbed truck. I suspect he moves with the seasons like the migrating eagles he loves.

Most of the rest of my family are settlers. Three of my siblings—a marketing manager, an architect, and a teacher—have established homes and professions. They plant gardens. They contribute to their communities. I admire that. I am not the kind of nomad who looks down on people who can plant roots and draw nourishment from their communities. I secretly long to settle, but it's just not in my constitution.

My father struggled all his life, pulled by the two impulses within him. The settler trying to make a home for his family. The nomad who would rather have wandered.

IT'S TOO SIMPLE, of course—this trying to divide all of mankind into two categories. It doesn't take into account the marauders both groups must contend with. Marauders roam into territory not their own, destroying and seeking plunder. Sometimes the marauders are other nomads as in the case of the Comanches who moved into the Southern Plains trying to displace the Apaches and Kiowa whose hunting grounds had ranged from the North Platte River in Nebraska to the Red River in Texas. The buffalo hunters who swarmed into the Plains killing off the herds were also marauders. The American settlers who moved into the Plains, though they certainly did not think of themselves as such, were indeed marauders taking plunder of the natural resources—the water, the grass, the hardwood forests along the rivers, as they moved west, finally wrenching the land itself from the population that had lived there for thousands of years.

Then there are the weekend marauders.

Every November the marauders came from the South—truckloads of pheasant hunters with their shotguns and seemingly unlimited ammo. Roads were clogged with pick-ups pulling campers as they moved north on the highways. My father would dutifully post our land. Posting meant putting up signs that said *No Hunting. No Trespassing.* No one actually paid attention to the signs. If the hunters were from Oklahoma, they drove onto the yard and asked if they could hunt. Dad always politely said no, but thanked them for asking, and they would go away.

But the Texans didn't even ask. They would come in caravans, park at the side of the road, and within minutes they would attack a field, spaced equidistant from one another, shotguns pointed into the air, marching in. Their *modus operandi* was if the farmer doesn't kick us off personally, this field is fair game. All farm work stopped for those days while Dad drove around in his pickup, virtually on patrol, rousting group after group, often having to wade deep into his now trampled fields to ask the hunters to leave.

Sometimes we stopped at the side of the road and just watched the Texas hunters in amazement. Twenty or thirty men, each maybe forty feet apart would systematically begin walking in to a field. As they marched in, startled beautiful birds would take flight, only to be shot. Very seldom did a pheasant escape the onslaught. The approach was methodical, almost like a combine harvesting wheat. But my father said we couldn't kill everything that moved. There had to be some birds left if there were to be baby pheasants for next year.

My father was not against hunting game, *per se.* He and my brothers went out several times during the season. Our Thanksgiving "turkey" was always a pheasant. Nothing tasted better in the world—or felt more authentically pilgrim. Sometimes when meat was scarce, Dad sneaked a pheasant when it wasn't hunting season. That was against the law, but we ate the evidence too fast to get caught. But my mom always felt guilty, so she referred to it as "prairie chicken," when we asked what we were having for dinner.

Jackrabbits were another story. You got two dollars for every pair of rabbit ears you turned in to the authorities because the voracious rabbits were eating our crops out from under us. It was always open hunting season on our Western Kansas jack rabbits, so big they resembled kangaroos with long ears as they sat on their back haunches, with their front legs up like little arms, just looking at us, daring us to shoot. The Odyssey drugstore sold postcards with trick photography—as my dad called it—of big mule-sized jackrabbits harnessed to a wagon. Jackrabbits could run faster than a truck. They often raced along beside our car as if to prove their prowess. (Years later on a trip into the Australian outback, kangaroos would race along my rental car, keeping up at 50 mph, just as the jackrabbits of my youth had.) My father explained that hunters had upset the balance of nature, killing too many coyotes, hence the rabbit population was out of control. So it was okay to shoot them. I learned to fire a rifle, and in fact, became pretty good at shooting tin cans. I'd go along with my big brothers on rabbit shoots and hand them ammo when they ran out, but I could never bring myself to aim a gun at any creature including a jackrabbit. (I won't tell you about the rabbit drives in our county where farmers lined up on all four sides of a section of land and walked in chasing the rabbits into a fenced-in circular enclosure and then clubbed them to death. Rabbit drives were too awful to imagine. My father wouldn't let my brothers go to rabbit drives. It was too cruel, even for jackrabbits.)

The Texans were hunting pheasant for sport, taking more than they could ever eat or pack out in ice. I imagine the Dallas housewives to whom they returned from their he-man adventures had little use for pheasant anyway. Probably threw them out, being more inclined to frozen fish sticks or TV dinners—something that I'd heard was the rage in places like Los Angeles or Dallas. Given that we didn't have TV, I had no idea what a frozen TV dinner was.

Adding insult to injury, few in our community felt as we did about the pheasant hunters. Odyssey put up banners at the stoplight welcoming them. As if it were their municipal duty to house these marauders, the town scrambled to provide lodging. Since there were only two motels along the highway, not nearly enough to accommodate all the hunters, the town opened up the high school gym for sleeping quarters. They put up cots. The men used the gym showers—even the girls showers. (I refused to take a shower after gym class one November day because I felt the room was contaminated. I was sent to the principal's office for an official reprimand, and given a C for the marking period.) The Lions Club cooked pancake breakfasts for the hunters, the Chamber of Commerce organized barbecues. When the pheasant hunters left, the townspeople would argue for days about how many hunters had come: 1,000, 2,000, no 5,000 some would claim.

But the worst part of pheasant season was that my brother and I were not allowed to go out to the pasture, our Indian ridge, or the creek. We could be shot by a stray bullet from some lone hunter my dad had failed to apprehend. In fact, we weren't even allowed to play in the yard. I ached to return to my village on the ridge, make campfires and to run free across the pasture with the wind in my hair or climb about the willows or play in the dry sand bed of the creek. Pheasant season was a cruel punishment.

My dislike of Texas and Texans—and I freely admit it is prejudice in its most naked form—stems from the many pheasant seasons during which I endured their onslaught on our land. I ache to think about how my father heroically tried to protect the land from their casual debasement, a battle he ultimately lost. As I think about it I can't help but fantasize that these rude, drawling men with their cigarettes and shotguns are the descendants of the men who slaughtered the buffalo for sport and pocket change on these same Plains a hundred years earlier.

I wonder, did my father know that his demise would come from the South? Was that why we never drove in that direction? Perhaps it was one of the Texas hunters he ran off our land who came back to take it away from us. Actually, the more I think about it, it seems very likely.

14

Buffalo

BUFFALO LIVE IN GROUPS. They roam in herds. If you ever see one alone, it is because it is lost or too sick to travel with its group. A lone buffalo is terrified and helpless. My father always said that like the buffalo we need our families, our clan. Alone we are powerless and without spirit. A family—and a clan—goes both forward and backward. With us are the spirits of many generations before us, as well as many generations who will come after us. They are all part of us. So we are never just one. We are everyone. And we live not in one day, but in all days.

There is something that *Our People* know. It comes to us as easily as breathing. We have always known it. Yet it is something that White Man does not know: All living things are one. They are connected. The grass and the soil are one. The wild geese and the lake are one. The earth and the sky are one. The coyote and his prey, the rabbit, are one. Nothing stands alone.

Because all things are one, we take from the earth only what we need, and we give back. Yes, we kill the buffalo. But we honor his spirit by using each part to renew ourselves and the earth. We drink his blood to quench our thirst and eat his flesh to feed our hunger. We preserve his hide to make our teepee, his coat to shield our bodies from the winter wind. His bladder becomes our water jug, his bones become our tools and our flutes, his dung feeds our fire. And so the mighty beast lives within us as we honor his gifts. Without the buffalo we die.

Without the grass the buffalo dies. In turn, the buffalo honors the grass and gives back dung to nourish it. All things are connected. I scarcely can explain it because we know this truth in our bones and in our blood and in our muscles. We know it as we know our own names.

Our spirits mingle and soar with the eagle, so we see down upon ourselves even as we look up into the heavens. We learn the wisdom of the fox, of the owl, of the rabbit and the quail. Every stream, every flower, every tree, every cloud has a purpose. Everything is connected to the next thing, just as the past is connected to the future and the mother is connected to the child. Nothing stands alone. This we know from birth. Yet White Man does not know it. White Man burns trees and tears grass from the soil. White Man kills a buffalo and dishonors it by leaving it to rot in the sun. When the buffalo hunters rode across our Plains with their big guns killing buffalo, it was the same as killing us. We smelled the stench on the wind and it was the stench of our own death.

Around the fires at our wintering grounds the old men grumbled. "If he could do it, the White Man would tear down a mountain rather than climb over it. He would rather stop a mighty river than cross it," they said.

"Do not talk like that," my father admonished the other men, "the White Man may hear your words and do it!"

It was not so long after those words were uttered in jest by our old men that we heard that white men were building great smoking wagons that moved like large snakes across the earth thundering and belching black clouds. And when their wagon snakes reached the mountains, we are told that white men chipped away at mountains, chopping them up to make a path through the mountains for their great snakes. What will be next? Will they drain the rivers of their water, the sky of its sun?

15

Buffalo Hunters & Sodbusters

THEY SWEPT ONTO THE Plains in groups, rough, crusty men flushed from the bloodcrazed Civil War, looking for adventure and pocket cash. It waited for them just beyond Dodge City. Great legendary beasts, in herds of thousands, roamed the hills—huge, hulking beasts with great ancient heads and dark eyes that glistened with fear and rage. Dragons to slay.

Dodge City, a frontier outpost on the banks of the Arkansas River served as their mustering grounds. By 1875, the Northern Plains were nearly devoid of buffalo, but the Southern Plains still teemed with great herds. According to the terms of the Medicine Lodge Treaty, buffalo hunters were not allowed south of the Arkansas River, but with hides going for two to three dollars a piece, plenty of hunters were willing to take a chance. Who was going to stop them? In Dodge, the buffalo hunters gathered supplies and joined with other men—skinners and cooks—organizing into hunting parties of a dozen or so, fanning out south and west looking for the herds.

Among their ranks were men whose names are legendary. Buffalo Bill Cody, Wild Bill Hickock, and a host of lesser known legends: Hoodoo Brown, Tom Nixon, Billy Dixon, Zack Light, Prairie Dog Dave, John Goff and George Brown, to name a few.

The best method for killing buffalo was to approach a herd carefully, slowly, and at about a hundred yards aim their .45 caliber Sharps rifle right for the lungs. The hunters called this method "killing in stands." If the shot was accurate, the wounded animal would puff hard and blow blood for a few minutes. Then, as he lay dying, the other buffalo would surround him. They didn't leave, wouldn't run away. Then the hunters would target another bull, then another, while the herd shuffled around, circling the downed animals, refusing to leave. This puzzled the buffalo hunters. The only explanation was that buffalo were exceedingly dumb.

I know why they did not leave because Gentle Wind told me. Buffalo live in groups. They do not know how to be alone. They would not leave their fallen brothers because they could not. It is not in their nature. Loyalty comes not from stupidity but from courage.

By killing in "stands" a good buffalo hunter could pick off a hundred or more animals in a day, or however many hides his wagons could haul back to Dodge.

I once read an account written by George Brown, a buffalo hunter with a touch of poet in his soul, of his hunting days in 1874. His story was published in a Guymon, Oklahoma newspaper in 1915. He tells of his trip into pristine prairie in search of herds, riding south out of Lakin, a small village on the Arkansas River, camping on the North Fork of the Cimarron, which from his description sounds very much like what would later become my grandfather's Willow Valley. There he killed eighty-five buffalo. Then he made camp the next night a few miles south at Wagonbed Springs before traveling further west and south in search of larger herds. Observing trails of beaten down grass from a large herd going westward, Brown's hunting party followed another ten miles until they came to a lake of water that covered about a quarter section of land. Recounts George Brown. "And all around the lake, as far as I could see, I could hardly see the ground for buffalo. This was a rainwater lake, and as my visit was in the fall of the year, this lake was covered with wild ducks and geese, and all kinds of waterfowl. This scene out on the prairies, long before the white man had taken possession of this domain was one of the prettiest scenes I ever saw in all my life. The lake and the wild water fowl, the buffalo, and also wild ponies running loose made it an unforgettable sight.

"It was at this lake that we made our good killing," remembers Brown. "We camped there for about ten days, and brought down 800 buffalo. Shooting was so good that we found that we were running short of ammunition."

The buffalo party would quickly skin the animals, leaving the carcasses to rot in the sun. So many dead buffalo littered the prairies during these years that travelers through the Plains reported that the smell was nearly unbearable.

The history books say the buffalo hides brought good prices back East, citing it as the primary reason for the slaughter. Buffalo lap robes were the fashionable way to keep warm in the open-air carriages on the streets of New York and Philadelphia. Furthermore, by 1875, Eastern tanneries had learned what the Indians had known for thousands of years, how to cure the tough buffalo hide and make "belts." I have seen the photos in the museum at Dodge City, great mounds of hides, higher than houses, as far as the eye could see, mounds and mounds of buffalo hides beside the railroad tracks in Dodge City waiting to be shipped. Between 1871 and 1887 five million hides were shipped out of Dodge alone. Even just a few mounds of buffalo hides, I reasoned, would provide enough leather to make a belt for every person living on earth. How, I have wondered, could there possibly be a market for so many belts?

In my life as a journalist and a student of human nature, I have learned that when all is said and done, only two things fuel the events of history. Need and Greed. There had to be some overwhelming economic reason for the slaughter of the buffalo. There had to be more to it than belts.

I found it as a piece of a sentence in a book written by a Western Kansas newspaperman who had gathered his bits of history by talking to the eyewitnesses of the era. It was just a phrase out of place, four or five words inserted innocuously into the middle of a sentence, that finally explained it. Belts, yes, belts. Oh, not belts to hold up pants, there weren't enough pants in 1880 to need that much holding up. It was discovered that buffalo hide, too tough to make good leather garments, were quite ideally suited to another kind of belt. Durable, nearly unbreakable, great wide, tough belts to turn the wheels and turbines of industry. Belts to enable the Industrial Revolution. The world's factories needed those kind of belts.

But there was more to it than that.

Industry might find uses for their hides, but railroads needed the beasts out of their way. Fueled by the heady Gold Rush to California, the railroads had linked the East and the West. Using the sweat and blood of coolies from China who were willing to work themselves to death to build them, railways stretched across the whole breadth of the great new continent, opening the way to all kinds of possibilities. One problem. Trains need to run on schedules. But on the tracks through the Great High Plains, trains were sometimes held up for hours, even days, as great herds of buffalo stumbled slowly and stubbornly over the tracks, making their way north and then back south following the bloom of the prairie grasses, a great, never-ending flow of massive brown beasts who seemed not to notice or care that a train sat waiting for them to pass. Something had to be done.

But there was something more.

There was an even *more* fundamental economic reason that the railroads needed to get rid of the buffalo—not some, but *all of them*. For the railroads to survive, they needed goods to ship. The native inhabitants of the Plains—the nomads who followed and lived off the buffalo—were neither producing goods in quantity that needed to be shipped east, nor consuming goods in quantity that needed to be carried west. As long as the buffalo herds provided everything the indigenous nomads needed to survive and thrive, they would stay and live as they had always lived. There was no business for the railroads in that great middle of the continent. The great expansive Plains needed to be cultivated, turned into goods-producing lands that required a railroad to carry their produce to the population centers in the East. Clearly, no one was going to make farmers out of these savages. The Plains must be emptied of its native population and settled by farmers.

But where was one to get enough farmers to populate and cultivate such a vast area? When the federal government granted the railroad companies millions of acres of land—ten miles to either side of their tracks as an incentive—the railroads placed ads in foreign newspapers and sent recruiters to Europe to cajole and entice solid European farming stock to immigrate to the American Plains. The railroad companies were willing to sell this land for pennies, hell, almost give it away to farmers willing to come. The government was also giving away land— Indian land—with Homestead Acts that offered free acreage to whomever would settle, live on it, and turn a plow to the native buffalo pastures. Sodbusters was what they would come to be called. For that is what they did.

That's how my great-grandfathers, on both sides of the family, happened to come from Russia to America. Santa Fe Railroad officials went to southern Russia, where my German-speaking forefathers grew wheat on the harsh steppes, and talked my mother's grandfather Isaiah into bringing his whole clan to America. My great-grandfather and his brother made an exploratory trip to America, paid for by the railroad, and when they got off the train at Newton, Kansas and looked around, they said, this looks just like our home in Russia. We can come here, and get away from those Cossacks who are riding into our villages and raping our women and burning our barns. We can come here. We are treated as foreigners in Russia because we speak German. We can be foreigners here just as well. They went back to Russia and moved dozens—and then hundreds—of families to the prairies.

In the same way, railroad officials convinced my father's grandfather to leave another Russian village for the plains of North Dakota. That family group found the Dakotas much too cold and windy, and later joined the Land Rush into Oklahoma territory.

All of them—both sides of my family along with the many other European immigrants who settled in their midst—would face harsh winters of starvation and disease and would somehow learn to survive on the American Plains, plowing under the buffalo grass of untold millennia, planting their grain, displacing a population that had laid claim to these hunting grounds for thousands of years—all so the railroads would have goods to ship cross-country. We repeat the stories of our forefather's struggles, turning their travail into heroic tales of courage and perseverance. They endured plagues of biblical proportion—sickness, locust, drought, storms—and too often, death of their firstborn—in order to lay claim to their promised land. Promised not by God but by the Santa Fe Railroad.

At first, as the native population was pushed out of the way, they struck back, raiding and killing and burning out settlers here and there. These random acts had a clear purpose: To send a message to the hoards of European settlers that it was not safe to come here. The U.S was obligated to send in their armies to protect the settlers. So Civil War-weary soldiers moved west to fight the Indian wars.

Just as the proper marching British redcoats were no match for the American rebels fighting guerrilla-style on familiar home turf in 1776, the uniformed, often very young, American soldiers were no match for the cunning of the Indians braves a century later. At first, the soldiers were losing. Ultimately, there was only way to win. The Plains Indians' whole way of life was based on the buffalo. It didn't take a genius to figure out that the only way to empty the Plains of these savages was to kill off their buffalo.

So the natives, those who managed to survive white man's diseases and warfare, were ultimately subdued by starvation. With the herds gone, defeated and hungry, the remnants of a proud people were at last themselves herded into reservations in Oklahoma Indian Territory, which in less than a decade would also be opened to settlement.

When the railroads and the government teamed up to defeat the Red Man by slaughtering the buffalo herds, there were plenty of men who relished the task. They killed the buffalo in such great numbers between 1865 and 1875 that the wind turned foul. Ironically, as the settlers moved into the emptied land now for the taking, farming was made difficult by the sheer volume of buffalo bones that littered the Plains, a curse that soon became a blessing. Starving settlers who found growing crops hopelessly difficult in the first years, made a living from gathering up the bones in their wagons, driving them to the railroad and selling them for six to ten dollars a ton. (Ironically, the bones themselves created goods for railroads to ship.) The buffalo bones were shipped east to make fertilizer and "bone" china.

Finally, the Plains were empty of Indians, buffalo, and now the litter of bones.

In Homer County, it is said that the last buffalo bull was found wandering aimlessly two miles north of Wagonbed Springs in the summer of 1889. How he got there, no one knows. Buffalo had not been spotted in the area in seven years. Charley McClay, the rancher who found the bull, didn't have the heart to kill it. He sold it to Buffalo Bill Cody's Wild West show.

In our part of the country, settlers often gave up after only a few seasons. Clearly, this arid land, which had been ideally suited to buffalo herds and roving nomads was better suited to cattle and cowboys than crops and farmers. Western Kansas with its inexhaustible expanse of dense buffalo grass became a ranching mecca. Dodge City, once the way station for soldiers fighting Indians and buffalo hunters exterminating their herds, now became an endpoint for cattle drives as longhorn cattle were driven up from Texas to be loaded onto the train at Dodge. And so Dodge City became the famous Wild West cowboy town, with its gunfighters and saloons and madams and lawmen. The stuff of legends.

Still, some settlers wouldn't give up. Living uneasily with the ranchers, fighting over fences and lifestyle, they flowed in, taming towns by building schools and churches. Trying to grow grain on these arid Plains that Coronado, who got it right from the beginning, called the worst, good-for-nothing desert in the world. The sodbusters were people who didn't know better, battling the elements, trying to tame the Plains. It was their plowing under of the natural grass that caused the great Dust Bowl of the thirties, when winds whipped up the sandy topsoil, darkening the skies all the way to Chicago and actually blowing dust particles as far east as New York City.

Finally, many sodbusters, themselves busted by sod turned to powder, facing starvation, migrated to California in search of salvation. Yet some wouldn't give up—like a handful of families in Odyssey who wouldn't leave, like my grandfather, who saw his sons pack up and move west, but who, even after he'd lost the deed to the Home Place, tenaciously clung to his lost paradise, waiting for rain to return so that he could buy back the land and coax his eldest son, my father, back to resume the struggle against nature to create the amber waves of grain for our national anthem.

Somewhere in the midst of all the struggle, the Plains got into our blood, and took over our souls. *How did it get into my blood? I left it as soon as I was old enough to flee.* Nevertheless, it got into our blood, *into my blood,* so we, *so I,* could hurt all over again when we finally lost it for good.

16

Buffalo Spirits

FIRST THEY KILLED the buffalo.

Then they came back with their wagons and hauled the bones away. As if doing so would get rid of the evidence of the slaughter. They could take the white accusing bones away, but they could not haul the spirits of the buffalo off the Plains in their wagons. They did not know that the spirit of the buffalo would remain in the wind. And just as the herds moved as great brown masses over the earth, their spirits would amass dark and threatening on the horizon, rolling and boiling, and then stampede in the wind across the Plains in blind, stinging retribution, choking life itself.

Other times the buffalo spirits rumble in great pillaring clouds above the Plains, brown with fury. And sometimes their fury whirls about and strikes down to the earth destroying everything in its path. Then the spirits pull back into the clouds and smolder in anger until the next time they boil over.

The buffalo spirits do not rest.

17

Horses & Gold

THE WORST THING THAT HAPPENED to our people was horses. We traded for them with the Spanish. At first our people believed it was a great gift. We became like gods as we rode these beautiful swift beasts. On their backs we became far more skilled at hunting buffalo. Moving camp became easier. The horses carried our teepees, our belongings. We no longer depended on little dogs or the backs of women. We could have large teepees. We could roam farther. And the horses did not compete for our food, as did the dogs. The horses ate the grass of our Plains, so their food was abundant.

Once we began to acquire horses, we began to acquire other things. Cooking pots, bigger and bigger teepees. Our belongings took on a spirit of their own. They became wealth. Once you begin to believe in wealth—which is putting value on worthless things—you desire your neighbor's wealth. Our people began stealing horses, not only from the white men, but also from their Indian brothers.

With horses we could travel farther, and clans began moving into new territories sacred to other clans. Suddenly there were no boundaries. Then war came to our land.

There have been wars from the beginning of time. But not like the wars we began to fight from the backs of our horses. And then came guns. Bows and arrows kill, but they kill when you are close. The guns we acquired from the French and the English could kill many, and kill from far away. When you do not look your enemy in the eye you do not see his spirit and it is easier to kill him.

Our clan did not like war. We wished to stay quietly beside our little river that nobody wanted. Our alliances made it possible. However, many of our young men wished to prove their skills in warfare and were drawn away from our hunting grounds to spill blood in needless wars. And so in every generation we lost half of our young men.

The war-loving Comanche eventually swept into our land. They had many horses and much wealth. They wanted everything. They did not need the bend of our little Buffalo River, but they wanted it to be under their command. So my grandfather, a great chief, made agreements with the Comanche chiefs. Comanche did not like agreements. But our young maidens married into Comanche clans, and softened the hearts of their husbands. And even the warlike Comanche finally agreed that we Kiowa Apaches—the name we were called by the White Man and the Comanche—were worthy to occupy the Plains and live as we had always lived.

Our people have a long history of understanding what the buffalo know. We are better in groups. We are helpless and spiritless without the love and understanding of our people. We travel together. We eat from the same flesh. We sit around our campfire together. We need to be together.

THE RED MAN LOVES HORSES. The White Man loves gold. They will chase it to the ends of the earth. They love gold more than they love their own children. They value it more their own souls. They will die for gold. We Indians do not understand that. Gold does not nourish anything. Despite its beauty and glitter, it is mere dust and rock.

White men love to tell a story about us that they find so funny, they roll in the dirt with tears running out of their eyes as they tell it. A war party of Indians captured a wagon loaded with twenty-five bags of gold dust. They dumped the gold dust into the sand and rode off with the twenty-five leather bags.

It is not so funny. The gold dust is mere dust, beautiful but useless. The leather bags can be used to carry food and important tools as we move from one hunting ground to another.

The stories repeated at our campfires say that the very first white man to wander into our lands was searching for gold. His name was Coronado.

He was a fearsome chief with many warriors from a different world who had been told there was gold in Quivera. We knew there was no gold. But our chief told him where to find Quivera because we wished Coronado to move on. He had taken many Indian slaves and we did not wish to also become his slaves. We sent him east.

Coronado and his warriors were willing to risk their lives to wander through a great desert in a land they did not know just to search for gold. Coronado, so the story is told, was very angry when he reached the village of Quivera and found nothing but earthen huts, fields of corn and happy people. No gold. Coronado first heard the stories of gold in Quivera when he conquered the Southern Kingdoms. The stories were lies to make him travel into the great desert and die. It was a clever ruse invented by some wise chief to rid his people of the suffering Coronado had brought to their land. They sent with him a guide, one of our own Plains tribesmen they called Turk, to lead him into the worst of our dry and desolate places. Then when Coronado and his men perished from hunger and thirst, as surely they would on this great flat desert, Turk, who had been a slave, was told he would be a free man and could rejoin his Pawnee clan just east of our hunting grounds. But when Turk was found sneaking off to the sacred spring at the Big Buffalo River to quench his thirst—after he had told Coronado he was lost and could find no water, Coronado killed Turk and hung his body from a tree so all could see his anger at being deceived.

RED MAN'S GREED FOR HORSES and White Man's greed for gold turned our hunting grounds into battlegrounds and made our land run with blood.

Three hundred winters after Coronado traveled through our lands, white men began traveling along our river trails across our hunting grounds on their way to the mountains of the West in search of gold. They heard tales of rivers flowing with gold, of mountains made of gold. They risked all—their homes, their families, their animals—to travel through our land, not knowing where to find food or water, not knowing if the stories of gold were true or tricks played by cruel fools. With them, came disease and starvation. Finally our warriors began to fight back because we did not want to see our land despoiled, our futures ruined.

When the invaders did not find gold, they came back for the buffalo.
When all the buffalo were gone, they came back for us.
Nadi-ish-dena.

18

Lost Treasure

I MEANT TO DRIVE OUT THERE and see it. I promised myself I would. But I can't do it. For ten years I have refused to even think about it. It's a kind of game I play with myself: that if I don't see it, talk about it, or write about it, it didn't happen.

I saw it once, accidentally, from the air. On flights between coasts, I now make a point of reserving aisle seats so I can't look out of the window. But on one full flight, I was stuck in a window seat, carelessly assuming it would be better than a cramped middle seat.

When I started seeing the huge green circles, out of habit I casually traced the Arkansas River, then the Cimarron, and then at the moment I decided to abandon the game, I noticed some sort of dark brown crop in the midst of the green circles. The brown fields were divided into small rectangular plots and some irregular trapezoidal shapes as they fanned out from what appeared to be the central farmyard with sheds and small silos. I wondered to myself what crop in Kansas would make the field appear dark brown.

With a horrible rush, it came to me. And I averted my eyes, tried to busy myself in my book. But I could not read through the tears welling in my eyes. Later, knowing I was well past the western border of Kansas, as the plane angled over the southeastern corner of Colorado, I looked out again. Periodically, I saw small rectangular clusters of brown fields. They must be feedlots, I realized. But none, not one, was anywhere near the size of that first one I saw nestled between the North Fork and the Sand Arroyo. I was sick with the knowledge of how large it was, how it changed the earth even from 30,000 feet up.

I meant to drive out there. To go the thirteen miles. When I was at the Willow Valley school yard, I could smell it on the wind. Semi-trailer cattle trucks rumbled by on the road, making the earth shake. But I chickened out and high-tailed it back to town, retreating back into my game: If I don't see it, talk about it, or write about it, it didn't happen.

Now, as step one, I'm going to at least put it on paper.

Dad doesn't talk about it. Mom does, but only when he's gone or out of earshot. As near as I can get from her, this is what happened.

One day in late November of 1974, a shiny black car drove slowly onto the yard. Mom saw it from a window. She was gripped by the very same fear that used to rise in her throat when she'd see Old Man Houston's black Model A drive down the driveway on the Home Place. Dad was outside repairing his Massey Ferguson tractor. He climbed off of it, wincing as that last long step down sent jolts of pain through his knees and hip joints.

Dad knew right away they weren't pheasant hunters. No pickup, no orange vests, no guns. Three men got out. They were dressed in expensive, well-fitting suits and dressy cowboy boots. The moment they moved toward him to shake his hand in a way-too-friendly manner, he knew they were Texans and that they wanted something that he was unwilling to give.

The men introduced themselves as representatives from a Dallas-based cattle company that was scouting out the Oklahoma Panhandle and Southwestern Kansas area looking for a good site for a feedlot. The spokesman, a tall man with a booming voice, came right to the point. His company wanted to buy Dad's land, they would pay top dollar.

"I'm not interested," was all my father said.

"Now, you know, Mr. Kluger, this land is worthless for irrigation. We don't have to tell you that. The hills, ridges, creek, it's not flat. And we don't have to tell you that dryland farming no longer makes sense. This is going to be a tough plot of land to sell when you want to retire, and we have a hunch that you're coming close to that time."

"I'm not interested in selling," my father repeated matter-of-factly.

"Now, Mr. Kluger, we know that you are thinking about selling. We saw your ad in the local paper three months ago."

"Oh, I just put that in to see if there was any interest. Just a feeler. It didn't mean anything. Farmers do that all the time."

"The price you asked, by the way, was way out of line. I'll bet you didn't get even one feeler, am I right?"

Mom by now was standing next to Dad in the yard. It was cold, but my mother was not about to invite the men into the house to continue the conversation.

"Now, here's what we'll do for you, Mr. Kluger. Even though we know the price you asked was way out of line, we are authorized to offer you that price. No haggling. That's what the land is worth to you. Fine. We'll pay it. We'll make the deal right now, today, if you're ready."

"Oh, I would have to think about it," said my father, trying to send a polite signal that he wished the conversation to be over.

"We need two sections," the tall man continued, as if he had not heard my father's polite no. "Four would be even better. Bosley, who owns the section just north of you, has agreed to sell. We're working out the deal right now."

"That would be news to me!" My father was now becoming a little bit angry. He rented the section from Bosley and farming that land had always been important to us: Western Kansas farmers generally had to till a lot of acreage to make a go of farming. Bosley, who was retired and lived in Wichita, had trusted my father to make good decisions about the land for years, and he had certainly not shared any plans about selling with my father.

My mother tried to make eye contact with Dad now, to warn him to talk no further to these men, but Dad was getting riled.

"I'm flat out not selling," he said. "Do you see this prairie here?" he motioned broadly to the pasture with its buffalo herd. "There's not much of that left in these parts and I won't see that become a feedlot."

"If you're worried about that buffalo herd, don't be concerned. We'd be happy to add a few hundred dollars per head into the contract and take them off your hands. You won't have to worry about moving them."

"No, it's a lot more I'm worried about. This land is not going to become a feedlot like that one outside of Dodge," my father said flatly.

"Are you saying you won't sell this land for any price?"

"I'd sell it to another farmer who was going to respect the land and farm it right." Dad said.

"So, it's just *us* you won't sell it to?"

Dad caught Mom's glance. "I'm not ready to sell it to anybody right now," he amended. "And I'm not interested in discussing it further."

The other two men stood awkwardly as the third man, the main spokesman of the group, reached into his pocket for a business card. "Mr. Kluger, here's my card with all my phone numbers, even my home phone number." He demonstratively wrote a number on the back of the card. "So if you change your mind or even have a question about anything, anything at all, you just give me a call."

The men all politely shook hands, their clean manicured hands tightly gripping my dad's rough, dry hands, which were undoubtedly smeared with axle grease from his tractor repair work. When the last man shook my father's hand and moved to go, he added in the manner of Texans who always need to have the last word, "Mr. Kluger, I think you will change your mind, once you have had time to think about it."

There was something menacing about the way he said that, my mother remembers in her telling. "He was like one of those pheasant hunters who hates to be told no, who figures that when the farmer's back is turned, he'll go in there and hunt anyway."

"Dad went right back to his tractor, not even stopping to talk about it," remembers my mother. "At supper, he didn't talk about it either but I could see he was stewing. His mouth was turned down into this frown and he was chewing on the insides of his mouth."

The FHA loan officer who handled Dad's government loan on the land stopped by the next morning. That wasn't terribly unusual. He was in the habit of stopping by from time to time to see how things were going. The FHA agents act as advisors from the Department of Agriculture, discussing the nitty-gritty financial details of the farms whose loans they hold. They are charged with keeping struggling farmers on their land. That's their job. Sometimes that involves adjusting payments and schedules, even suggesting new crop ideas, giving financial advice, just generally keeping an eye out for the farmer. More than once over the years, Dobbs had come out to arrange skipping payments when drought made times tough, or to refinance under better terms.

Dobbs—I never heard his first name—was a short man who always, even in winter, wore a short-sleeved sports shirt that was slightly rumpled like he'd slept in it. We didn't know much about him. Both his personality and appearance were nondescript except for his flattop haircut, which resembled a thick stand of lawn grass which the barber somehow cut off as flat as if a lawnmower had moved an inch above the head. The hairdo was popular in the fifties. I wondered if he still wore his hair that way in the seventies on the fateful day of his unannounced visit to my dad. I'd bet he did. The thing I most remember about that haircut was that when Dobbs lowered his head as he worked on figures at the kitchen table, in the center on top, the prickly hair was so short, you could look right through it and see bare skin.

"How old are you now, Joseph?" asked Dobbs as his opening remark.

"Sixty-seven."

"Maybe the time has come to sell the land."

"I'm doing fine, except for one pesky knee."

"Joseph, it's come to our attention that you've had an offer. A very good one. The likes of which you'll never see again."

My father didn't ask Dobbs how he knew what had transpired the day before. Dad merely said, "I'm not ready to sell just yet. Not to a feedlot."

"Joseph, you have a lot of principal left on the loan. You're getting older. You need to get out of farming. None of your four sons has shown any interest in farming. At some point you're going to have to sell. It might as well be for a good price." My dad didn't respond, so Dobbs continued. "This is worthless land, nearly worthless. It's a wonder you've made any kind of living off it at all. If it wasn't for the goodness of the FHA, and the way I've bent the rules for you over the years, you would have lost this land long ago. You know that, Joseph."

He was making a lot of sense, my Mom admitted in her retelling of the story. "Dad was listening to him. I suppose he *has* been very good to us over the years."

"I'm not against selling, *on principle*," my dad explained to Dobbs, "I'd consider selling to another farmer. Someone who will take good care of the land. I just can't see a feedlot coming in here, stinking up the place. Ruining the land. The neighbors, I can't do that to them."

"Joseph, you have to be practical. You have to think of your future, not your neighbors."

They were sitting around the kitchen table, as they had so many times before, usually after a crop failure, when things looked desperate and Dad was begging the FHA officer to let him miss a few payments. "Just work with me," was what my father was usually saying to Dobbs on these occasions. Dobbs would have spiral notebooks out and be looking through tables with numbers, furiously scratching out ideas. Mom and I both remembered those tense scenes, followed by the sighs of relief when Dobbs finally worked something out. He'd always leave by saying, "I'll have to talk to my bosses about this. But I think I can convince them."

"Dobbs had no notebooks this time. Not even a pen. So I knew things were serious," my mother intoned to me, nervously watching the window to see if Dad was home from church choir practice yet. She needed to finish the story before he got home. We were sitting in the living room of their trailer, which sat precariously on top of cement blocks on a dusty lot facing the highway a mile outside of Odyssey. Mom was trying to tell me the whole story as best she could, but she kept stopping to dab her hankie at her eyes. The rest of the world had switched to Kleenex, but my mom still believed in cloth handkerchiefs imprinted with mock embroidery-stitch designs that came five to a package from Duckwall's.

"Then Dobbs leaned back in his chair," my mother continued.

"Joseph, I didn't want to tell you this."

A pause.

"Joseph, we're calling in your loan."

Any lender can call in a loan at any time. Whether it's a home mortgage or a business loan, lenders always give themselves that back door. If "confidence is low," as they like to call it, a lender—be it a bank or the government—can *call in the loan*. However, the whole point of the Farm Home Administration Loan program, started at the height of the 1930s Depression, was to assist low-income farm families in staying on their land and to keep them from becoming tenant farmers. In other words, the Department of Agriculture established the program specifically to *not* call in loans.

My mother, who usually did not join in business discussions, and did not necessarily share my father's trust of Dobbs, interjected at this point, "So you call in the loan at the same time the feedlot tries to buy our land."

Dobbs faced her quiet wrath. "Mrs. Kluger, it's true. Word of the Texas company's offer did reach us. But you don't understand. My bosses have been trying to call in this loan for years. I've fought for you. But at some point, when a way out is clear, I can no longer justify my stand. That's what's happening here."

Then he turned again to my father. "This is a blessing in disguise, Joseph. No one is going to pay even half what they're offering you for this land. Face it. This is a way for you to pay off all your debts and have enough left over to retire, buy a nice little house in town, move to Phoenix, whatever you want. It's what's best for you. Look at you. How long can you keep climbing on that tractor? We're in a drought cycle again. You don't have irrigation. How many more crop failures can you withstand at your age?"

"My neighbors would be terribly angry."

"In your fix, they'd do the same. Perhaps they will do the same. The feedlot would like to buy up all the adjacent property. They have big plans, plans, by the way, that will be very good for Homer County."

My father pleaded with Dobbs to give him time to put an ad in the paper, find another buyer. Time to figure things out.

"I can give you until tomorrow," Dobbs said. "We call in the loan tomorrow. We take the land. The way land prices have dropped, it's not even worth the balance of your loan. You can let that happen and lose everything. Or you can call the feedlot company and tell them yes, and retire with something for all the years of hard work you've put in."

"It was the last thing Dobbs said, on the way out the door that really hit us," said Mom, dabbing at her eyes again.

He said, "Either way, it becomes a feedlot."

Dobbs left.

And that's how Dad lost the farm. He never really had a choice.

Within days, the whole county knew. Neighbors were furious. My father was denounced in community meetings and pilloried in a barrage of nasty letters to the editor in the *Odyssey News.*

Within thirty days he was off the land. Machinery, movable sheds, implements, and excess furniture were sold at a farm auction. My older brothers and sister came in to catalogue, price and help conduct the sale. My parents hastily bought a trailer home and a small plot of land to park it on a mile outside of Odyssey. I did not come home to help with the move. I could not bear it. Thomas was not reachable. But the day of the farm sale, Thomas suddenly showed up in a gigantic cattle truck, with three horses and two Mexican cowpokes and they herded the buffalo into the cattle transport while the feedlot officials screamed and hollered. They had considered the buffalo part of the sale.

No doubt, they planned on some buffalo burgers.

The cattle company was not really a Texas company at all. They were, we were to discover, a huge international corporation with big plans. They began bulldozing and rearranging the landscape immediately, building pens, installing lights, and transporting in cattle, in a matter of weeks creating a cattle finishing enterprise that would soon grow to be the largest feedlot in the world. There were other things we learned. The feedlot people hadn't even contacted Bosley before they talked to Dad. Bosley only sold to them because they told him Dad had sold and was retiring, so he figured he might as well.

As my parents tried to start a new life on the barren edge of town, controversy swirled around my father who never explained his plight to anyone, who never defended himself against the accusations. A man so innocent he did not comprehend the conspiracy against him. He thought that his refusal to sell to the feedlot and his loan being called in shortly thereafter was a coincidence—like a hailstorm coming the day before he was set to begin harvesting his wheat. He did not comprehend the evil ways of greedy corporations or corrupt government. And so he was a lamb led to slaughter, made to endure his neighbors' wrath. To them, he was a greedy farmer wanting to cash in at retirement time, a traitor who had caved in to the offers of an enemy—an outsider from Texas—come to despoil the landscape and foul the air for miles around.

He worried about the neighbors, the same neighbors whose irrigation wells had sucked the water out from under us, rendering our once rich bottomland worthless, our creek dry, our trees dead. He went silently. Had he ever confided the blackmail plot against him, those same neighbors might have rushed to his side to expose the misconduct of the Farmer's Home Loan official or perhaps even offered to buy the land to keep it out of the cattle company's reach.

And where was I? Big crusading reporter, always fighting for the little guy, exposing the corruptions of city hall and big business. Where was I when my father needed my help?

He went silently, asking for no help, offering no explanations. He went silently. And he suffered silently. And when his mind could live with it no more, dreams of buried gold filled his imagination and lifted his hopes.

PART TWO

Far From Home, 1968–1995

Perhaps she has gone to the other side of the sun
where children rule as kings. Perhaps she has journeyed
in search of new and happier spirits.

19

University

MY LAST YEAR OF HIGH SCHOOL was unbearable. I was seventeen and itching to leave Odyssey. My teachers were tedious, except for my art teacher, a bouncy, free spirit accidentally deposited on the prairie from who knows what planet. The blowing dust, the irrigation well across the road, the long bus rides to school, all of it was unbearable. I needed to go. Away. Somewhere. Anywhere. I was beginning to see the Plains as an outsider would—miles and miles of nothingness. The familiar mirage on the road, that shimmering pool of illusory liquid that disappeared as you drew closer, was no longer a marvel, but a harsh reminder that the unbearable flatness was playing cruel tricks on me. On clear crisp autumn mornings, the grain elevators of distant towns, elongated into shimmering skyscrapers by the morning mirage-like phenomenon, no longer thrilled me. Instead, I longed for a real city on the horizon, filled with exciting places and people.

I did not go out to the pasture anymore. The willows along the creek were slowly dying out. Protruding from the tops of the cottonwoods in the U-bend, a few leafless bare arms reached out, beseeching the heavens for water. I felt the same way. I was pleading not for water, but for something I could not name. Aching for someone I had not yet met. Praying for one day to be different from the last.

If I had a daughter, I wondered, would she one day feel the same way at seventeen? Or was it only me? (It never occurred to me to ask my mother if she had once felt this way. We baby boomers always assumed we were the first generation to feel the emotions that blew into our charmed and tortured lives.)

The unhappiest day of that year was when I was elected homecoming queen. How could that be unhappy? Was that not the zenith of acceptance and the ultimate fulfillment of a teen fantasy? Me the brainy, country girl winning out over cheerleaders who went steady with football players. But the honor of winning the popular vote of my peers was overshadowed by the humiliation of not having a date to the homecoming dance. Having grown up in a household with four brothers, I had acquired a hundred more. I was every boy's favorite sister. Boys I had crushes on would ask me to go Christmas shopping with them to help pick out gifts for their girlfriends, and eager for their friendship and approval, I would go. Not one boy in my class thought to ask me for a date to the homecoming dance. Certainly not the homecoming king, His Honor Luke Mahoney, captain of the football team.

I had known Luke, sort of, since we were children because he also attended a one-room country school—one located about ten miles south of Willow Valley. I saw him at county track meets, spelling contests, pioneer days and other shared country school events. He always won the top medals in the county track meets—in the boys' division, that is. I always won the top medals in the girls' track events. There was no girl in Homer County who could run faster or jump higher than I could. But when we entered high school in town as freshman—I couldn't help but believe it had been as frightening for him as it was for me—instead of being my friend, he pretended he didn't know me.

As soon as it became clear that he was the best quarterback to ever play for the Odyssey High School football team—he could run faster than the wind—he transformed from shy country boy to arrogant hero. Every girl in school worshiped the ground he walked on—except me. The thought of having to sit next to him and be totally ignored at the homecoming dance was unbearable. You see, Luke and I had not been on speaking terms since a December day when we were juniors in high school and I made him stop his car to let me out. He had been spinning the car 360 degrees on an icy street in Dodge City. I was among the carload of teenagers Luke had driven to Dodge for the State Championship Basketball Tournament. "I don't want to be in this car when you wrap it around a tree and kill everyone. I'm getting out," I demanded.

Stunned, he stopped, and I got out. In a near blizzard I called my father, who had to drive ninety miles to get me at midnight. Luke never spoke to me again. I had challenged his manhood and humiliated him in front of his friends.

When we were seated alphabetically in physics class our senior year, we ended up having to sit next to one another at a small table for two. The tension was so obvious our teacher called us in after school three weeks into the year and asked what was going on. We refused to discuss it and asked if one of us could be moved. Mr. Moore wouldn't do it, said we had to be mature enough to work out whatever it was. So we sat side by side at a table for two in the front row, demonstratively chatting with everyone around us, never acknowledging each other's presence.

And now as homecoming king and queen, we had to stand awkwardly next to one another during the halftime crowning ceremony, which was traditionally followed by the king kissing the queen. This year it didn't happen.

"You don't have to look so worried," he had whispered to me just before, as he stood next to me in his grotesque padded shoulders, holding his helmet in his hands so a crown could be placed on his head. "I'm not going to kiss you. Jessica would kill me." I was certain he resented the fact that I had won the vote, when by rights it should have been his steady girlfriend, Jessica. That's how it had always turned out other years. That's how it was supposed to be. A couple. A king with his queen. I struggled to keep up my fake smile during the ceremony though tears threatened just back of my eyeballs. The dust was blowing that night. The air looked hazy under the artificial yellow floodlights. And my eyes were stinging. I felt like a usurper. I didn't even want to be homecoming queen, but it happened so quickly during the senior assembly when somebody put my name into nomination that, well, it just . . . *happened*. Standing there in my taffeta dress with puffy sleeves, and a silly dimestore-cheap tiara on my over-teased, over-sprayed, beauty shop hair, I half wondered if voting for me had been my classmates' conspiratorial sadistic joke to irritate Luke and humiliate me.

So I slipped away moments before the end of the football game and Luke's final crowd-pleasing touchdown, slithered through a gap in the bleachers, stealing around to just under where my father was sitting, and whispered to him that I wanted to go home. He and Tommy joined me in back of the bleachers and we walked quickly to the car. The three of us silently drove the thirteen miles home. My dad didn't even ask me why I was leaving early. He probably thought I was having female problems, or maybe he thought I was upset about Mom being in the hospital—she was in for "testing," and my parents were being mysterious about what it was for.

Yes, I was worried about Mom. But in truth, I was more absorbed in my own misery that night. My throne would just have to sit empty at the homecoming dance. As for Luke, well, there was no other way to put it—I hated Luke. Now, more than ever.

At the end of the semester, I dropped physics, angering Mr. Moore, who I guess wanted to make a rocket scientist out of me. I explained that I had enough math and science credits to graduate and there was a course in photography I really wanted to take. "You would choose playing with a camera over physics?" Mr. Moore was red in the face. "Do you know what opportunities lie ahead for a young woman with your aptitude for math?" In reality, I just couldn't bear sitting next to Luke another semester.

But it was more than Luke, it was *everything*. I just wanted my senior year to be over. I wanted to be done with high school and done with Odyssey.

AND SO, FINALLY, COLLEGE. What a relief it would be.

My parents loaded up the trunk and back seat of the Oldsmobile— I had selected only three stuffed animals to take with me so as not to appear immature to my future dormmates—and we traveled four hours east to Mt. Sinai College, a small religious school where my brothers had attended, where my grandfather, the artist-writer-preacher, had been part of the first graduating class, where my father had studied history and music until the Depression hit and Grandpa Kluger called him back to the farm.

My first trip back home, six weeks after school started, was on the Kansas City Chief, the same train that would later carry me home from Chicago. I admit here, now, for the first time, that I cried all the way home, overcome with homesickness mixed with relief that I would soon see my parents and Thomas. Drying my tears only moments before arriving in Dodge City, I stepped off the train and tried to greet my parents as if my homecoming was a casual thing. I didn't fool them. My mother bawled in relief with me. My father viewed the road ahead through moist eyes. Being the fifth in the family to go off to college and come home for a first visit, you'd think they would have been used to it by then.

My first year in college was a disaster. Not because I didn't enjoy it, or make lots of friends, or pile on good grades. I did all that. But I hated the fences. The women's dormitories in this small, protective college were surrounded by walls and fences and locked gates. The hated wall surrounding the quadrant of women's dorms was created by cement blocks arranged in staggered patterns to appear decorative, but we all knew what it was: a wall. To quote the great poet: "Something there is that doesn't love a wall."

Curfews were 10:30 on weeknights, 11:00 on Friday and Saturday nights. After that, the wrought-iron gates both at the front and at the back entrance of our dorm swung shut. The curfew, with its gates and walls and fences to enforce it, was designed to keep college girls chaste. A web of other rules regulated nearly every aspect of college life. I admit to being ringleader to many pranks to taunt the institution's rule makers. Our freshman dorm had a developed a rivalry with the senior girl's dorm down the street, partly out of jealousy. It was not part of the walled-in quadrant of underclassman dorms. To get our older "sisters" in trouble we bought condoms, made them look "used," and dropped them haphazardly in the dirt parking lot behind the back entrance where boys dropped off their dates and often tarried until the mad dash at 10:59 p.m. on Saturday nights. We thought our prank was exceedingly clever, but it backfired. The president of the college called a special "closed" meeting of all girls, including freshmen, to lecture us passionately about the evils of unbridled sex. The Dean of Women sat on the podium behind him, embarrassed, fidgeting in her chair. Dr. Williard lectured us on virtue, complete with statistics and case histories of ruined young women. Were we going to throw our whole lives away for one night of sinful pleasure?

"And don't tell me you are all virgins," he thundered. (We *were*, nearly every one of us.) "I'm not stupid. I've seen the evidence," he whispered into the microphone in a dramatic closing, red-faced with excitement.

Then President Williard passed out a paper, and the Dean of Women got the crummy job of reading the new rules out loud. All curfew extensions were cancelled. Until then we'd been allowed three midnight extensions per semester with written permission from the Dean of Women. Furthermore, effective immediately was a "three strikes and you're out" policy. Caught coming in late three times and you were expelled from the college. No recourse. Until then, you needed five violations before coming before the disciplinary board, which had wide discretionary powers on meting out punishments.

I had two curfew violations at the time. One more and I would be out. This meant I didn't dare so much as go to a movie in Wichita, because if traffic was bad coming back, I could easily miss the 11:00 deadline. I was pretty much stuck in the middle of Kansas at a stifling college in a self-righteous small town. I longed for Odyssey.

Two of my Odyssey "brother" friends had been keeping me sane up to this point, coming down from a nearby state teacher's college on weekends to cheer me up (and meet my cute dormmates). It was one of these friends who had failed to drive fast enough on the previous Saturday night, contributing to my second violation. Despite my pleading, he thought it was unsafe to drive 90 mph on the thirteen-mile road shortcut that led from the main highway back to town. "You want me to get us killed?" he protested.

After Dr. Williard's sex talk, I kept my curfews, but I started climbing over the wall for risky forays into the night. I had always been a nocturnal creature. Many a night in my teen years I would become engrossed in a book or writing poetry into the late, late hours, a practice my parents tolerated as long as I didn't keep anyone else in the family awake. (My parents, I was discovering, had been very tolerant of a lot of things.) At college, my creative juices only flowed when everyone else was asleep. So I would write my papers in the middle of the night in the dorm lounge so as not to keep my roommate awake. And then I would get so hungry that the front and the back of my stomach would stick together, and every internal organ in my body would scream out for food—real food, not just candy bars or crackers or popcorn. So I'd call my best friend, Mark, an artistic literary type like me, who was widely rumored to be a homo (the word "gay" had not yet entered our lexicon). "I'm starving," I'd whisper into the lounge phone.

"Meet me at the corner," he'd say. The boy's dorms had no curfews, I suppose that the school felt that if all us girls were locked in for the night, there was no trouble the boys could get into that amounted to anything.

Wearing dark clothing, with hair tucked into a baseball cap so my silhouette would look masculine if caught in someone's headlights, I'd scurry up and over the cement block wall at the back of the dorm. The decorative arrangement of cement blocks provided plenty of foot and hand holds, making it easy to climb. Then I'd lurk in the shadows behind the lilac bushes until Mark appeared in his beat-up Buick. I'd hop into the back seat, crouched down out of sight while he drove five or so miles out of town. Then Mark would stop and I'd come up front. We would open the windows and let the radio blare as we headed to an all-night pancake house in Wichita. In a back booth, surrounded by drowsy truckers, we would order pancakes and eggs with hash browns and bacon. Just before dawn I'd slip over the wall, and ease into bed in my dark room. My roommate assumed I'd been studying all night—this was one secret I didn't even share with her. Those mornings after, I'd snooze through the mandatory chapel service—also an infraction of the rules, but one not punishable by death. Sleeping in chapel was common and merely resulted in a reprimand in the Dean's office, coupled with a motherly, concerned conversation about getting more sleep.

You know where this is leading—my third and final curfew violation.

One night, about four weeks before the end of the school year, the town's perverted cop (I could tell you a few stories about him) saw me shimmy over the wall. Several miles out of town, after following us with his lights out, he appeared out of nowhere with his siren blaring, lights flashing. He stopped us, shined his monster flashlight menacingly into our eyes, and demanded both our driver's licenses.

"She's a passenger. She doesn't have to show you a driver's license," Mark protested.

"If you are in the process of committing a crime, she is an accomplice. She will give it to me. And you! Let's see your car registration, if you have one."

The officer kept us sitting a half hour while he checked via radio "to see if we were driving a stolen vehicle." He returned to the car, shining the light into my eyes once again. "I called your Dean of Women. Boy was she mad that I got her out of bed," he smirked as he handed back my driver's license.

Flashlight back onto Mark, "I suggest you drive the lady home right now. Someone will be at the front gate to unlock it for her." Flashlight back to me, "I've been asked to convey a message to you, young lady. You are to report to the Dean's office immediately after chapel tomorrow morning."

So that was my third curfew violation.

My parents were asked to drive in to attend the disciplinary hearing a few days later. The "hearing" was conducted around a large, oval mahogany table in the library conference room. In attendance, the President of the College, the Dean of Women and her assistant, three student representatives, my housemother, two teacher advisors—one of them my English teacher, a tall, sophisticated single woman, who was called an "old maid" behind her back. When she read Shakespeare in class she would electrify the room. Even the dull farm boys would sit up straight and pay attention. I worshiped her. I dared not meet her eyes to see if she was disappointed in me. Instead, I stared at the reflections in the polished tabletop, struggling to keep my tears in check as the charges were read by Dean Williams. Then I was asked for comment.

I stood and apologized as politely as I could. "I was hungry, that's all. I couldn't think of any other way to get something to eat."

She followed with some questions of fact. Had I called Mark to pick me up, or was it his idea? (Mine alone.) What time did we leave? (Around 1 A.M.) Mercifully, she failed to ask if this was the first time I had done it. I answered each question straightforward in a few syllables. There were a lot of awkward silences. The sexual preference of my comrade in crime was well known but not acknowledged. Homosexuality did not officially exist on our campus. Since he was clearly not my "boyfriend," it was hard to turn this into a sexual escapade, which would have delighted the college president who could then have launched into a fire and brimstone lecture. Normally, Dr. Williard did not sit in on disciplinary committee meetings, but he had chosen to be part of the meeting "in deference to my great-grandfather's name," as he had put it. (My mother's grandfather Isaiah Werner had been one of the founders of the school.) He gaveled the meeting to order, then turned it over to the Dean, only to take back the lead almost immediately.

"Rebecca," he intoned compassionately, "your three older brothers graduated from this institution with college careers of distinction. I looked up your records. Straight A's. Your professors have the highest regard for you. Our expectations for you far exceed that of the average student. I admit that places extra stress on you. You are as precious to me as if you were my own daughter . . . "

I wanted to duck my head under the table and gag.

". . . but climbing over a wall. Wearing a disguise. This is a very deliberate, well thought out act. I wish you could make me understand it."

There was a long pause and I suddenly realized he was waiting for a response. I wanted to shout, *I threw those condoms in the parking lot, you dirty-minded son of a bitch. You couldn't see through a silly college prank. And furthermore, I've climbed over that wall for breakfast dozens of times. And tell me, what is the town cop, that sleazy creep, doing parked outside a girls' dorm in the middle of the night. What about that?*

I didn't. I merely choked away tears of humiliation that he thought was contrition, and said. "I was hungry. I have nothing else to add."

He didn't seem to hear me. He continued. "In their collective twelve years here, I never had one of your brothers come before this committee."

If any one of those three brothers had been in the room they'd have popped him in the mouth. I was sure of that, as only a girl with four brothers can be. The very image of it gave me a courage and calm I'd lacked until this moment. "My brothers were boys. They had freedom that girls here aren't given."

Again, fortunately, Dr. Williard pretended not to hear. Perhaps I only thought I said it.

"Do you have anything you want to say," he asked my parents, seated in a row behind me.

My mother stood, my grave-faced father solidly at her side. I turned to see, with pride, that my mother was staring straight at Dr. Williard with a look that would make a tree's roots wither. "When Becky was in high school, she often stayed up real late to study, and then she'd always need something to eat before she could get to sleep. She'd tiptoe to the refrigerator in the dark, so as not to wake us up. She's always gotten hungry in the middle of the night. I'm sure it was nothing more than that."

"In all due respect, Mrs. Kluger, we have refrigerators—actually a whole kitchen in our women's dorms for student use."

And now Dr. Williard—who had completely taken over the meeting, leaving the Dean of Women powerless and nervous in her chair at the head of the table—went back yet another generation. "Your great-grandfather, Miss Kluger . . . You *do* know about your great-grandfather?"

"Isaiah Werner," I said, hoping to end the lecture.

"He was our patriarch, a man of great vision and courage, our Moses, who led our people out of Russia. You might say it is because of him that this institution was founded. What was he seeking, Miss Kluger?"

"Freedom. Religious tolerance," I said, with just a note of smart aleck in my voice. "Like myself, he valued freedom. The ability to make choices for ourselves."

Dr. Williard did not even get my drift. My mother did. She edged her foot forward and gently kicked mine in a wordless warning. My cousin Caroline's roommate at Senior Hall, one of the students on the committee, had warned me privately that if the Dean of Women was the decisionmaker, I would be able to defend myself and she would listen, but if Dr. Williard became involved, any attempt to explain myself would be viewed as rebellion and I would be crushed utterly. My only hope, she had warned, was to appear very repentant.

Dr. Williard was not done with great-grandfather Isaiah. (Williard was also the History Department chairman and loved to lecture on history, particularly that of our German-Russian sect on which he considered himself the prime expert.)

"Yes, freedom, but freedom for what? Not to break the rules that bind us to one another in love. Not to disregard our traditions and beliefs. But freedom to build a life for ourselves, to follow God's covenants without interference from unbelievers. The Bible tells us 'teach your children in the way that they should go and when they are old they will not depart from it.' That is what we do here at Mt. Sinai College."

The only way I was going to live through this was to imagine it differently. "With freedom, young lady, comes responsibility," hissed Dr. Williard. My fantasy self retorted, *I only climbed over a wall that shouldn't have been there. I didn't gather our tribe's jewelry and melt it down to make a golden calf. I only want the freedom Great Grandfather Isaiah came to this country to find.* And then I saw the ancient Isaiah Werner with his immense white beard—in death grown down to his ankles, rise from the middle of the reflection in the table. He shook his bony fist at Dr. Williard. *Do not take my name in vain. And leave my great-granddaughter alone!*

Fortunately, Dr. Williard was finished with his lecture and was ready to pronounce his benevolent decision. I shook myself out of my reverie and tried to listen. An exception would be made. Instead of expulsion, I would be suspended for five days, which I was to spend with my "wise and godly" parents, and hopefully I would return to school the following week repentant and ready to turn over a new leaf.

"And one more thing, young lady," he added sternly. "You are to go out and buy some groceries and stock your dorm refrigerator with emergency food." There was a self-satisfied twist of a smile on the president's face as he finished the sentence. At that cue, nervous, quiet laughter of relief erupted from the whole committee, including the three student peers who had been nearly as uncomfortable as me during the meeting.

Back at the dorm, I gathered some dirty laundry and a few textbooks, and within an hour we were driving west toward the flat land, into the big sky with mirages dancing on the road ahead. My mother and father—how I love them—never said one word about the meeting, or the incident. Not that day, nor any day that followed. As we drove, my mother bubbled on with Odyssey gossip, with talk about her garden, news about my sister's new baby. My father was silent, but smiled at Mom's stories, adding in his own tidbits when she stopped to take a breath. When we got home, Thomas, now fourteen years old and six feet tall, was waiting for me on the porch, just as I once waited for my big brothers to come home from college. He saddled up two horses, insisting that I ride his beloved Evening Star. We rode along the ridge, and sat quietly watching the sunset.

It was good to be home.

In the dusk, as we rode back to the house, I thought I saw fluffy white chicken feathers fluttering in the breeze.

ON THE LAST DAY HOME before returning to school to finish out the four remaining weeks, I casually mentioned during supper. "I think I'll apply at KU for next year. I'll try to get a scholarship."

"That sounds like a good idea," said my father matter-of-factly.

"It's a lot farther away," said my mother, quickly correcting herself, "well, only four hours further east."

My father's oldest brother had a barbershop in Lawrence and a lovely Victorian farmhouse seven miles out of town. I would have Uncle Paul and Aunt Lilly nearby if I got lonely.

"They'll be tickled pink," said my mother. "I'll write them a letter tomorrow."

I LOVED THE UNIVERSITY OF KANSAS. It was a serene and beautiful campus with stately limestone buildings topped by red-tiled roofs scattered over a series of green rolling hills. Flowering shrubbery, full, spreading shade trees. Weeping willows. Little bridges over ponds where mallards floated while preening their iridescent plumage. The carillon bells in the evening. I loved everything about the University. The witty professors—and the boring ones, the large lecture halls and the crowded hallways, the students—thousands of students—from all over the world mixed together. Endless numbers of new people to meet.

I especially loved my dormitory: East Women's Scholarship Hall. A kind of sorority for girls of a certain GPA, no, not girls, here they called us "women."

Fortunately, I had taken very little with me on the train—just one large suitcase, a duffel bag and my favorite pillow. My parents didn't drive me. Instead, I took the train, which gave the trip an air of formality. This time I really was leaving home. Attending Mt. Sinai College had been like going away to summer camp, in a town still on the flat Plains, a little town no bigger than Odyssey, clustered around grain elevators, a farm community town where the college's four-story red brick administration building had stuck out rudely. Lawrence, Kansas, on the other hand, was beyond the Flint Hills, in the land of gentle green hills and valleys, lakes and wide rivers, a land of humid air, flowering bushes and vines that grew like weeds clamoring over walls and fences. Lawrence was an old frontier town situated on the banks of the Kansas River at a point shortly before it emptied out into the Missouri River. It practically wasn't Kansas anymore, way up there in a foreign-looking, jagged corner of the state, practically Missouri. It was, in a phrase, "Back East."

We waited beside the train tracks in Dodge for the Kansas City Chief, which was now a half-hour late. "I've never known this train to be late," complained my father. "It's always run like clockwork." I was happy for the extra half-hour to spend with Mom, who found this whole thing difficult. Now finally, she felt she was giving up her little girl. She dabbed her hankie at her eyes, though I didn't see any actual tears. When we heard the train whistle and saw it coming, she felt obliged to give some advice. And here it came. "Becky, you are going where I have not gone. I don't know what to say to you." Suddenly resolute, she said, "Yes, I do know. I have no advice to give you. You don't need any advice. I have taught you everything I felt you needed to know."

The thing I most regret about not having children, about not having a daughter, is that I will never have the chance to pass those words on. My only answer to my mother's advice was a hug so tight, my father had to pull me away as the train squealed to a halt. The conductor grabbed the suitcase from my father, for the stop was only a fraction of a minute. The train, after all, was already running late.

It was a relaxing trip. I daydreamed and dozed for the first four hours. I didn't pay much attention to the thunderheads and lightning that began around dusk. Nothing unusual about that in Kansas. When it began hailing and pouring rain, the train slowed to a crawl, then stopped at some point not far from Topeka, last stop before Lawrence. For more than an hour we sat on the tracks, with no explanation except that there was a problem ahead, "due to weather." Finally, Santa Fe officials boarded the train and walked through each car to make an announcement. There had been a tornado ahead. In fact, the train depot, tracks, and much of downtown Topeka had been destroyed. We were instructed to gather our luggage. A bus would soon transport us into Topeka where it would drop the Topeka-bound passengers, then go on to Lawrence where another train was waiting to continue on to Kansas City and points east.

At first, there was a lot of nervous talk on the bus. One man held a portable radio to his ears, reporting back to the other passengers the news of the tornado that was being described as the most destructive ever to hit the state. When we reached the center of the darkened city the chatter stopped. Not another word was spoken. We were totally unprepared for what we would see as the bus wound through littered side streets, trying to find a path to the train station through the debris. It looked like a war-torn European city in a World War II movie. Brick buildings in rubble. Electric poles and lines down. Uprooted trees blocking streets, overturned trucks and cars wherever you looked. The city was dark; no lights anywhere except for red flashing lights of police cars. No sounds, except for wailing sirens of ambulances trying to get through. And yes, wounded people in the street. Many more stunned people stood in small groups. I saw one man lying on a stretcher, unattended. His shirtfront was soaked in blood. I saw a child clutching a mother's hand while blood trickled down from a gash across her forehead.

It didn't seem real. From the inside of the bus, looking out the window, it seemed as if everything was playing in slow motion. It was raining, but no one seemed to notice. The only sound inside the bus was the two-way radio crackling as the bus driver was guided into the city by a voice at the other end. A few passengers left the bus at the dark train station, which was still standing, but without a roof. The bus drove on, trying to find its way out of town like an animal caught in a maze. It was midnight by the time we arrived in Lawrence.

I HAILED A TAXI AT THE train station—my first taxi ride. After repeatedly ringing the doorbell at East Scholarship Hall while the taxi waited to see if he had dropped me at the right place—I hadn't known the exact address—an older woman answered the door. I had clearly awakened her. She wore a flowing, long, white nightdress. Wavy gray hair tumbled down her back. I'd swear she was holding a candlestick, a figment of my overactive imagination, I'm sure. But she did look like a character from a Dickens novel, and would remain so in my mind over the next three years.

"First call your parents collect," she motioned to a phone in the foyer. "They will be very happy to hear you have arrived safely."

"Becky, Oh Becky, you're okay. Thank God. The tornado hit at 8:45. Do you know that is exactly when your train was due into Topeka?" gasped my mother. "Here, talk to Dad."

My father said just one thing. "The train was a half-hour late. It's never late. That was God's hand. Never forget that."

Until that moment it had not occurred to me that if the train had been on time I would have been pulling into downtown Topeka at the precise time the tornado ripped through the capital. The gods were angry that I was leaving the Plains, yet they spared me.

I had survived yet another tornado.

Miss Dickens, actually, Victoria—she insisted on being called by her first name—showed me to my second-floor room, up a sweeping plush-ly carpeted circular stairway. I was astonished to see it was a room without a bed. Just a desk, a six-drawer bureau, a matching armoire which served as a closet for hanging clothing, and a corner sink with a mirrored cabinet above it. And one other item of furniture, an upholstered easy chair which looked as if it could be adjusted to a reclining position. There was one of everything. Obviously a single room.

"I don't have a roommate?" I asked, astonished.

"No, every woman has a room to herself. We find it makes for better study habits."

"And where do I sleep?" I sucked in my breath as the question popped out of my mouth, for suddenly it occurred to me that perhaps I was expected to sleep in the recliner.

Victoria saw me looking at the chair as I asked the question. She was amused, but clearly I wasn't the first one to ask it.

"No, no, the chair is for sitting, not sleeping. Oh, perhaps a nap, now and then. We have a common sleeping room. I'll show you your bunk. We'll have to be very quiet, to not disturb the sleeping women."

We tiptoed into a long chamber, a second floor veranda-like screened porch running the entire width of the building. The room was lit only by streetlamp light wafting into the open screened windows along with a cool breeze—it was late August. Dimly, I could see rows and rows of bunkbeds. Mine was third row to the left, second bed over, lower bunk. My name could be made out taped to the headboard beside a gold plate bearing the bed number which corresponded to my room number, 233. Crisp white sheets were on the bed. Victoria listed a few facts as we left the sleeping room and headed back to my study room: linens would be changed once a week by the chambermaid, fresh towels would be left at our door every three days, shared bathroom with showers at the end of each hall. "You will like the dining hall on the lower level," she said. "The food is rumored to be the finest on campus. Our chef is excellent."

"Chefs? Chambermaids?

Victoria left me back at private study room 233, with the invitation to knock on her door, just left of the entranceway hall, if I had any questions. She assured me that my floor's resident assistant would fill me in on further details in the morning. "Oh, I almost forgot, we knew your train wasn't due in until late. Chef Angelo thought you might be hungry, so he left a turkey sandwich, a plate of cookies and a glass of milk in the refrigerator at the end of the hallway. It has your name on it."

I had arrived in heaven.

After my snack, I unpacked a few essentials, donned a long white t-shirt, and around 2 A.M., I slipped quietly into the sleeping porch. I found my bed and stretched out on top of the sheet. Whispers of cool night air stirred the white cotton curtains at the windows. As my eyes grew used to the dark, I could see the whole room clearly. Rows and rows of sleeping young women, their rhythmic breathing rising and falling, creating a wave of comfort. Once in a while someone stirred or murmured in their sleep. I expected to be uncomfortable, as I'd been at summer camps as a child. Instead I felt enveloped in an indescribable calm. I fell asleep almost immediately that night and every other night for the next three years. I had found the cure for insomnia.

The few nights over the next three years that I tarried, often on purpose, not allowing myself to fall asleep, or on those infrequent occasions when I momentarily awakened during the night, I saw them. Women in ethereal white flowing gowns in a slow choreographed dance, swaying to music I did not hear, moved through the aisles, between the bunks. Spirits perhaps of generations of East Scholarship Hall residents come to soothe our sleep, enliven our dreams, assuage our self-doubts. Or were they reflections of the moonlit, white curtains stirred by the night breeze?

Mornings were equally mystifying. Alarm clocks were not allowed. Yet somehow, we all managed to rise and silently glide from our sleeping chamber at the right time. In the beginning of a new semester, there was always someone who awoke naturally at the right time. She would know who else in the porch had a similar schedule and she'd tiptoe around gently waking each of her schedule comrades. A half-hour later, another round of silent wake-ups would be in progress. But by the third or fourth week, everyone rose on cue with no help from anyone.

We were teased, not kindly, on campus for our sleeping arrangements. "Oh, you live at Dyke Hall," classmates would say when I mentioned my dorm. Only we fortunate dwellers of East Scholarship Hall knew the truth. We drew strength from one another and from the spirits of the night, as we slumbered (we didn't sleep, we slumbered) in our communal sleeping porch. It could not be explained. It was as if we were able to plug into the umbilical cord of all knowledge, of all peace, of all being each night and rise each morning refreshed, with minds pure and receptive. We were the women of the future, invincible. We all felt it. But we did not talk about it.

I loved the University. I loved East Scholarship Hall. I loved autumn, winter, and spring on the University of Kansas campus. From 1965 to 1968 I trudged up and down the hills of the campus thinking deep collegiate thoughts, developing massive calf muscles and creating new neuron pathways in my brain. I took to writing poetry under a flowing weeping willow tree I named "Bower" inspired by Adam and Eve's idyllic love nest in Milton's Paradise Lost.

Best of all, in Lawrence I was reunited with many of my Odyssey high school pals. When we crossed one another on a path, or spotted one another across a crowded bar, we'd shriek and run to each other. We had all discovered in our first year away, to one degree or another, that the rest of the world was not like Odyssey. Few of my comrades had found the discovery as painful as I had. What made us different, we wondered? Was it the flatness of the Plains that made us believe there were no limits? Was it something in the Ogallala Aquifer water that made us drunk with cockiness? Had the irascible quirkiness of Odyssey itself invaded our DNA and now pulsed through our cells forcing us to attempt the impossible? We couldn't define what set us apart, what made us loathe fences and boundaries. We bear-hugged in celebration of our oddity. It was good to be known by our own. To talk in abbreviated language. To read one another's minds. We took to gathering most Friday nights at Looney's, the rowdiest of off-campus bars.

"Do you realize that all of us Feisty Five (our term for five of us who had vied for valedictorian our senior year, our grade point averages all within a few decimal points of one another) are here, in this room, drinking lousy 3 percent Coors," shouted Matt over the barroom din one December night when we should have been studying for finals.

"All except Luke," Matt corrected himself. "Do you believe the son of a bitch got accepted at Yale?"

"I didn't think they let farm boys into Yale," added Miriam (the only other girl in the group).

"They do if you're one-half Cherokee," said Mike.

"It's one-quarter," corrected Matt. "And not Cherokee. It's Cheyenne, I think."

And then the conversation moved on to other things.

I was quiet for the rest of the evening as my pals consumed pitcher after pitcher of beer. (I was never a beer drinker— hated the taste—but enjoyed the company around the table so I'd nurse one sour mug of brew to be sociable.) I excused myself and walked home, up the hill, in softly falling snow. The snow sparkled under the street lamps. The wind kicked it up, blew snowflakes into my face, but I was thinking of dust, blowing dust and the trails left by pickups that raced past our farm on hot summer evenings going south.

My sisterability had persisted into my university years. It didn't matter, I told myself. Romance just wasn't in the cards. The male students I met were immature. I preferred Shakespeare, Ibsen, Robert Frost and D. H. Lawrence. My Odyssey friends—I dearly loved them, but any romantic involvement would have felt, well, incestuous. Once in a while, in those three years, I was momentarily felled by an overwhelming crush that left me debilitated and morose. But it happened less and less frequently. I dated one shy math major for nearly a year because he bought front row tickets to a Peter, Paul and Mary concert and took me for lavish dinners in Kansas City's nicest restaurants. When he proposed marriage to me near the end of my junior year, I realized how selfish and callous I had been. The role of heartbreaker weighed heavily on my conscience. I hadn't meant to be one.

Shortly thereafter, Uncle Paul asked if I wanted my cousin Donald's old VW Beetle, which was just sitting in the yard after he joined the army. "But it's Don's," I protested.

"Nah, he told me to sell it. It's that crazy orange color he painted it. Nobody wants it," complained Uncle Paul.

"If you ask me, it's a piece of junk. It won't last long," said Aunt Lilly. "But it will get you here and back for Sunday dinner."

I gave Uncle Paul a dollar, and he signed the registration over to me and told me how to transfer the license. So now I had a car. A kind of replacement for the math major who had once occupied my free time. The car mostly sat in the dorm parking lot, but sometimes when I was overcome by restlessness, I would get behind the wheel and drive around the countryside, stopping at random to hike. After finishing semester finals at the end of my junior year, in giddy sleep deprivation, I and a few of my dorm sisters painted black spots all over my orange VW, effectively turning it into a "ladybug." That summer, I drove the ladybug home to Western Kansas, waving broadly when truck drivers honked at me, barely making it to the outskirts of Odyssey before it choked and died. Another cousin—I have an unlimited supply—who happened to be enrolled in an auto mechanics school in Garden City, took on the car as his class project. He rebuilt the engine and turned my ladybug into a tiny tank.

My last year at the university, with nearly enough credits to graduate, I treated myself to what I loved. I enrolled in Professor Wolfe's creative writing course and the short stories poured out of me like honey and bitter herbs. For a final grade in a theater-directing course I staged *Of Mice and Men,* transforming two randomly picked guys with no acting experience into the characters I willed them to be. My professor took credit for my directorial blossoming, but in truth it was merely a throwback to the days when Mrs. Shaw allowed me to create something out of nothing on the little stage in the Willow Valley one-room schoolhouse. Yes, it was a good year. Yet, the last semester of my senior year the restlessness set in once again. I wanted to be gone. Off to the next thing. Enough of the protected campus air. The cities were on fire. The world was falling apart. Many of my friends planned to join the Peace Corps after graduation as homage to John F. Kennedy, whose death still pained us deeply. We were thrilled when Bobby Kennedy visited our campus during his presidential campaign. I reached out and touched his hand. A couple of weeks later he was shot. We had not yet recovered from the loss of Martin Luther King. It just wouldn't end.

But more than anything else, in that crazy year of 1968, the war defined us. Viet Nam raged, and our leaders were willing to sacrifice our generation to make some macho mumbo-jumbo domino point they could not even articulate. I threw myself into protest marches. In Kansas, our generation was not all of one mind. The campus was evenly divided for and against the war. ROTC boys hated the war protesters and sometimes things got nasty. This was the heartland where farm boys did what they were told just "becuz." And they were dying because of it. When Dr. Spock visited our campus I was assigned to be his escort. A friend and I greeted him at the Kansas City airport. The school had given us one of KU's official Lincoln Continentals for the purpose—fortunate, for the doctor would have never fit into the ladybug. He was an enormously tall man who towered above us, radiating warmth and love into the upper stratosphere. That evening, backstage in the auditorium, I and five other of the rally organizers sat at his knees and listened to his wisdom as we waited for the rally to begin. "You are my babies," he said, with tears in his eyes. "And I cannot let you be sent to your slaughter." And he unfolded himself out of the chair on which he sat and walked into the auditorium to speak to 3,000 assembled students.

The Democratic Convention was coming up. It was clear. I had to go to Chicago. So after graduation, I emptied the meager contents of my dorm room into the front-end trunk of my ladybug—clothes, books, papers, and my new typewriter purchased with the $125 cash prize I'd just received, winnings from the university's short story writing contest. Then I stopped by the bookstore next to my uncle's barbershop and bought a road atlas, said goodbye to Uncle Paul and headed further east to the city that would become my destiny.

20

City by the Lake

I HATED THAT "Oh, you're from *Kansas,*" business I'd get at parties that first year in Chicago. It was usually followed by, "So, where's Toto," or "Been through any good tornadoes lately." After a while, I tried to avoid the where-are-you-from question. Chicagoans always ask it. They know the minute you open your mouth you are not one of them. I couldn't produce that flat "a" sound they do somewhere in the upper reaches of their nasal cavities no matter how hard I tried.

When the tiresome psychology graduate students who seemed to dominate the parties I attended failed to exploit the *Wizard of Oz* line, they fell back on the "Oh, you're an English teacher. Why couldn't I have had a pretty young English teacher like you when I was in high school." That line was invariably followed by long descriptions of their various unattractive and bizarre English teachers and the poor grades they undeservedly received in English.

When the newness of the urban life wore off, I was forced to admit that Chicagoans, by and large, were a provincial lot. Few of them ever ventured outside the city limits. Oh, perhaps two hours north to visit the Wisconsin Dells, a tacky tourist trap of lakes and water shows, and maybe east to Michigan to discover whether the eastern shore of Lake Michigan was any different than the Chicago side of the lake. But for the most part, none of my newfound contemporaries had seen a mountain or a desert. Few had climbed into their cars and just driven somewhere. In all fairness, during a Sunday afternoon drive into the countryside around Chicago, all anyone would encounter for miles were cornfields and such stellar examples of small town life as Peoria. So who could blame them? Chicago offered all the excitement one could possibly want from the world.

I loved it though, at least in those first few years. So many people to meet. So many possibilities. I could barely breathe knowing I was passing hundreds of people on the streets each day. I wanted to know their stories—who were they, what did they think about things. I actually felt guilty about not saying hello to everyone I passed on a sidewalk or in a hallway—no urban person can understand that. But when you are conditioned to feel connected to every other human being in your sightline, it feels utterly, insanely unnatural to be alone in a crowd.

It took a long time before I could walk down a city street, head down, oblivious to strangers around me. Margaret once told me she went through the same thing when she moved to Denver.

How did I end up making Chicago my home? Very simply, I went to the Democratic Convention in 1968 to protest the war and never left. That summer I found purpose and camaraderie. I crashed temporarily at a hippie commune on the North Side. Everyone loved my anti-war poetry, which I read in coffeehouses, sitting on tall barstools with a microphone which allowed me to read oh so softly and put the right amount of whisper, pause, and intensity into my lines. My verse could make people cry. Men said I was beautiful and intelligent and refreshing. I was treated with respect. It felt good. So I stayed.

But that's not the whole story. The whole story was that I fell madly in love, with a tall, dark, earnest psychology graduate student whom I met through my anti-war activities. He was as passionate about his beliefs as I was about mine. At last, a soulmate, a match. I was introduced to John, quite literally, by my ladybug. I had parked on a side street near Lincoln Park to attend a protest rally. When I came back to the car, he was standing beside it. He said he wanted to meet the owner of the coolest Beetle he'd ever seen.

My friendship with John was just that at first, a friendship. He was enmeshed in a long-term relationship with a girl, which had become fraught with emotional turmoil and guilt. He asked my advice constantly. When he broke up with her, I just waited for him to notice I was a woman. He was everything Western Kansas boys were not. Sensitive, artistic, literate, passionate about his beliefs, thoughtful, and now fresh out of a stifling relationship, he was also fun, lively, and full of surprises. Once we slept out all night on blankets in a lakeside park in Evanston so we could watch the sun rise over Lake Michigan. We took lakefront riverboat rides like tourists. With me, John was seeing Chicago anew through the eyes of a fresh observer. Things between us were uncomplicated. For several weeks, we were friends, not lovers.

John was an only child, son of first-generation German immigrants. Father an alcoholic. Mother domineering and possessive. At age twenty-two he still lived at home. He called his mother several times a day from his downtown campus, and, if she as much as said she was out of milk, he would skip class and rush home, driving forty minutes north just to go to the neighborhood store and get it for her. I tried to never offer advice to John on how to separate from his mother, though he constantly berated himself up for not being strong enough to move out. In those days, with apartment rents so cheap, staying with one's parents past the age of twenty-one was unheard of. You could share an apartment for as little as $30 a month.

I quickly became tired of the physical and emotional messiness of the commune where I was staying, and while I was waiting for my first paycheck so I could move into my own apartment, John insisted that I stay at his home for a couple of weeks.

John's mother was gracious and welcoming. I was given the spare room, and treated to the finest bratwurst and sauerkraut ever served. But when I tried to use the basement washing machine to wash a load of my underwear, she had a fit. "No one touches that machine but me." And once she caught me washing dishes—usually I didn't get a chance because she would swoop up a dish or cup before it was half empty. (She kept plastic covers on the sofas, and we took off our shoes upon entering the home lest we spoil her pale pink carpets.) When she turned her back for a moment one evening, and I started washing dishes after a meal, she shrieked, "You're our guest. You do not wash dishes."

Feeling quite wounded, I meekly left the kitchen. The very next morning she pulled her son aside and said, "I can't be cleaning up after your friend. She won't lift a finger to wash a dish, and she even expects me to do her dirty laundry."

When John dithered about which version to believe, I promptly packed my big duffel bag and headed back to reclaim a corner of my former room in the commune.

Three weeks after I began my teaching job, and soon after I moved into my apartment, John sheepishly showed up and re-entered my life—he had noticed the ladybug parked on Sheridan Road. Just as he had done weeks earlier, he waited by my car for me to appear.

He apologized for the mother episode. "She tries to spoil every relationship I make. She's so afraid of losing me that she goes to great lengths to hold me there."

Then he made an announcement. He had moved into his own apartment, which he was sharing with three other guys. One was a guitar player in a folk club, one was a psych grad student like himself. And the third—"Richard, he's the son of a very famous writer, you'll figure that out the moment you hear his last name. But don't let on. He deeply resents being a famous son. He's a math major—I guess to get as far away from his father's profession as possible."

"Mum's the word, John. I'll never let on. But you know it's going to be very hard. I love his father's books."

And bingo. With his new independence it happened. The friends became lovers.

It was in late October. I remember no details except the love beads. How could such an important day in my life leave so few neuron paths in my memory banks? I had started the day—it was Saturday—with a cup of tea and a good novel, first feeling immensely guilty that I was not grading papers or making lesson plans. Then I got over it and decided I owed myself a solitary walk along the lake. It was a beautiful day. Autumn is Chicago's best season. Mid-afternoon John picked me up— he had a VW Beetle too, a dark green one. And we went to a movie: *A Man and a Woman*—with French subtitles. After a lazy dinner in a popular country French bistro near his apartment, we stopped at a blues club. It was our usual Saturday night routine, where we ended up back to his apartment, which was crowded with each roommate's circle of friends. We shared a glass of wine with his roommates and assorted friends, and turned down the passed communal joint—neither of us believed in drug use, not even marijuana. As I began to collect my purse and keys around two in the morning, he begged me, don't go home tonight. Stay over.

When we ducked into his bedroom, the only private place in the busy group apartment, I knew this would be the night. A long string of love beads had been ceremoniously draped from the light fixture hanging above his bed. I still have the love beads, stuffed in my Civil War trunk somewhere—properly organic brown seeds interspersed with some dried purple berries, strung together in a twelve-foot length. I could see the bizarre shadows they created on the wall in the dim light that filtered in from the window, with the bits of orange-yellow street lamp light diffusing around the edges of the cheap, roll-down shade. I could hear the screeching of the El as it rounded the curve two blocks from his apartment. But that's all I remember about that night.

I felt strangely removed from the details of what was transpiring between us. And furthermore, I have no memory of any of the intimate encounters with John that occurred in those ensuing weeks and months.

That first morning-after, when I had tossed and turned for what seemed like hours, John finally woke up. I nestled in his arms and murmured. "The love beads were a nice touch."

"Richard sneaked in and put them up sometime during the evening, for good luck I guess," he announced, sleepily.

I felt slightly taken aback that someone else—outside of our couplehood—had predicted our night of love. Our privacy felt breached. But those were the times, the magic late sixties, when our generation shared our wine and dollars and digs, when all of us felt connected, laced together with common goals, common fears, common passions. What happened to one happened to all. We were the baby boomer generation, united like a great river. We flowed in the same direction. We were one.

And now John and I were tied to one another by an ancient bond. We both were innocent and serious beings adrift in a society of chums for whom a Saturday night sleepover was no big deal. But for us, both of us, it was a big deal. He was my first. I was his second. Considering it was the sixties and we were both over twenty-one, that was in itself amazing.

Below Richard's dangling love beads we had begun a journey. It was the romance I'd always dreamed of. Staring into one another's eyes— the phrase "adoring gaze," comes to mind. Once grounded firmly in my work inside the classroom, I now became a clock watcher, living for the weekend when we could be together.

John was secure and happy. I was elated. At last, I had found someone like me, someone to whom I could talk, talk, talk, into the wee hours, then talk some more. Within weeks, we were spinning webs of dreams. Elaborate road maps to our future.

"I want six children," he announced one day. "Lots and lots of children running through the house. I hated being an only child."

"How about five. Would you settle for five?" I'd cajole.

"You are going to make a great mother!" he would shout.

Marriage was completely and totally assumed. The only question was when.

"I need to finish graduate school, so I can start earning a wage."

"We could live off my teacher's salary," I'd offer.

He'd fret at the thought. "My ego could never take being a kept husband."

But there was the draft. That was the thing that kept John up nights. He had manipulated his student deferment about as much as could be done.

"I'm not doctoral material. And even if I was, I absolutely want to stop this academic shit and get into real work. But the minute I do, my number will come up."

We puzzled and fretted about it. John applied for conscientious objector status. "It's absolutely in the Methodist tradition," he'd assert, knowing full well the draft board was going to turn him down.

John was my life. Marshall High was my paycheck. Shortly after arriving in Chicago, I had applied for a teaching job with the Chicago Board of Education. All you needed to do in order to get a teaching job was to pass a test any sixth grader could ace, submit to a chest x-ray and produce a birth certificate. I did okay on the first two counts, but when I called home for a copy of my birth certificate, it turned out that I didn't have one.

I was my mother's first baby out of five to be born in a hospital. When she went into labor three weeks early, my father insisted that this one would be born in a hospital with a real doctor. So he loaded my mother into the '45 Dodge truck and trekked the ninety miles to Dodge City—the closest hospital—in the middle of a rare late-November blizzard. The blizzard was so bad the doctor and most of the nurses couldn't make it in to the hospital and I was born mostly through Mom and Dad's well-honed home birthing techniques with a little help from one inexperienced nurse. And in all the ensuing confusion, my birth was never properly registered. So after the discovery of the missing birth certificate, there started a process whereby various Odyssey officials—such as our family doctor and school superintendent—had to swear to knowledge of my birth.

While waiting for a document—officially called a "delayed birth certificate"—to be issued by Topeka, the Chicago Board of Education, although desperate for teachers, couldn't assign me a school. Without the generosity of the commune, I would have starved. When the document finally came in, dated September 14, 1968, the certifying clerk rejected it, saying that the rules stated that no document could be less than five years old.

One of my commune buddy's father who had clout with Mayor Daley, marched in with me, read the clerk the riot act, and somehow they found a way to place me in a classroom. Of course that classroom was in the deepest West Side ghetto, in the most dangerous—or so everyone said—high school in all of the city, Marshall High.

The principal assigned a student bodyguard to shadow me in the hallways for the first week. He was big, he was bad, he was fearsome-looking—in truth, he was really a pussycat. His name was Tiger. And he taught me how to survive. In the hallway, everyone deferred to Tiger, and my proximity to him bestowed on me a kind of respect. Tiger was nineteen—he had been held back a few times. When I asked about it, he swore me to a secret. He didn't know how to read. I made a deal with him. I promised him he would be reading at an eighth grade level by the end of the semester. We worked after school. I used the techniques we country kids practiced on each other. With only one teacher for all grades, it had been necessary for older kids to teach younger ones how to read. I knew exactly how to do it. I would soon discover that every student in my English class shared the same secret. So I threw out the books, wrote my own materials and began to run my classrooms like Mrs. Shaw had run Willow Valley School. All we lacked were the tumbleweeds, but I entertained them with my stories. Eventually I became known as Miss Buffalo, or to those who didn't like me, "The Tornado." The principal continually called me in for "meetings" to tell me my classrooms were too noisy. But somebody liked me, because an Illinois State Teacher's College education professor started sending in graduate students to sit in my classrooms and observe my "revolutionary tactics." The professor once asked me what my method was called. I told him it was the Shaw Six-Shooter method. He wrote that down.

• • •

SPRING WAS IN THE AIR. The trees in Lincoln Park near John's apartment were finally boasting a green haze. "It's time for you to meet my Great Aunt Gertrude," John announced to me during a leisurely walk through the park. "She's invited us to go up to Michigan for Memorial Day weekend."

I had never heard about the great aunt. I soon discovered she was a wonderful Old World lady with a New World mouth who'd outlived four husbands but never had any children. She now lived alone in a gigantic three-story Victorian farmhouse on the outskirts of a charming Northern Michigan town called Silver Bay, a three-hour drive from Chicago.

It was the first of many wonderful summer weekends with Aunt Gertrude who, unlike John's mother, loved me. Her house was gigantic, had been in need of remodeling for fifty years, and was bursting with twelve unused bedrooms. "It used to be a boarding house. In fact, I used to board here as a young woman when I first came from Germany. And then I had an affair with the owner of the house," asserted Gertrude who never minced words. "Ended up marrying him when his cranky wife died. So here I am, but no way am I going to run a boarding house. Too much work for an old lady."

"This would make a great bed and breakfast during the summer months . . . you know, like they have in Europe," I said to her one day.

"I know what a bed and breakfast is," she reprimanded me. "I'm okay with beds, not okay with breakfast. But when you kids are married, and this house is yours, you can make it into your bed and breakfast. I'll just live in the back bedroom, if I'm still alive. Just don't expect me to make breakfast."

It was her second mention of "when this house is yours." I never thought much about it. Gertrude's sense of humor was blunt and her banter was always peppered with surprises.

But I asked John on the drive back, why she was always talking like that.

"It's in the will, didn't I tell you? She put it in her will that I get the house when she dies. Actually, she's always told me its mine any time I want it. No waiting. As long as I move up here and help fix it up."

And so our wandering dreams took on a giddy air of reality. Our life became planned out to the smallest detail. When he finished grad school, we'd marry and move up here. I'd teach in the local high school.

"They must be desperate for teachers up here," John would say. "And I'll be a family counselor. I may have to drive in to one of the larger towns to start a practice. Or, who knows, if that doesn't work out I could teach psychology at the local junior college, and then there's always educational testing. Educational psychologists are in high demand now that most states are requiring special ed classes.

"After we're settled in we'll have children." He would glow and look lovingly at me when he talked about our future children. He'd describe how they looked, how they would act. He had it all down. Never had I seen a man so taken with the idea of fatherhood.

All this, of course, if Viet Nam didn't intrude on our lives. The war was always lurking in the background. But now our protests took on an urgent personal meaning. We were fighting for our lives and for the permission to build our version of the American dream in Silver Bay, Michigan. We had to individually and collectively stop the war in Viet Nam.

Between marching and organizing, we continued to daydream. "And when the kids are off to college, the last one, and the house becomes empty again, we'll start that bed and breakfast," I'd muse. And then we'd start planning in detail how we'd fill the house with bargain antiques and paint each room a different color.

And so, for a whole year and a half, I taught English in the roughest ghetto school by day, and by night spent glorious hours in love. That first summer, John came home with me to meet my parents and find out about his country girl's childhood. He could only stay three days. He had to get back for his summer job with the city park district. So I drove him to Dodge and put him on the train back to Chicago. He pretended to be disappointed to leave, but I knew that our unfortunate run-in with the rifle-totting Bob Houston the day I showed John the old Home Place had put wings on John's feet. I suspected he found the Plains and its inhabitants a bit intimidating.

The remaining two weeks I stayed home, moping about, missing John so much I wrote twelve-page letters every night.

"Maybe you should just go back to Chicago," my mother said. "You are miserable."

"No, Mom, it's good for me. Now I know for sure I have to spend the rest of my life with him."

• • •

WHEN SCHOOL STARTED IN September, the bloom of first love was off. Now the relationship was deeper—and yes, duller. More like real life. Sometimes our togetherness wore thin. I began to be irritated by his constantly feeling guilty—he had replaced his guilt over his separation from his mother with guilt over school. He didn't like his courses or his professors. Grades were becoming a problem, but mostly he fretted over his low draft number. I understood his worrying. And so did his new very understanding neighbor who moved into the apartment above him.

John was totally in awe of a thirty-seven-year-old woman who had decided to change her life, get out of the suburban rut and go back to school. "I can't wait for you to meet Lillith. You are going to love her," he bubbled. "She insists I bring you up for tea next time you're here. She really wants to meet you."

Lillith answered the door and gushed warmly all over me, "I've heard so much about you. John utterly adores his Kansas 'Dorothy'—I heard you've survived three tornadoes. How cool is it, actually *being* from Kansas!"

She was a tall woman with overly broad hips, curly brown hair and twenty-five different kind of herbal teas. It took me no time at all to realize that she was jealous that she had been born ten years too early, and was afraid she was going to miss out on the flower child/peace now/sexual revolution. As we chatted—and Lillith glowed with excitement—I learned that she had left her husband of sixteen years and two children, a four-year-old boy and a two-year-old girl. She had said, "I need my space, I need to find myself." And just like that she moved out of a four-bedroom home in Palatine, Illinois, taking only one suitcase of clothes. "Mostly underwear," she giggled, "and one box of odds and ends—can't live without my hair conditioner with this awful hair which turns to frizz on humid days."

Lillith had taken an apartment in this run-down building, which had become a Mecca for students on a budget. Then she had visited the local Salvation Army store and bought a few pieces of furniture and some mismatched dishes, and registered for classes at DePaul University. She had also obviously paid a visit to a Rush Street hippie shop, because she was wearing a flowing Indian-print skirt, which emphasized her wide hips, and a too-tight ribbed sweater that accentuated her Mrs.

Shaw-sized bosom. Her outfit was trying too hard and all slightly wrong, like trying to match a picture of a Haight-Ashbury waif from two years ago. And now, she was a student, like us, ready to live life to the fullest and to find her essential self—and, of course, protest against the Viet Nam War.

John was impressed. I was horrified. Stunned that a woman could walk out on two young children. How was their father explaining why Mommy had left?

When I gingerly asked how the children were handling her absence, she replied. "My husband is a great father. He will be coping just fine. I'm not worried. He's a husband kind of guy. He'll find another woman and get remarried. I'm sure of that. So the kids will have another mommy before you know it."

I asked to see pictures of her children.

"I didn't bring any. I really needed to start my life over," she explained almost crossly.

As we sipped another and yet another cup of tea, and Lillith continued to explain her "journey," John kept saying, "Isn't that great?" He was filled with admiration for what she had done. I was filled with revulsion. It suddenly occurred to me that this was the first time John and I had ever disagreed on anything. I was puzzled. But then I realized that what you see is dependent on what you yourself have experienced. John saw Lillith's leaving her family as a bold stroke of independence, not unlike his moving out of his mother's house and sphere of domination. I empathized instead with Lillith's children, imagining two sobbing youngsters unable to comprehend a mother walking out on them. I was raised within a tight, warm, solid family. I couldn't imagine a child not having a mother to depend upon. But trying to see Lillith's actions through John's maternal trauma calmed me. I would not let Lillith become an argument between us.

Still, Lillith's cavalier attitude toward her escape from family bothered me, even as I realized there must be more to it—perhaps a cheating or abusive husband. When our friendship seemed secure enough, I asked her. She laughed. "George was a dull accountant"—she used the past tense as if he'd died. "He didn't have the gumption to have an affair. But he is quite emotionally dependent, so he'll look for a woman right away. But hell, no, he was a good enough husband, just so incredibly boring. He's an accountant, for God's sake!"

Visits to John always included that cup of tea upstairs. Lilly—the name had gradually shortened—always seemed to be home. Textbooks would be spread out on her coffee table, which was a piece of glass held up by two cement blocks, but she was never studying. Instead, her focus seemed to center around her most recent decorating touch, as she laboriously hippie-ized her apartment. Glass—actually, plastic—beads hung in her bedroom doorway. Her mattress sat on the floor—"no bed frame, cool, huh?" She bathed me in praise, impressed at my willingness to teach inner city kids and face daily danger. She massaged John's ego as well, encouraging him when his interest in his psychology studies flagged. She seemed good for us. A kind of mother who always approved and lavished praise. I found myself confiding in her, asking her advice. We would often invite Lillith to join us when we went out for a bite to eat in the neighborhood.

But yet, it chaffed on me—her leaving her children. Even her name chaffed on me.

"Isn't that the greatest name?" John asked me. "Do you know who Lillith was?"

"You mean Adam's legendary first lover—an evil sorceress. God had to create Eve just to give Adam a proper woman. Is *that* who you mean?" I think my edginess showed.

"Well, you don't have it quite right. She was, however, the first goddess—a free and lovely erotic creature. Can you imagine parents having the courage to give their daughter that name?" he mused dreamily.

I couldn't let it pass.

"Her parents didn't *give* her that name, John. I accidentally saw some forwarded mail sitting on her kitchen table once. It was plainly addressed to a Judith Hunter."

I saw a hint of anger and defiance pass ever so briefly through his eyes. But it was gone in an instant. He didn't argue with my unwelcome offering, just shrugged and said. "Even if she took that name for herself later, it still took real guts to pick out such a name."

By November, our friendship with Lillith/Judith began to wane. We saw less and less of her. John no longer suggested going up for tea when I dropped by. When I asked how she was, he'd answer distractedly, "Oh, I guess she's really busy with her classes now. Not so easy to be a student after being away from it for sixteen years."

I was relieved that Judith was no longer a prominent feature in our lives. It was good to be free of her bubbly optimism and overly warm advice. Anyway, John was way too busy fretting over the looming draft and the stupidity of his professors and their inane exams.

Face it, John was a worrier. But I could understand it. Being a graduate student kept you in a kind of suspended animation, waiting for real life to begin. That's why I'd opted out of graduate school. I much preferred learning from life, in my case by trying to hold my head up in a messy, noisy, classroom of teenagers on the brink of disaster, and hope that I was doing something right. I was certain John's moods would change when he was out of school, and when the war ended. Viet Nam was a gloomy cloud that hung threateningly over his head. I could wait it out. Nothing he could do or say could shake my steady commitment to him and our life together.

That next Christmas, the plan was for John to come home with me again, and this time meet all my brothers and sisters and their offspring to see what Christmas is like in a big family. He was thrilled with the idea, but as we drew closer to the holiday, he became more and more morose over finals, gripped by his insane fear he would flunk out of school and then suddenly become subject to the draft. His grades had mysteriously dropped to C's. He was distraught and distracted, unable to concentrate.

"Honey, I have to stay back and study for finals," he finally decided.

I was disappointed. I said I'd stay back in Chicago too. He became upset at that. "I will not let my finals ruin your Christmas," he demanded.

So after my last day of teaching, I boarded the 4:00 P.M. Kansas City Chief for a solitary train ride home. This might be my last trip home as a single woman. Perhaps it would be good to be alone.

When I returned to Chicago that thirty-first of December I came back to a changed world. Nothing would ever be the same again. I had rushed back to spend the last day of the sixties with John. I called him the minute I'd had lugged my bags up the three flights. Still out of breath, I dialed.

"I'm back. Let's party. It's New Year's Eve."

Dead silence.

"I'm back. This is Rebecca."

Had I just woken him from a deep sleep?

"I can't party tonight. I have to study." Then he followed this blunt statement with a lame, "I didn't know you'd be back this soon."

He sounded irritated, almost disappointed that I was home.

"I'm tired anyway," I lied. "I'm going to stay in and go to bed. Call me when you come up for air." I hung up the phone without hearing so much as an *I love you* or a *glad you're back.* John called the next day to set up a Friday night date—dinner at my house.

"Let's make it a quick dinner. I have to get back to my books. But we need to talk."

Need to talk? A phrase I'd never heard from him before. Our relationship was not one of "needing to talk." Neither of us had ever *needed* to talk with one another. That was like telling a baby it needed to suckle.

When he didn't show up at the appointed time, and with the spaghetti getting soggy, I called. He seemed in a daze.

"I'm sorry. I just couldn't make it over."

I didn't even answer. I didn't want to have our first fight.

"But we do need to talk."

"What is it you want to talk about?" I asked.

"I think it's gotten too intense between us. I think we shouldn't see each other for awhile. I have a lot on my mind. With finals coming up, and . . . "

"It's not finals that's bothering you." I said it flatly, like my mother would state a fact that was obvious. "Are you trying to say that you don't want to see me again?"

"Not exactly," he hedged. "I just think maybe for awhile, we should . . . yes, not see each other for awhile . . ."

John was dumping me. And he wasn't even man enough to dump me in person. He was so chicken he had to do it over the phone. And me, how stupid could I have been? How blind to not see something coming. To not pick up clues, whatever they were. The called-off Christmas trip. The worry over finals. The Cs, from a formerly brilliant student. I was being dumped. Furthermore, he had been worried about doing it for a long time now. I now recognized the distracted fretfulness I'd seen in him when he was struggling with the dumping the last ex.

In past relationships, I had always been the one to do the dumping when I sensed something wasn't right for me. I was good at it. John wasn't. He was being a gutless ass. Too gutless, too dishonest to say why, to explain, to give me something to walk away with. It wasn't like we were on the third date, for God's sake. What about the six children? The bed and breakfast in Michigan? What about the whole life we had laid out—which *he* had laid out, which I had agreed to, like a puppy dog, lapping up, then embellishing every detail while gazing lovingly in his light gray, soulful eyes. Worrying along with him every day about the goddamn draft. And his goddamn finals.

I was stunned.

January 3. I went back to my classroom. I let a week go by. Then another. I called. Whichever roommate answered would always say that John "wasn't there."

Finally, one day after school, I did what I should have done the very first day. I bundled up in my coat. I drove to his street. I parked. I walked into the building. I pounded on his door. Richard answered.

"I'm coming in," I announced. No asking *is he there* this time. No allowing the answer *sorry, can't find him.*

I walked right past Richard and barged into John's room. It was empty. Cleaned out except for a naked sagging mattress on a naked bed frame. Nothing. He was gone.

I sat on the edge of the old lumpy mattress I'd slept on so many times, with backaches to prove it. Richard came in and sat beside me. He said nothing. Just sat there a few inches away from me and waited. He was clearly uncomfortable, but he stayed nevertheless.

"When did he leave?"

"Couple of weeks ago."

"Where did he go?"

"Didn't say."

Rich wouldn't look me in the eye. He was like a kid who can't think of an excuse when he hasn't done his homework.

"Did he quit school?"

"Yes."

"Did he go to Canada?"

"I don't know. He didn't say."

"Oh come on, he must have said something to you."

"No, he just moved out. But I think he's left town."

Suddenly I thought of something. "Lillith will know. He always confided in her." I stood up ready to bolt upstairs.

Richard stopped me. "She's gone too."

I sat back down on the edge of the mattress. The cliché is that your whole life flashes in front of you in seconds when you think you're going to die. Well, when love dies, the truth behind a relationship can flash instantly as well. Foolish is not a strong enough description of how I felt. Maybe the Old English word, cuckolded, has the right ring for what had transpired in the last four months.

"Richard, did they leave together?" I looked at him hard, trying to force him to look into my eyes.

"I don't know."

"Come on, Richard."

"Well, they left at the same time."

"He was spending a lot of time up there lately, right?"

"He always said he couldn't study down here. We were making too much noise."

I stood up. I wasn't about to break down in front of Richard. It was enough that I was blind and stupid, even worse, everyone around me knew what I couldn't see. I grabbed my coat from him. For some reason he had been holding it, clutching it in his nervousness.

"You and your lovebeads." I spit out the words.

He finally looked me in the eye, and I could see how much I had hurt him. He didn't say it, but I saw it in his eyes. They were saying, "Those beads were from me to you. I would never have run away from you like John did."

I walked down the flight of steps with the dirty striped carpet that the landlord was never going to get around to replacing, shoved open the heavy entrance door that would never quite shut on its latch, tripped down the five cracked cement steps that were never going to be repaired, and got in my ladybug and made my way through traffic up Lakeshore Drive through a fog of tears.

I pulled myself wearily up the three flights of stairs covered by equally stained carpet runners to my third floor apartment with the back window view of the lake. I did not feel anything. I was not cold. I was not hungry.

I stayed not hungry for several weeks. Every time I tried to eat, it came back up. When my weight fell to 105 pounds and my pelvic bones

were beginning to stick out weirdly, I went to see a doctor. An exami-
nation ruled out any physical illness to explain the weight loss. On my
second visit, by which time I had dropped to 102, the doctor wasn't
polite about it. He looked over his reading glasses at me and said. "You
will come back next week. If you don't start eating, I'm putting you in
the hospital and feeding you through your veins." I didn't argue with
him. He instinctively knew, without probing, that my rejection of food
was a rejection of life. Uncharacteristically docile, I accepted his author-
ity and obeyed. By the next visit, I had gained three pounds. I had
found my way out of the willow woods.

In the beginning I tried to make it political. I would even make
speeches at rallies how I had lost my boyfriend to the Viet Nam War,
explaining that my man had to secretly steal away to Canada. In the
middle of one speech, it finally hit me. He didn't leave the country. He
left me. He didn't skip out on the war. He skipped out on me. I would
have gone along to Canada with him—he knew that. He chose to take
someone else into exile with him. And then in the next split second,
while I still stood at the microphone leading a chant, another truth hit
me. John's painful attempt to extricate himself from his mother had
failed. A replacement had stepped in, offering saccharine nurture laced
with manipulative domination that outmothered his own mother. It
had nothing to do with me. I had not failed in love. He had failed in
his attempt to become free. And that day I stopped blaming myself, and
became angry with John and ashamed of my own meekness. I didn't
like what I'd become. The suffering, supportive farm wife, standing by
while dust blew and crops failed. In short, a suffering settler. I needed
to escape the dirty dishes and run out to the pasture again.

The next day I spotted a brochure in the English department office,
and on little more than a whim, signed up for a summer course at
University College in London. Next, I quit my teaching position—two
years was enough—and applied for an entry-level job at the *Tribune*.
Writing was all I ever wanted to do.

WHEN I RETURNED FROM London in the fall, I became cub reporter,
the new girl at the *Tribune*, shakily launching a career that would eventually fling me across the globe as a foreign correspondent, then settle
me into a coveted desk as editor of the paper's *Sunday Magazine*.

Years later, I once drove through Silver Bay and passed by Aunt Gertrude's house. I wanted to stop and knock on the door. But I was afraid, not that Lillith and John would be there living out a cozy life, but afraid that the woman who might answer the door would be me— a split of me, another dimension in which I was a settler, not a nomad. I pictured confronting my mirror image, an aging hippie in a flowing skirt and boxy sandals with long hair pulled into a messy knot in back. She would be shocked to see my face—*her* face, except framed by an easy-care, close-cropped haircut. Black trousers. Casual sweater. Tortoise-shell glasses. A sharp contrast to the earthy careless Michigan mother of five. There would be children laughing and playing and teasing each other in the background, their games spilling out onto the veranda. You could see the striking resemblances in these children, clones of John and me.

"Honey, who is it?" John would call from his study, to the right of the large staircase. He would come out, still holding his book, marking his place with a finger. The hair at his temples would be gray, he'd be wearing reading glasses—I'd never seen him in glasses. Still dark and lank, still handsome, in a professorial kind of way.

I couldn't possibly knock on that door and accidentally discover that he had not run off with Judith, but with me in a life we'd planned and were now living out, and discover that world-trotting reporter Rebecca was the figment of *her* imagination.

I even carried a memory of another shadowy existence. Sometimes I awoke from dreams thinking I had children to get off to school. Some mornings I awakened certain a sick baby had just been laying in my arms, who, exhausted from crying, had finally fallen into a fitful sleep with her damp head nestled against my chest. I would be sweaty from it.

Maybe I was a settler, and my nomad self an illusion.

I tried to shake myself out of my reverie. Needless to say, I did not knock on the door of that well-tended, freshly-painted house in Michigan.

Ten years later, I drove past it once again and noticed a *For Sale* sign and wondered for a fleeting, eerie moment, had my life fallen apart? Had we gotten a divorce? Were the children sad to be moving out of this house? Was I sad?

That was a few days before my unexpected trip to Utah.

21

On the Trail

I AM WIND STORM, DAUGHTER OF Gentle Wind. Perhaps it is for this day my name was given me, for a storm is blowing from my breast. We left my mother at the sacred springs of the Big Buffalo River they call the Cimarron. I wailed, I begged, but the soldiers would not let me stay beside her. Her breath came in rattles. Her eyes no longer saw me. She said, Let me die here. I will ask the vultures to carry me back to the ridge to be with the children. Already they were circling, waiting for her death rattle to cease. Her eyes fluttered. She looked at them. She spoke to them. They understood what they must do.

As I watched the turkey vultures with their black underbodies and white-tipped wings hanging lazily in the air, waiting, I remembered the words my mother once spoke when I was a child and frightened by these birds. They do not create death, they only clean up after it, she said. For that purpose were they placed in the heavens. They are black, the color of death, but see the white tips of their wings, she said, pointing at the creatures I feared. The white edges are from the great burst of light as the spirits of the dead join with the spirits in the sky. So do not be afraid of the big black birds. They come to feed, yes, but also to heal and comfort.

There is no comfort for me. On the trail, I pray for death to take me, for vultures to circle and to eat of my flesh so through their droppings my spirit can also stay on the Plains I love. But there is no comfort, no death for me. Only marching to a dark fate.

I loved a white man once. We made a secret place and a secret vow under the willows of the Buffalo River, where our bodies and spirits mingled. Our love was fierce and consuming. Some of my people were ashamed of me. But my mother said, make the white man your husband and come to live in my teepee. He learned my language. I learned his. A language I now hate because I can understand what the soldiers are saying. He did not wish to live in my mother's teepee. I went with him north to a place near the Great River.

I called my white husband Prairie Dog because one minute he was there, quivering in excitement, the next moment he was gone. He was even more restless than a red man. Always thinking of a new place. A new adventure. Perhaps a new woman.

I tried to live in his house, in his ways. I prepared for him the food he wished to eat. I loved him with a passion deep and forgiving. And when our baby son was born I was happy beyond words. Our son had my husband's pink-white skin and my raven black hair. But my husband was not happy. And when our son died of White Man's fever, I was no longer happy.

I wish I did not know their language. I wish I could not hear what they are saying.

In the morning when I left my mother, the soldiers made us walk east. In the evening of that day the sunset was the most beautiful I have ever seen on the Plains. In the midst of the red and brilliant orange glow was a sudden burst of gold, a ray shooting, reaching, flying to the heavens. I knew it was the spirit of my mother. And then a cool breeze reached out to caress my checks, to play in my hair, and I loosened my braid and let my mother's gentle spirit lift my hair and whisper in my ears.

22

The Canyon

WE MARCH FOR TWO DAYS on the trail. The earth is as flat as it is east of the Little Buffalo. Then suddenly we come to a great hole in the earth. I have heard of this place. Palo Duro Canyon, they call it. We have another name for it. It was known to my father as Deep Winter Place. It is impossible to know it is here until you reach the rim of the canyon and look down into its depths. We make camp here on the edge of the great canyon. A scout they call "the half breed" tells them another party is marching to meet us. So we wait two days for another group of soldiers who are bringing more prisoners to join our march.

They come, and we see that they are ragged and hungry. They are Kiowa and Comanche, and a few Cheyenne, mostly young ones. They once hid in this canyon, below the vision of White Man. Until the day Bad Hand found them. As we continue our march, the stragglers tell us the story of how Bad Hand and his soldiers surprised them in the cool season just before winter, in the dark part of morning while they still slept.

A young boy, nearly a man, tells us the story: "Our braves fought them off, but could not win. There were too many soldiers and not enough of us. Most of our fighters had been lost or captured in battle, and our remaining warriors were sleeping because they had just returned from a raid on a buffalo hunter's camp. Bad Hand's soldiers sneaked in just before dawn. We had two lookouts, but the soldiers killed them immediately. Our horses were in the front pasture of the canyon. We were mostly women and children. We fled out the other

side of the canyon. We could not get to our horses. They killed our horses, a thousand horses. Killed them and left them to rot. I have never before
seen anyone kill horses just to kill them. Then they burned our teepees,
our buffalo robes, even our dried meat and stores of grain. They burned
everything in a great fire whose smoke could be seen darkening the sky."

"They were cowards!" These words were spit out by the thin girl
with the burning eyes and scars on her arms, who until now did not
speak. "They were cowards, too cowardly to kill us, so they destroyed
our horses so we could not travel, our teepees and our robes so we
would freeze in the wind, our food so we would starve. That was the
coward's way of killing us," she said.

Those were the only words she spoke. She chose to walk beside me
silently, her eyes cast down on the ground. When a soldier rode by on
his horse, only then did she look up, and then with burning hatred in
her eyes. I have never seen such a look in eyes before.

Others told us around the campfire in the evening that nearly all the
dwellers of Deep Winter Place who fled the attack had wandered on
the Plains all winter, hiding in small groups, and most had frozen or
starved in the cruel days that followed. It was the beginning of spring,
and only a few had survived—the two dozen or so who stumbled with
us on the journey to Indian Territory. But they were too weak and hungry to flee when the soldiers found them this time. "Until we saw you,
we thought we were the last of our people left on the Plains," said the
young man.

The girl, almost old enough to be a woman, eyes downcast, thin,
hungry, angry, stayed walking at my side. She wanted to be with me. I
do not know why.

When the sun hung low and red in the west, I spoke to her. "My
name is Wind Storm," I said.

"I am called Burning Fire," she answered.

"My daughter is dead," I said.

"My mother is dead, frozen in the winter wind," she said.

There was no need for me to say you will be my daughter or for her
to say you will be my mother. It hung in the darkening air, the words
we could not say. And we walked side by side, and would come to live
side by side in the reservation, me old with cold anger, her young with
hot anger.

23

Words & Pictures

THE PICTURE OF MY NEW EXISTENCE in the City by the Lake is not complete without explaining about Bill, who has become the inconstant constant in my life. We first met when he was assigned to shoot photos for a "Neighborhoods of Chicago" series I was writing for the Perspective section. My job—a plum assignment for a reporter only on the job a year, according to envious colleagues—was to go into a different ethnic neighborhood each week to produce a color piece. His job was to provide the photos. We clashed right from the start when I began telling him what pictures to shoot. He quickly let me know that no one told him what pictures to shoot—not in Viet Nam, not in Panama, and certainly not in the back alleys of Chicago on his home turf.

David William Condell (who prefers to be called Bill) is a Pulitzer prize-winning photographer, seasoned at an early age on both the battlefields of Viet Nam and South Michigan Avenue during the Democratic Convention. His portrait of a defiant Abbie Hoffman raising his fist is known around the world.

On our first assignment I found myself reluctantly following him around—he was shooting the pictures, I was filling in the space between his images. That's how it would have to be on the streets of Chicago. But I vowed that someday—when I was a little less green around the edges—he would have to follow *me* around and fit his pictures to *my* words.

Despite our bad start, we fell in love.

As with all good photographers, Bill's camera is an extension of himself. He wears a camera bag over his shoulder as a woman carries a purse, never without it. Bill is also never without his multi-pocket olive green gadget vest, which holds various lenses and equipment at the ready. I've never seen him touch a comb to his thick mantle of dark brown hair, yet he fusses over and constantly trims his short beard—his one and only vanity. Now twenty years after our first assignment together, his gadget vest has faded to a pale shade of an indeterminate color and his close-cropped beard is salt and pepper.

Our romance was born in the dim corners of small family-owned storefront restaurants in neighborhoods across the city. As part of our on-going assignment, we were expected to sample and review neighborhood ethnic fare. And we delighted in finding these gems—for instance, one Guatemalan place without a name or phone number. You could reach it only if you happened to know the number on the pay phone in back by the bathroom door. What the restaurant saved in advertising costs, signage and phone bills, it poured into ingredients. Huge, succulent shrimp swam in broth seasoned by lemon and cilantro—I have never tasted such a soup before or since. There were Indian restaurants along Devon Avenue with curries so hot you had to follow them with sweet lassi, a yogurt drink perfumed by rose water. Lassi, I discovered, was an elixir that coaxed overactive brains into blissful sleep. I had found my new cure for insomnia. In the neighborhood just west of the Loop, Greek restaurants—usually reachable only by traversing a narrow corridor through a storefront Greek grocery—came alive after dark. You could always count on flaming saginaki, platters of roast lamb and herb potatoes, live music and dancing till dawn, along with a fair share of broken wine glasses. In Bill's boyhood Rogers Park neighborhood, corner delis served corned beef on rye stacked so high, you had to remove half of the corned beef just to fit the sandwich into your mouth. In Mayor Daley's neighborhood, there were rowdy Irish bars, and further south, blues—Chicago Blues—in smoky clubs such as the Checkerboard Lounge. And then after clubbing nearly all Saturday night, you could rejuvenate your soul with rousing gospel music at the South Wabash Full Gospel Assembly followed by a soulfood buffet at Gladys' that could provide enough calories to last the week.

Each week another neighborhood, each week a continuing education for me—not only in ethnic Chicago but the world at large—and Bill.

Most of Chicago—all of it except the Loop and its near north high-rise neighborhoods—was Old World ethnic. Italian, Polish, Jewish, Mexican, Irish, German, Greek, Lithuanian, Swedish—every wave of immigrants had claimed their section of the city. Store window signs signaled the language of the neighborhood, restaurants served their fare with ingredients shipped from overseas for authenticity of taste. Within the neighborhood, people retained their language, their customs, their prejudices, their blood feuds. Serbs and Croats clashed in the street in front of their nightclubs, which they had placed teasingly close to one another. Moroccan-born Israelis and Jordanian-born Palestinians argued passionately each morning in Arabic in the falafel cafe that demarcated the border between their close-set neighborhoods. When Bill and I left a southside Lithuanian restaurant—where we had been stared at as if we had disembarked from an alien space ship—the cook stood in the kitchen doorway in his dirty apron muttering as we paid our bill and left. I heard within his guttural stream of Lithuanian, the words "Jew Communist." I thought I saw him, out of the corner of my eye, spit on the floor as he said it. Fortunately, Bill's camera was rewinding and he was too distracted to hear what I heard. How did they know, I wondered, that Bill was Jewish? Everyone born in Chicago instantly knew the ethnic derivation of the strangers they met. That's why they always puzzled over me. They could not quite place me within the ethnic grid of neighborhood Chicago.

The ethnicity of every neighborhood went deep, keeping in its grasp the young, who were expected to marry only within their own, and usually did. A young, vivacious Lithuanian reporter I worked with dated sophisticated Near North men—mostly commodity traders or lawyers. Then one day she surprised us by announcing her marriage to her Lithuanian betrothed—the young man, electrician by trade, whose family lived next door to her grandmother. She had grown up with him and it was always understood they would marry—regardless of her fancy dating. Bill's fashion photographer buddy whose family hailed from Southern India was a man about town and a regular of the night-club scene. But one day he married an Indian pediatric surgeon from Orlando he met only the day before their wedding. The marriage had been arranged by their parents in New Delhi. A baby followed within the year. His bride changed from scrubs to a sari the moment she arrived home from work, and each night she ate separately from him in the kitchen despite her doctor's degree.

Bill was my first love after John. I had taken a long time to trust another Chicago street boy. Unlike John, a man of wondrous words, Bill's sensitive side showed only in his photos. He had little to say. But he captured strangers' souls in black and white. During the early weeks of our romance he followed me around lovingly with his camera lens. And later, when I spread out his black and white glossy love offerings on my kitchen table in private, I learned to know myself. The camera had captured me at my desk, in my kitchen, reposing in the park, napping on my couch. It was odd what his camera could see. Brooding, regret, elation, exhaustion, satisfaction, amusement, boredom. In every photo, emotions sprang from my face. I thought I had a stoic face.

Mirrors can bend reality. Photos do not. Sometimes I stared for hours at Bill's pictures, which displayed a different me than the mirror. I learned, for instance, that I had one eyebrow that arched much higher than the other, as though always asking a question. Perhaps that is why people spilled out information to me, even before I began asking questions. I saw that my thin, wispy, "dull" hair was in fact beautiful. In constant motion, with a life of its own, my hated hair actually enlivened my face, rather than distracted from it. And my eyes. I saw other worlds in my eyes, which were so clear, so light, so haunting, that I now feared for anyone to look deeply into them. Bill had captured my soul.

The ancients were right.

When Bill went to Pine Ridge in South Dakota to shoot pictures for a medical magazine story on the poverty, alcoholism and diabetes problems on the reservation, the Sioux refused to allow him to photograph them. Bill respected their wishes and came back with landscapes and buildings and a few shots of the backs of Indians walking on trails through the prairie. Actually, the photos were beautiful, despite not one face showing. The editors were furious. They ended up superimposing some old Oklahoma Indian man's face onto a Pine Ridge landscape to create their cover. ("The *Tribune* would have never done that," said Bill, and he stopped doing freelance magazine assignments, deciding to stick to news photography.)

Bill hated color photography. For him, black and white was the language of reality. When newspapers started printing color photos on their front pages, Bill said it looked like a child had taken watercolor paint to photos, sloshing outside the lines and choosing inappropriate colors. Nor did he allow a lab to develop his film, insisting on his own secretive dark room techniques. Eventually, he had to give up on that as the *Tribune* grew and the news cycle shortened.

While I loved Bill's stunning black and white portraiture, we disagreed about color. For me, the colors of the world, of a particular place, is key to understanding its essence. Every place has a color. For instance, the color of Chicago is gray. The cloudy brooding sky in winter, the buildings—from the stately stone edifices of the University of Chicago to the steel and glass Mies van der Rohe boxes of the city's modern skyline—are all shades of gray. Even the gleaming "white" marble Standard Oil building—if you look closely, the marble is light gray with tiny flecks of darker gray. And the "black" John Hancock building—look again, dark gray steel. Yellow-gray soot drifts across the city when winds carry it from the belching steel mills at the bottom of the lake at Gary, Indiana. And on winter days even the lake abandons its blue and reflects the gray of the sky above.

You know the color of a place by how they paint their woodwork. In Chicago, the back porches and courtyard stairways of apartment buildings are painted dark gray. No exception. During my many years in Chicago I have never seen a back porch *not* painted gray. On the shelves of neighborhood hardware stores, you'll find paint cans labeled "porch gray." I have repeatedly asked my building superintendents, teased them, cajoled them, to paint our building porches another color, say yellow or blue. Every one of them—and I have lived in buildings all over the North Side—has recoiled in horror at the suggestion. "I would be fired," they've said. "Why?" I've asked. No one knows the answer. But painting *not gray* is out of the question. That is because everyone knows the color of Chicago is gray. A friend and co-worker, fresh from Minneapolis where color is lavished on buildings to contrast with the snow, painted the steel gray back door of her condominium townhouse yellow. She ignored a warning letter from the condo board that demanded she adhere to the bylaws that specified the color for doors. Her newly-painted yellow door was, after all, hidden from sight behind a high patio fence. So why should anyone care? Nevertheless, the condominium board began legal proceeding to take her townhouse away for violating the condominium covenants. My Minnesota friend would not relent, refusing to repaint her door. She lost her townhouse in court. She did not understand the power of gray.

The statue on the Civic Center plaza—Picasso's grand joke on the city of the big shoulders—is reviled. Not because of its curious creature shape, rather like Snoopy of the *Peanuts* cartoon, but, I maintain, because of its rust color. All the other sculptures gracing Chicago's many lovely plazas are gray. Check it out. Gray, and graying more as pigeons and pollution do their duty.

But gray—with the exception of the porches—is not necessarily ugly. The stately columns of City Hall, the regal lions that guard the entrance to the Art Institute, the sparkling Buckingham Fountain in Grant Park, all gray. Gray, in all its infinite shades and moods and nuances, can be beautiful. Yet I long for color. Especially in winter when even the pure white snow turns gray within a day of falling.

What then, I have asked myself, is the color of the Plains? I am finding the answer in my clothing. As I grow more and more homesick, here in my adopted city "back East," my wardrobe has changed. I have stopped wearing the hippie rainbow of reds, purples, golds and indigos, which were my initial reaction to this city of gray. Instead, I have begun wearing pale blue—supposedly to match my eyes—and light sandy beige—supposedly to match my hair, but in truth they are the colors of the overwhelming sky and the parched, blowing dust back home. Once in a while, I allow a pale gray-green—I suppose you could call it sage—to briefly enter the blue-tan combination—perhaps, to celebrate the stubborn tufts of buffalo grass, sagebrush and cactus still gripping the sandy soil where plows have not penetrated.

It was unconscious. I didn't *decide* on these colors. They found me. And when they did, shopping became easy. I now stick to denims, the pale, washed out kind. And khaki, in the lightest shades. In winter I wear sweaters of sky blue. Even my one business suit is pale blue wool, which I wear with a golden-beige silk blouse.

So I walked the gray city in my blue and beige, unaware of my colors until my friend Jenny pointed it out to me. Once I became aware of it, I remembered something Gentle Wind whispered to me when I was trying to make my t-shirt dress resemble her lovely fringed doeskin dress. "These are the colors of my tribe," she had said. "The color of the sand, the color of the sky, the color of the grass, and the color of the sun." Once in a Smithsonian museum, I saw an exhibit entitled, "Shirts of the Plains Indians." I had earlier marveled at the bright colors and bold ornamentation of the clothing of Northern tribes, such as Crow, Sioux, and Blackfeet. When I reached the exhibit for the Southern Plains, I was disappointed to see a sign informing that most of the Plains tribes chose not to contribute to the display because they believed their spirits resided in their clothing. But the exhibit did feature a few color photographs, and one sign explained that of all the tribes, the Kiowa Apache's clothing was the simplest. Their shirts and dresses were of pale buckskin or doeskin, devoid of decoration except for a few painted designs in soft blue, pale green and yellow.

Gentle Wind's whispered words, and her tribe's magnificent palette, had crept into my wardrobe and now I knew the colors of home.

During my on-going color versus black and white arguments with Bill, I have always conceded that perhaps color would indeed cloud Bill's photographic explorations of human faces. And one day, after sharing my thoughts on the grayness of Chicago, I even admitted, "Okay, in Chicago black and white is appropriate, but when you come west with me, you must load color film into your camera. There is no way to capture our sunsets, prairie wild flowers, mountain vistas and towering thunderheads in black and white."

To which Bill replied, "Tell that to Ansel Adams."

BILL AND I HAVE BEEN a couple of sorts, sharing our meals and our bed when we wished to. Walking together on streets, down alleys and across pristine wilderness landscapes, he with his camera, me with my pen, soaking in the world, sometimes on assignment together, sometimes on our own time without clock or duty.

In that first year, we almost got married once or twice. Then we would think better of it. Why change from something comfortable to something frightening? My friends would pull me away to cluck and commiserate about Bill's "fear of commitment," so prevalent in the men of our generation. When I waved them away, they would begin whispering about *my* "fear of commitment," which they said revealed the underlying insecurity of feminists of our generation. But neither Bill nor I are strangers to commitment. He is fiercely committed to his pictures, I to the words that spill from my pen and clatter from my typewriter. But we are not the kind of couple to build a nest and raise offspring. I regret that, but I always understood it. I never found a better man than Bill. And so I never built a nest.

I regret even more that Bill never photographed my home before it disappeared. I almost got him there, that time he left me for the Flint Hills. Of course, even then, so much of my childhood landscape had changed that there was little to shoot. Home can only exist in my head. I have no proof of its true existence. The few poorly-focused photos my parents keep in shoeboxes display family members lined up on porches squinting into bright sunlight. Sometimes there is a glimpse of the Home Place dugout or the Golden Hill stucco barracks house, the brick schoolhouse or white clapboard church in the background. Once or twice a car or a beloved dog hangs on the edge of the photograph. But we never captured the willow woods, the cherry orchard, the creek, the swimming hole, the ridge, the cottonwoods or the pasture on film. No one thought to do it. And now I have no proof of home, only what rattles around in my head until I wonder, did I concoct a fiction of my life on the Plains? I can only see it in my eyes in the photos Bill shot of me when I was unaware that his camera lens was pointed into my soul.

Will Bill and I grow old together? I think not. One day Bill will stay one minute too long in harm's way to shoot the photo that must be shot. Perhaps he fears the same for me, that one day I will stay one minute too long to understand what I must understand and record. But we do not live in fear. It is not a matter of duty or dedication to our trade. It is our love of pictures and words.

24

Wind Storm's Story

I GROW OLD NOW IN INDIAN TERRITORY between the Canadian River and the Red River with many tribes and many clans bunched so close together that it is difficult to keep from quarreling. Some we know because our fathers once wintered together by the Great River. Others we know because of the legends we heard when we were children, stories told around our campfires by the Dog Soldiers who once rode through our land on their magnificent horses, seeking white invaders to kill. In those days, we gave the warriors food around our fires and rest in our teepees. Their horses drank the sweet cool water of our spring.

After we left the deep canyon, Bad Hand—whom the white people call Mackenzie—and his soldiers marched us south many days to a place called Fort Sill. There were already many Comanche bands there. Some had surrendered to the soldiers because they were starving in the winter out on the Plains. With the buffalo gone there was nothing to eat. Others, both Kiowa and Comanche groups, had been found and forced in, as we had been. They locked the warriors in a damp dungeon under the guardhouse, where they could barely see any daylight. Other men and boys were herded into a horse corral with high walls made of stone. They did not even clean out the horse dung before forcing the men into the enclosure. We women and children were allowed to camp along Cache Creek nearby but soldiers kept an eye on us.

Once a day an army wagon would drive by the stone corral and toss raw meat over the wall to the men as if they were animals to be fed. We women worried how they would cook the meat without us there. Perhaps they ate it raw. We learned later that the meat was half-rotten and tasted so bad that the braves were sickened by it, but they ate it because they had no choice. Sometimes the soldiers drove thin, sick-looking cattle into the corral for the Indian braves to butcher and eat, but there was not enough room to do it properly and it stank. The meat of a White Man's cow is not sweet like the flesh of the buffalo. But our braves ate what they could. They needed to live so they could fight off our oppressors when their strength returned. We were also brought food by the soldiers since we had no men to hunt game for us. They gave us the same kind of spoiled meat thrown to our men. But we are women. We could cook the meat until it was tolerable to eat. They did not give us enough cooking pots, but we shared what we had.

When the wind blew from the west the stench was unbearable, for as they brought in bands of Comanche and Kiowa, the soldiers killed the warriors' horses and mules so they would have no means of escape even should they be able to climb over the stone fence. Hundreds of carcasses lay rotting to the west of our camp, so many that there were not enough vultures in the world to clean up after the kill.

Gradually, as summer came and turned into autumn, they allowed some of the men—the old and the very young—to come live in our women's camp. They sent the chiefs and great warriors, whom they suspected of leading raids on buffalo hunters and settlers, away to prisons in a dreaded hot place far, far away, a place they call Florida. We have heard stories of this Florida, where men were sent to die like animals locked in cages. Finally, they released the rest of the men, those they considered too old, too young, or too peaceful to be a problem, and took all of us to our permanent reservation camping grounds on a bend of the Washita River. The Comanche, Kiowa, Cheyenne, and our little ragged band of *Nadi-ish-dena* all camped near one another. Many other Indian peoples, some of them from beyond many rivers to the east, lived nearby. We did not know their languages or their ways. Some of them were content to live in houses.

The white masters from the Agency, using their Indian interpreters, pleaded with us to walk the road of peace, to be content to live in one place, to sleep in houses not teepees, to farm the earth not hunt. They pleaded with us to foreswear revenge and accept that the world was now a different place and we could never change it back to the way it was.

Some of our great tribal leaders also believed Indians must make peace with the White Man. Black Kettle, of the Cheyenne, was one of the great old man chiefs who talked peace. Ten years before they found us, Black Kettle was camped with five hundred men, women and children at Sand Creek, a place north of the Great River, two days journey northwest of our Little Buffalo River. The White Man's army said that Black Kettle's clan could stay and hunt buffalo until the winter came, and then they would have to move to the Indian Territory in the south. Black Kettle agreed. He placed an American flag on his lodge to show his peaceful nature. One beautiful autumn day, after his men had returned from a buffalo hunt and the whole camp had eaten well, soldiers rode into camp. They were from an army called the Colorado Militia. Black Kettle told his people not to be afraid. He held the pole with the American flag in greeting to show the soldiers that he was a man of peace. Suddenly the soldiers opened fire, shooting and clubbing at anything that moved. Two hundred people, mostly women and children, were killed that day. Black Kettle escaped the flying bullets, and in the midst of the battle, ran to pick up his wounded wife and carried her in his arms into the sand hills above the camp. The soldiers took scalps from the dead—even from the children—to show to their comrades in Denver. They were very proud of their victory and claimed to have killed 800 fierce Indian warriors at Sand Creek.

The survivors of Black Kettle's band were marched to Oklahoma Indian Territory where they were given a place to camp on the Washita River, near the Kiowa and Comanche villages where we would eventually come to live. Even after the massacre at Sand Creek, Black Kettle still spoke of peace with the White Man. More killing and raiding would only make things worse, he counseled his people. Many of his Indian brothers hated Black Kettle for these words.

Even though Black Kettle preached peace amongst his people, and even though Black Kettle went freely to live on the reservation where White Man promised his people would be safe, just four winters after the bloody day on Sand Creek, another army band, this one under the command of the hated General Custer, rode into Black Kettle's camp on the reservation and attacked his village. Custer's soldiers killed many people before braves from neighboring Indian villages came to drive Custer's soldiers off. Black Kettle and his wife were killed, but some say it was one of his own Cheyenne warriors who shot Black Kettle in the back.

Whenever anyone around our campfire speaks peace, the braves say, remember Black Kettle. Whether we talk peace or war, killing or mercy, the White Man will kill us. If we are to die, we might as well die fighting our oppressors.

That is how my adopted Cheyenne daughter, Burning Fire, feels. If she were a man, she would ride out at night on secret raids as do the strong young men in our camp. We *Nadi-ish-dena* and other Plains tribesmen live now in a camp on the Washita River, which is to be our home forever. We have placed our camp far from the Agency so White Man cannot interfere with our ways. And our braves sometimes ride out at night to continue raiding buffalo hunters on the Texas plains. But some say it is no longer necessary. There are no more buffalo left. There are no more of our people living on the Plains. There is nothing left to save.

The man we have come to revere as our great leader is Satanta, a Kiowa chief who is much loved. My brother, Two Eagles, respected Satanta. My Kiowa husband lived and died following Satanta, so it was a great honor when I could meet with the great leader and pass him greetings from my brother, Two Eagles, the fallen chief of our little clan of *Nadi-ish-dena* and remind him of my husband's loyalty to him.

Satanta was the chief who represented our people at Medicine Lodge many seasons ago, when all the great chiefs met to talk with men sent from the White President to make an agreement that would end the wars between us. He listened to the white men promise to bring the Indian people to a homeland a few days journey south of the Arkansas River where they would build houses for us. We were to live on three large reservations where white men would not be allowed to intrude or settle, but our hunting parties would still be allowed to hunt game anywhere between the Arkansas and the Red River. On the reservation, they would teach us to grow our food in the earth and keep flocks of sheep and goats and cattle for meat in case we could not kill enough game to feed our children. Furthermore, because the world was changing, they would teach our children the ways to prosper in the

White Man's world. My brother was at Medicine Lodge and he told us that when Satanta rose to speak to those assembled at Medicine Lodge, everyone listened. His words could make tears flow, even from the eyes of the white men who listened.

He said, "This talk of building houses for us is nonsense. We don't want you to build any for us. We know how to make our own shelter. We want to travel and live on all our land from the Arkansas River to the Red River. As for farming," he said, "land does not want to be worked. Land gives you what you need if you are smart enough to take it. We know this land. We know how to take what it gives us and to care for it in return."

Ten Bears of the Comanche, also known for his wise words, then rose to speak. "I was born upon the Prairie, where the wind blew free and there was nothing to break the light of the sun. I was born where there were no enclosures, and where everything drew a free breath. I want to die there, and not within walls. Why do you ask us to the leave the rivers and the sun and the wind and live in houses?

"I know every stream, every wood between the Rio Grande and the Arkansas," Ten Bears explained to the gathering. "I have hunted and lived over all that country. I lived like my fathers before me, and like them, I lived happily. Now whites have taken the best places where the grass grows the thickest and the timber is the best."

"The White Man has taken our country," Ten Bears conceded, but he pleaded with the men sent by the President to not force Indians to live in houses. "We only wish to wander on the prairie until we die." It was the lament heard round the meeting place by all the Indian leaders: Just let us live and die on the Plains we love.

But ultimately, facing utter ruin and annihilation, the great old man chiefs lent their signatures to an agreement that seemed to save at least some of our sacred hunting grounds. We would be allowed to hunt between the Arkansas and the Red River, as "long as the grass grows and the water flows in the streams." That was the language, repeated by my brother and many lesser leaders around the campfires when they returned from Medicine Lodge. Two Eagles reasoned that as long as we were allowed to hunt these grounds, and as long as we did not make trouble for the White Man, we should be allowed to camp on our hunting grounds as well. How else can you hunt if you cannot camp? And that's why we stayed so long by our Little Buffalo River. We saw no reason to come in to the reservation. We could take care of ourselves.

Satanta, who represented the very large tribe of the Kiowas, agreed to move his people to the reservation in Oklahoma. "But do not build us any houses," he warned the white men. "There will be time enough to build houses when the buffalo are gone." Less than ten years after he uttered this prophesy, the buffalo were gone. Satanta became angry. He had placed his signature and his blessing on a document that turned out to be lies. When white buffalo hunters rode onto the hunting grounds promised to his people forever by the treaty, Satanta struck out with raiding parties across the Plains.

After one bold and successful raid of a buffalo hunters' camp by Kiowa braves from our reservation, Satanta admitted he had led his warriors in defiance of the authorities. In truth, he never left the reservation and did not go on the raid, but he was protecting the young warrior who he expected to become chief when he was gone, a brave warrior whose name we do not speak because we wish to save his life. The army sent Satanta to a jail in Texas for two years. When my band of *Nadi-ish-dena* were brought in to Indian Territory, Satanta had just been released from that Texas prison. That is when I met the great leader face to face. It was a great honor. I will never forget how tall he was, and how kind his rugged face was. He reminded me of my grandfather. But as with all old men, he decided to follow peace. We had lost our precious land. No raid would get it back for us. So he instructed his followers to cease their raids. But the young men were angry and were becoming more angry each day. Our secret young chief continued to lead raiding parties into the Texas plains. The authorities believed Satanta was behind the new raids so they sent him off to jail "for life." This meant he, one of the greatest chiefs to ever live, would grow old alone locked away in a cage like a White Man's animal until he died. Satanta was too noble for such a fate. He pretended to be sick, and then when they sent him to the prison hospital, he jumped out of a window to fly like a bird with no wings into death where his spirit could be free. When word reached our camp we mourned for many days. We fasted and we danced slowly around the campfire and we cried until our tears ran dry. If Satanta was gone there was no hope for the rest of us.

• • •

AND SO WE LIVE HERE in sadness that deepens with each day.

White Man wishes us to live in houses they have built for us. Our dogs like the houses, we do not. We prefer teepees if it is cold and windy, and we prefer sleeping under the stars on warm summer nights for as we sleep the spirits of the stars send sparks into our souls which keep us alive. Without the sun, the wind, the stars, we would die.

The Agency gives us bundles of things and expects us to be grateful. Silly red flannel clothes, so when we wear them they can laugh at us. Smelly food to make our bodies stink. Stiff bristly blankets that rub harshly against our skin. They want our children to go to school instead of learn from their elders. They want our men to plow and plant seeds and tend fields even though it is women's work. We don't know what they want women to do. They do not even understand what a woman is. That she gives and receives and nourishes life, in the image of Mother Earth.

They want us to imprison animals behind fences—sheep, goats and cattle—White Man's sad-faced animals. And they want the animals to die behind fences.

They want us to live and die behind fences too.

When I look at the young white soldiers I am happy that my pink-faced son died. If he had lived, would he have become a white soldier, herding his Indian brothers into fences? I do not talk of my white husband even though he is loved in my deepest memories. It was long ago when I was very young, yet the smell of his body still haunts me in my dreams.

When my heart healed, in those precious last seasons on my beloved Plains, I took a Kiowa husband. He came to live with my clan and hunt with my brothers. I loved him with a calm love, quiet as the spring in the bend of the Little Buffalo which bubbled effortlessly from deep within the earth, replenishing the pool of clear sweet water. That is the love I had for my Kiowa husband and father of my children.

But when White Man came deeper into our lands, plundering and killing, my husband became more and more angry. One day he and my oldest son left to join a Kiowa raiding party to stop the buffalo hunters who had swept into our hunting grounds killing without reason. My husband and my son did not come back. While I grieved, my mother, Gentle Wind, and my brother, Two Eagles, cared lovingly for my young children until I could join the living again.

My mother named me Wind Storm because I was born in a storm. The wind blew the teepee away as I came from the womb. As I drew first breath, Gentle Wind held me tight to her breast so the wind would not blow me away. Even when I was young, there were streaks of silver-white in my black hair, marks from the wind that blew through my mother's tent. So my fate was sealed. I would forever be in the eye of a storm. Great storms. Many storms. When one storm passed, I always knew another one would come.

"Why did you curse me with that name?" I would accuse my mother in my tempestuous youth. "It is not a curse," she would say. "It is a name of great strength. You are as strong as the wind itself. Nothing can move you. Your feet will forever hold to the earth."

I wish it were not so. Why must I stay on this earth when my mother is gone, my husbands are gone, my children are gone? Why must I stay with my feet still planted on the earth? I wish the wind that blows red dust in our mouths here on this reservation would blow me away. Away. Away from this land which is not my own.

But I stay. I stay for Burning Fire.

BURNING FIRE LIVED WITH ME in the teepee that I pitched beside the log cabin the Agency provided me but in which I refused to live. I taught her to plant corn and beans and squash and I taught her to cook. The food the Agency gave us was not fit for our dogs.

She often cried out softly in her sleep. But one hot summer night she began screaming. I tried to wake her from her nightmare. But even when she was awake, she still lived in her dream. "I left my baby brother to burn in the fire," she sobbed into my neck.

I asked questions, gently as my mother would have, and learned what burned in her heart. In their camp in Deep Winter Place Canyon, it was her duty, as it is of all young girls, to help her mother care for her baby brother. Sometimes she strapped the beautifully decorated baby carrier onto her back and took her baby brother for walks. Other times her mother worked about the camp with the baby carrier on her back while the baby napped inside. In the canyon when Bad Hand and his soldiers came to capture her tribe, Burning Fire had been asleep and was abruptly awakened by the shouts of women. Her mother had risen before dawn, as she often did, to begin the morning duties and was not in the teepee. Burning Fire ran from the teepee to find out what was wrong. Everyone was running. There was confusion and shouting. Soldiers and horses were everywhere. Gunfire blazed. Smoke obscured the view. She was running and running, calling out in fear for her mother. When she found her mother at the edge of the camp, her mother said, "Where is the baby?" Then Burning Fire saw that the baby was not on her mother's back. She knew then that the baby was still in the teepee. Burning Fire ran back. Everyone said, "Do not go back. You will be killed." But she did, running swiftly. Teepees all over the camp were on fire, flames leaping high in the air, the white soldiers rode on their horses, shooting into the air, screaming animal sounds, and tossing burning torches into teepees. Her mother's teepee was on fire, but Burning Fire ran into the teepee anyway. She grabbed her baby brother and fled, with her own dress on fire. She ran and she ran, clutching the baby. But the baby was dead, burned like meat in a fire.

THE HORROR OF THE BURNING FIRE could not leave my adopted Cheyenne daughter's heart. I knew then that she was not given the name Burning Fire. It was the name she chose for herself. I rocked Burning Fire in my arms until the daylight, until her tears were spent, until her sobs subsided. In the morning, I spoke with her gently.

"What was your name, the name your mother gave you before the fire?" I asked.

"Running Antelope," she said. "Because I could run as fast as any brave in our clan. My ancestors were runners chosen to carry messages from one village to another over great distances."

Then Burning Fire turned her face away from me. "I am ashamed. I ran from the tent, without thinking. I ran too fast. I left the baby to burn in White Man's fire."

"I will call you Running Antelope from this day on," I said. "The spirits gave you the gift of speed. They are not angry that you ran. You did not cause the fire. You could not stop the fire. Fire does what it will. Your baby brother's death is the evil doing of the White Man's heart, not of your own."

"You will call me Burning Fire," she said, angrily. "I am *only* Burning Fire. The heart of Running Antelope died that day in the teepee. Do you not see the marks on my arms and legs? I am Burning Fire."

Then she ran, fast as a pronghorn antelope, out of my tent, and I did not see her for many days.

Then one night when the wind was cold out of the north and there was no moon, I heard a sound at the flap of my teepee, and I awoke in fear from a deep sleep. But quickly I understood it was no intruder. The girl knelt beside me shaking from cold, and in a small and quiet voice, she said, "Is it agreed? My name is Burning Fire."

I said without hesitating: "You are my daughter, Burning Fire. Fire can destroy. And fire can cleanse and make way for new life. Have you not seen that after a prairie fire, wild flowers burst up from the charred earth?"

And we lived again, Wind Storm and Burning Fire side by side, in harmony, but with few words between us.

IN THE THREE YEARS WE LIVED together in our reservation village on the large bend of the Washita River, I watched Burning Fire grow from a young girl, thin and straight as a willow sapling, to a young woman of soft shapes and graceful movements. When her breasts began to form, she was unhappy because she said now she could not run as fast or as free. So I taught her, as Gentle Wind had once taught me, to wind soft cloth about her chest, tightly binding her breasts close and firm to her body so that she could run swiftly, yet gracefully. And when her bleeding began, I taught her the purification and counting rituals to mark the cycle of womanhood, which follows the cycles of the moon. I believe that she was grateful for my teachings but she never said so. I did not require the words. I was happy that I could guide her into womanhood as I would have wished to do with my own three daughters who did not reach womanhood.

Burning Fire was beautiful to look at, and I saw how the young braves in our camp became silly in her presence, they so longed for a kind word or glance from her. She seemed not to notice. Her name now held new meaning, for she ignited a burning fire in the hearts of the young men who lingered lovesick about our campsite.

As Burning Fire journeyed into womanhood, she wished to learn the ways of her people, the Cheyenne, so she began to visit their camp, a short distance from ours. One day the proud band led by the legendary Chief Dull Knife came into Indian Territory. Dull Knife was the great old man chief of the Northern Cheyenne who came from the far north country of pines and mountain meadows. His people were very unhappy and became sick after their arrival. They loved snow and cool mountain air, just as we Plains people loved sun and wind. Their babies and their old people were dying of the sticky, hot Oklahoma air and the putrid food. The Agency had promised that if they did not like Oklahoma Territory, they would be sent back north the following year. Dull Knife wished to live in the Sioux reservation with Red Cloud in the north country. Chief Red Cloud had promised to welcome Dull Knife's people. When one year was up, the Agency broke its promise. Instead they asked Dull Knife to stay another year, and then perhaps they could move north. Dull Knife answered, "If we stay here we will all die. We will go home." So, cloaked in the greatest of secrecy, he and Little Wolf, another Cheyenne chief, began making plans to lead a large group of Cheyenne men, women and children out of their intolerable conditions. They would leave under cover of the night, taking food and weapons and horses. A number of warriors of the revered Dog Soldiers, who had fought many battles at the side of Dull Knife and Little Wolf, were ready to ride on the flanks and provide protection. Some of them had fought and defeated Custer in the Great Battle of the Little Bighorn. It was agreed the warriors would fight only when attacked. Dull Knife and Little Wolf were very wise. They explained to their warriors that the purpose of the journey was not revenge, but to reach their homeland.

I knew that Burning Fire had made friends in the Cheyenne camp. She would often sneak away at night and not return until dusk. I thought perhaps she was in love with a Cheyenne brave but was embarrassed to tell me. I remember only too well my behavior when I was young and full of the juice of life. One morning she announced her secret to me. She had been training in the cunning art of defense and survival. She had learned to use a gun, and even a bow and arrow. Dull Knife was going to lead the Cheyenne people north to their homeland.

And she was going to go with them. My heart was heavy, but I helped her pack for the journey. I gave her secret medicines and potions. I gave her a beautiful soft, doeskin dress that my mother once wore, decorated with beads and fringes. It could one day be her marriage dress. I told her the spirits of my people would protect her as she traveled through the Cimarron country where my people had lived and died.

She was excited and happy as I had never seen her before. And so I hid my heavy heart and feelings of dread as I said my motherly good-byes. I prepared her last meal before the journey and I walked with her to the Cheyenne camp. I did not allow my tears to run until Burning Fire was on her way to a new life, out of my sight.

Dull Knife's group successfully fought off attackers along the way, including a company of soldiers and buffalo hunters at the Cimarron River's Sacred Springs where I left my own dear mother to die. I know that she made it past the South Platte and the North Platte Rivers. After being surrounded by troops from all directions, Dull Knife and most of his band surrendered at Fort Robinson in Nebraska and were allowed to stay for the winter. Their horses were taken away. But they were given plenty of food and were well treated. But after that, the stories are not happy ones. At first they were promised they could journey on to the Red Cloud Agency after the winter, but then the white masters, as always, went back on their word and ordered the Cheyenne group to return to Oklahoma Indian Territory. Dull Knife refused. His people—all of them—agreed they would rather die than return. So the army locked them all in barracks—men, women and children—and cut off all food supplies for eight days. Some of the children died of starvation. Still they would not agree to go. Then their water was cut off. They licked the frost off the windows to cool their dry tongues. Some died of thirst. But other survived. Rather than die imprisoned in barracks, they planned a daring escape, for just before they had been taken by troops, the women had taken apart a few guns and hidden them in their clothing along with some knives. And so they overcame their guards and escaped from the barracks windows in the night. Many were killed, but some fled into the surrounding hills, where they preferred to battle the harsh winter than be captives to the White Man. A few of Dull Knife's band—mostly old people—were captured and sent back here against their will. That is how I know these stories. The survivors tell me that Burning Fire made her escape into the night, and they believe she lived because she was a fast runner, and was skilled with a gun and unafraid to use it.

I have heard nothing more in the ten years since she left. I have lived these years without the sparks and warmth of my Burning Fire. But I will stay alive and grow old here, in hopes one day Burning Fire will send word that she is well. Perhaps by now she has a child.

On long nights alone in my teepee, I long for my children who are not, and I grieve for my grandchildren who will never be.

Some nights I think of the day I spoke with Chief Satanta. He wished to know how my brother Two Eagles died. So I told him about that day, and about the riddle. Satanta, when he heard my story, said to me, "Your most esteemed brother was not the only one of us to fail to understand White Man's riddles. At Medicine Lodge they spoke a riddle and no one understood. All the great chiefs of all our peoples were there. And not one, not even the wise Ten Bears, understood that their promise was a riddle—a lie in the form of a riddle." Satanta spit out these last words.

"White Man told us, and they swore to it on their Holy Book and they wrote it on their papers, that our people could hunt and roam freely on the land south of the Arkansas River 'as long as the grass grew and the water flowed in our streams'. We did not understand then that one day the grass would not grow. See what they do?" Satanta threw open his arms wide, motioning toward the field of corn growing within sight of our camp. "See how they dig up the earth and destroy the grass? And not only must they do it, they wish for our Indian men to learn the ways of the plow."

The great chief was silent for a moment. His eyes stared out to the distant horizon. Then he spoke slowly. "First they killed the buffalo and drove us from the land. Then they plowed under the earth and killed the grass."

"Soon they will find a way to kill the water," I said quietly, knowing those words were in the heart of our great chief Satanta, whose voice now failed him as he struggled to keep his face strong and not show the sorrow of his heart to me, a woman.

• • •

WHEN I WAS FIRST AT THE RESERVATION, I was consumed by the need to tell the white masters what had happened. A Kiowa chief arranged for me to go to the authorities at Fort Sill to tell my story. But I did not want them to know that I spoke their language. So I took a translator with me to the fort. In my own language, I told them what happened on the ridge.

The army captain's steely gray eyes looked through me and he pretended that he did not understand what I told him. He said thank you and dismissed me, as if he heard such stories every day. He did not believe me. White men often do not believe what women tell them, not even white women. I saw that long ago when I lived with my white husband in their settlement on the Great River.

When I became old, I did finally tell someone who believed me. There was a round and merry white woman who came to spend long mornings with us. We taught her how to tan and weave and bake bread our way. She was sent by the Agency to teach us to bake bread but when we explained we did not like bread made of white powder because it had no taste, she laughed and said she also hated white powder bread. She ground her own grain to make brown bread. After that we knew she was one like us. And so I spoke to her in her own language. She promised never to tell that I could speak it. I taught her my language and she loved the sound of the words in her mouth. One day when my heart was heavy and my tears were dripping unbidden from the corners of my eyes, she noticed, and so I told her what happened.

She could not contain it. It broke her heart. I should not have told her.

THERE IS NOTHING LEFT for my people except the Dance.

I do not believe in the Dance. Nor do the elders of the *Nadi-ish-dena*. The Comanche chief forbids it. But the young people amongst the Kiowa believe it and embrace it with fervor. And secretly, some of the Comanche and Apache also do.

The Ghost Dance came to us from a Paiute Indian named Wovoka who has created a story that is a crazy mixture of White Man's religion and Indian People's longings. He said that the Messiah—the Chosen One—had come to the White People but they had rejected him and killed him. But now he was going to come to the Red People. For he knew the Red Man was wise and would welcome him. When the Chosen One came, he would bring a new earth. Vast herds of buffalo would once again fill the grass-covered Plains. The railroads and telegraph lines would disappear. All white people would suddenly be gone, and the land would be as it had been before they came to destroy and deface it. Wild ponies would roam free. Rivers would run with clear, sweet water that would never dry up. All the Plains Indians who had died would rise again and help bring the new earth into being. There would be no more sickness or war or death.

To bring about this new earth, said Wovoka, Indian people must pray and do the Ghost Dance. Some people believed that perhaps Wovoka himself was that Messiah and that the day of the return of the buffalo and the old way of life was very near.

And so they danced. It was not like a war dance with drums and quickening rhythm. It was a slow, dream-like dance that would last for three days. The dancers did not eat or take water. By the second day they would begin to swoon and see visions, visions that brought joy to their hearts. Some fell into trances and saw their beloved dead ancestors.

We heard stories that in the Northern Agencies, the white authorities feared the Ghost Dance, and there were bloody massacres when they tried to stop the Dance. In our Indian Territory, the white authorities also feared the Dance but did nothing but watch and hope the people would grow tired of it. Quanah Parker, the great Comanche chief whose mother was a white woman, forbade his followers from taking part in the Ghost Dance. It was better, he said, to partake of the ritual of Peyote if they needed visions to keep their spirits alive. In my village, half of the people believed. Half did not. Many wanted to believe it, for without the Ghost Dance, they could not go on living. I did not believe it, yet deep inside my soul I too wanted to believe.

I must admit that once I did join the Dance. I fell into a trance and I saw the visions of the brown beasts. It is my mother's vision. The hills are covered by brown beasts, as far as the eye can see. But they do not move. They do not flow north or south with the seasons, seeking new pastures. They stand in their own dung, sinking deeper and deeper into the brown mud, waiting for their death. But in my vision I see something my mother did not see. I see fences. They cannot move, they cannot escape, because the beasts are encircled by fences.

But the young ones, even the young *Nadi-ish-dena,* see other visions. And when they collapse on the ground, flushed with excitement, they believe their visions. They believe that the buffalo will again roam free across the Plains, and with them, our life will return.

I am Wind Storm, and for me the storm is never over.

25

Thomas

THOMAS BROUGHT BACK the buffalo. Not the herds of thousands as far as the eye could see, as Gentle Wind had described to me, but a raggedy dozen or so grazing behind high fences on our virgin prairie pasture.

Thomas loved animals, and they loved him back. Besides the ever-present dogs, cats, chickens and assorted farm animals, Thomas filled his existence with pets—from parrots to tropical fish to hamsters to his famous dwarf pony. Add to that goats and a donkey at various times. When Thomas was fifteen he acquired a magnificent part Arabian horse, dark brown—almost black—with a star on its forehead. He traded a painting for the horse. That was Thomas' other love. Painting. He was born an artist. Whatever was in his mind appeared almost magically on the canvas. "He needed no training"—this I heard from the high school art teacher at my ten-year class reunion. "I gave him some paint, just pointed him in the right direction and he just took over the canvas."

"He was especially good with painting animals," she recalled. "Eagles, especially. He used to drop in and we'd talk after school. There was a pair of golden eagles on your farm that he'd get real close to. He spent a lot of time observing them, understanding them."

I was surprised. I couldn't recall ever seeing any eagles on our ridge. Lots of hawks, circling all day long. But eagles? But then I had been away at college during Thomas' teen years, and obviously out of touch with my little brother's life. Yet . . . it wasn't the first or last time the possibility flitted through my mind that maybe Thomas was making things up—that maybe he had trouble separating fantasy from reality.

I had grown out of my Gentle Wind days. Perhaps Thomas had not.

"In class once, he just painted this eagle from memory," continued the art teacher, "I could never understand that—how you can remember what something looks like and just paint it. I always have to have the subject in front of me," she mused. "That was the best thing he did in my class—the eagle portrait, don't you agree? He deserved the award he got for that one."

I nodded in agreement, embarrassed and frankly miffed that I'd never heard about, much less seen, his eagle portrait or his "award."

But Thomas' crowning achievement in animal husbandry—and later the paintings it inspired—had been the buffalo herd. When Dad quit raising cattle and the pasture sat empty, Thomas had the idea of repopulating it with buffalo. He talked a few of his high school buddies into helping him construct a buffalo fence—one much higher than the normal pasture fence. And then he set about building his buffalo herd.

He found a pair—one of his famous cashless trades—then a few more. When I would come home from college on spring break, the first thing Thomas would do is take me out to the pasture to see the new buffalo calves. More of them were surviving each year. The herd had grown from seven to eighteen in three years.

I was afraid to go out to the pasture now. I didn't trust the buffalo. Thomas did. He would walk amongst them and they hardly paid him any heed. Thomas did talk me into riding Evening Star into the pasture so I could see the buffalo up close. They were magnificent. Big ancient heads, hulking, shaggy shoulders, eyes that looked both confused and incredibly sad. They were wary of me. White girl. It was as if their genes carried memories of doom that my presence evoked. They didn't seem to react that way to Thomas. He was one of them.

On long weekends home, I was no longer free to take my meandering, contemplative walks along the ridge overlooking the creek. I grumbled about it to Thomas, but he always said, "The buffalo were here first, not you." It was useless to argue that this particular herd had arrived on this pasture twelve years later than I had. Instead, I walked outside the buffalo fence along the gravel road down to the creek and sat under one of the few old cottonwoods still surviving in the small U-bend of the creek—the fenced-in buffalo pasture stopped short of the creek. The swimming hole had long dried up. The spring that once fed it no longer bubbled to the surface, but a few willows remained to mark the spot. I could remember the days when my three older brothers and their friends held contests on how long they could stay under water, frightening me witless. Would they ever emerge from the muddy, murky depths?

When Thomas graduated from high school, he attended art school in Wichita but was soon discouraged by his professors' and peers' derision of his animal paintings—too realistic, too uncool. A professor flunked him on the very buffalo portrait that would one day draw a $12,000 sum in a Taos, New Mexico art gallery—the one about which a New York art critic wrote that "the tragic wholesale slaughter of Native American culture lurks in the eyes of this magnificent, noble bull."

Thomas came home for Thanksgiving during his second year of art school—shortly after I started my reporter job in 1971. That Thanksgiving he asked Dad if he could have the 1945 Dodge flatbed truck. Dad said yes, if you can get it running. It's just sitting out back rusting. Thomas began working on it—not an easy task for him. Like me, Thomas did not communicate well with machines. They didn't hear his voice like the eagle and buffalo did.

I was there for that Thanksgiving. It was a good time for me. I was three months into a job with the *Tribune*, and had several by-lined clippings to bring home, the kind that make your parents proud. In the first few months, I had already established myself as the reporter who went "behind the headlines," finding the human stories that others overlooked.

It was a special Thanksgiving, a feast of pheasant from my dad's last hunt. I didn't know it, but it was the last time I would sit around my mother's table with my younger brother. It was a memorable holiday. Just us two kids—our older four siblings now had spouses, children, suburban dining rooms with chandeliers and turkeys roasting in their own ovens. Thomas and I were still our parents' children and this was still our home.

Thanksgiving on the Great Plains can be either in the middle of a sub-zero blizzard or in the last warm, yellow rays of summer. This particular day was sun drenched with warm, mischievous, light winds out of the west. We sat cross-legged on the back lawn after the midday meal. Thomas brought his guitar out and he strummed and we sang the old songs we used to love as children.

I left for Chicago on Sunday. He left in the truck—when he finally got it running two days later—and just disappeared from our lives. No one heard from him at all for two years. In fact, I didn't see him again for fifteen years. All we knew was that he was living out of the truck somewhere in the West.

Though I didn't see him for fifteen years, my parents did. With no forewarning, and as casually as if he lived next door, Thomas would appear at the farm, and later at my parents' retirement apartment in Denver, for an afternoon. He would sit and talk with Mom and Dad, who adored him with that special love reserved for the baby of a large family, and he'd be gone as quickly as he appeared. Never a word about where he lived, where he was going. He'd climb back into the cab of the '45 Dodge, and off he'd go.

"Mom, why don't you ask him where he goes, how he lives, does he have a job, why won't he call me, do you give him my phone number like I ask, why won't he call me, do you tell him how much I miss him?"

"Oh, we just visit," Mom would say offhandedly, "he doesn't seem to want to talk about what he does, so I don't bother asking, I'm just happy that he's well. Whatever he does, it's outdoors. He looks good, Becky, very tan, his hair is long and bleached by the sun, he puts it in a kind of ponytail. He has a beard. Tommy's very handsome—in a pioneer man kind of way. He seems to be happy. He asks about you, Becky, just like you ask about him."

I'd hang up from these phone conversations and just cry. I missed Thomas very much. I missed our childhood. I missed running free on Indian Ridge. I missed not knowing what he was like as an adult. I had only memories of him, like one has of someone who died young. I could only picture him as a tow-headed little boy running beside me, his bossy twelve-year-old tomboy sister. That's how I thought of him. Trotting alongside, contented inside his own little world, totally willing to play my Indian Ridge games, as lost in the ancient world as me.

"Doesn't he say anything about where he spends his time?" I queried Mom over and over again.

"Well, he *did* say something about the river. Spends lots of time on the river."

"What river?"

"He didn't say what river."

It was maddening. Did my parents not care where he was? What he was doing with his life? Surely if they asked him a direct question, he would answer. *They* could be calm about it I suppose. After all, he visited them—perhaps irregularly, but as my mother once pointed out, he showed up more often than I did.

Thomas must have been devastated by the loss of the farm; that pasture and its flora and fauna were part of his soul. He knew every inch, communed with everything that grew, grazed, or flew over our eighty-acre patch of virgin prairie. He loved his buffalo. Before he left that Thanksgiving, he had arranged for a high school friend to look after the herd in case it became too much for Dad. No need. My father had become as obsessed with the buffalo herd as Thomas was. He organized tours in town and people came out to see the herd and hear my father's lectures about the days when buffalo ruled the Plains. He would tell them how the herds were so large that they covered the prairie for as far as the eye could see. I once tagged along when he spoke to a fourth grade class field trip. The boys and girls were plastered against the buffalo fence enthralled with looking at the big, gentle beasts. "The herds were once so large, the train would be held up for days waiting for the herd to pass. That's why the buffalo hunters started killing them, you know, so the trains could get through." Then my father pointed out mysterious circular spots in our bottomland where the alfalfa grew in a little darker. "That's where an old buffalo wallow used to be. The ground water would seep up in those low spots and the buffalo would roll around in the mud to coat themselves with it. You know why? There was this pesky little fly that used to drive the buffalo crazy, stinging them. They actually had a very sensitive hide. The mud coating helped protect them from the insects."

My father became a trove of little-known buffalo facts, some gleaned from books and other obscure notions borrowed from Thomas' nearly endless supply of Indian lore. God knows where Thomas got his information, he rarely picked up a book.

The loss of the farm that fateful February day in 1975 had happened quickly, at a time when Thomas was out of touch. I imagine he must feel as guilty as I did about not being there to somehow stop it. I would have called our congressman. I would have started an investigation. I would have turned the Department of Agriculture upside down, if I had only known. If I had only been there. If Dad had only told me what was happening. Why did he not call on the help of his children?

Surely Thomas felt the same way. But then, Thomas, the last of his sons to leave the farm, never said "Dad, I'll stay and work the farm with you." Even though he was a product of the land and loved it dearly, Thomas wasn't a farmer, just as none of his big brothers had been. We had all valued the life farming gave us, but none of us wanted to stay and continue the Western Kansas struggle against the elements. Yet we wanted the luxury of running back to our special patch of the Plains when we needed it.

I wondered, did Thomas paint? I imagined him sleeping on a bedroll on the flatbed truck under the stars, tucked between easels, buckets overflowing with tubes of paint, and in-progress canvases. What did he do if it rained? Did he pull a plastic tarp over the truckbed, like a covered wagon?

"He has a dog," my mother once mentioned. "A mongrel of some sort. Follows him everywhere. I don't think he has a horse. Once Evening Star died, he wouldn't buy another horse."

I wondered what Thomas looked like. Mom's descriptions were suitably evocative. I could imagine him. Would I recognize him if he walked by on the street? I wondered until my best friend showed me a picture of him. I recognized him immediately.

I GUESS I HAVEN'T MENTIONED my friend Jenny. A product of a small Illinois town, Jenny is a sassy, street-smart, fast-talking, idealistic romantic. I know those traits don't belong together. But that was Jenny—a bundle of contradictions that somehow made sense when you were with her. She had over-bleached blond hair, a voluptuous figure, a sense of humor and the ability to charm any man who came into her radius—and she commanded a very wide radius. Jenny sold ads at the *Tribune,* and while immensely effective at what she did, was nevertheless perpetually in conflict with her bosses for breaking *Tribune* rules of propriety in her pursuit of ads.

Our friendship was struck when we frequented the same hot dog stand for lunch. We soon took to meeting for lunch every day and laughing over the impossible things that happened to us in the Tribune Towers. We both colored outside the lines.

Jenny is the one who gave me my Chicago name. I had graduated from Becky to Rebecca when I left for college, but everywhere I've landed, people have always insisted on giving me nicknames. In the freshman dorm at Mt. Sinai, I became Klugie. Later, Rebecca slid back to Becky when my Odyssey friends found me at the University of Kansas. In my early Chicago days, John had dubbed me his "Dorothy from Kansas." Fortunately, I was able to shed that misnomer when he dumped me. But now Jenny had her crack at it. The first day we met, she looked at me, cocked her head and said, "Forget this Rebecca stuff. It's too Victorian. You seem like a Becca to me." It stuck.

Jenny was always madly in love with someone. She seldom met a man she didn't adore. At first I thought it was fake, but at some point I realized that she really loved men. She had none of my wariness or weariness over the faithlessness and fickleness of that gender. In fact, our attitudes toward nearly everything in life were opposite, and no one, least of all the two of us, understood how we could stay friends. We were such good friends that when Jenny suggested we become room-mates, I was smart enough to say absolutely not! I knew we would be annoyed at one another's habits over the long haul. But I liked being refreshed by someone so different than me. Jenny from Kankakee.

"The only thing weirder than Kankakee, Illinois, would be if it were Kankakee, Kansas," Jenny would say. She took me to her home once, a time-forgotten Victorian frame house on a corner lot surrounded by a lovely garden and an honest-to-god white picket fence, all of which was fussed over by the most old-fashioned, sweet mom I'd ever met. Her mother baked cherry pie and wore a bib apron. Jenny explained that her father, who had been the most handsome charming man who ever lived, had divorced her mother when Jenny was twelve.

And that was the one man Jenny hated. She wouldn't talk about him, except to say that after he left, she went through his desk in an attic study and found a diary wedged behind a drawer—obviously hidden—that he had forgotten to take. She had burned it after reading it, and wished to God she'd burned it *before* she read it.

Nevertheless, Jenny fell in love with charming men just like her father over and over again. I've seen her in and out of four marriages. She won't take my advice to give her romances time to cool before walking to the alter.

But I must say, Jenny is always happiest after her divorces. In those weeks our time is filled with impromptu lavish dinners, sneaking off from the office for afternoon movies, weekend picnics in the forest pre-serve. Then she falls in love again and our contact retreats to lunch at 12:30 every day—under-the-El-tracks hot dogs on nice days, sand-wiches in Grant Park on even nicer days, and soup at no-nonsense lunch counters on lousy days. Every lunch became an occasion for laughter—not quiet, girlish tittering, but belly-jiggling, roll-on-the-sidewalk guffawing. That's the only way a Kansas farm girl tomboy and a small town Illinois hussy can survive the *Tribune* year after year. I wished I'd known her back in the days after John dumped me. She would have gotten me over him in two days flat.

After a particularly bitter divorce in 1979, Jenny decided she needed a major change of scenery so she signed up for a whitewater rafting trip down the Colorado River that originated from Moab, Utah. As near as I could tell from her description, Moab was a dusty Western town very much like my own hometown of Odyssey.

Despite my advice, she packed all the wrong things. High heels, slinky dresses—her usual tools of conquest. The river rafting outfitters provided her with a waterproof duffel bag and a sleeping bag, but when they saw what she was trying to stuff into the duffel, they sent her to the local dry goods store for cut-off jean shorts, t-shirts, rubber thongs and a supply of sunscreen. And then started what must have been an unforgettable adventure for the outfitters as well as for Jenny.

Jenny's recounting of her journey on her return was nonstop gushing. But she gushed not about the magnificent river, its dangerously thrilling rapids, the stunning red rock cliffs of the canyon or the serenity of sleeping on sandbars under the stars. No, all she could gush about was the river runner who piloted her raft.

"He was the most beautiful specimen of mankind I've ever seen. Tall, lanky, tanned limbs, flowing, long locks, bleached nearly white from the sun. He never wore shoes. He seldom talked except to tell us Indian lore and point out every ancient ruin, every petroglyph carved into the cliffs. He knew so much about the Indians who once inhabited the canyon, he must have been one of those archeologist dropout professors. Gorgeous, Becca, he was incredible."

"What was his name?"

"Tom. But I called him River Jesus. That's what he looked like, a beautiful, blond Jesus with flowing hair. I had to stop calling him that because it offended this uptight fundamentalist couple on my raft. They said, 'Excuse me, but you are taking the Lord's name in vain.' I thought they meant my swearing, but it was the River Jesus thing that got their noses out of joint.

"Of course everything about me offended them," continued Jenny. "Especially my swimsuit. There was no point in wearing anything else because we were always getting wet."

"If it was that green bikini of yours, you wouldn't have to be a fundamentalist to be offended at that," I countered.

"Another reason I called him Jesus is he had these scars on his hands. You know, like nail marks, but not in his palms, but on the outside of his wrists, actually. Several long scars, like he had cut markings into the skin. I couldn't make sense of them. It wasn't like scars from slashing your wrist—God knows, I've seen enough of those—it was on the outside of his wrist. Maybe some ritual thing." (Jenny had a younger sister who had repeatedly attempted suicide by slashing her wrists, and eventually did so successfully. That was another thing Jenny never talked about. Only once, when she was very drunk did she tell me about her sister. Until that moment I never knew she had one.)

"He was a real Jesus, must have taken a vow of celibacy. Nothing I did or said had any effect on him. He never once looked at me like men look. But I know he wasn't gay. It wasn't that kind of disinterest. I was just a person to him, not a woman, if you know what I mean."

I knew what she meant. "Story of my life. Go on."

"The wet t-shirt, nothing worked on him."

"Jenny, aren't you going to tell me about the trip?" I asked. "What about the rapids? What about sleeping in sleeping bags. I can't even imagine you . . ."

"He was a real river rat—that's what they called each other. There was this other boatman, I think he was the owner of the outfitter company. Joe, good guy. I should have turned my attention to him. Not bad, fairly good looking, but the kind of guy who probably drinks too much. And frankly he was too much like my last ex. Depressed, a little grumpy. Anyway, just before Brown Betty—that's the name of one of the rapids, the two of them pulled the rafts off to the side, told us to get out, and they hiked up ahead and just sat on a boulder looking down at the rapid. For a half-hour, maybe an hour, just looked. Didn't talk. Just stared at it.

"Joe finally came back. But Tom stayed. 'What's he doing?' I asked Joe.
'Talking to the river.'
'Talking?'
'Tom believes you gotta talk to the river, get its permission before going down the chute.'
'What's a chute?'
'You'll find out, Miss Illinois.'

"By the third day," continued Jenny, "I decided I had to crack my blond Jesus. So I waited until everyone was asleep. We all just dragged our bedrolls out onto the sand, no tents, no privacy. Only the fundie couple insisted on a tent. God knows why. They would have been too afraid to get it on, in case one of us might hear some grunting.

"So, anyway, I snuck out to where the river runners slept, near the campfire and the beer coolers. I thought I'd have a quiet conversation with Tom, just wake him up with some little emergency or something.

"He wasn't in his sleeping bag. Joe was, and he woke up and asked what I wanted. 'I have to ask Tom about something. Where is he? Doesn't he ever sleep.'

'Naw, he goes up to the top.'

'What does he do up there?'

'Talks with the coyotes, prays, does rain dances. I don't know what he's doing. Maybe he wants to get some sleep away from pesky passengers with dumb questions.'

"Like I told you, Joe was grumpy. Then I noticed, Tom left to climb into the cliffs every night. Never came down until morning. Strange man. But beautiful."

There was no point in asking Jenny any questions about any other aspect of the trip. The raft trip, the side trip to the Grand Canyon, or her week in Vegas. There was only one thing on her mind. I had forgotten how annoying Jenny could be when she set her sights on an unattainable man. And I was particularly annoyed about this one.

"If he's so beautiful, did you bring home any photos so I can see?" I asked.

"Of course, but I haven't taken them in for processing, yet."

A week later, after daily reminders about where the photos were, and her telling me she didn't have time to pick them up, I demanded the Kodak stubs from her, and went to the Jewel and picked them up myself.

I ripped open the envelopes. Good close-up taken from the back of the raft aiming forward at the river runner straining through a rapid. Good action. Water spraying, droplets caught in mid-air. There he was. This god in flowing blond locks—part of it pulled back in a ponytail, strands slipping out, muscles rippling as he rowed, a look of innocent joy on his face.

It was Thomas.

26

The River

IT WAS FOR THIS MOMENT, June 19, 1979, that was my friendship with Jenny was born.

I glanced at the clock. 6 P.M. First I called Jenny and asked her to look after my cat and water my two sickly plants, telling her to look in the usual hiding place for my apartment keys. Then I left a message on my editor's voice message tape at the *Tribune* saying I was off to follow an important lead on a story and would communicate later. Then I called for a taxi, grabbed my small suitcase which was always packed with basic essentials so I could leave on a trip at a moment's notice, first pulling out the business suit and heels, and replacing them with jeans, boots, khaki shorts and sandals. Within fifteen minutes, I was on my way to O'Hare, a new record. I've always kept track of the time such departures took. The one thing I didn't do was call Margaret. Whenever I leave for somewhere, I phone my older sister Margaret—it's a deal we have—to let her know where I'm going. I didn't this time because she wouldn't understand my coming through Denver and not stopping to see her or Mom and Dad. Plus, I didn't want to tell her about Thomas. No need to raise her hopes until I found him. If I called, I wouldn't be able to keep the excitement out of my voice and somehow she'd know.

I blustered my way onto the first United non-stop to Denver, getting in at midnight, crashed a few hours in the airport, still not calling Margaret, and took the first early morning commuter flight to Grand Junction, Colorado, where I rented a car. Heading out I-70 West into Utah, I turned off on Highway 128 which, judging from the map, appeared to be a shortcut to Moab. Soon I found myself angling through Castle Valley, a beautiful, pristine desert landscape of red rock towers. Only then did I begin to reflect on the upcoming reunion. I was going to see Thomas. I was bursting with joy and anticipation. It had been so many years. Already, I knew the basic outlines of his life. He was a river runner, and his river was the magnificent Colorado River, which flowed west from its trickle-beginning at the Continental Divide, cutting the deep gorge of Glenwood Canyon before it left Western Colorado and crossed into Utah. There, it widened to a red desert river skirting Arches National Park filled with its mythical towering shapes and wind-carved arches. Highway 128 was now twisting and turning as it followed along the banks of the Colorado River. I mentally added this road to the list for my book on the most beautiful highways of America.

I had picked up rafting brochures in the Grand Junction airport as well as maps of the area. Jenny's four-day raft trip had been with an outfitter called Travis Tours. Her trip had originated thirty miles southwest of Moab and traveled through Cataract Canyon, passing through several rapids, terminating in the locally-hated Lake Powell, created by a dam that obliterated miles of beautiful canyon habitat and ancient Indian ruins, all to create a "recreational" lake for boaters. (This I learned from my seatmate on the commuter plane flying into Grand Junction, a Utah rancher who had bitterly opposed the dam.) Further downstream, this magnificent river carved the Grand Canyon, and then, as the river headed west, its water was stolen to satiate the thirst of Los Angeles before it crossed, now reduced to a trickle, into Mexico.

Driving into town, I noticed several billboards advertising river rafting outfitters, all competing loudly to introduce tourists to the thrills of whitewater rafting. I didn't see a billboard for Travis Tours even though their brochure said they were the first in the area. But I found their place: a low, ranch style log building with a wide front porch. The parking lot was empty. Out back behind a high wire fence, were old repainted school buses with rubber rafts lashed to trailers behind them, as if ready to head for the river. When I reached the door, a hand-lettered sign said, "CLOSED FOR BUSINESS." Someone had scratched out the word "business" and written in "Good." I knocked several times and tried to peer through the windows to see if anyone was inside. I saw desks messy with papers and coffee cups, giving the place the look of having been evacuated suddenly rather than deliberately cleared out.

Not willing to give up easily, I went around to a back door and pounded. It was no use. The place was deserted.

I drove to the center of the town, finding where Moab's main street intersected the highway. If this town was anything like Odyssey, and I had a hunch it was, any local person could tell me exactly where to find Joe, the name I remembered from Jenny's speculation about the owner of Travis Tours. Their tour brochure offered no names, but described Travis Tours as "family owned and operated for three generations."

But if I was to get any cooperation I needed to look like I belonged, not like a tourist from "back East." My traveling clothes were wrong, so I u-turned at the center of town and headed back to a gas station a mile out. There, I rolled my suitcase into the restroom and hastily changed into jeans, t-shirt, and cowboy boots, pleased that the boots looked scuffed and in need of polish. I scrubbed off any remnant lipstick. No doubt I was walking into something potentially unpleasant. The hand-scrawled "Closed for Good" looked angry.

There were several pickups parked in front of a bar named the Cottonwood. So I walked into the drug store a block down from it. A rotund middle-aged woman at the register looked local and chatty.

"Have you seen Joe? He's not where he was supposed to meet me, and he sure as hell isn't at Travis!" I said.

"Who knows if he's still in town," she shrugged. She was trying to figure out if she recognized me.

"I know he's in town. I just talked to him this morning. He doesn't move that fast."

"You telling me?"

She paused. Then she passed judgment on me. "I'd try the bars," she said nonchalantly. She chewed gum like a teenager.

"Cottonwood still his favorite?"

"Ain't it everybody's?"

"Not mine. It's seen better days."

"You telling me?"

It was midday but so dark in the bar I couldn't make out anything when I first walked in. The building must have once been a retail store of some sort. A wall of windows facing the street had been painted black from the inside to keep out the light. I was pretty sure I would recognize Joe from the photos "temporarily borrowed" from Jenny. On the plane I'd picked out who I guessed was Joe loading provisions onto a raft. He was red haired with a scruffy beard and a perpetual sunburn.

Sure enough. I had no trouble picking him out, once my eyes adjusted to the dark. He was alone at a booth. I walked over and sat opposite him.

"Joe Travis, I'm guessing?" I was taking a calculated risk that the tour company name was also the family name. I was right.

He looked up from his beer, his eyelids heavy, his whole face tired and sagging. "So you found me. Hooray for you." He acted like he knew who I was and why I was looking for him.

"It wasn't that hard."

He didn't respond.

"To *find* you. It wasn't that hard," I repeated.

"So which are you? The victim's relative, come to shoot me? Or the victim's lawyer, come to sue me?"

"Neither."

"Okay. You want me to guess." Joe Travis' speech was slurred. "You're somebody I laid back in college but can't remember because I was drunk. I'm the father of your child who you just found out needs braces. And you want a little belated child support."

"Wrong again. I've never seen you before in my life."

"But you look familiar. Come on, you're an old girlfriend, right?"

He was wearing a dirty white t-shirt with the sleeves cut out. His arms were covered with dense soft reddish-gold hair. That, plus a dusting of tiny freckles on his arms and face is what made him look sunburned in the photo. Obviously weathered beyond his years, I guessed he was late-thirties. I wasn't sure if he was sober enough to hold a real conversation.

"Actually, I'm not looking for you. I'm Tom's sister. I'm looking for *him*."

"Well he's left town. I doubt I'll ever see him again. He shouldn't, but he feels responsible."

"For what?"

"You don't know? The accident. The *death,* for Godssake. Everybody knows about it. Ten o'clock news every night. Every tourist who drives into town knows about it. You the only one in Moab who doesn't know every bloody detail?"

"I just flew in from Chicago. I haven't seen a local newscast. Was

Tom involved in some accident?"

"No, *I'm* involved in some accident," he said sarcastically. "They were on *my* J-rig."

"I'm sorry," I mumbled.

"I should've never let that girl ride bronco on the tip. She and her mother both fell off on Big Drop Number Two. But her mother did what I'd told them, went feet first through the rapids, kicking off the rocks. The girl didn't. She just panicked, I guess. Head first into a boulder, ripped her skull open. I couldn't do a damn thing." He rambled on as if talking aloud to himself. "I had twelve other people on my boat to get through. Tom was down below. He made it through the chute just fine. Saw it happen too. He couldn't do a damn thing but collect her body down below.

"You know, they all sign liability waivers. They're warned that anything can happen. This isn't Disneyland, you know. This is the River. It's unpredictable. The Grand Canyon is actually safer for tourists, the rapids are always the same, day after day, because they let out the water from that goddamn Glen Canyon dam at a steady rate. But this is the real thing up here. The River is never the same one day to the next. They sign waivers, you know."

He lifted his bottle in a mock toast. "My lawyer says those waivers mean shit."

"So you're being sued for wrongful death?" I hated myself for sounding like a reporter.

"Hell, no. But I will be. As soon as they find me. Next person to walk in the door could be serving me papers. No point in hiding. Here, have a beer with me."

"I don't like beer."

"Tom won't drink 'em either."

That reminded him. "Oh yeah, you're Tom's sister. That's why you look familiar."

Joe Travis was just like the guys I went to high school with in Odyssey—tough and vulnerable at the same time. I needed to get him out of the Cottonwood before a real lawyer walked in there to see him recklessly, remorsefully drunk. I slipped his keys, which were laying on the table, into my pocket and told the bartender I'd settle up later, I was driving Joe home.

"Don't worry about it. He's got a tab of sorts. And thanks, you're sav-ing me the trouble of doing it myself."

Joe was puppydog grateful for me to drive him to his ranch house three miles east of town, directing me down a dirt road that kicked up a dense cloud of red dust behind us. There were two horses in a fenced-in pasture behind the house, some deteriorating sheds and barns out back, and an old rusting windmill. The yard was clearly the remnants of an early Utah ranch, probably back from the days when Moab was lit-tle more than a wide spot on the road. Joe was wobbly but not falling-down drunk. Once on his home territory, he became embarrassed and awkwardly gracious. "You can stay here, so you don't have to pay tourist robbery rates at a motel. If you want to. I've got three extra, unused bedrooms. Just pick the cleanest one. When I'm feeling a little more steady, we'll go looking for Tom."

I was relieved. I didn't want to let him out of my sight until he could lead me to Thomas.

"Are you hungry? Aw, I shoulda got you something at the Cottonwood. Best burgers in Utah."

"I'm fine. You sleep. We'll worry about dinner when you wake up. I got only three hours in that crappy Denver airport last night. I could use a long nap myself."

He disappeared into his room. (Inviting me—a near stranger—to stay at his home was such an "Odyssey" kind of thing to do, I felt com-fortable about accepting.) I brought in my suitcase and chose the small-est of the three bedrooms and fell into a long, deep sleep.

It was dark when I awoke. For a few minutes I didn't know where I was. I smelled coffee.

"You're an angel, you know," Joe Travis grinned, pulling out a chair for me as I wandered into the kitchen. "Elmer says they did come look-ing for me a half-hour after we left. Process server, lawyer, he doesn't know who. Thank God I wasn't there. Elmer sent 'em over to my lawyer's office so they wouldn't come here to the ranch. This is serious business and I shouldn't be running off at the mouth with them."

"Or with you, for that matter. Sorry," he added shyly.

"It doesn't matter what you told me," I assured him. "You were with a friend."

As I'd guessed, the Travis family was one of the original families to settle the Moab valley. Their ranch predated the town. Joe's grandfather was one of the first to go down the Colorado on a raft, and his son, Joe's father, was chosen to guide the Army Corp of Engineers in their charting of Cataract Canyon. He and Joe's grandfather informally took wealthy industrialist adventurers down the river and eventually turned it into a business far more lucrative than cattle ranching. The Travis family sold off most of their ranch to the growing town and continued to live on their home place.

Joe was left alone on the family ranch and with the family business because his parents had decided to retire in Tucson. "They wanted a dry climate. Do you believe it? How the hell can any place be drier than Moab?"

"We were here first, hell, we pioneered the outfitting business," Joe explained. "My dad and I, and our guides know this river better than anyone. These other outfits came in here from Wyoming and Montana. They're actually big corporations. They've had accidents and don't think anything about it. Their insurance pays out. They don't care. They don't miss a beat. Oh, we got insurance too. But our family never lost anyone before. Lawsuit or not, I'll fold the company before I ever let it happen again." Joe was silent for a moment. "Maybe Tom is right. He says the river is telling us to stop taking people down."

I was grateful to pick up information about Thomas without even having to ask a question.

"No matter how careful we are," Joe continued, "we're destroying the canyon one grain of sand at a time. Tom told me that day that the river was angry. He said we shouldn't do Big Drop that morning. I said we got to, there's a helicopter coming to pick up our people at Lake Powell tomorrow noon and we have to be there. What could we do? Hike twenty-three people out of that canyon? The river is the only way in or out.

"Tom kept saying, 'Big Drop is boiling with anger.' See, that's why he felt responsible. He saw it coming. We've been down the river a hundred times or more together. Tom never said anything like that before. I didn't listen. When I insisted we were going down, he said he'd go first. I should watch him.

"He made it through. When I went, we got caught in a hole. Almost turned us over. Coming out of it we got hit from the side. It shot us into the air. It's a wonder everybody didn't fall off. It's a wonder we lost only one. She was only sixteen years old. I'll never fall asleep again without seeing her face."

Joe was clearly devastated by the event. I wasn't sure if talking about it helped him or pulled him deeper into the vortex of his anguish.

"How can I find Tom?"

"I know of a few of his favorite places. Old Indian sites, mostly. But the only way to reach them is to go down the river, and I'm never going to run it again."

"It's been your life, Joe. You have to go down the river. Take me. I want to see these places Thomas loves."

We barbecued steaks on a greasy grill out back and wrapped corn on the cob in foil and put it on the grill. While cooking and while eating, I cajoled, then pleaded with Joe until he said. "Alright. I'll take you down. I can't promise we'll find Tom. He could be in Mexico by now for all I know."

Joe said most of Thomas' favorite spots were not more than a half-hour's hike from the river. "But we're putting out before Big Drop if I don't feel comfortable about running it. That means a two-day hike out of there. No complaints."

"Deal."

"You got hiking boots?"

"Of course."

We sneaked into the Travis Tours office before dawn to pack provisions and gear. Joe chose a four-man rubber raft, without a motor. "I like to run quiet," he said. Towing the raft behind his pickup, we drove to a put-in spot on the Green River. The dirt road down into the Green River canyon—where Joe says they captured Butch Cassidy and the Sundance Kid—was steep and hairpin. Below, the meandering, orange colored river was thickly lined with apple-green tamarisk trees. Once the Green joined the Colorado we were sheltered between the high, sheer, red walls of a canyon so lovely I understood why Thomas had made river running his life.

Every place has a color. The color of Moab, this canyon, this part of Utah, was orange. Not a simple orange, but a complex array of colors from yellow gold to rust to salmon to vermilion to hints of purple. It was a palette of colors so warm, so overwhelmingly joyous, I could hardly contain myself. On the Plains, the overpowering sky displays a never-ending variety of blues. Here, the blue of the sky, while no less beautiful, merely provided a contrasting backdrop for the heroic orange. On the Plains, the horizon stretches forever, with you standing tall on top of the surface of the world. Here, surrounded by the magnificent canyon walls with their spires and arches and fantastical shapes carved by rushing wind and water, here, you stood in the depths of a great bowl looking up. It was the exact opposite of the Plains, yet I felt the same sense of awe mixed with calm.

Most of the first day we floated in what Joe called "flat water," where the river flows gently with no rapids and barely a ripple. No need to paddle. Most of the time we didn't even need to steer. The river moved our raft along effortlessly. We began to talk about Thomas.

I explained that Thomas had been out of touch with me for years, which I couldn't quite explain to Joe, except to say that Thomas was like a beautiful wild animal not bound by time or space. But I felt, in my soul, that he would be happy to see me if I found him, that we shared a common bond of love for the earth from our childhood days on Indian Ridge.

Joe said that he understood. That his own friendship with Tom was deep but transitory. Even though Tom was his best river runner, he always knew one day he'd wake up and Tom would be gone, moved on. "I'm surprised he stayed with me for eight years. Every year, when the season was over, about October, he'd disappear, and I'd never know if he'd show up in that damn truck in time for the first trip in April.

"One time, a couple of years ago, he didn't show up for the Monday four-day. I figured he'd moved on, didn't think much about it, except I was a little pissed he didn't tell me, so I could replace him. Then when I come back in after the four-day, the sheriff says, 'I got one of your river rats in my jail. Wanna get him out?'

"It seems they picked him up because the truck didn't have license plates," recounted Joe. "They claimed it was stolen. Who'd want to steal a truck like that? I was really pissed."

"Thomas didn't call you to get him out?"

"To tell you the truth, he was in really bad shape. Never saw him anything like that before or since. Couldn't stand being in a cage. I knew how he felt. Happened to me a few times, back when I was drinking hard. But he was wild, pacing, talking nonsense. Something about a buffalo fence."

"He had a buffalo herd in our pasture. Did he ever tell you about his buffalo?"

"Can't remember him ever mentioning it. The sheriff brought in a forensic psychiatrist from Salt Lake City to examine Thomas," Joe continued. "I think they had him pegged for some psycho serial killer who'd struck in Salt Lake City years ago. Anyway, they examined him and said he was schizophrenic—apparently Tom was hearing voices. They asked me if he took medication, and if he did, could I go find it." Anger rose in Joe's voice just thinking about it. "I told those sons of bitches that Tom was saner than anybody in the room and didn't take medication. And please, let me make bail. I needed him back on the river, since he was my most reliable runner."

We fell silent. I think Joe saw the tears in my eyes despite my sunglasses. I felt deeply pained, thinking of Thomas stuck in some jail. He must have felt like one of his buffalo. He was always talking about how it was a shame to have to keep them behind fences. They were born to roam. This land belongs to them, he'd say.

Finally I asked Joe, "Do you think Thomas is schizophrenic?"

"Nah," he said, slowly and deliberately, "It may be true that schizophrenics hear voices, but not everyone who hears voices is schizophrenic."

On the Colorado River, by day, the sun beats down relentlessly until you long to hide from it. And sometimes we did. Joe would row over to the edge of the river and stop in the shade where the steep canyon wall blocked out the sun. Or we'd disembark on a sandbar and seek shade behind tamarisk trees or a boulder. (Joe hated the tamarisk which he said didn't belong on the Colorado River. The shrub had been brought in from Asia for erosion control and had spread rapidly, now choking out the willows and cottonwood that once lined the banks. The parasite-like tamarisks were literally sucking precious water out of the river, said Joe.) The sand was white and fine, so fine it would fall through a flour sifter, just like the sand in the dry riverbed of the Cimarron at Wagonbed Springs. As we rested, I let handfuls fall through my fingers.

After lunch, Joe took me upriver a bit, hiking over boulders to a sheer wall a few feet from the river's edge. "There's something I want to show you," he said. "Do you see it?"

Like many of the canyon walls, this expanse was coated with a kind of black, iridescent smear, looking almost oily. "This sooty stuff, I asked?"

"That's desert plaque, sometimes called patina or desert varnish—everybody's got a different name for it. Locals call it slick rock. But it's not soot. It's formed from certain bacteria on the rocks attracting natural minerals in the air—mostly iron oxide. But that's not what I was referring to. Look lower down, about five feet up from the bottom."

Then I saw them. Intricate drawings carved into the stone. Some of it stippled, like we used to do in Vacation Bible School class on copper sheets. I could make out what appeared to be a bear, some antelope-like creatures with long horns, a row of abstract, geometric-shaped human figures carrying round things, perhaps shields, and holding tall spears at their sides. The figures had elaborate headdresses.

"The canyon was inhabited from ancient times, as early as 10,000 BC," Joe explained. "The Paleo-Indians probably hunted mammoths as well as bison and antelope. Then around the first century A.D. came the Anasazi cultures, ancestors of the Pueblo Indians. We find a lot of their pottery. Some of these petroglyphs were carved and stippled onto these desert walls perhaps 5,000 years ago—that's around the time the pyramids were built in Egypt," Joe explained, lapsing into his tour guide voice. "Some are more recent, but still many centuries old. They tell stories of hunts, of brave warriors, of celebrations, who the hell knows what all. I am amazed and humbled every time I look at them."

So was I. And I was even more amazed that no one had put up a fence to protect this treasure. What if some tourist just walked up and tried to add his initials to the scene? Some half-drunk teenager out to impress his girlfriend. And then I thought with a silent giggle, maybe this was ancient graffiti left by some peyote-stoned teenager doing just that, impressing his girlfriend in 3,000 BC? I kept this irreverent thought to myself.

"There are hundreds, no thousands of these, on walls all over these canyons," Joe said, as if reading my mind. "Locals are used to finding them. I've never heard of anyone trying to deface them, though I'm sure it has happened. We grow up here with a respect for the petroglyphs."

"No one knows more about them than Thomas," Joe continued. "I've seen him stand here five hours without moving, just studying every detail, thinking. Not saying a word."

As we floated down flat water, sometimes the silence would be broken by the sound of a tour group's motorized raft or J-rig coming downriver. We'd pull off to the side to let them pass. The J-rigs, which were three pontoons lashed together, could hold a dozen or more passengers. The tourists would shout and wave as they passed. "I hate motorized rafts, they're so noisy, it destroys the peace of the canyon," Joe would mutter.

The tourists were noisy too, I noticed.

In the late afternoon, the moment the sun fell below the tops of the canyon wall, relief set in. The whiffs of the wind carried an undercurrent of delicious chill.

Nights are very special in the canyon. We were blessed with a full moon, and at that magic moment when it rose above the canyon wall and entered our available sky, the sandbar was instantly flooded with light. It was almost too bright for sleeping, and I could hardly close my eyes because there was so much to see. When I finally did, I noticed there was also much to hear. I unrolled my sleeping bag far enough away from Joe to maintain privacy, but close enough to feel protected from the coyotes that howled somewhere out of sight. I felt twelve years old again, sleeping under the stars, listening to coyotes in the heady days before the Clutter incident and irrigation wells changed our lives.

By the second day in the canyon, I had decided, as I've decided so many times before, that it was time to leave Chicago. Find a place that I really loved.

"This is where I belong," I said to Joe, as I lounged back on the raft marveling at the pink-orange rock formations of the canyon walls.

I was miffed when Joe said, "That's what everyone says on the second day." I wondered if that's how he viewed me. Another city tourist naively discovering nature, spouting cliches I'd later forget. I decided to keep my mouth shut and enjoy the beauty of the canyon in private if he was going to mock my sincerity. I had, after all, grown up on an old Indian campsite overlooking the confluence of the Sand Arroyo and the North Fork of the Cimarron. How dare he treat me like some city slicker out for four days of bought-and-paid-for self-discovery.

Brown Betty broke the silence. That was the first of several rapids, and apparently not one that Joe feared. Even so, he pulled the raft to the side and got out above it, scrambling over the boulders to find a good vantage point, then he stared at the rapid hard and long before he said, "Okay, ready for the first one?"

I'll admit I was afraid. But we slipped through the rapids smoothly and effortlessly, with little more than Joe's upper body muscles and a set of oars to get us through. I realized that Joe was a very skilled white-water rafter indeed. He made it seem easy, but I saw how he anticipated every movement, every nuance, how he watched and waited and moved at the right moment in a dance with the river. It was like sex. Very, very, good sex. Once in the pool below, looking up at the power of the rapids we'd come through, I realized how addicting the rush from running a rapid must be to a true river rat.

I forgot that I was irritated with Joe.

Brown Betty was enough for me. I wondered, with not a little panic, how massive Big Drop Number Two must be. For my sake, I hoped Joe would decide not to attempt it. But for Joe's sake, I knew he must.

My heartbeat had just returned to normal, and I was feeling good about flat water again, when Joe said. "We'll make camp early tonight. We're near a favorite spot of Tom's."

While we unloaded the raft, Joe explained. "Tom always insisted on making camp here, then after supper, he'd disappear. If I asked where he was going he'd say, 'Gotta go talk to my eagles.'"

It was more than a two-hour hike to Thomas' spot, mainly because Joe didn't know exactly where it was. He said he'd recognize it when he found it. Dark had fallen before we spotted it. Above us on the edge of a cliff we saw a silhouetted figure. We first mistook it for a tree stump. Quietly we picked our way around for a better view. We saw him, kneeling with both arms outstretched horizontally, forming a human cross. His head was bowed. His whole body motionless. Joe and I glanced at one another and instinctively remained motionless as well. Then an extraordinary thing happened. An eagle swooped in and alighted on the wrist of one outstretched arm. Moments later, a second eagle alighted on his other arm. For some moments Thomas remained motionless. It was as if his arms were indeed the limbs of a tree. Then slowly he moved his head up to look left then right at his eagle companions, then lowered his head again and remained motionless.

"Now I know how he gets those scratches on his wrists," whispered Joe. More silence, we didn't even move. Joe finally asked, "What do you want to do?"

"We need to leave him, let him be alone," I whispered.

Moving silently, praying the rocks wouldn't slide as we inched down, we moved out of sight. Then wordlessly we started hiking down.

"I know a fast way to get back to camp," said Joe. We were on the edge of a precipice with a kind of crack in the sandstone wall filled with sand, sort of a rockslide composed of loose sand. The moon disappeared behind some clouds, and momentarily the canyon became dark. "Sit down, butt in the sand, and shove off," Joe instructed. "Think of this as a very long slipper slide. I'll go first. If you get stuck, push off, get sliding again."

Joe sat down on the sand and was gone. I shoved off. And then I was sliding, sliding, sliding down a chute of fine sand on the world's longest natural slide, being helplessly pulled away from my little brother. The night breeze was playing in my hair. Then I was laughing. A child on her first carnival ride. Lost in some crazy, surreal dream. This could not be real. Sliding, slipping down the walls of an ancient canyon on an exquisite moonlit night. My breast felt as if it was bursting open. The human heart cannot take such beauty and joy. It was too much, simply too much joy.

I stopped moving. Too giddy, too dizzy to stand. Joe was there to help me to my feet.

"You'll never see anything like this again. This is an original," he stated matter-of-factly. "I save this treat only for the tourist groups I really, really like. Last year that was only one group. They get harder and harder to like every year."

I followed after him reluctantly, as we picked our way the remainder of the way down to our white sand campsite.

"We'll get up early and find his camp in the morning. Can't be too far from where we saw him."

At dawn, with nothing more than a drink of water from our canteen, we set out to the top. We looked in every direction, back and forth, searching for his camp. There was no trace. No tell-tale truck tire marks in the sand, no footprints, no remnants of a campfire. Nothing. At noon we gave up.

Two days, four rapids, and one helicopter ride later, we were back in Moab having a greasy hamburger at the Cottonwood.

"I'm going to stop drinking," said Joe.

"I'm going to start," I replied.

We had reduced our conversation to one-liners. I'd reverted to Western Kansas man talk, which I'd guess is pretty close to Moab Utah talk.

"You want me to keep trying to find Tom?" Joe asked.

"You won't find him. He belongs to another world."

Joe nodded in agreement.

I added what Joe already knew, "You can't go to him. He can only come to you."

"I don't think he's ever coming back here," said Joe. "Something tells me that he was up there saying goodbye to the eagles."

I went home empty-handed, heavy-hearted. I had missed my one chance, but it had been my own decision. I could never have interrupted Thomas' communion with the eagles in the spiritual quietude of that moonlit canyon. I could only console myself with the knowledge that I had at least seen him.

On the plane, I brooded about homelessness, his and mine. Perhaps Thomas did not feel homeless. Perhaps, like the eagles, he alighted where he wished and all the world was home.

While I long to wander, and feel a kind of envy for Thomas' nomadic life, somewhere down in the pit of my being I do feel homeless. I long for the gray-green pastures of home.

But I have no home.

27

T. S. Eagle

EVERY SINGLE TIME I GET UP the courage to quit my job and leave Chicago, something intervenes. When I returned from my unauthorized week in Utah, my boss was livid. It was not the first time. I was in fact famous for leaving town without permission or notice, other than my usual after hours answering tape message. Sometimes my sudden departures were for legitimate stories, but more often they were to bolt back to Kansas for a "family emergency," which, in reality, was feeding my own need to return to my geographical and metaphysical center. So after reading the seething memo waiting in my office mailbox, I began to compose my resignation letter. It was good that it had finally come to a head. It was time for me to head west if not home.

I can't go home. I have no home.

When I knocked on my boss' office door to deliver my letter, he ushered me to a seat, thanking me for coming by as if he had called for the meeting. He was remarkably cordial, asking me about Utah as if he had no memory of his scathing memo. (If I do not use a name for my boss, it is because the name constantly changes as positions shuffle in the company. Lucky for me. If I'd had the same boss during my whole tenure at the paper, I would have been fired years ago.)

"I have something to give you," I said, proffering the letter.

He waved it away. "First, let me tell you what I have on my mind. A vacancy has just come up for foreign correspondent covering Western Europe. Are you interested?"

• • •

FOR THE FIRST FEW MONTHS I was based in London, a city I knew and loved from my University College days there. Within a few months, the paper moved me to Paris, where I rented a small flat in the St. Germaine des Pres area on the Left Bank. From my bedroom window I could look directly out on the bell tower of the eleventh-century church of St. Germaine, and I woke to its deep melodic tolling at ten o'clock on Sunday mornings when I had the luxury of sleeping late. In Paris, I found myself blending into a culture that I curiously knew little about. At first, I spoke not a word of French and knew even less about the country's history. Nevertheless, I sometimes rounded a street corner at night, and a scene would pack such a wallop of déjà vu—one of the few French terms I knew—it would take my breath away. The glittering lights. The blended musical sounds of conversation in the sidewalk cafes. Paris was strangely familiar and comforting. I would have been content to stay there forever.

My beat was all of Western Europe, which meant I was always rushing off to another capital. I will never forget the excitement as I watched the Berlin Wall being torn down, stone by stone, by both West and East Germans. *Something there is that doesn't love a wall,* said the poet Robert Frost. Objective reporting out the window, I cried and screamed in joy, and jumped in to tear pieces of concrete away with my own hands. I could never be a TV reporter, because I cannot feign aloofness with the surge of history around me. Given a short lapse of time, I can fake it on a piece of paper. But in the moment, I am part of it. God, I loved being there when the wall came down.

Bill, my photojournalist buddy, was assigned to Europe as well. Our schedules seldom allowed us to be in the same city at the same time, but there were some three-day weekends when we slipped away to Cannes, the French Alps, or castles along the Rhine.

There were times in France when I traveled on my own, discovering vast flat wheat fields and roadside sunflowers in the Loire Valley and I was strangely reminded of Kansas. One weekend, I stayed at a small chateau in central Normandy, and as I was coming down for breakfast, I passed a portrait on a stairway landing. I felt a jolt of recognition, as if I knew the man in the painting, deeply, intimately. Despite his dandy eighteenth-century garb, his curly, white wig and powdered checks, he looked like someone I knew. Even more strange, he knew me. His eyes followed me down the stairs. I was so shaken, my coffee cup rattled in my hand as I tried to have breakfast.

I don't believe in reincarnation. And if I did, I surely was not the consort of some effeminate, overbearing French nobleman with pale skin, I kept telling myself. I asked the host of the manor, a disheveled little man with dirty oversized glasses, who insisted on being addressed as "Prince," about the portrait. "That is Sieur de Bourgmont, an eighteenth-century adventurer briefly granted this estate by King Louis the XV when he returned from exploring in the New World in 1725. He died without an heir and the property was restored to its former noble inhabitants, my family." The prince then launched into a detailed history of his own rather boring ancestors.

I kept trying to ask questions about Bourgmont, a name I'd never seen before in the history books. "Why was Bourgmont granted a noble title?"

The prince, annoyed at my questions, finally informed me that Bourgmont was a thief, a scoundrel, once even arrested in his youth for poaching on this very estate. He was not of noble lineage, explained the prince. "He literally fled to the Americas to avoid prosecution for various crimes, and then into the uncharted American interior to avoid arrest for bedding the wife of his commanding French army officer.

"An explorer? Hah! A fugitive, more precisely. But apparently King Louis XV believed him to be responsible for making peace between the warring Apache Indians and the Osage and Kansa tribes in the Missouri Valley of the Americas. He probably did so to save his own skin after who knows what predicaments he brought upon himself in dealing with the natives, if you know what I mean.

"According to our history books," continued the prince as if quoting from a script, "he brought a band of the Apache savages back to Paris to impress the Boy King, Louis XV, who gave the Indians free rein at his summer palace, Chateau de Fontainebleau. It is said the Boy King stripped naked and hunted pheasant—or was it peacocks—with bow and arrow in the royal woods with the Indian warriors until not a bird remained in the forest. The impressionable teenage King Louis XV was so delighted by his frolic with the noble savages that he gave Bourgmont both a title and land to go with it. Fortunately, with no surviving heir—only daughters—on Bourgmont's death, the land was returned to my family."

The prince sniffed, and made that French face of disdain that is very like my cat's response to unwanted attention from a stranger. (I missed my cat. Jenny had adopted Diva, with a promise to give her back if and when I returned to Chicago—which turned out to be sooner than I expected.)

I couldn't resist asking my host as I was checking out, "If Bourgmont was such a scoundrel and imposter, why do you have his portrait hanging in your home?"

"Madame, it is not my choice. The French Historical Ministry requires me to display it in order to collect the funds that are offered for maintaining a historical site." Then he added snidely, "If you ask me, the only reason they wish it displayed is to give tour guides an opportunity to tell the stories of French exploration in the Americas. It interests our American tourists."

The prince's facial expression left no doubt as to his feeling about American guests. "As you notice," he continued, "I've put it on the top stair landing, so only the chamber maids, and of course the third floor guests must pass it. I cannot bear the man's eyes. Do you not agree?"

"I do agree," I assured him. At least we had that in common. I almost told him that I was leaving one day earlier than planned just to avoid those eyes, but thought better of it. No need to increase the animosity between the two gentlemen further. Making a mental note to research this Bourgmont, I wondered if his travels took him through present day Western Kansas. If the treaties he made were with the Plains Apaches, it was very likely.

My golden days of foreign correspondent journalism came to a halt in 1990. The *Tribune* has a funny habit of moving people out of their positions just when they get really good at what they do and begin to feel comfortable. I was feeling comfortable in Paris and beginning to acquire a glimmer of an understanding for European culture and politics—just enough that my stories were beginning to lose their naivete. So of course I was called home. But on the bright side, they offered me a job I had long coveted, editor of the *Sunday Magazine.*

WHILE I DEEPLY REGRETTED departing from Europe, I was happy to be at the helm of the *Sunday Magazine.* I was brimming with ideas for improving the focus and look of the magazine. Furthermore, with my parents entering their eighties, I had begun to feel uncomfortable about living an ocean away. Dad was walking with great difficulty, his knees barely able to bend. And he had begun to suffer little strokes, almost imperceptible seizures that passed within seconds, as Margaret described them.

"Something is affecting his mind," my mother whispered into the phone to me every time I called from Paris. "He's not the same." Though his speech was slightly slurred, Dad seemed sharp enough to me. "Your mother," he'd complain quietly into the phone, "is losing her memory. Sometimes she can't remember what time of day it is. She made me eggs and toast for supper yesterday." I tended to place more credence on Dad's assessment since Mom always asked about the weather in Chicago, totally unaware I was calling from Paris no matter how many times I reminded her. Now I really would be in Chicago, and only a two-hour plane flight away in an emergency.

The best part of being back in Chicago was having Diva back. At first, my cat seemed not to know me. It would take time—after all, I had been away for five years. After three months, Diva was again curling up beside me while I watched TV news and sleeping at my feet at night. Things were nearly normal. One year back and I was a workaholic again. A second winter arrived.

My new job at the *Tribune* involved very little travel. I once loved Chicago. Now it had turned into a gray prison. Jenny was married once again, and this time a full year into it, the union was working out. Her new passion was trying to get pregnant despite her forty-plus age. She insisted she was thirty-five, even to her doctor. I was getting tired of hearing her theories on positions that were sure to promote conception. Bill was now assigned to the Middle East and thoroughly enjoyed risking his life daily as unrest flared in rhythm to the desert heat. I seldom even heard from him.

I once looked forward to Chicago winter weekends. Unrushed, lingering Saturday afternoons at the Art Institute. New plays at the Goodman. Tantalizing little neighborhood ethnic restaurants my friends and I would find, whose locations we would then jealously guard. But this was the very first winter I had stayed in Chicago for the whole season. The cold was settling in my bones. The hot, dry, indoor heat was cracking my skin. The sullen skies were dulling my senses. The wind was brutal on the way from the bus stop to the Tribune Towers, some days nearly knocking me down.

Furthermore the natives were becoming increasingly hostile with each new snowfall. There is a curious Chicago neighborhood tradition that first baffled then amused me. However, with each passing winter this tradition was becoming more annoying. An alien landing in Chicago in February would assume these were a people who worshiped broken down chairs, often two of them set out on the street with a broomstick stretching from one to another. These and other elaborate constructions of damaged furniture would begin appearing on the streets after major snowstorms. At first, I half believed they were some sort of altar built to appease the Gods of Snow.

That first winter, my building superintendent explained it to me with the impatience of a man talking to an idiot. Most of the apartment buildings in Chicago were built before the arrival of automobiles. Hence, parking spaces were not designed in. So many city automobile owners are at the mercy of available street parking. Now when you have spent hours digging out a curbside spot for your car after a snowstorm, it would not do for another person to simply take that cleared space while you're out buying groceries. Therefore, the chair constructions save your space, just as a coat on a theater seat might save a place for the moviegoer who has run out to the popcorn line. To steal the spot would require the offender to first remove the chairs before parking, an act that would bring down retribution from the entire neighborhood. Homicides have resulted from less.

However, by March this ritual was losing its charm. There was hardly any snow left, yet people were still hogging their spaces with chairs and broken down tables. I was beginning to fantasize about lighting a match to these shabby altars. Clearly, I was becoming as irritable—no, *more* irritable—than most of my neighbors. Furthermore, this year, my indoor respites were not satisfying me. I was no longer thrilling to the Art Institute's Monet collection. I needed to be on the road. Away from Chicago.

Editing the *Sunday Magazine,* I had discovered, meant tedious, never-ending hours of trying to salvage poorly-researched, badly-written features. "I might as well be writing them from scratch, it would save a lot of time," I would complain to my colleagues, who then countered that I was simply unable to "let go." I didn't realize that being an editor was synonymous with letting go. Furthermore, wasn't forty-three years old too early to "let go?" The 30 percent increase in my salary was worthless. There was nothing I wanted to spend the extra money on.

So in mid-March, as the restless, never-ending Chicago winter was coming to a close, soon to be replaced by the dirty slush and pothole hell Chicagoans call spring, I marched into the general manager's office. *Being editor is not my cup of tea. I need to write.* I had rehearsed my deal, canned and sanitized, the night before, and again in the shower, complete with facial expressions and body language. I would lay it out simply and forcefully: I would research and write four stories a year, handing over more day-to-day editorial control to my second in command, yet retain my salary. And I would take a two-week leave within the month, provided I brought back a suitable story for the magazine.

"I agree to your proposal," Jones said, leaning way back in his brown leather executive chair. "You're a damn good writer, and the paper has been missing your by-lines too long. You need to get back into some writing."

Oh Boy. What's coming next, I thought. He was being a pushover, not his usual style.

Here it came. "I have one other thing to throw into this deal," Jones added, folding his arms, looking way too satisfied. "I pick the topic for your first of four features."

Management is not supposed to impose its editorial ideas on the news people. I was being asked to do something I shouldn't agree to. These too-easy negotiations had put me in a position of weakness. But I sorely needed two weeks in Utah. "Okay, let's hear it."

"There are exciting things going on at the Chicago Art Institute and no one covers them." Then I remembered, Jones' wife was a major fundraiser for the Art Institute. I was about to be snookered into getting him brownie points with his independently-wealthy wife who was the biggest charitable giver in the city. This year, I'd heard, she was on the board of the Art Institute. She probably busted his balls every night about the Institute's inadequate coverage in the *Tribune,* couldn't he do something about it. After all he was the general manager of the goddamn *Chicago Tribune.*

"You've got a deal—provided you leave in my hands the decision on just what aspect of the Art Institute we're going to cover," I chicken-heartedly agreed. "You know, I'm a great fan of the Art Institute. I spend my lunch hours there. You don't have to convince me. Their extraordinary collection is underexposed, taken for granted in this city. I just need to find the right hooks to give the story the freshness it must have to meet the *Tribune's* standards." (That was always a good turn of phrase to throw around—*the Tribune's standards.*)

I couldn't believe I was compromising my editorial judgement—just for two weeks in Utah. *And,* don't forget, a chance to write again. But I had a plan. I would go to Utah, find a place somewhere not too far from Moab, quit my job, move there. I'd be a few hours' drive from Margaret as well as my parents, who at the time lived in Denver. Furthermore, from Moab I could spend weekends combing the back-roads of the Southwest looking for a '45 Dodge truck with specious license plates.

Jones was ecstatic, but also feeling guilty. "Now you do understand, this is a gentlemen's agreement. It's just an understanding between you and me."

"Of course."

"Get yourself a nice gown," he announced patronizing. "Here are tickets to the Art Institute Winter Ball next week. Most people, you know, are paying $1,000 for these tickets. Yours free, for you and a guest. The speaker is fabulous. He's talking on Southwest art with a particular emphasis on native painters. It should be quite good."

I took my slinky, black velvet dress out of mothballs, had highlights put in my hair, and imposed on Bill—temporarily back in town—to rent a tux and be my escort. I ate the rubber chicken. Drank the vinegary wine. Enthusiastically applauded for Jones' impossibly thin wife with her upswept flaming red hairdo with its few artfully careless tendrils spiraling into her neck when, as chairman of the event, she introduced the speaker. And I picked at my inedible dessert while some art professor from the University of Arizona droned on about Navajo and Ute painters. When he mentioned several Kiowa artists, my ears perked up. I'd determined that some species of Kiowa-Apache had last inhabited the Western Kansas Plains before they were moved off wholesale to reservations. I was reminded that I had failed to follow up on that French explorer and his Apaches.

Then the speaker started a slide show. I waited for the Kiowa painters to come up. They were at least interesting to me. "Now I know what all of you really want to hear about is T. S. Eagle," monotoned the professor. "He's the hottest topic in art circles these days, but no one is sure whether he is Native American or not. Obviously his heart is clearly one of a Plains Indian, but his style differs enormously from the Kiowa Five, and since no one has met him—or her—we cannot really classify T.S. Eagle as Native. So what do we know? He mysteriously ships paintings to a Taos Art Gallery, where, as you might suspect, they draw enormous sums of money and often end up being sold at auction. Yet even the Taos art dealer is unsure of Eagle's identity and has never met him."

The professor began displaying T.S. Eagle slides on the screen as he further expostulated. The artist's style seemed somewhat familiar to me—hyper-realistic with subtle colors and light effects. But I paid little attention. My pantyhose were cutting into my waist—I hated wearing pantyhose. He continued to speculate on the painter's true identity as he flashed two or three other paintings on the screen. It was on either the fourth or fifth T.S. Eagle slide, that I suddenly snapped to attention. On the screen was a scene that took my breath away. An encampment of Plains Indians on a ridge, women cooking, children playing around a campfire, dogs chasing about the tepees—a languid summer afternoon scene with towering thunderheads teasing in the background sky. The ridge had a peculiar indentation, as if a cave dug into the ridge had fallen in on itself. I knew that landscape. I knew that sky. And I knew the girl in the foreground—copper skin, her purple-black hair half out of her braid, strands blown back across her face by the wind, as she knelt, bending her slender, agile body over a grinding stone.

Thomas was painting again.

The speaker moved on to other topics, but my heart beat rapidly throughout the next fifteen minutes of his droning presentation. The applause had barely finished when I was pushing up to the front to ask questions about T. S. Eagle, questions he brushed aside arrogantly.

"I refer you to any art journal," he sniffed. "Eagle is all the art critics like to talk about these days. Their speculations run the gamut. If you ask me, it's a clever commercial ploy on Eagle's part to build a well-crafted mythology around himself. In fact, I suspect he's really two or more artists. Some of his painting are landscapes, others are portraits—his buffalo and eagle subjects, for instance. In my opinion, the two styles differ too much to be coming from the same painter."

The professor patronizingly sideswiped my spilling questions. "I am not really a champion of his work. Too illustrative. You need to read the journals, particularly a collector's magazine called *Southwest Art*, quite enamored with him, I'm afraid."

I was in the Chicago Public Library when it opened the next morning, combing through the art magazines. I tried to disregard the pompous critics who thought they understood T.S. Eagle's message, skimming instead for bits of useful information. T.S. Eagle indeed shipped or secretly delivered his works to a small art gallery in Taos, New Mexico. Yet many people who had staked out the gallery had never seen him come or go. The gallery owner, Robert Jensen, despite his insistence to the contrary, was believed to know T. S. well, but was sworn to protecting his identity.

One story caught my eye. An art dealer in Texas believed he had found some early T. S. Eagle paintings—a group of five golden eagle portraits acquired by an elderly rancher and horse breeder in the Texas Panhandle. The man, now deceased, was said to have traded an Arabian horse for the first painting, and thereafter acquired more paintings by trading bison from his experimental herd in the rolling hills near the South Palo Duro River. The rancher's son knew only that the artist was a shrewd teenager who extracted four buffalo calves from his father for the last painting. "My father obviously had a good eye for art," the son was quoted as saying. The article went on to say, "The paintings were signed with the initials TSK, not T. S. Eagle, but the style is so similar there is little doubt they are the early work of the artist. The rancher's son, who was not living at the ranch during the period when his father acquired the paintings, does not remember his father as saying the teenager was an Indian. But his father did say that he repeatedly offered money to the kid, but he only wanted buffalo, not cash."

So *that's* what happened to the eagle portraits.

I had my first feature topic for the magazine. I called the airlines and changed my flight. I would be going to New Mexico instead of Utah for my two-week respite from the gray gloom of Chicago in March.

• • •

IN THE ALBUQUERQUE AIRPORT, a Pueblo Indian musical group entertained with instrumentation and melody lines so sweet and calming I actually stopped for ten minutes and tears welled in my eyes. This was the Southwest, an American treasure. Not just a place but an attitude. I heard it in the lyrics even though I did not understand the language. *Slow down. Inhale.*

The drive from Albuquerque to Santa Fe was up an Interstate not unlike any other one in the West, a new river of commerce once again following an ancient route—in this case, the banks of the Rio Grande River. I buzzed through Santa Fe, not stopping, and began ascending the mountains to Taos, home of the oldest, continuously inhabited dwelling in America. The Taos Pueblo is an ancient condominium of sorts. The structure itself has been occupied for at least six hundred years, thriving as a trade center for centuries. Long before Spanish and French traders stumbled onto this artisan's Mecca, the nomadic Plains Apaches, who inhabited my part of the country, traded with Taos, bringing them dried buffalo meat and robes—the essentials of life, in exchange for art—pottery, and decorative cotton blankets, as well as obsidian, turquoise and shells for ornamentation.

No wonder the artisans of the twentieth century gravitated to Taos. I had never visited Taos despite its popularity with my generation in the late sixties and early seventies. Strange that I had never been there, considering it had served as an inspirational hideaway for two of my favorite authors, D. H. Lawrence and Willa Cather. The first time I read a Cather novel as a young girl, I was enthralled to find someone who understood the soul of the prairie. She had grown up on the windswept Plains of Nebraska and was haunted by its pull even though she left it. Later in life, worn out by the literary pulsebeat of New York she had come here. I understood why.

As I drove into Taos, I was first struck by the colors. All the structures, from modern bank buildings to ancient homes, were of the same round-cornered warm tan adobe. The dust that puffed everywhere—many of the streets weren't paved—was that same golden tan. Yet tan was not the color of Taos. It merely provided the backdrop to set off blue. The sky was a special, rich hue, a color so unique it could only be called Taos blue.

I quickly found the central plaza and angle-parked in front of the

Jensen Gallery. The low-slung building that housed the gallery—all the buildings on the plaza were connected—was the usual adobe tan with the posts painted blue. I quickly noticed that everywhere, any exposed wood, such as beams, doors, or porch rails, was painted blue.

Every place has a color. Moab, Utah is orange. Chicago is gray. Blue was the color of this town. Everyone instinctively knew it. What I didn't know at the time was that this particular shade of blue is the sacred color of the Taos Indians, so sacred that they do not even talk about it. Of course. One had only to stand under this sky, in this place rimmed by mountains of a complimentary darker shade of blue, to sense that this color was sacred.

I stepped into the gallery and took off my sunglasses. The gallery walls were white, simple white. Exposed wood beams at the top of the high ceiling were bleached to a light white-beige. I looked around and was disappointed to not see any of Thomas' work hanging.

I was the only person in the gallery, so I could hardly browse anonymously. A middle-aged man hastily ended a phone conversation and stood up from behind a small desk at the back of the gallery to greet me. He was ruggedly good-looking, his wavy silver-streaked hair—probably once light brown—pulled into a ponytail at the back of his neck. He had a kind face, heavily lined from sun exposure, and gentle mannerisms. I guessed he was one of the hippies who gravitated to Taos in the sixties and stayed, becoming a model citizen and town father.

"Most of T. S. Eagle's painting are spoken for long before they arrive here," Robert Jensen informed me when I began querying him on Eagle's recent works.

"Whatever you're pricing him at, I represent a buyer who will pay double any offer," I told him.

"And let me guess, the condition is that the buyer gets to meet T.S.," Jensen offered dryly.

"Not at all," I protested.

"And let me guess, you're not a buyer at all, you're really a reporter from *Southwest Art,* looking for an exclusive."

Did my pores reek of newspaper ink? What gave away my profession?

Getting Jensen's trust was going to be difficult. He was a devoted protector of Thomas, a worthy friend. I didn't want to push too hard.

There must be a reason why Thomas was being so reclusive. Maybe there was something about my baby brother that I did not know or comprehend. But if it could be known, I was the only person in the universe who had any chance of understanding. I had found him on the Colorado River, and then lost him. And I was not going to lose him again. Like a household pet who has run away and cannot remember his owner and will not risk coming in from the wild, I knew my brother Thomas carried a reluctance—perhaps a fear of—being tamed back into our family and the family of mankind in general. He was like a wild animal, beautiful and free in an environment he loved but saw slipping away. His ridge and pasture were gone, his buffalo dispersed. His eagles banned from their roost. He, more than I, suffered the loss of our bit of virgin prairie. But I felt certain he would be happy to see me, once he actually saw me. He would remember our childhood bonds. He would sense that only I understood his restless journey into the wilderness of the past. He would understand I was still a part of him, whoever or whatever he had become as an adult. I ached just to see the shy grin spread across his face when we shared an inside joke. If I had to stake out the gallery, go through Jensen's garbage, whatever it took I would do it. Thomas would not slip through my fingers into the sand again.

Across the plaza stood the La Fonda Hotel, an old historic inn creaky from age. The uneven lobby walls showcased local artists' paintings, massive dark wood beams held up the two-story lobby, stained red-carpeted stairs led to various levels. I asked for a room that looked out onto the square. The one room in the hotel that featured a balcony overlooking the plaza was indeed available, but the elderly Mexican desk clerk warned me that it didn't have a TV or a working phone. I took it without even asking to see it. As I passed through the second floor hallway, I noticed that the doors to each room were painted in bright colors, featuring various Indian symbols that I did not understand. Everywhere I saw that Taos blue.

From the balcony, I could look across the bare cottonwood treetops directly at the door of the Jensen Gallery. I was disappointed that spring had not yet arrived in Taos even though the temperatures hovered in the balmy sixties and the sun radiated warm on my bare limbs. The cottonwoods did not even show buds. Did these hearty trees bear the ancient wisdom deep within their trunks that, despite the seductive warmth of the sun, a March blizzard could blow out of the mountains with little warning? Three gigantic cottonwoods graced the plaza, along with a few younger ones. The old tree trunks were massive, gnarled and twisted. The lower branches were marred by a great deal of trimming. But unlike the cottonwoods in Western Kansas whose top branches were sparse and often dead, these ancient treetops were a gray-white haze of little filament-like branches bleached white by the winter sun, frizzle-full, like an old lady's unkempt hair. I sat under the cottonwoods on uncomfortable wrought iron benches watching people pass through the plaza. Joggers and citified dog walkers in the early morning, local Indian women in the late morning, and finally, a hoard of trinket-chasing tourists by mid-afternoon when tour buses from Santa Fe rolled into town. I enjoyed thick black coffee and extraordinary breakfasts—everything served with a side of black beans—at a warehouse-like bakery a block off the plaza presided over by a motherly Hispanic woman. Her chef, a middle-aged white man with a gray ponytail, labored over a huge iron stove in back, with his bicycle parked right beside the stove—no wall separated the front dining area from the kitchen, bakery and storage areas. (I was discovering that every white man in town over the age of fifty had a ponytail). Late at night, there was noisy brew and greasy food at the Alley Cantina, a rambling multi-room complex tucked into an alleyway off the plaza. The whole town was built like the famous Pueblo itself, in interconnected pieces, extra rooms added to existing buildings, growing organically, and haphazardly. I was reminded of the ancient marketplaces of the Middle East. The alleyways and little streets branching off the plaza in an unplanned maze of delight offered every imaginable Southwest Indian artifact—pottery, silver jewelry, blankets, masks—most of it produced by local Pueblo Indians. Here and there were hippie teahouses offering healing herbs, new age literature, tinkling bells and unsolicited advice. But most of the time I stuck to the plaza with my eye on Jensen's door.

The third day in Taos, I realized that I was getting nowhere. The fact that this gallery sold his paintings didn't necessarily mean Thomas lived nearby. Furthermore, even if Thomas personally drove his paintings to the gallery, he could be months away from delivering his next one. How stupid of me to sit on this balcony or in the plaza, staring at Jensen's front door. Thomas would undoubtedly back his truck up to the rear entrance of the gallery, which opened up into a small parking lot hidden behind an adobe wall—I had checked that out the first day. And he would do so under cover of night.

I consoled myself with the fact that Taos *was* a fascinating place, and I began leaving my watching post on the plaza to explore the town. I browsed through every museum and art gallery in the days that followed. Kit Carson's home. The impressive residence of Mabel Dodge, the scandalous, wealthy New York socialite who ran off to Taos and took as her fourth husband Tony Luhan, a Taos Pueblo Indian. She built a rambling adobe home on the outskirts of the town which became the center for the literary and artistic darlings of the 1930s, a place they could come work, be entertained and fed. Mabel had provided lodging for the likes of D. H. Lawrence, Willa Cather, and Georgia O'Keefe, to name a few.

And of course I drove out to the six hundred-year-old Pueblo itself, a wonder of ancient architectural endurance and mystery, with its akivas and top floors reachable by ladders. I wandered through its surrounding alleyways, embarrassed to be there. I had been told by townsfolk that until recently, the Pueblo had been strictly off limits to tourists, photography forbidden—even from a distance, with the complex jealously guarded by secretive elders who refused to answer even the simplest questions. But now, between noon and four o'clock, the Pueblo opened itself to the stares of camera-toting tourists and their stupid questions. A local Indian shopowner, who moved out of the Pueblo when she married outside of the tribe, told me that the Pueblo people are still secretive. "We never ever talk about our religious beliefs. From toddler age, we learn to never repeat outside what we are told inside. I do not live there. But I still observe the rules. The things they tell the tourists," she laughed, "are lies, total lies."

So I wandered through the Pueblo feeling awkward. I did not take out my camera. I did not ask any questions. The fees they charged for admittance, for taking pictures, for entrance to the museum, plus the tacky, hastily-built casino on the edge of the Pueblo grounds were bringing in much-needed cash, but at what cost I wondered. I left the Pueblo an hour after arriving.

I should not have come. It is their home.

Never for a moment in my foraging away from the plaza, did I forget I had come to Taos to find Thomas. But by day five I was painfully aware that I was no closer to finding him than the hour I arrived. I needed to study all his work for the subtle clues that only I would understand. Jensen perhaps would have a portfolio, maybe a book of slides of all his work. I'd noticed that most of the galleries kept binder-style notebooks on their featured artists, filled with plastic page inserts into which they slid photos of artwork, including pieces already sold, plus magazine and newspaper clippings about the artist. I hadn't noticed such a binder on T. S. Eagle in Jensen's Gallery.

When I entered the gallery again, Jensen greeted me coolly, but nevertheless offered me a cup of espresso. "Here's the deal," I began impulsively. "I wasn't being quite honest. I do not represent any buyer. I'm the interested party myself. I have very personal reasons for my interest, which I'm not prepared to share with you. I don't have a lot of money, but I will beg, borrow, or steal to own one of Thomas' paintings."

I didn't even realize that I had used the name Thomas, instead of T.S. Eagle in my outpouring. Nor did Jensen react to it. He was silent a moment. Then he put down his cup of coffee. "You are in luck, my dear, a new painting came in this morning. You will be the first to see it."

He locked the front door, and turned the sign around to read *Closed*. Then he disappeared into a curtain-covered back room doorway and emerged moments later with a large unframed painting—perhaps five feet across and four feet tall, still wrapped in bubble.

As he unwound the bubble wrap, I felt as if I had entered a great empty cathedral in an ancient city and was about to be visited by a mystery of profound beauty. I was going to be the first to see what I knew would somehow change my life. Even Jensen, my brother's protector, had not yet seen what lay under the layers of bubble wrap.

When I saw the painting, I fell to my knees and wept like a peasant woman who has just been visited by the Virgin. I wept in joy and sorrow. I use that word—weep—because weeping is something different from crying or sniffling or sobbing or bawling. I wept.

The painting was a grand panorama of the ridge on Golden Hill. The sky was that clear shimmering blue that you only see in April or May on the prairies. The soil of the ridge was dry, with dust puffing where the children ran. It was his usual Plains Indian encampment scene, women tending fires, dogs fighting, braves home from a hunt resting in the background oblivious to the everyday commotion of a spring afternoon. Horses could be seen in the background, cotton-woods and willows in the U-bend of the North Fork were visible in the far right corner of the canvas. But what was different—utterly, shockingly, different—about this familiar T. S. Eagle tableau, was that two golden-haired children ran with the other raven-haired youngsters, a tow-headed boy, perhaps three or four years of age, and a long-limbed girl, perhaps eight or nine, her hair flowing in the wind. Their faces turned to the sunlight, delight shining from their eyes. The golden-haired girl held hands with an Indian girl about her size. The little boy ran behind with a small mongrel dog nipping at his heels.

Jensen just let me weep. Finally, awkwardly, he offered me a Kleenex.

"This is Thomas," I said, pointing to the boy. "This is me. And this is Gentle Wind. We told each other our secrets. I didn't even know Thomas could see Gentle Wind. But that's her on this canvas."

"I want to see my brother," I pleaded. Jensen walked to the back of the room, held the curtain aside, and Thomas came slowly into the room. He pulled me to my feet, and held me until I stopped crying.

And then I saw his little grin. "This one's for you, Becky. And you don't even need to double anyone's bid."

Then we were babbling. Jensen along with us, as if he were one of the family.

"When Bob told me a reporter was snooping around asking stupid questions, I knew it was you," said Thomas. "I got here as quick as I could. The Dodge doesn't move too fast."

"Thomas, how did you know about Gentle Wind? How did you know exactly what she looked like, right down to that stupid braid down her back? She hated that braid."

"You think I didn't see her?"

"Thomas, she was a figment of my imagination."

"Then I guess I was in on that same figment." Again that little boy grin.

"I gotta show you my place. I've actually got a roof over my head, so to speak, even though I'm not there much. Pretty rustic though. Bring any camping clothes?"

"Of course."

I packed my bag, left my car in the hotel parking lot, and climbed into our old harvest time truck. I remembered riding in it beside my big brother, Jim, when he'd take the wheat to the elevator. It was so exciting, rushing our bumper crop in from the field. I think it was our only bumper crop. I still don't know what bumper means.

Thomas' home was somewhere in northern New Mexico. We traveled down so many curving back roads and trails I would never be able to trace our four-hour journey, though I remember crossing the Canadian River and recall a signpost for the Kiowa National Grasslands. His home was a natural cave into the side of a hill to which he had added an adobe front with open windows, out of which he had a magnificent view of a purple mountain range. Out back, to the east stretched a vast flat expanse of grass-covered plains.

The cave home—I suddenly realized it was a primitive dugout—was devoid of furniture except for a futon, a small table and two chairs. In the middle was a woodburning stove with the chimney disappearing into the ceiling of the cave. The floor was hardpacked dirt. The walls were the earth itself, covered in some places by what seemed to be buffalo hides. The only decorative touches were a painted clay water pot and a Navajo rug beside the futon.

"This is my winter home," Thomas explained. "I mostly use it to store my paint and my lodge poles. I pitch a teepee in the summer. Actually, I live mostly out of the truck. I'm always on the road exploring. But here is what's great about this place." He pulled back the buffalo hide wall hanging to expose a cacophony of petroglyphs.

Then he painstakingly translated the pictures. I was amazed. From what I'd heard, no one had every successfully deciphered the abstract meanings of the petroglyphs. At best, the experts viewed them as a celebration of hunts and mysteries of native religions, only guessed at. Thomas understood the details, the nuances.

"I do not doubt that you understand this. But how?" I marveled.

"I spend a lot of time studying these messages on the canyon walls all over the Southwest. After you see enough of it, you begin to understand. I don't know how, but I know. The language of the petroglyphs is quite complex. And beautiful. Like your poetry, Becky. Do you still write poetry?"

Without waiting for my answer, he exclaimed, "Hey, I forgot to show you something. Hop in the truck," Thomas drove two or three miles, then stopped by a high fence. "Look out there," he said.

"Oh, my God, Thomas, is that your herd? The ones from home?"

"Yup, several hundred head by now."

"Dad loves to tell the story of how you appeared out of nowhere with a huge semi, backed it up and loaded the buffalo right in front of the Texas company men. He loves to tell the story."

"You didn't think I was going to let them make buffalo burgers outta them for some Texas politician's barbecue, did you?"

"The cattle company claimed it was part of the land sale. Buffalo meat was a rare delicacy back then. Brought a good price, as Dad tells it."

"I just told them they weren't Dad's to promise. The herd belonged to me. Everyone in the county knew that. What were they going to do? Shoot me?

"These guys started babbling about restraining orders. I said to Mom, 'Go call the newspaper, get Photo Joe out here right now.' And I just kept loading.

"This is only a fraction of my herd," Thomas informed me proudly. "I've given away buffalo to many tribal groups. There are herds all over the Plains from this stock. Why there's one herd in South Dakota that numbers in the thousands now."

I wondered what Thomas was doing with all the money he was making from the paintings. I saw little evidence of it around me. Thomas explained that he had started departments in "bison management" at several Indian schools with his anonymous contributions, as well as contributing to programs to restore grasslands and protect public lands in the West. "I have fun with my money. I don't need it for myself," is the way Thomas put it, as he flashed his modest, little-boy grin.

Over the next week, Thomas took me to site after site, translating the mysteries carved and stippled into canyon walls and caves. He showed me granaries and ruins. We slept out under the stars. He taught me how to pitch a teepee—I couldn't get the hang of it. We hunted game—I was very bad with a bow and arrow. We cooked over campfires. We worried together about Mom and Dad.

When I asked Thomas, as a big sister inevitably will do, if he had a

girlfriend, he answered. "Not one that ever lasted." Then smiling sheepishly, he added, "Camping in a teepee and cooking on a campfire, for
most women is fun for about . . . three days." But I saw a look pass over
his face, a look I know well, of unhealed heartbreak. And he added,
"There was once a Navajo girl who liked this life for . . . well, let's see,
for almost two years." He was silent a moment and then said, "She made
beautiful jewelry."

One night, staring at the stars, he casually asked, "How's your friend
Jenny?"

"Married, would you believe," I retorted just as casually. "Wait a
minute. How do you know she was my friend?" Funny, we hadn't even
talked about his river days yet.

"The third night on the river, for a moment, she dropped her the-
atrics and started talking," said Thomas. "She talked about how much
she admired her friend Becca. She said I reminded her of you, and then
quickly reasoned that was because she grew up in Kansas, which was
practically the West. I knew right away she was talking about you."

"She's a real piece of work, isn't she. I'm sorry she was such a pest."

"Hey, it's gringos like her that made it easier for me to quit the river
job. And it got me back to painting. Maybe I have her to thank."

"I have her to thank for *almost* finding you five years ago. The minute
I saw her pictures I flew to Moab, but you'd already left."

"So, did you meet Joe?"

"Yeah, he even took me down the river. It was hard for him. He
folded the company after you left. The accident really broke him up. By
the way, he's afraid you feel personally responsible somehow. He's worried about you. You should go see him sometime."

"No one was responsible. The river can't be completely tamed or
understood. It was trying to remind us we are not in control." Thomas
was quiet a moment. "I miss the river."

At the end of the week, as I reluctantly prepared to leave, I extracted a promise from Thomas, that just like he kept in contact with Mom
and Dad on his own terms, he would also stay in touch with me. He
agreed. But I knew that he was not tamed, he had merely allowed me
to enter his world ever so briefly. I was certain he had picked an
impossibly circuitous way to reach his cave home so I would be unable
to retrace the journey. But I did not doubt that he loved me and

thought of me sometimes. I saw it on the canvas.

I left Taos for Chicago with my precious painting, meticulously bubble-wrapped and crated. I asked Thomas what the painting was called. "Let's leave it 'Untitled,'" he smiled.

BACK IN CHICAGO, I CAREFULLY picked my way through the gray slush and entered Tribune Towers, two days late from my two-week leave. "Where's your story on T. S. Eagle?" the sleazy Mr. Jones demanded late that afternoon.

"Not much of a story there. Anyway, I didn't solve the mystery of his identity. But I could do a great piece on the nuances of meaning hidden in his paintings. I've got a real good feel for it."

Then it dawned on him. "Wait a minute, what does this story have to do with the Art Institute?"

"Yeah, we need to talk about that," I added. "The Art Institute needs to add some of his work to their collection. Otherwise, I don't have a local angle."

"I'll see what I can do," he grumbled, virtually stomping from my office.

28

Buried Treasure

WE BURIED ĐAD TODAY, as Mom wished, in my grandfather's old churchyard beside the Cottonwood River. I remained behind after everyone had left just to be alone with him and breathe for him the clear spring air that could no longer fill his lungs. His last few years, a haphazard journey from the trailer park in Odyssey to the apartment in Denver, and finally to the retirement community in a little Kansas farming town a few miles from here, were not particularly happy years for Dad. I console myself with the knowledge that at least his last few weeks were happy. Thanks to Thomas.

In those first few years after the loss of the farm, they lived in a trailer house on the outskirts of Odyssey, as if afraid to stray too far away. My father was not the kind of man to go to the local greasy spoon and sit over coffee with the other retired farmers. He had a project—a kind of reverse farming project that consumed him: trying to make buffalo grass grow in the dusty acre in front of the trailer. He first tried seeding, but it didn't take. So he asked a rancher out near Wagonbed Springs if he could dig up bits of sod from his pasture. Dad painstakingly transferred the sod to his front yard, but most of it refused to send down roots into the new soil. Furthermore, weeds—Russian thistle and Mexican sandburrs, mostly—overpowered the clumps of buffalo grass. Mom missed the soapweed plants we'd had on Golden Hill. So Dad transplanted some of them too. They died. It became clear that the natural flora of the prairies chose not to respond to man's gardening endeavors. It took millions of years to create the shortgrass prairie, and it could not be recreated in a season by man, as my father was discovering. Still he would not give up, bringing in more sod, pulling out weeds. It was a losing battle, but one that he refused to concede.

Dad's other projects were his church and his music. Unfortunately, the church was falling apart. Power struggles and infighting, which happens in so many little churches in the Bible belt, had moved into high pitch. Town people against country people, brother against brother, father against son, cousin against cousin. My dad, the peacemaker, was in high demand, deciding squabbles, trying to get warring factions to talk to one another. It kept him busy, but was as hopeless as the buffalo grass project. That did not deter him.

And there were the obituaries—coming faster than ever. My father owned an Underwood typewriter. He had once been the only man in the county who could touch-type. Not even the newspaper editor could type his own copy. So whenever someone died, the grieving family, clutching photos and tiny scraps of paper, showed up on our door for Dad to write the obituary. That was his job in Odyssey, whenever he wasn't making peace between two fighting brothers.

From as early as I can remember, even back on the Home Place when our only light was an oil lamp, I recall strangers coming in, people from town I'd never even seen before, sitting around our table with him. Often the whole family would come. They'd sit around the kitchen table—later on Golden Hill Farm, around the mahogany dining table—sniffling into their handkerchiefs. Sometimes breaking out into sobs.

My dad would ask them questions. Then type a sentence or two. Followed by some more questions. He had it down to a science. Where were they born? Names of family members. Organizations belonged to. Honors and accomplishments. Sentence by sentence, he would construct a thorough obituary. By the time the obituary was done, the sniffling had stopped. Somehow the grieving father or son, wife or daughter, would come to terms with the finality of their loss as Dad pecked away. It was on paper now. It was final. A kind of gentle shutting of the door. Then I'd hear the familiar sound as he rolled—kind of ripped— the last page out of the typewriter carriage. He'd hand it to the family and tell them to take it to the office of the *Odyssey News*. They would murmur thanks and try to give him money.

"Oh, no, that's not necessary." He'd never take even a dollar, no matter how badly we needed it. He never thought of writing as a vocation. It was something he did because he owned a typewriter.

Dad also had his music. He was one of the few in his family to go on to college where he'd majored in music. He didn't graduate because at some point Grandpa had needed him to come back and help on the farm. My father had a stirring tenor voice. If he'd been born Jewish he would have been a cantor at a great synagogue. If he'd been born Italian, he would have been a great opera singer—that's how extraordinary was his voice. He sang solos in church all the time. My older sister played piano for him. Then when she left home, I became his accompanist. I knew just where to pause, where to crescendo, where to make my fingers soar along with his voice.

Often a couple of days after grieving families left our home clutching their typewritten pages, they would return. Sheepishly at first, pretending to be back to thank my father once again, they would stammer and say, "We ah, heard that you sing at funerals. Would it be possible . . . I mean, we would be so honored if you could sing at our dad's service."

Of course, he'd say yes. That meant I had to brush up on "Nearer My God To Thee," or "Jerusalem, City of Gold" and accompany my father on some unfamiliar piano or organ in some unfamiliar church in town with stained glass windows while I averted my eyes from the inevitable open coffin. One time it was a fourteen-year-old boy, sickly all his life, who used to live just down the road from us. That was really hard. But my father's sweet and soothing tenor vibrato opened the doors of heaven for his young soul to pass through.

Sometimes they'd call him before they were dead, especially those who didn't go to church, with a plea for Dad to come sit at the deathbed to hear their confessions and "last words." He'd sit there and hear all their sins, their regrets, their deepest, darkest secrets. These were the people who felt so sinful they couldn't call a preacher. My father would listen, offer no advice. No counsel. Just listen. And then he'd tell them that God had heard them, and had forgiven everything. My father told them they would go to heaven, even if they'd been a stinking drunk most of their lives, because no matter what they'd done, God was a loving and forgiving father.

There wasn't a preacher in Odyssey who was more godly than my dad.

He even had people confess murder to him. It never left his lips, except maybe to my mother behind a closed door. And that was the end of it. I know that because he once said he'd heard a deathbed confession of murder, but no matter how we kids begged to know who it was, he wouldn't say.

But after they moved to Denver there weren't any quarrels to negotiate or obituaries to write. Only gossip around the card tables. And my dad didn't play cards. Or even bingo. That would be gambling, which was a sin.

The retirement building population was mostly widows. Few men. "All those widows are just waiting for me to die," Mom would dryly remark, "because they like Dad so much. They call him if a light bulb needs changing instead of dialing the janitor."

"There's something wrong with his mind," Mom confided in me, on one visit. "I don't know what to do. He's not himself."

It first manifested itself in a sweepstakes obsession.

My father had gotten himself on the sucker list—all those sweepstakes that tell you in big letters to pick up your prize, you've won a million bucks. Dad believed it. "It says so right here," he'd insist. And indeed it did. Printed right on the letter, "Joseph Kluger is the winner of . . ."

He couldn't read the tiny print—with his one fogged eye, and failing eyesight in the other—those throwaway sentences that used the qualifying word "if" or "when." My parents' mailbox was clogged with magazine subscriptions to obscure publications and their tiny apartment was beginning to fill up with junk—cheaply framed little paintings printed on textured cardboard, tacky clocks, widgets of every description—bought in my father's attempt to increase his chances of winning a prize.

His elation each time he received an envelope telling him he was a winner, and later, his profound, begrudging disappointment when it turned out he had not won, was wearing everyone out, especially my Mom, who would go in the bathroom and cry over his naivete. Later, on the phone, she'd rant to all of us children about how unfair these "lies" were. How could anyone get away with outright lies sent through the U.S. Mail?

So my brother Jim, who had just recently moved to Denver, made a secret deal with the post office. All my parent's mail would come first to his house. He would take out the sweepstakes mail, and then it would be rerouted to my parent's address.

After that, Dad would wait in the lobby every day for the mail to arrive, then walk slowly to the elevator and up to his apartment with great difficulty—his knee continued to worsen—bowed further in keen disappointment when nothing arrived from the various sweepstakes he was sure he was about to win. The rest of the day would be spent grumbling about something being wrong with the mail. He would talk of nothing else.

Until he started talking about the buried gold.

"I've finally figured it out, after all these years!" he'd exclaim with excitement. "I know where it's buried."

"Joseph, what are you talking about?"

"The gold. The bend that Mexican was looking for was not the bend in the creek at Willow Valley. It was the bend right on our land, our second place, two miles upstream. He got confused. He was looking in the wrong place. Believe me, it's easy to get confused. They both look alike. He buried it in an awful hurry. He had a posse after him. Both places had that large grove of cottonwoods in a kind of circle, they both had a spring and a round swimming hole. No wonder he couldn't find it when he tried to dig for it."

"Joseph, what on earth are you talking about?"

"The Mexican that Old Man Houston and his buddies hung, the one they claimed was a horsethief."

"A horsethief?"

"Yeah, that's what they claimed. But I've got it figured out. The Mexican had a shovel. Why did he have a shovel? It never occurred to Houston and his gang why he had a shovel. They'd been drinking. They weren't thinking clearly."

"Joseph, don't tell me you believed Houston's tall stories."

"I know the Mexican had a shovel. Because Houston's words, exactly, was that when they found the Mexican on Carl Sandbottom's horse they told him, 'Good thing you got a shovel, you stinking horsethief, cause you've gonna have to dig your own grave.' They made him dig it. Then they hung him off that dead cottonwood tree near where Pappa planted the cedars."

"So why did he have a shovel?" Mom sometimes found it easier to go along with Dad's stories than to continue arguing some sense into his head.

"He must have been the guy who robbed the stagecoach from Colorado bringing back gold nuggets back in the 1880s. He held up the stagecoach near Wagonbed Springs, then he rode north. But like I said, a posse was after him, and at some point, he buried the gold, and then escaped by shooing off his horse and hiding in the willows. But he was so scared of being caught he just took off. Then years later, he comes back to claim the gold. He was sure he knew where he buried it. So he's back with his shovel, after all these years, but things look a little different. He rides north from Wagonbed, but he's off by a mile, just a bit off to the east, and lo and behold he comes upon the bend with the circle of cottonwoods, the willow thicket, it looks like the right place. He's just fixing to start digging when Houston rides up. And he looks and acts so guilty—maybe he stole his horse, maybe he didn't— that Houston's gang, half drunk decide to harass the Mexican and things get out of hand."

"Houston didn't hang anybody. He's a bag of wind. Him and his stories."

"No, this one's true."

"Joseph, you know everything Old Man Houston said had to be taken with a grain of salt. No a *box* of salt."

When Mom recounted this conversation to us some months later out of Dad's earshot, when our family was gathered for Christmas, my brother Harold stopped her.

"No Mom, this story *is* true. Don't you know about the digging Uncle Bill and Dad did when they were teenagers, and how much trouble they got into with Grandpa for doing it?"

Then Harold told us the story. He knew it because Uncle Bill told it to him once years ago. Dad had never mentioned the story. I guess he didn't want us to have nightmares about it. After all, we were living a few mere feet from the spot.

Apparently, when my father was sixteen and Bill was fourteen, they overheard Old Man Houston bragging to Grandpa about how he hanged a horsethief from the dead cottonwood after making him dig his own grave. Houston specified the spot where they buried the

Mexican as being close to where Grandpa had planted the cedar trees.

A few days later, when Grandpa had gone into town for supplies and my father and Uncle Bill were supposed to be mending a fence, they got shovels and started digging under the dead cottonwood.

They dug up a skeleton, complete with remnants of a noose around its neck. They were hurriedly trying to rebury it and cover over the hole when Grandpa came home. He gave them a licking, even though they were big teenage boys.

Grandpa himself had never believed Houston's "tall tales." This brought into question a whole lot of Houston's other wild stories. How many more were true?

Grandpa told the boys to never tell anyone about what they had found, especially not Grandma or their sisters. Apparently Dad kept his word, until old age released his stored-up memories. Uncle Bill was never one to pass up a good laugh and he thought the story was hilarious. Nevertheless, when he told it to Harold, it was on condition that he never repeat the story to anyone.

Shortly after that Christmas reunion, Dad suffered a big stroke, which left him paralyzed on his left side, totally bedridden, and at first, unable to talk. My mother refused to send him to a nursing home, and with help from Margaret and Jim, she managed to care for Dad herself. My father was determined to recover, and before long was pulling himself from wheelchair to bed, bed to wheelchair, and managing little tasks like brushing his teeth and combing his hair by himself. Key to his recovery, according to my mother, who shook her head in shame and helplessness when she told us, was his desire to get well enough to go dig for the gold.

Browsing through Dad's bookshelves one day when I had come to Denver to help care for Dad those first few difficult weeks, I discovered several books that detailed stories of buried gold in Kansas. A couple of chapters were bookmarked with margins scribbled full of notes. Wagonbed Springs and Point of Rocks, both on the Cimarron River, were important camping spots on the Lower Springs shortcut of the Santa Fe Trail. This faster though more dangerous trail was a favorite route for the Colorado-bound gold seekers as well as merchants and traders heading for Santa Fe in a hurry. Santa Fe Railroad payroll shipments also moved along the Trail. Another important trail, a military road called the Palo Duro Trail, also ran through our territory. It connected Fort Elliot in Texas to Fort Lyon in what is now Eastern Colorado. Army payroll monies and supplies ran up that trail as well. These desolate, unprotected trails were a gold mine—no pun intended—for bandits. According to Dad's books, legends abound of miners returning east from the gold fields who were surprised either by raiding Indians or outlaw bands, who then hastily buried gold, silver and other treasures, intending to return to claim them later.

Many documented robberies did occur—and plenty of murders as well. Respected locals say that robbers stole more than $90,000 in gold from one party of returning gold seekers, but before they could escape, another group of wagons approached, so the bandits buried the heavy bags of gold intending to return, but never did. The exact location is debated, and the $90,000 has never been found. A second tale, duly bookmarked by my father, claims that in the 1850s, a man named Alexander and his three partners traveled that route from Illinois to Santa Fe with wagonloads of calico, which they sold in Santa Fe. When they headed back home with their profits, which were in silver bars and silver bullion, the men were surprised by Indians along the trail somewhere between Point of Rocks and Wagonbed Springs. The Indians stole their animals, leaving them stranded but unharmed. Fearing the Indians would return at dawn, the men buried the silver then overturned the wagon on that spot and burned it—very clever, since no one would attempt to look under hot embers for treasure. The Indians did not return and the men somehow hiked out of there and continued east. But when they came back two years later to dig up their profits, they could not locate the spot, the burned wagon's ashes having been dispersed and obliterated by the winter winds. They eventually gave up looking.

In Homer County, a legend about buried gold at Wagonbed Springs persists, though no one has any proof. Gold miners returning from the California Gold Rush camping at the Springs were able to bury their treasure before being attacked by Indians. Supposedly, one man survived to tell his story to a local rancher—no one seems to be able to say who that rancher was. The gold was never found, but plenty of people have looked for it. And more than one person who has stayed too late at Wagonbed Springs tells of seeing ghostly guards protecting the treasure.

Little credence has been given to these sightings since excessive late night drinking parties are a tradition at Wagonbed Springs.

There is even one story of found treasure. In 1914, a farmer only a few miles from our old Home Place, dug up a ten-dollar 1847 gold piece while plowing. Further digging in the area turned up three more. A Topeka newspaper article reported the incident: "Farm hands are quitting work on the ranches to join in the search for gold and part of the Santa Fe's extra gang, at work repairing flood damages on the Dodge City extension, deserted work to make a 'gold rush' to the 'find.' So far, only four coins have been unearthed, but a first class job of plowing is being done on the Anderson and adjoining farms."

As I read story after story in Dad's books, I was discovering that my father's obsessions were fueled by more than his own imagination.

In the late summer of 1990, my parents suddenly decided to move from Colorado back to Kansas—I suspect the reason was so they could die in a familiar place and not have to be buried in some suburban mountain-view plot they regretted buying. They had located a retirement community in a village a few miles from where my mother had been born. There they sat contentedly on their little porch, Dad in his wheelchair, Mom in an outdoor folding chair, and remarked how "Eastern" Kansas looked more like Western Kansas used to look now that so many trees were dying here too. Thomas and I helped them move into their apartment. Mom had hoped the move would distract Dad from his buried gold obsession. But once they were settled, he started up again about digging for the gold.

When I listened to his story, asked questions, and generally appeared to believe him, Mom was mortified. "Why are you encouraging this nonsense?" she complained to me.

I wanted to explain to Mom that the story was symbolic. Dad sensed a great loss. In losing the farm, he had in effect lost his gold—his bumper crops, his dreams for a bright future. But as I tried to find a way to verbalize it, I realized this symbolic explanation would be painful to Mom—she too had lost her "gold." So instead I approached the truth differently, in fact, probably more accurately though less poetic. "He's lost much of his memory from the stroke," I explained to Mom. "The older stored memory is more resilient, so he's caught up now in the memories stored during his teen years when he and Uncle Bill dreamed about the buried gold. They must have come up with the buried gold scenario when they heard the shovel detail in Houston's story. That's how teenage boys think, always looking for mystery, for excitement. I'm guessing that when Grandpa caught them digging, it was probably gold they were looking for, not a corpse. So Dad's stuck in this moment in the past, and there's nothing we can do about it but listen," I explained to Mom. "So I'm listening," I shrugged. "He can't help it. I figure, at least he's talking. A few months ago, he couldn't even talk."

Then feeling guilty about my somewhat smug advice to my long-suffering mother, I added. "I realize it's easy for me to listen. I'm not here all the time. I know you get sick of it. So would I. About all you can do when you've heard as much as you can stand, is help him think of other things by distracting him, like you might do if he was a toddler."

My ideas made sense to Mom and she became less frustrated and embarrassed by the buried gold talk. Furthermore, she now had a sensible explanation she could pass on to others—relatives, visiting pastors, nurses—whose ears were being bent by Dad's incessant stories of buried gold.

My last visit with Dad was in January of 1993. It was bitterly cold and windy. Chicagoans complain about their cold wind, which they call the Hawk. They know nothing of a Kansas wind in January, which whips through heavy coats and multiple layers of clothing as if you are naked. Thomas and I were both home. Not long after we arrived and had downed the customary *borscht* Mom had waiting on the stove, Dad got wound up in his gold story.

Thomas sat there and listened in rapt attention. The kid in him clearly wanted to believe the story. I watched, touched by the simple kindness of my brother. Perhaps Thomas sees the poetry in it as well, I thought to myself. Or perhaps he just loves Dad so much he is able to get into Dad's passion just to please him. Thomas is the consummate listener. He listens to rivers. He listens to eagles. He listens to Dad. And then Thomas did something extraordinary. He pulled some of my father's old typing paper from a drawer in the hutch and began drawing maps. The two of them pored over their maps, pinpointing exactly where the buried treasure was likely to be. Then Thomas promised Dad he'd go dig for the gold.

No one reminded my father that the spot on Thomas' map was now covered by a feedlot holding thousands of cattle.

Thomas left the next morning, clutching his hand-drawn map, assuring Dad he was going to buy a good shovel, go to Odyssey and begin digging for the gold. The gray cloud that had settled over Dad, turning his mouth down into a perpetual frown, suddenly lifted. His facial muscles relaxed. He smiled. He began noticing and hearing the conversation around him.

I left a few days later. In the days that followed, my mother reported to me that Dad stopped talking about the buried gold, but he asked Mom every day, "Did you hear from Thomas yet?"

The winter was nearly over. The winds were turning warm. My father was at peace because someone was looking for his gold. He was at peace when he died a few days later, March 11th, secure in the knowledge that the gold would be found. His youngest son would surely recover the treasure. My father moved on to reclaim his gold in heaven.

There was never a man so pure. So trusting—yes, you could also call it naive. So convinced in the deep down good in every man that he couldn't even imagine much less detect evil intentions in those around him.

Just as my father's God forgave all who confessed their shortcomings to him while he sat with them in their waning hours, God forgave my father's impossible dreams, his foibles and obsessions. For while my father never found his buried gold on earth, his treasures were stored up in heaven.

Actually, the more I think about it, as I stand here at the foot of the mound of earth beneath which he rests, he had his gold all along. But instead of hoarding it, my father had been distributing little nuggets of it all his life to family and friends and strangers. Little nuggets, from the books read around the lamplit kitchen table, to his peacemaking between estranged fathers and sons, to obituaries and songs for grieving families—nuggets here and there.

29

Death on the Plains

WE DO NOT BURY OUR DEAD like the white men do.

We wrap our dead in ceremonial robes and place them on high willow scaffolds facing the sky. We do this to offer their spirits to the sun and the wind. And that is why our ancestors' spirits hover in the heavens and whisper in the wind.

Across these great flat Plains our kinsmen know of the departure of our loved ones even before they approach our camp. They see our grief, our love, etched in sharp silhouette against the morning sky.

When we have laid them in their high resting place, we beat our drums slowly and our songs of grief pour from pained throats and reach into the heavens. But we know they are not gone, only their bodies remain, the bodies that hungered and grew thirsty, the bodies that felt the bite of winter cold and the swelter of a summer day. The bodies that endured the pain of an arrow, the gore of a stampeding buffalo, the frailty of old age or the ache of unfulfilled love.

They go, the fortunate dead, on the fourth day, to mingle with their ancestors and the spirits of all other living things. They go, and yet they never leave us. As their strength wanes, our strength grows. As their vision dims, we see more clearly.

They are part of us. We are part of them. We are part of the great whole of everything.

Many winters ago, when I was still a child, we placed our shaman's body high in the cottonwood trees that line the Big Buffalo River so that his spirit could rest near the sacred springs from which his healing powers flowed. Three white men in a wagon pulled by oxen, came to the springs and when they saw our shaman, they climbed the tree and cut him down. They dug a hole in the earth and placed him in it and covered him with dirt. Then they stood around the covered hole and took off their hats, and one man spoke an incantation of magic words and they stood silently looking at the ground. Then they got into their wagon and continued on the trail.

One of our young warriors had come to the springs to drink after traveling from the Great Deep Winter Place. He watched them from behind the bluff. He rode swiftly to our camp and told what he had seen. The next morning, angry young men of our clan rode out and killed the three white men, leaving them dead in the dusty trail beside their bawling oxen.

Our people did not understand why anyone would desecrate the dead. I now know that white men bury their dead in the ground. It is their way. I know that they do it, but I do not know why. Why would they cover them and leave them in the dark? If we were to hide our dead in the earth, we might forget. High above in scaffolds of willow, or in the limbs of gentle old trees, we see and know that we are one.

Nadi-ish-dena.

30

The Other Side

IN THE MONTHS FOLLOWING my father's death, Mom, now distracted and even more forgetful, lived each day, talking only about her girlhood in Eastern Kansas, barely mentioning Dad or our lives in Western
Kansas. She was clearly lost without anyone to care for after eighty-five
years of tending to brothers and sisters, students, husband, children and
grandchildren. Out on her front porch, she complained bitterly that she
could not tell east from west, north from south. Without strong wind
blowing from the south, without mountains to the west, but mostly
without the compass of a husband, one day melted into another day
with little reason and less purpose. Thomas stopped by often now.

I flew into Wichita every couple of months, buying another piece of
sunflower pottery from the airport's corner gift shop each time I passed
through. I now had a sugar bowl and creamer, a milk pitcher, four mugs,
two plates—I was on my way to a place setting for four—a piece at a
time—as a way to mark the passage of time until my mother would be
gone too.

On my third plate, Mom died. I was there for a weekend visit when
she had a massive heart attack. I called for the ambulance while beating
on her chest and begging her to breathe. In the hospital they made me
sign forms about taking no extraordinary procedures even though they
had a copy of her living will which clearly stated her wish not to be
kept alive through artificial means. The cardiologist made me sign it
even before he allowed me to call my brothers and sister.

I made the first call to my sister who called everyone else and within hours all five were on their way to say goodbye. No one called Thomas of no fixed address because he had no phone, but he showed up the very next day. I knew he would. He lurked at the edges of my parents' lives like an eagle looking down knowing when to alight.

Her "three days to live" turned into eleven. No one on staff at this small Kansas hospital understood how a frail eighty-five-year-old woman could tarry with only 15 percent of her heart working. We, her children, could understand. She had always refused to give in to the elements.

Eleanor had come to the desert of Western Kansas at the age of twenty-two to teach at a country school, answering an ad she saw in the newspaper on little more than a whim. For her, leaving her home in Eastern Kansas for a town on the frontier of the state in 1929 was as gutsy as my move to Chicago had been in 1968.

The first thing she noticed about Odyssey was the great big windmill and cattle tank in the middle of the town. "People actually drove their stock into the center of town to water the animals. It was so primitive," she remembered. The streets were wide and consisted of rutted, packed dirt. "And everything was dusty, with tumbleweeds piled up everywhere," she recalled.

The school was poor, but the community was supportive, eager and curious about their young beautiful new teacher. She was tall and thin and her hairdo and clothes had a hint of flapper about them, though her demeanor was down to earth. She always wore a hat to school, firmly attached to her hair with a large hatpin. When she got to school in the morning the first thing she did was deposit her lunchbox on a shelf in the cloakroom, and remove her hat and place it on a high shelf.

This teacher meant business, but she also somehow thought schoolwork was fun. Two weeks into the school year she had not yet enumerated the rules. That's the first thing Mr. Schneider had done. Sour, dour, old Mr. Schneider had a long list of rules he read the first day of school, which he made the children memorize and repeat back to him.

There's a photo, tiny and out-of-focus, in Mom's photo album. In it, seven or eight gangly boys, ranging from age twelve to sixteen are standing on the roof of a small building. They are stretching their arms up and clearly shouting. You can almost hear as well as see them jumping up and down on this roof.

Here's the story as we heard it from Uncle Art, Dad's youngest brother who was one of the boys on that roof. Mom, who acts like she has forgotten why the picture was ever taken, has herself never mentioned the story.

Puzzled by the nonchalance of their new teacher, the children finally brought up the burning question on their minds. What are the rules of the school?

"Do you think we need rules?" was Mom's reply.

"Well, yes, every school has to have rules."

"Well then it's your job to come up with the rules." She told the students to make a list of the rules they felt were necessary, and when they agreed on the list, to make a clean copy of it and present it to her. There began a long process of arguing and hammering out the rules that lasted most of the morning.

Curiously, number seven on the list the children finally presented to her was NO CLIMBING UP ON THE ROOF OF THE COAL SHED.

So Mom thanked the children for their long and careful deliberation and posted the rules on a bulletin board at the back of the schoolroom.

That afternoon when she rang the bell to mark the end of recess, the younger children and all of the girls came in and took their seats. Clearly, the room was missing all the boys in the upper grades.

"Where are the big boys?" she asked the younger ones.

"Dunno," they mumbled, and looked down uncomfortably.

No one would answer her repeated inquiries. Finally, she left her desk and walked outside to look for them. When she rounded the back of the red brick school building, there they were—all of them, up on the roof of the coal shed.

"Stay there, don't a one of you move," she demanded in her sternest voice, and ran back to the school building.

They stayed, unsure what the next move was. Would she return with a whip? That's what Mr. Steiner would have done. Now was the moment. They were about to see what their pretty lady teacher was made of.

My mother, as Uncle Art tells it, returned carrying a camera, as excited as if she had just discovered the Grand Canyon. Trailing behind her were all the little kids. "Come on, wave your hands high. Smile," she seemed utterly delighted, as she snapped her photos.

When she was done taking photos, she said. "Okay, now climb down and let's go back to our lessons." Stunned, not sure what to think, they climbed down and returned to the schoolroom without further ado.

When Mom developed the photos, she posted one next to the rules. That's why the picture has a thumbtack hole in it.

There's another story from my mother's first year of teaching at Willow Valley School that we love to repeat. A few weeks into the school year, the kids were talking about a "horny toad." She inquired what one looked like. They tried to describe the creature, surprised that she had never seen one.

A few days later, the older brother of one of her students entered her classroom as she was cleaning up after school. He carried a small, care-fully-constructed cage of wood and wire screen. Inside the cage was an ugly little toad with bumps all over it, looking more like a rough rock than a reptile. The shy young man with white-blond hair introduced himself as the brother of Artie. "I heard you had never seen a horny toad. Here's one for you and your class."

That's how my mother met my father.

But I best know my mother as a gardener. Throughout the very worst years of the fifties drought, she always had a lush garden. Now that we had an electric pump on our well, water was easily available. She grew corn and green beans, squash and pumpkins, cantaloupe and watermelon, onions and potatoes, leaf lettuce and cucumbers and toma-toes. My favorite was radishes. I would pull one up every time I passed by the garden, wash it off under the garden faucet where the mint bush-es grew like weeds. And I'd eat it, one zingy bite at a time. To this day, I never eat a radish without thinking of my mother's garden. And whenever I smell a vine-ripened tomato, I feel my mother's nearness. Her tomatoes were plump and red, and tasted delicious sliced with a touch of sugar sprinkled on them. She always won blue ribbons in the county fair for her vegetables. But she grew her garden not to win prizes but to feed her family.

We ate vegetables in profusion all summer long. And she canned and canned and canned, and on Golden Hill since we had electrici-ty and a big freezer, she also froze vegetables so they would taste "fresh" all winter long, including corn frozen right on the cob so we could eat corn on the cob in January.

We grew everything we ate. Beef from our pastures, chicken from our yard, eggs I collected each morning—like a treasure hunt because we allowed our hens to roam the yard and they picked the most intriguing hiding places to lay their eggs. Vegetables from our garden. Eventually, fruit from our small orchard—once the Russian olive tree hedge grew high enough to shelter fruit trees from the wind.

The boundaries of Mom's garden grew larger each year. "Joseph," she'd say each spring, "Let's plow up a little more on the north side. This year I want at least two more rows of corn, and the melons need a lot more room too." So Dad would use his hand-held plowing device to turn more soil, and the garden fence would be moved over. The garden was getting closer and closer to the pasture. Before long, the garden was a full half-acre.

My mother was a practical woman—she had to be practical to balance off the dreamer in her husband. But she was also spiritual and creative. Her garden was the proof that she could create something out of nothing. In a life and a landscape over which she had little control, her half-acre garden was totally under control. Working in it gave her peace.

When I awoke on a summer morning, she was already in her garden, dressed in denim overalls and a gigantic straw hat, bending over, tending, weeding, watering, harvesting, lost and happy in her green, green garden from sunup until noon, often singing softly to herself as she toiled. She only came in when it was time to fix dinner. We called the noon meal—the largest of the day—"dinner." It consisted either of beef pot roast or fried chicken, mashed potatoes, a green vegetable, lettuce and cucumber salad, and something wonderful for dessert—such as peach cobbler. The evening meal when Dad and the boys came in from the fields was called "supper," and it was lighter and sometimes little more than a large bowl of *borscht* or a prune and raisin pudding called *plumma* mousse, and bread. Oh yes, she baked all our bread too, from grain we grew and ground by hand as we needed it. Slathered with sweet, white butter we also made ourselves, Mom's whole wheat bread was the zenith of wholesomeness.

And now she is dying. All they feed her is chicken broth and Jell-O squares. Thomas and I spoon it to her lips patiently, coaxing her to have another bite.

We are amazed that a dying woman can retain a sense of humor. The dinner tray comes. Her eyes are still closed. She says dryly, "Let me guess. Jell-O."

She's also become quite irreverent, making fun of the earnest young preacher from her church who feels it his solemn duty to visit each day. "Not him again, with all his long prayers," she sighs when she sees him enter the room. When he leaves, she remarks, "I think he's disappointed that I'm not dead yet."

I start intercepting him when I see him coming down the hall. "She's really very tired today. She can't have any visitors," I tell him.

When not dozing in morphine-induced oblivion, she reflects in a clear and steady voice on her life and her death, telling us over and over again that she is not afraid of dying, that when it comes our time, we should not be afraid either. Always the teacher, always the protector. She now had all six of us to protect once again. We fill her room—fortunately, the nurses do not kick us out—and there is more laughter than silence, as we remember old times, swap memories, entertaining our mother until she falls asleep.

After five days, each of our older siblings said their goodbyes and returned to their jobs, families and lives. Thomas and I, the homeless ones, stayed on, not allowing Mom to be alone for even one moment. I had taken a room at a motel nearby, and stole off to sleep sometimes. Thomas was supposed to use the room to shower and rest while I sat with Mom. But he refused to leave her side, except to slip away for ten minutes at a time now and then.

On day eleven, shortly after Thomas left for a walk around the hospital parking lot, she motioned for me to come closer. Her voice was weak. I leaned over her to catch her words.

"Other side." She repeated it several times.

Assuming she wanted me to move to the other side of her bed, I did.

"No, other side," she motioned. So I switched back.

She shook her head in frustration. "No. Other side. I can *see* the other side.

"The other side?"

"Becky, it's beautiful. Can't you see it?" She pointed in the corner of the room, toward the bathroom door. "It's green. The light is so bright, and it's green. Pink, too. But mostly green."

Suddenly, I understood, she was seeing another dimension, that famous tunnel of light in the often-described death experience. But it was not simple white light, but brilliantly colored. Green like her garden.

"Dad is singing to me, don't you hear him?"

Thomas was now back at her side, her other side. We held her hands.

"Shall I go?" she asked.

"Yes, if you see the light you should go. You have our permission," I assured. Thomas nodded. We said goodbye. He kissed her right check. I kissed her left.

"It's beautiful. I wish you could see it. Dad is singing. His voice is so sweet."

Her eyes closed.

We thought she was gone.

"Do I have great-grandchildren?" she suddenly asked, opening her eyes turning her head to me and then to Thomas.

"Mom, you have two great-grandchildren, and a third one on the way."

"My great-grandchildren, all the ones who aren't born yet, will you tell them that I love them?"

"Yes, Mom."

"The light is very green. Oh no, the door is starting to close. Shall I go?"

It was the hardest yes I ever said.

We buried Mom beside Dad, and just behind Grandma and Grandpa, in the country cemetery beside my grandpa's church. Except my grandpa's church, like everything else from my childhood, was no longer standing. It had been demolished many years ago. Aunt Catherine saved me one wooden railing from the balcony and I made it into a candlestick. Now just below the cemetery, on the other bank of the creek where my grandpa conducted baptism is a RV camping ground.

So now Thomas and I are fatherless and motherless. We are homeless and childless. I have my always shifting apartments, my cat and my laptop. Thomas, of no fixed address, has his paint and canvas and flatbed truck, now with a genuine Kansas license plate, though he does not live in Kansas. He has his cave and his buffalo.

What do I have?

I will have, once the railroad freight service ships it to me, Mom's hutch. I asked my brothers and sister if I could keep it. They were all more than happy not to take it. The hutch is huge, awkward and ungainly to most people's taste, but to me it is treasure beyond worth. The hutch, handmade by my great-great grandfather, was one of two pieces of furniture brought from Russia by my great-grandfather. A hutch so sturdy it survived the trip. The family's baby did not. However, the handmade rocking cradle that soothed the sick child in her waning days did survive the tempestuous passage, only to break my great-grandmother's heart over and over again each time she looked at it—until there would be another baby to replace her daughter lost at sea, my grandmother Sara, born in this country.

My mother got the hutch after Grandma died. Aunt Catherine got the cradle. The hutch, painted a sickly green color, stood filled with junk in a corner of our back utility room, too ugly for company to see. My father complained about the space it took up. No one seemed to like it except me. I decided it was the green color that offended everyone else. So when I was sixteen, I bought an antiquing kit from the hardware store, scraped the old green paint off the hutch, discovering in the process many other coats of paint beneath the green, and then, following the kit's instructions, I very methodically brushed on a new coat of streaked light brown paint to mimic English pine. My handiwork was not very thorough, for if you look closely you can see traces of yellow and green paint shining through underneath. For that, I am now thankful.

My father then replaced the cracked glass in the doors of the upper shelves. And, suddenly, it seemed—at least to me—to be a worthy addition to our dining room. However, the hutch continued to sit hidden from the world in the utility room. Until we lost the farm. When my parents moved to the trailer, and then later to an apartment in Denver, the piece achieved the status it always deserved as a prominent feature of their dining area. Mom kept her white and gold wheat pattern china and matching wine goblets in the top shelves so they were visible behind the glass doors. (She soon discovered that it was easy to slip snapshots of grandkids on the glass panes securing them in the corners of the wood frame, which fit loosely to the glass. And before long the pictures were obscuring the view of her china.) The slanting, hinged secretary top when pulled down revealed numerous little compartments for ink, pens, stationery, scissors, nail clippers, odds and ends. Below that, a large middle drawer held table linens and embroidered tea towels. Covered door shelves below held vases and large platters. The hutch was useful, but more than anything, for my mother, it was a reminder of her forebearers, as well as something solid and steady to depend on. Something that survived every move—from Russia to Eastern Kansas to Canada to South Carolina to Eastern Kansas to Western Kansas to Colorado and back.

And now in Chicago, it does that for me too. Behind the glass doors, sit my incomplete sunflower pottery dinnerware and my mismatched wine goblets. The middle drawer holds notebooks and folders full of handwritten poetry. Candles, baskets and keepsakes of all kinds occupy the lower shelves. Its sheer size at six and a half feet high looked awkward under the low ceiling of my parent's trailer home and later, their cramped Denver apartment. In my high-ceilinged, late nineteenth-century Chicago apartment, the hutch finally looks right for the space it occupies.

When the hutch arrived at my apartment a few days ago, the two delivery service men, seeing a twenty-dollar bill in my hand, uncrated the piece and offered to move it into place where I wanted it. After they left, I set about cleaning it, dusting out the shelves, polishing the glass. When I opened the secretary part revealing the little dusty cubicles and began wiping them out with a damp cloth I saw it. An old emory board wedged in a crack against a shelf. Stuck there until I pulled it out. It was white with the dust of my mother's nails. I remembered how she would sit in her swivel chair at the dinette table in her Colorado apartment, and swing around and reach for that emory board to file a rough spot on her nail, then replace it, all without looking. I looked at the emory board.

You might think I would have broken down and cried hysterically at the thought of my mother's remnant nail dust. But I did not feel grief. I felt anger. Anger that all that was left of my mother—that beautiful, tall, articulate, strong, brave woman—was this dust trapped inside the texture of an emory board. I was filled with rage, terrible rage, that this flimsy object that probably cost less than a penny, essentially a worthless piece of stiff paper with a sandpaper finish, this *goddamn paper nail file* had outlasted my mother.

Is it possible that this is all I have left of her?

Weak and shaken from the anger that had surged through me, I replaced the file, slid it back into the crevice to reside there for however many more generations. I wedged it back in the corner of an ink-stained compartment in the old hutch. All that is left of my mother.

Dust to dust.

PART THREE

Home Again, 1995

My story spilled out through the brown eyes of the white beast. I did not mean to tell her. But I could contain it no longer. When there is too much joy, or too much sorrow, some must spill out.

31

The Feedlot

I FLEW INTO WICHITA YESTERDAY. I really will be fired this time. I told no one at the *Tribune* that I was leaving. Of course, I gave Jenny a key so she could feed Diva. When I was changing planes in St. Louis—I hate that airport—I did call and leave my usual message on Jones' voice mail. I don't really have a boss these days since I've gone up the ladder about as far as you can get. I'm one of the big bosses myself. But Jones is still around, needs his general manager job more than ever since his rich, bitchy wife divorced him. Instead of lying about following up a lead on a super secret story, which is what I used to do in my earlier days—which got me into trouble because then I really did have to produce some great story—I more or less told the truth. Since I'm about to resign anyway, what's the point in making up a story. So on the recorded message, I simply said that I needed some personal time to "reflect and refocus." I didn't tell him where I was calling from. But I promised I'd be back in one week.

This is my last time here. I knew it when I tried to buy a piece of sunflower pottery in the Wichita Airport gift shop. "Oh, sweetie, that's been discontinued," the lady with the big hair said. "Just yesterday, we sold the last piece of it off the mark-down table."

But along Highway 54 through Kiowa County there are real sunflowers along the roadway to welcome me. As a child, I believed sunflowers were not rooted to the soil as most other plants but had the magical ability to move around where they wished. I believed this because instead of growing all over the fields and pastures, scattered at random as the other wildflowers are, they always seemed to be clustered at road sides as if having run there to greet passersby.

And while one might assume from their name that they turned their heads to face the sun, in truth they turned their faces in a welcome greeting toward sojourners along their roads. I tested this theory many times while riding my bicycle down various roads around our farm. As I approached they looked at me—I could almost detect excitement on their brown fuzzy faces—as they stared, unblinking at me. Then after passing a cluster of sunflowers I would stop, hop off my bike and look backward. And sure enough, they had turned their heads to continue staring at me. I tried to fool them. But always, they turned toward me. This held true if you passed in a car as well. Once I started driving at age fourteen, I tested it out, coming to a screeching halt and looking back. Always, they were looking at me.

Years later, I noticed the same phenomenon along country roads in France, also crowded by sunflower greeters. I wondered if French explorers brought back the sunflower from America or whether the flower was native to the European continent as well. I suspect they loved our sunflowers so much they brought them back, just as they did our corn and tobacco and cranberries. If so, lucky for Van Gogh. I will have to check that out one day.

I'm sure a botanist would tell me that sunflowers tend to cluster at sides of roads because the runoff in the ditches provides the necessary moisture. Plus there they are safe from the farmer's plow. I don't believe it, because many of the sunflowers are not growing down in the ditch, but on the elevated roadway, just on the dry, gravelly shoulder where cars and trucks pass, just where it is hardest to grow. I remain convinced of my childhood explanations. I'm 49 years old, driving in a rental Oldsmobile, and still, I swear, the sunflowers have rushed to the side of the road to welcome me, their faces turned toward me in curiosity and unabashed excitement. *Rebecca has returned home.*

I have always loved sunflowers. The yellow-gold of their petals is so bright they seem to generate light from within. They are the exception to the pastel and grayed-down hues of the prairie. I have noticed them standing in defiance, even in hard times, with tumbleweeds and dust dunes blown against their stalks. Despite the droughts that indiscriminately killed off both weeds and wheat, sunflowers raised their heads proudly and stubbornly, standing tall at the roadway. When I was nine years old, I decided that if they would not go away, then neither would I. I would ride my bike even in the blowing dust. I would be a sunflower. How I would like to rekindle the strength of my nine-year-old self. Is it possible that I am facing fifty? A childless fifty.

Does being childless mean I am doomed to forever look backward, never forward?

In defiance of my age—I'm not about to become predictable and plodding—I varied my pattern, sailing past the cutoff to Dodge, city of my birth. Instead I stayed on the road as it turned ever so slightly south and out of my way. When I passed a signpost pointing to Meade Lake, I took the road south to the lake even though it would put me several miles further off track, on this my last odyssey to Odyssey. What a magnificent lake it used to be, with a slipper slide going down into it. When I was a child, our big family plus a revolving assortment of uncles, aunts and cousins would pack a picnic lunch and come here to swim and play all day, usually on a Saturday after harvest was finished. Then, when the sun was low in the west, the grown-ups would coax us kids out of the lake and we'd barbecue hamburgers at one of the grills scattered under the cottonwoods. We wouldn't leave until it was so dark we could hardly find where we had parked the car and the cicada noise would be so deafening we couldn't hear one another speak.

I remember the lake being azure and so wide across you couldn't swim it. When I stopped by in 1985 it had receded into little more than a muddy pond because the springs that fed the lake had dried up. So I was pleasantly surprised this time as I came around the bend and dropped down into the valley, that the lake was back—as large and blue and tranquil as ever. I got out and walked under the cottonwoods, bursting with little new apple green April leaves.

I found myself alone except for one fisherman in a rowboat. When he paddled in, I moved out onto the dock to greet him, brimming with questions on how the lake had reemerged from its near death. I took the line from him and the old man stepped out of his boat with arthritic difficulty and said howdy.

He told me how folks in the area were so devastated at losing the lake, they raised money for an irrigation well to pump the lake full of water again. "We wanted our grandkids to grow up with this lake like we did," he said. "Why, we got checks sent in from all over Southwest Kansas, hell, checks all the way from McPherson. Then Topeka matched what we raised, made it into a state park, and before you know it we had the lake back."

The lake was quiet. Too quiet. I suddenly realized what was wrong.

Where were the peacocks? When I was a child the wooded picnic areas around the lake were filled with peacocks—dozens, maybe hundreds of them crying, crying, crying as if they were lost. Whenever I asked how the peacocks got there—they certainly didn't seem to be a Western Kansas kind of bird—no one ever seemed to know. Meade old-timers would say, "Well, they've been here as long as I can remember."

But now they were gone. The fisherman didn't seem to know where they went. "I don't remember seeing any dead birds around. Maybe they got rounded up and shipped out of here when the lake was about to go dry. I think that's what mighta happened."

Then I asked him the question I'd been asking Meade old-timers since I was a child. "How did the peacocks get here in the first place?"

He thought a little bit, then said. "I dunno. They was here when I was a child. That's seventy years ago."

Funny, every time I have asked that question over the years, it's as if it's the first time anyone has ever asked it. No one seems to have an answer or to even have given it any thought.

Less than an hour after Meade Lake, I drove into Odyssey, up that last hill out of the river bottom, past the big cement O our high school pep club installed into the side of the hill. It needed a coat of yellow paint—the current pep club must be falling down on the job.

This is my last time here. I do not intend to ever return to Western Kansas again. But this time, this final time, I must find the strength to go the thirteen miles.

A Homer County "tourism" brochure I found in the motel lobby stated that the West Kansas Feedlot offered tours. But when I called the feedlot, I was told that tours could be arranged only for groups of five or more. In response to my disappointed silence, the receptionist added that the Kansas Adventurer's Club was coming on Saturday, in case I wanted to join them.

I got the Adventurer's Club phone number from the motel clerk who happened to have booked their rooms. "Sure you can go with us," chirped the organizer when I called. "But you can't just pay to see one stop on the tour. You will have to pay the whole ten dollars for the day, even if you join us for only one event."

"Ten dollars? I'll be happy to."

It was Thursday. That meant I had two days to wait in Odyssey. So I did what I used to do when I was a restless teenager waiting for summer to be over. The library was still housed in the same building adjacent to the courthouse shaded by Chinese elm trees that were much taller now. Twice as many books had been stuffed into the same space. If I'm ever rich I will donate money to build a new wing.

"I wonder if I might view microfilm of old *Odyssey News* issues?" I inquired, almost sheepishly.

"What years?" asked the librarian, a chunky, sixty-ish woman with a boyish haircut and a brusque manner. She might have been the same librarian who'd put up with my endless Saturday afternoon requests some thirty-five years ago. But I couldn't be sure.

"Oh, fifties, sixties, maybe seventies."

"Perhaps I can narrow it down for you. What topic are you looking for."

"Dust storms," I improvised.

"Then you're talking fifties, maybe some sixties. Not seventies. Once irrigation came in, crops held the soil. Some blowing, but not like before."

"I just want to see the changes in the town over the years, so I'd like to go up to the mid-seventies."

"If you insist." She looked at me keenly, as if wondering why I was so stubborn as to not take her word for it. "I hope you have a lot of time. That's a lot of years."

I spent some time scrolling through the fifties. Dust-storm headlines week after week. I made a few copies of stories and photos showing Main Street practically blown under by dust, tumbleweeds piled up twenty feet high against the old hotel. Then I skipped to the year 1975.

This was going to be almost as hard as driving out there. I waded through the first front-page story announcing the land sale to the Texas-based cattle company. Then I scrolled to the editorial page. The letters to the editor, while angry, were not nearly as critical or insulting as my mother had described them at the time. My father's name was never even specifically mentioned. Perhaps I've become jaded by years in Chicago where political fights are brutal in comparison. But then I suppose for a man like my father, who had given a lifetime to his community, the word greed, used more than once in these letters, would sting. In addition to his unofficial community service of obituaries, solos, and deathbed confessions, my father had worked in an official capacity for the county welfare department distributing food to the poor, sometimes taking food out of our own freezer when county funds dried up and he knew families were going hungry. Greed was not in my father's nature.

I copied those letters, I don't know why. Then, scrolling week by week for the next five years, I charted the progress of the West Kansas Feedlot, its buying up of adjacent land, its rapid growth into the three-square mile, 150,000-head lot it became by the mid-eighties. I had been given free rein in the microfilm room once the librarian got tired of coming in to open new drawers for me. She just unlocked the cabinet, lectured me on putting the years back in the right drawers and let me browse. At one point when a front-page story on the lot's expansion was on the screen, she walked in. "I see you're interested in the feedlot."

"It's pretty amazing. One that big, out here in the middle of nowhere."

She took umbrage, showing it ever so slightly. "Well, that's the whole point. In the middle of nowhere. So you don't stink up the air for too many people. But then again this really isn't nowhere. This is where they grow the feed grain. This is close to cattle breeding ranches in the Panhandle. It is the perfect location. They were certainly smart about that."

"It looks like people were pretty upset when it came in. Were you living here then?"

"Was I living here? I've been living here forever." She laughed. The ice was broken. "Yes, they were pretty upset, mainly at the first farmer to sell land to them. But funny how everybody got over it once money started pouring into the county."

"What do you mean, like tax money?"

"No, more than that. Jobs for one thing. They employ two hundred people over there. That's someone from every family in town. That's two hundred people who didn't have to move away to find a job. That's more money for all the merchants, banks, grocery stores, house builders, you name it. But it's especially been good for the farmers. Now they sell their grain directly to the feeders. The feedlot pays them the going rate and cuts out all the middlemen, including those vultures on the commodities exchange in Chicago."

She was really wound up now. "Look around this town. Compare it to all the other towns around here and in Nebraska or the Dakotas. Most small towns here on the Plains are dying, losing population, just plain disappearing. Look at Odyssey. It's growing. Great schools. New businesses coming in. Did you notice, we've got five motels, a bunch of restaurants and all those franchises—KFC, McDonald's, Subway, Burger King, Taco Bell. Do you find that in any other little towns around here? It's the feedlot that's saved this county. This town should bless those farmers who sold. They'd be called visionaries now."

"From what I'm reading here I bet they'd be surprised to hear anyone say that!"

"Well, just look in this week's paper and you'll see everybody's up in arms about those pig barns coming in south of town. Sure they stink. Stink a lot worse than the cattle do. But give it fifteen years and people will be happy for the hog feeders too. Funny what people forget when they got some money jingling in their pockets."

Then suddenly embarrassed at her boosterism, she laughed, "Oh my goodness, it's past closing time. I got so wound up."

I assured her that it was me who kept her talking. I gathered up my stuff and said I'd be back the next day.

Since I had just about exhausted my "research" into the feedlot, the next morning I began aimlessly browsing through other microfilm drawers and was astounded to find a reel of *The Golden Gazette,* a newspaper from the late-1880s. I had no idea that the town on whose edge our farm perched had once supported a weekly newspaper. In its pages I found glowing editorials that called Golden City "the great metropolis of southwestern Kansas—the Queen of the West." Ads in its pages boasted that it was "surrounded by the prettiest, richest and most productive valley in the world, and is destined to be a great commercial center." I read stories complaining about the mail being delivered "two hours late on Wednesday," moony descriptions of one resident's new bride who had come in from Illinois, with the editor's injected complaints about his own dreary bachelorhood. On every page were comparisons of Golden City to the town of Odyssey, the prose virtually foaming with rivalry.

Ads talked about the plentiful and good tasting water that flowed a mere five feet underground and ascribed all sorts of healing properties to it. As for the name "Golden City," one letter writer flatly admitted, as if responding to criticism about the town's misleading name, "a name will boom a town more than any natural advantages it my possess. Don't kill a town with a harsh sounding name."

At least they were right about the water. It had always tasted good. Ice cold even in the middle of July and almost sweet, seductively beckoning you to drink more and more. I had loved it best sipping it out of my cupped hands under the garden faucet.

By now, the librarian, whom I'd determined was indeed the more solid, older version of the wispy young woman who once supervised my Saturday vigils hunting Indian lore, was wondering who I was, and why I was there.

"Where you from?" she asked me a few minutes after I'd settled back into the microfilm room.

"Chicago."

"You don't seem like a Chicago person to me," she said flatly. "We once had a Chicago woman and her son come to town. They opened up a pizza place. She had quite an accent and an attitude, if you know what I mean. You seem more like a small town person."

"You're right about that. Have you ever heard of a town called Kankakee, Illinois?"

(I didn't say I was *from* Kankakee. I only asked her if she'd heard of it. My father would have called that a lie. I thought of it as a clever evasion.)

"Can't say I heard of it."

"Few people have. I've lived in Chicago now for quite a few years, but I guess I haven't developed the Chicago attitude yet."

The librarian proceeded to tell me how the tough Chicago woman who looked *Eye*-talian and had bleached blond hair as tough as straw and a fat, lazy nineteen-year-old son, had no decent explanation for why she'd moved to Odyssey. "We all figured she was hiding out from a crazy husband or maybe even the law. But she made good pizza so no one gave her a hard time. Then one day, the boy got a little drunk and started bragging about his mobster uncle, and wouldn't you know it, the next day they were just gone. Moved.

"You ever heard of the witness protection program?" she continued. (Western Kansas women talk a lot.) "That's where the FBI hides people, gives them a new identity. That's what we figure it was. What better place to hide someone than Odyssey. No one would ever look for you here.

"You know," she added wistfully, "they were just startin' to fit in."

I'd forgotten how suspicious small town people were of newcomers. They could accept any oddity in "one of their own," but outsiders were judged by a harsher yardstick. Having chosen not to identify myself on this my final visit, I was the outsider now, but clearly I had met the librarian's approval. Well, almost . . .

"So how did you end up here, in Odyssey? All the way from Chicago."

"Oh, just passing through on my way to Denver. I have some time to kill. I liked the name of your town so I stopped."

Rushing to steer the conversation in a new direction, I asked, "How did the town get a name like Odyssey?"

"No one knows," she shrugged. "Whoever came here first, I guess thought of it as an adventure, you know like in Homer's *Odyssey*."

Almost as an afterthought she said, "You know, this county is Homer County."

It hit me like a brick. Me, once an English teacher and always a student of literature, having never made the connection—Odyssey-Homer County. I'd always believed Photo Joe's yarn about the Englishmen. I felt foolish for a moment. In the next moment I wanted to argue with her. The county was named after Reginald Homer, one of the first ranchers in the area. But that was something a stranger wasn't supposed to know, so exercising great self-control, I virtually stammered, "Well, of course. Why didn't I notice that?"

While we spoke, I struggled not to mirror her accent or use Western Kansas phrases. It was so easy to slip back into it. Just this morning, for instance, I didn't know I was doing it, until the waitress in the cafe adjacent to the motel studied me hard at breakfast and said, "You from around here?"

I said no.

She said, "You shur talk like it."

"Oh I just pick up accents easily. I lived in France for a while and in no time I was talking English with a French accent."

"We don't have an accent here," she said. "Not like they do in Texas, anyhow."

It was still on her mind when she came back to refill my coffee ten minutes later. "Funny, not too many from these parts ever go to France."

I guess I didn't fool her. She knew I was a local. I hoped the librarian wasn't that perceptive. I needed my anonymity. I needed to feel invisible.

This was no longer my home.

My morning chat with Miss Collins—I had finally remembered her name—moved quickly back to the feedlot. She was perceptive enough to know what was really on my mind. "Before you leave, why don't you go out there and take a look," she suggested.

"I'd like to, but they say only with an organized tour. But I did hear that some club is going out there tomorrow."

"Oh yeah, that Adventurer's Club. We have their brochure in the vestibule. Maybe it's got a phone number you could call."

I thanked her, took the brochure and made an exit. I had the feeling Miss Collins, now probably with a different name, was just a few more sentences away from remembering who I was.

THE GROUP SEEMS TO BE composed entirely of elderly widows hoping—I'm guessing—to meet some widower farmer by joining such an activity. The first Saturday of each month, the Kansas Adventurer's Club met in a central place and journeyed by bus to a different location. Last month it had been the salt caverns underneath Hutchinson. The month before that, they had explored the Indian ruins in Scott County. This Saturday it was Homer County. The group had started with a sunrise breakfast at Wagonbed Springs, then spent two hours touring the county historical museum followed by a Mexican buffet lunch in town. The feedlot was the first afternoon stop, and was to be followed by a visit to the Helium Plant—this was the heart of Natural Gas country. Then they would join the local Senior Citizen's Club for a potluck dinner and a square dance in the 4-H building. It was a full day and the ladies were more than up to it.

I joined them for the Mexican lunch, explaining that I had missed the morning tours because of "previous commitments," yes, I regretted missing a fabulous sunrise cowboy breakfast at Wagonbed Springs. I assured the ladies, who were bubbling with Kansas hospitality, that I would stay for tonight's dinner and square dance.

As they started loading into the bus, I realized that I really wanted the privacy of my own car. "I will meet you there," I told the bus driver.

"You'll never find it," insisted the driver.

"I'll follow you."

As if I didn't know how to go down this road blindfolded. Past the Coop Elevators. Turn south right after Uncle Sam's farm. Over the railroad tracks. It was tedious to drive so slow. As a teenager I could make this thirteen miles in ten minutes. But not behind a busload of Kansas Adventurers. Every so often a large sign would direct drivers to West Kansas Feeders six miles ahead and so on. All traffic, most of it trucks, seemed to be headed there.

After passing the old school site, we came up over the gentle rise out of Willow Valley—the *former* Willow Valley, and I saw it for the first time—a brown haze of bovine bodies stretching to the horizon. Looking in from the outside, the feedlot was a great brown seething thing, alive. Closer, it was a sea of sad eyes, a few dirty-white cows mixed in with all the browns and occasional blacks. I followed the bus down the driveway into the middle of the compound, where a two-story brick office building occupied the exact center of the feedlot. In pens to either side as I drove in, I notice a few animals standing foolishly atop mounds in the center of their pens, mounds of dried dung, I presumed. What are those mounds for? Have they been bulldozed up to give the cattle a chance to stand on dry land for a moment? To be king of the mountain? For an instant not to be mired ankle deep in dung and urine-churned mud? Here and there, a steer futilely, absentmindedly, mounted a heifer for just a moment, a feeble pretense that progenation was an option. They are all on their way to the slaughterhouse.

We moved slowly into a paved parking lot in front of the main building. I parked beside the bus and joined the ladies as they filed out. "The second biggest feedlot in the world, can you imagine that?" They seemed genuinely excited to see it. "Bigger even than Dodge City," one of the ladies filled me in.

The local-sounding name belied its ownership by a big international agribusiness conglomerate—except of course they got it slightly wrong. No one would call it "West Kansas" unless they were from East Kishniev. (It's *Western* Kansas.)

In the lobby, we were greeted by a tall friendly man with jet black hair and a well-oiled handlebar moustache who introduced himself as the general manager and chief janitor. I couldn't decide whether he looked more like a Texas rancher or Salvador Dali. But his aw-shucks, down-home language soon had the Adventurer ladies charmed. Only once in a while did he lapse into agribusiness mumbo-jumbo.

I tried to look inconspicuous by pulling my straw hat down low and adopting an osteoporosis posture. Mr. Moustache drove us around in a minibus, and, using a small microphone, which was totally unnecessary, stopped now and then to explain. Mostly about the feed—it's perfect mixture of proteins and carbohydrates, and yes, in answer to my question, perhaps some antibiotics and hormones—he wasn't sure. Animal nutritionists with PhDs behind their names regularly assessed the needs of the cattle at various stages of their feeding cycles. "And believe me, we never put anything in there the government doesn't allow. You wouldn't believe the FDA regulations we have to adhere to." This remark was greeted by clucking and sympathetic murmurs of pity amongst the ladies. Everyone here loves to decry government interference—except when the farm subsidy checks come in. We drove past towering feed storage elevators, huge heaps of silage covered by black plastic with rubber tires to hold the plastic down, and storage sheds for bulldozers and feed-dispensing trucks—all this operational support structure formed the center of the property, the hub of a wheel. Then while he spouted statistics about the operation, our host insisted on driving the perimeter of the property, perhaps to emphasize its sheer mass.

"We own those fields west of here, two whole sections. We grow some feed on them, but mostly we just let it sit. We re-stock it with pheasant every year. If you look closely, you'll see some of the ring-necked pheasants in there, beautiful birds."

Restock? I could just see it. Every November all the company offi-cials, many of them undoubtedly from Texas, probably come in and trample through the field. Now, without some pesky farmer in overalls telling them to get off the property, they would have free rein to shoot every single bird in sight. So, *of course,* they would have to restock every year.

The bus returned to the center of the property and began slowly inching down lanes past the various pens, which fanned out like spokes of a wheel, pens and pens and pens packed with cattle. Each pen in a different stage on its journey to death, all computer regulated and timed. Each pen ripening for slaughter on a different day with feeding regimens that changed as they neared their date. This pen is on finish-ing rations. That one on a starter regimen. As we passed slowly in this surreal journey, the cows stared blankly at us. I felt their eyes on me. The gray-haired ladies surrounding me, chatted and giggled and exclaimed over this and that, as if they were on a tour through the Universal Lot in Hollywood. Only I made eye contact with the ripening produce. I felt hot, flushed, suffocated.

The bus continued to slowly roll. Salvador Dali continued to drone on about "finishing." One small pen, where the cows had green labels instead of the customary orange ones stapled into their left ears, was the "hospital" where animals were sequestered if the vets felt anything was wrong. They were never placed into the regular population again, even if they became healthy, assured Mr. Moustache. At one pen we saw a gigantic transport being loaded. One obese lady who regularly wiped sweat from her brow wanted to know how long the cattle would have to be in those hot trucks on their way to market.

Mr. Moustache explained that the animals were mildly tranquilized and fed moderately in the day or two prior to their trip. "We make sure they are as unstressed as possible. And we send out only to packing-houses within ninety miles of this location. They are harvested within four hours of leaving here."

"Harvested!" The muscles in my stomach contracted. Harvested.

Okay, I'm a farm girl. I've seen my father hoist a dead steer up on a cable hanging from the yard light. With a huge plastic apron tied around him and a knife bigger than a man's arm, I've watched him carve a car-cass into sections, all the while looking at a book with diagrams showing him where to cut. My mother at a folding table beside him would wrap the meat in butcher paper and mark each one, and I would shuttle between her and the house, rushing the bundles into our freezer.

Yes, I know we eat cows and I know we have to kill them first. My father used one quick bullet to the head, but I was never allowed to watch. And I know that all cattle, except those who die of old age and disease, wind up in a packinghouse. It's just that these gentle beasts, in another era, had some kind of life before the day of their demise.

Whether being driven up the Chisolm Trail, or herded into roundups at the OK Corral, or munching at midday in our pasture, there was adventure along the way. Cowboys and horses, wide-open space, prairie rattlers to watch out for. Here it was dead-end boredom, no day different than the next, no hour different from the previous one. No plodding home at dusk on a narrow, winding path with a collie nipping at your heels. No jackrabbits to startle along the way. No shade trees to stand under. No standing head to tail with your buddy, flicking flies out of each other's eyes, tails in perpetual mutual precision. Who says cows are dumb? Not really dumb, just slow-moving—and pragmatic. I have often noticed while driving through the Flint Hills, where cows are still allowed to be free, that in the heat of the day with no trees in sight they find shade, bunching up behind billboards that line the highways. Cows are not dumb. They know where to find water. They know where to find shade. They know how to flick flies out of each other's eyes with the absolute minimum of energy output.

In my youth in our buffalo grass pasture studded with soapweed and prickly pear cactus, I shared a path with our cattle, stepping over their fresh dungbeetle-filled piles, sensing that by staying on their path I was safe.

These poor beasts packed in shoulder to shoulder knew only standing in their own dung in the hot sun and howling wind. Each animal looking ridiculous with a coded orange tag stapled into its left ear. They stood, they ate, and then they died.

Harvested.

The bus was swinging past the parking lot on its way to another section of the yards. I stumbled to the front and asked the driver if he could let me out. "I'm not feeling well. My car is just over there."

Mr. Moustache abruptly stopped and opened the door. "Sometimes the smell affects city folk," he drawled into the microphone. "Me? I don't even notice it. I guess it just goes with the territory. Anybody else feeling a little green?" To me he said, "There's only ten minutes left in the tour, if you want to hang on."

General quiet laughter followed. No one else wanted off the bus. In fact, clearly, the ladies were all having a great time, and they were, frankly, amused by my request. I nodded that indeed I did want to get off. And without a word, I left and hurried back to my car.

The smell, though strong, had no effect on me. It was not nausea, but tears that threatened to undo me. I had walked through littered battle-fields in the Middle East and stayed steady as steel. But somehow, here on "my pasture" turned feedlot, I couldn't withstand the assault of the brown eyes on me, blaming me, beseeching me. I stopped and returned the dull gaze of one dirty-white heifer who moved close to examine me. She was not asking for food, nor curious about me, as had been the cattle in my father's pastures. This animal's expression ranged between the blank of depression to the mildly resignedly accusatory. And then, her eyes spoke to me.

Behind the wheel of my stifling hot rental car, I fled from the parking lot to the road leading off the property. The entrance road was lined on either side with spindly little cedar trees trying to hang on until the next watering of urinatious irrigation. I drove past all the warning signs, too fast over the speed bumps and the final animal guard at the gate— the last line of defense should an animal break free and make a run for it. Then I turned south and inched along the gravel road perimeter of the property trying to regain enough composure to safely drive back to town. I could not. I felt horror, a horror I cannot explain. I could not stop seeing the white cow. I could not erase those brown eyes staring at me, into me. Revealing. Accusing. Pleading. I pulled to the side of the road.

I'm not sure how much time passed. A woman in a van with kids in the back, stopped to see if I needed help. Flustered, I said I was looking for the entrance to the feedlot.

"You missed it. Go back a mile. Turn left at the sign." She gave me this look that said, *How could you be so stupid. You just drove past a sign with a big arrow.*

Two miles later, beside the Old Golden City cemetery, I stopped the car, got out and surveyed the brownpacked hill. Only my disposable panoramic camera, purchased that morning at Duckwall's, could capture the whole scene. I needed to take that picture to convince myself it was real and irreversible. And then I vowed I would never drive out here again. I reached to open the car door to the back seat for my camera. The door was locked. I tried the others. With motor running, air conditioning blasting, radio blaring, I was locked out of my car. A safety feature of the new Olds, doors automatically lock when car is running—even with driver outside of car and even when car is in park and idling. Technology without a brain. I was locked out in the middle of what God intended to be a great desert, with the noontime sun straight above, with the temperature hovering above 90 degrees—highly unusual for April, but then weather on these Plains is always unusual. I was locked out. All windows rolled tightly up to keep in the air conditioning. No weapon to break a window. There was nothing else to do but walk the two miles back to the feedlot perimeter, to a long, dirty-white, stucco-covered house with four bedrooms, now surrounded by dying elm trees and piles of wind-whipped sand. The house where I grew up. A house where I hoped someone lived and would be home to give me a glass of water and allow me to use a phone. I walked past the cemetery. I walked head down and kicked at the loose gravel just as I used to do thirty-some years ago, when my brothers forgot to pick me up from the Willow Valley school on their way home from high school. I would wait until four o'clock, and then if no one came for me, I would start walking. In the blowing dust and hot wind. Five miles. It was at about this spot, when I had two more miles to go, that I would start crying. My tears would drip off my chin as I kept walking. But in this high-noon heat, today, they were drying before they reached my chin.

I was nine years old. And I would cry. Why did I have to walk home from school? Why had everyone in the family forgotten about me? I only wanted to be home. Home to fling my lunchbox onto the kitchen counter, gulp down some cold water and head out to Indian Ridge with my little brother to build campfires, sit in the shade of our father's teepee, and, on tiptoe from the highest point of the ridge, survey the horizon looking for buffalo herds.

When I reached the driveway, I noticed with a shock how stout the trunks of the four elm trees had grown—not unlike the inevitably thickening torsos of old ladies. Could that many years have gone by? It seemed only yesterday that my father had fastened wire to the finger-thin trunks of the saplings and staked them to the ground to keep the wind from bending them. Many thick, lower branches had been trimmed down to ugly stumps, and those few remaining branches sprouted few leaves, like old ladies' thinning hair. Where did the sparrows build their nests now that so much of the foliage was missing? Our elms, lovingly watered twice a week, had created an oasis of protection for birds and shade under which to park our car.

I approached the house. A tricycle was on the porch. Yes, someone lived here. I saw how the porch steps were cracking. I knocked. A young Native American woman answered the door, holding a whimpering baby in her arms. Her hair was streaked with silver-gray, but she didn't look older than perhaps twenty-five. I explained to her how I had locked myself out of the car while I had been visiting a grave at the cemetery and accidentally closed the door.

"I'm so embarrassed. It was so stupid. I need to call a locksmith. Could I use your phone?"

She surveyed me warily. Then mumbling about how messy her house was, with the baby being sick and all, she held open the door with her one free hand and said, "Come in. The phone is in the kitchen."

All the rooms were now covered in a cheap, dark brown fake wood paneling. It made the rooms look hot and small and mean. And so bare. No paintings with brilliant sunsets graced these walls. The wood floors were now covered by the cheapest imaginable, early-eighties, multi-brown shag. The kitchen counter Formica was peeling. The feedlot, which was obviously renting out the house to an employee, had not bothered to keep up the dwelling. The house had served as the company's temporary offices while they were building their two-story headquarters. I guess the feedlot thought wood paneling would make the house look more office-like. Behind our house where barns and sheds once stood, there were now rows and rows of trailer homes to house workers. No trees, no bushes. It looked more like a compound I'd seen in the Australian outback for Aboriginal mine workers than my former farmyard. In fact, it was nothing like our former vibrant Golden Hill farmstead. There was no garden with corn, beans, and endless rows of radishes for the picking. No bushes of mint plants to absorb the dripping garden faucet. No little lawn to water daily. No croquet game perpetually set out on the lawn. No locust tree to give shade. No Russian olive tree hedge to break the wind. No lilac bushes under the kitchen window. No horses, no chickens, no kittens tumbling outside the back door. No pasture.

No pasture. No buffalo grass. No buffalo. No hill. No creek. No swimming hole. No willows. No cottonwoods.

I asked to use the bathroom. That gave me a chance to peak into my room. I remembered what my mother had told me a few months after they sold the farm when she had to go the feedlot office to pick up some legal papers. "There's a great big Xerox machine sitting in your room now, Becky. And would you believe it. Your room is still lilac."

Crazily, I half expected to see the pale lilac walls I'd painted myself, white lace curtains at the window—the ones that had to be taken down and washed once a month because they trapped the fine sand that the wind somehow mysteriously drove into the house even with the windows closed, a large fluffy lilac rug beside the bed. But no, just more dark wood paneling and brown shag carpeting. A baby bed. Toys.

As I passed back through the kitchen I looked into the utility room. More wood paneling. Gone was the pot-bellied gas stove that once stood in the center of the room for those cold winter days when the electricity lines went down and our electric-powered furnace along with them. We would huddle around that stove for heat and light as blizzards raged. I did see the gun closet in the corner near the back door, now with a proper folding door, instead of our hanging canvas curtain to hide the hole. In the other corner was the entrance to the cellar "tornado shelter."

A window over the kitchen sink was cracked. Did the feedlot company not have the money to maintain the house in livable condition? Did the young Native American father, no doubt grateful for a job off the reservation, lack the guts to ask Mr. Moustache to fix the windows, or install air conditioning, or recarpet the floors, or at least tear the dirty shag out to rediscover the fine wood underneath? I wondered how much rent they were paying to live in this firetrap of a dwelling.

I did not tell the young mother, worried over her child's fever, embarrassed about toys strewn on the floor, I did not tell her I used to live in this house. That the walls beneath the dark paneling held the sweetest memories any child could cherish, that the laughter of six children once echoed wall to wall. That the lovely wood floor under the dirty old carpet was once soiled by Johnny, my brother's dwarf horse when he brought him into the house to scare my mother.

I will never forget the look on Mom's face. She was washing dishes at the sink, back turned to my brother who had quietly entered leading the horse into the kitchen. The radio was playing and she didn't hear the clank of Johnny's hooves on the linoleum. I looked up from my freshman Algebra homework and my mouth dropped open.

"Mom, he's hungry. Do you have something for Johnny to eat?" Tommy said gently, all smiles, about to burst into laughter. Mom turned around absently, her hands dripping soap water. And shrieked. Her shriek scared Johnny. When he bolted, all four legs slid out of control like Bambi on the ice pond.

By the time Tommy and I had Johnny under control, the kitchen floor was, well, dirtied. After we tied Johnny to the honey locust out back, we came back in to find my mom sitting on a kitchen chair laughing so hard she was shaking and tears were pouring out of her eyes. It's a wonder she could still have any sense of humor after raising six children, four of them rambunctious boys, and one of them a tomboy always disappearing into the pasture when there was housework to be done.

Always there were animals in this house—pets of every possible species, birds and fish and furry things. The only time mom got angry about any of them was when Tommy's pet snake got out of his homemade cage and was lost in the house for six days. "He's just a bull snake. Not poisonous," Tommy kept saying. One day she found him curled up on her pillow. She did not laugh that time.

The town's only locksmith was not listed in the Odyssey yellow pages. I guess everybody in town knew his name. But a reporter knows what to do. The sheriff's office gave me his number. I kept dialing it. No answer, not even an answering tape message.

I was overstaying my welcome. The young woman was clearly uncomfortable. I heard a kind of muffled whimpering, like a child having a nightmare. It seemed to source either from the back bedroom that was once the boys' room or the guestroom next to it. (It always puzzled me that Mom insisted that one room sit unused, perfectly orderly, waiting for possible guests, when our large family could have used the space. Perhaps that one uncluttered room helped her feel that some measure of order did exist in our turbulent environment, or perhaps she lived with the fantasy that one day an important guest would come up our driveway and change our lives in ways we could not even imagine.) The young woman nervously glanced at me to see if I had heard the sound. I guess she saw me look in the direction of the back bedrooms. "My other children," she mumbled as if ashamed, "are not well today." I did not reply but merely nodded and smiled for I had the phone up to my ear. I had dialed the number once more. Finally, after perhaps a dozen rings, an answer. The town's only locksmith was back from lunch. He promised to come out immediately. "It's those new Oldsmobiles," he drawled sympathetically. "You're not the first one."

"Where did you live before this?" I asked, trying to make small talk with the shy Indian woman. "Oklahoma." She did not elaborate. I asked her for a drink of water. She brought me a huge plastic glass stamped with the feedlot logo, which she filled from the tap. It tasted terrible. Funny, the water from our well used to taste so good, so sweet. I hated to think what was seeping into the well water nowadays. Maybe that's why her baby was always sick. But I had to drink it. The inside of my mouth was cotton. And I had two miles to walk back to my car under an unrelenting sun.

I exited the stucco house, water in hand—she insisted I take the plastic glass with me—with profuse thanks and apologies. Down the dusty driveway. I left a house I'd long ago left, and trudged down a dirt road I used to bicycle down on cool evenings. I was thirteen. Riding my bicycle, dreaming of the young bronze boy I loved, the one who could run as fast as the wind. I cherished the sweet northerly breeze with its surprising bursts of coolness as dusk fell. I pretended I would meet him accidentally as he rode by in his pickup. I would see a dust trail over the horizon. I would dismount my bike and wait by the side of the road for the pickup to pass. He would slow when he saw me, then suddenly stop. He'd lean out and drawl. "Do you need any help?"

"Oh no, my bike wheel is a little flat. I'm just walking it back to my yard."

"Oh, I'll give you a hand." He'd jump out, and cockily lift the bike into the back of the pickup. He'd catch me in my lie. The tire was not flat at all. But he'd pretend not to notice.

I would shyly open the passenger door and hoist myself in. No four-teen-year-old boy in these parts would be gallant enough to open a door for a girl. It would be way too embarrassing, but the thought would cross his mind and he would blush.

But then instead of turning into my driveway, he'd go past it. "Wanna go for a little ride." He'd say it as a statement, not a question. And we'd head out, going south—into the unknown. ("There's nothing impor-tant south," my father would say on our Sunday drives. He'd always turn either north or west, and sometimes east. Never south.)

My girlhood was made up of such daydreams—delicious, warm, tin-gling daydreams with mystery, intrigue and romance just around every bend. The vast, terribly blue Western Kansas sky, the flat, pale earth with its sun-washed greens and golds, the shimmering mirage on the roads— all of it lent itself to endless daydreams.

I walked back to my locked car. The breeze was in my face. But thir-ty years later, the breeze had turned acrid. I could even taste the foul air. The subtle scents of grass, wild flowers, cactus and soapweed were overwhelmed and extinguished. The land—even the air—was forever changed. The past no longer existed. Where the once-proud, beautiful Gentle Wind gazed outside her father's teepee hoping to catch sight of the brave she secretly loved, another bronze-faced and old-too-soon young Indian woman waved goodbye to me, as she clutched a crying child on the porch of an old stucco home standing on the edge of an artificial, bulldozer-arranged slope covered with soylent brown. The landscape had forever changed yet again.

THROUGHOUT MY ADULT LIFE, I've had two reoccurring dreams. In one, I get into our turquoise and white Oldsmobile with the tailfins and I head south from our farm. The road suddenly curves southwest— very curious. Roads don't go at angles here. They are laid out in straight miles. Each section of land a perfect square. Every mile anoth-er dirt road. Rivers curve and meander as they wish. But roads go east and west, north and south. But now, this road is defiantly slanting and curving. At some point, I go over a hill and see trees, lots of them. Dark green trees. Thick and thicker. Forest-like. I keep driving, amazed. I did not know they were here. I'd assumed that if I drove south, I would merely see more dust-blowing fields, more flat-as-far-as-you-could-see landscape. Yes, a lone tree here and there. An abandoned homestead, a rusty windmill. But forest? Never. Dusk is falling. And suddenly I am in a town, a small city, actually. The streets are lined with dense pear-shaped trees filled with little blinking white lights. Like Christmas, but it's summer. The street is filled with little cafes with tables and light spilling out on the sidewalks. Waiters balance trays of food as they serve the outdoor diners. Along the street, interspersed with the cafes are all kind of little shops displaying amazing beautiful things. People are strolling arm in arm. I park and begin to walk in a daze. I didn't know this was here. In all those years I lived in Western Kansas, I never knew that a few minutes from my home there was a delightful, lively, sophisticated city. If I had only known this was just over the horizon, I would have never left.

A SECOND DREAM—one from which I awake in a panic: I am playing with my baby in a sandbox. My baby is only a half-inch long. Miniature, but perfect. I love my baby. It's difficult to feed and care for him because he is so small, but I do it, with a heart bursting with pride and joy and love. The phone rings. I go inside for just a moment to answer it. When I come back out to the sandbox, the baby is gone. Disappeared. I frantically sift through the sand with my fingers, trying to find my baby. He must have sunk into the sand. After all he is so small. He will be smothered. He can't breathe in that sand. I run back into the house and get a tea strainer. I sift through the sand, hoping I will find my baby. How could I be so careless, so stupid to leave my baby for a moment. I awaken from this dream crying, my heart beating so fast that I cannot calm down and go back to sleep.

I would much rather dream about the city over the hill where all things are possible. Even though it makes me ache with possibilities lost, opportunities spurned.

• • •

DOWN THE ROAD IN A TRAIL of dust comes a pickup. It's the lock-smith. In moments, his little wire contraption does the trick. The charge is $30. When I try to give him an extra ten dollar tip he is insulted. He's gone. I'm alone in my car. I contemplate turning around and heading back to town. It would be good to take a shower.

No. I want to finally go south. It's about time.

The road does not slant, does not curve. There are no forests. South indeed is as I've always known it would be, miles and miles of flat, dusty landscape. It will be this way until I hit the Cimarron River. And then it dawns on me. Yes, there is something waiting for me south. To get there I must double back within a mile of the feedlot, go east and rejoin the highway going south toward Oklahoma.

32

Ridge of Blood

I TOLD HER. I SHOULD NOT HAVE. My story spilled out through the brown eyes of the white beast. It was wrong. But I could not contain my darkness. Too much sorrow, just as too much joy, must spill out.

She is an old woman now, almost the age as I was when I died along the trail. But she does not look old. Perhaps she went to the other side of the sun and the young king renewed her body. Her hair is still golden. She walks nearly as easily as she did as a child. I did not mean to tell her. But her morning sky eyes sucked the truth out of me. I did not mean to tell her about the Morning of Blood.

We were the very last ones. The very last of the clans of the Plains to leave. My son, Two Eagles, was once a great warrior. He rode with the Dog Soldiers attacking, fighting, killing, trying to save our land from the invaders. He lived to see all of his companions killed or captured. He said there must be another way. He prayed to the Great Spirits who told him to return to lead us and they instructed him that our clan should plant ourselves, as the grass, on this sacred ridge beside our ancestral Little Buffalo River. We will stay here, he told our small clan. The Treaty at Medicine Lodge promised our peoples all land south of the Great River. This is two day's journey south of the Great River. This land belongs to us. When they come, if they come, we will trust the spirits to keep us safe on our sacred summer hunting grounds.

For a long time they did not know we were here. The willow woods were thick. We could hide. We sent our horses away, because, said Two Eagles, if they saw horses, they would know we were here. Then we killed our dogs, because if they heard our dogs howling, they would know we were here. It pained us to kill our dogs but you cannot send a dog away. He will stay by his master forever. We taught our children to not cry, to not make a sound if white men were near. We had special hiding places. We dug one hiding place into a hill and covered it with willow branches. Safe inside the dark of the earth we hid. But we were too many. At night we came outside our cave to see the stars and we burned our campfires to stay warm. They saw our smoke. Our days of hiding had come to an end.

They rode in on many horses and asked to speak to our chief. "You must leave this land, you must go to a place called Oklahoma where the dirt is as red as your skin," they said with mockery and derision in their voices.

"Why do white men call us red?" I would ask my father when I was a child. "Why do we call them white?" he answered. My father often answered a question with a question. He was a wise man and part of wisdom is teaching others to answer their own questions.

"We call them white only because they insist on being called white," I answered, then added, "White is not such a good color, it is the color of bones. We are not red. Red is the color of blood.

"Perhaps their blood runs white," I said. "No," responded my older brother, who was a warrior and once killed a white man. "Their blood is red, the same as ours."

"Perhaps when they see us, all they see is blood," I said. "Because that is the future they want for us. Blood spilling out on the land." I was a child when I said that. I did not understand that it was a prophecy.

The soldiers were becoming impatient with Two Eagles, for my son continued to repeat the words of the Medicine Lodge Treaty. "It was promised to our father, our great chief, that our children and grandchildren and their grandchildren will stay on this land forever."

The chief of the soldiers said, "You want your children to stay on this ridge? Is that what you want? Okay that is what you will get. If you have not packed for moving by the morning, I promise you your children will stay on this ridge. You, however will go," they said to Two Eagles.

"He promised me," said my son around the campfire that night, "that if we do not pack our things by the morning that our children will stay on this ridge. Yet, he said it in anger. I do not know if I should believe him, but that is what he said." So my son told the clan, "Do not dismantle your teepees. Do not pack your things for a journey. Sleep." But Two Eagles stayed up all night puzzling over the meaning of the soldier's words. He repeated them to himself over and over: *Your children will stay on this ridge. You, however will go.* They mean to take me away, but let the clan stay, reasoned my son. Then I will allow myself to be led away, even put to death, so that my children might stay.

The next morning, we had not packed. The soldiers gave us shovels. Dig a deep ditch twelve feet long. We did. Perhaps they will make us bury our belongings because we refused to pack our things, we thought.

Then they lined up the children from the tallest to the smallest along the ridge. There were only twelve children in our clan. Many others had died of sickness and hunger. They instructed the children to put their hands over their eyes. And then while we looked on, dumb, understanding nothing, they began to fire their rifles. Boom, boom, boom. Just as if they were shooting buffalo. Blood ran everywhere. The children fell into the ditch. When the soldiers were finished not a child stood. The chief of the soldiers said, Are you satisfied? Like the Treaty said, your children will stay on this land forever.

We could not make a sound. And then came our sounds. Wailing and wailing. Shrieks and cries reaching to the heavens. My son, filled with horror at this trick, held himself responsible because he did not discern the meaning of the white chief's words. So in front of me, my beloved firstborn thrust a spear through his own heart. And his blood ran with the blood of the children. We had killed our dogs and sent our horses away. But the dog spirits howled, and the horse spirits whinnied that high shrill sound horses make when they are afraid.

If I had a spear I would have run it through my heart just as my son did.

The soldiers took their shovels and covered the children with earth. I saw one young soldier, no older than some of our young boys in the ditch, look at me. His eyes were clear like the sky and I could see he was ashamed. While he was shoveling he started to vomit. Two other young soldiers also became sick. Their chief screamed at them. "Be men," he shouted.

How, I ask you, do they call themselves men?

We are like buffalo to them. I am surprised that they did not leave our children's bones to bleach in the sun like they did the buffalo. My daughter says they buried the children not out of respect but out of fear and shame. They did not want anyone to know what happened here.

They made us begin our march after we had packed our camp.

My daughter Wind Storm, a mother now without children, said, "I will tell. When we get to Oklahoma I will tell someone what happened. Somewhere there will be one good white man. I will tell him what happened."

She talks that way—believing in one good white man—because she once loved a white man, a trader who wore garments of skin and braided his hair as do our braves. He loved her too. But when he built himself a house beside the Great River, he sent for a white woman to join him from the East, so my daughter walked away from his camp and came to live again with me. Her heart was broken. I told her that children would mend her heart, so she became the wife of a brave who had lost his wife to sickness, and when my daughter bore children they were a comfort to her.

I was wrong. It would be better if she had died of a broken heart. Better had she not borne children than to see them bleeding in this ditch of horror.

We did not go far before I died. We made it only to the Buffalo River, which they call the Cimarron. They stopped to let us drink from our people's sacred spring they call the Lower Springs. Even with the water on my dry and burning throat, I knew I could walk no further. "I will die here by this spring," I said. My daughter begged to remain behind to honor me as I drew last breath, but the soldiers said no.

"Please go," I told my clansmen, "and tell the white men I do not wish to be buried in the ground along this trail. Instead leave me to die alone in the sun caressed by the Spirit of the Wind." They granted my wish. As I lay dying, I asked the vultures circling above to take my flesh back to the Ridge of Blood so my spirit could be with my grandchildren.

Nadi-ish-dena.

33

Wagonbed Springs

AT THE POINT WHERE THE highway curved east, I kept going straight onto a familiar gravel road. I felt a tightness in my chest and throat as I passed rows and rows of pig barns and had to pull to the side of the road as a Hog Express truck passed, leaving a horrible pigshit smell and taste in the air in its wake. Soon a second hog truck passed. Is it possible they had despoiled the Cimarron River too? Was our one historical spot also gone, bulldozed to make way for hog-growing chambers? I was relieved to see the familiar signpost. Yes, Wagonbed Springs still existed. I slowed, entering over the cattle guard into a landscape so exquisitely beautiful that tears began to sting as I drove down the hard-packed dirt trail to our holy site.

The deep wagon wheel ruts of the Santa Fe Trail were still visible on the hillside to my right. All around me, the soft, rolling hills were covered by buffalo grass, sagebrush, prickly pear cactus just starting to bloom, soapweed, and a profusion of wildflowers—white and yellow and lilac. These were the muted colors of the prairie I loved so much. A meadowlark sang its throaty song from a fencepost. A startled jackrabbit ran from his hiding place as I neared. I stopped the car, and pulled on the cowboy boots I'd thrown into the back seat. Then I headed across the grassland to the river, choosing each step slowly and carefully looking for rattlesnakes. I was alone—with no snakebite kit. No one could save me from their bite. I hadn't intended to end up here.

I had to know that someplace sacred still existed, that my childhood was not a mirage. There had been a paradise once, and pieces of it still must exist outside my heart.

I was not disappointed. I picked my way to the edge of a ravine, and climbed, mostly slid on my butt, down a steep embankment into a large dry bend of the river that was covered in the whitest of sand—a pristine beach minus its ocean. There were tracks in the sand of birds, of jackrabbits, but no slither lines from snakes. I felt a bit safer. I lay down on the sand and felt its warmth on the whole length of my body. Then I climbed up the other side of the bank seeking the shade of a large cottonwood tree.

There had once been many cottonwoods and dense willow thickets along these banks. Now, with the water table sucked out from under them, only a few cottonwoods remained. These hardy survivors had leaves on their lower branches, but the top branches were bare, dead horns sticking out into the pale blue. Trees not willing to die. Hanging on for dear life. I sat down underneath the largest of them.

I had forgotten the sound of the wind in a cottonwood tree. The leaves tinkle, mimicking falling rain. A sound so soothing, so hopeful, so utterly peaceful, it is virtually an invitation to fall asleep. Above me, on the healthy limbs, seed modules were bursting, but their cotton was not yet flying about. In a week, the white fuzz would fill the air in a feeble attempt to repopulate the banks of the Cimarron. There was little chance that any seed could find the moisture to even sprout, but like the stubborn breed of people who chose to live on these windwashed Plains, they never gave up.

To the east and to the west of where I sat, the riverbank was lined with the remains of once proud cottonwoods. Massive fallen trunks bleaching white in the sun like giant bones. Sometimes a branch stuck up like the horns of a fallen longhorn steer, whose strength wore out before reaching the end of the trail. But a few trees have made it, testament to a time when water actually ran down this river.

No longer would giddy teenagers have to worry that they might fall into the quicksand that once sucked naïve, thirsty settlers to their death when they waded into the shallow water for a drink or drove their wagons across what looked like innocent sand. That danger was gone. Gone too was the danger from Indians lurking in the willows to kill settlers or scouts who had reached the Lower Springs so desperate for water that they did not look for attackers.

Many died here at the legendary Wagonbed Springs—the only water on a sixty-mile stretch of the Santa Fe Trail cut-off after it left the Arkansas River at Dodge City. It was a shortcut that only the foolhardy would take. They arrived thrilled to reach water, only to be pierced through the heart by a carefully aimed arrow. Kit Carson frequently came through here on his way to Santa Fe. He survived. Jedediah Smith, another famous explorer of the West, was not so lucky. In 1831, Comanches surprised the thirsty traveler as he bent down to drink. In 1864, fifteen men were killed at the Springs by Indians within a two-week period. We were, after all, the invaders. We had come to slaughter the buffalo, drive the Indians from their lands, and then as a final insult, plow under the buffalo grass and destroy the landscape forever.

Another invasion was now in full swing. Now the invaders had business plans cooked up in boardrooms. Now it was vulnerable farmers, hot and thirsty, bending down to drink from the Springs, and like Gideon's men, not looking. How many more, after my father, had bled from the heart to make way for feedlots and hog barns, packing plants and chicken sheds? In other places in this country it has been strip mines and suburban developments with English country names that forever changed the landscape. How many more, like cottonwoods and cactus, coyotes and deer, would be blinded in the headlights of progress?

But I was tired of carrying historical catastrophe on my shoulders. I only wanted to sit under the tinkling cottonwood to watch the sun go down. And after the sunset colors faded from the sky, I would return to the white sand just below me, take my shoes off and savor the last time I had walked barefoot on this sand. *I dare not, I dare not think of it. I dare not.*

I had come home to say goodbye before leaving for London. He had come home to say goodbye before leaving for Viet Nam. He called me up. Why was he calling, how did he even know I was here? We had not spoken since graduation day. More accurately, we had not seen each other since graduation day. In truth, except for the few words whispered at the football homecoming ceremony, we had not spoken since that December day when we were juniors in high school and I made him stop his car to let me out.

Luke and I had to walk down the aisle together at graduation because our last names were alphabetically near one another. But he made sure we were always out of step, and that our shoulders never touched. That was the last time I'd seen him. Our paths had not crossed in five years. He went to Yale. I went to the University of Kansas. He had gone to Marine bootcamp. I had gone to the Democratic Convention in Chicago. He wanted to kick Charlie's butt in Southeast Asia. I wanted to stop the war. We had nothing in common except . . .

He called my parents and asked for me.

"How did you know I'm home?"

"My sister works with your cousin at the bank. I'm taking you out for a fancy dinner."

"There's nothing fancy for miles."

"I'll pick you up at seven."

So ten years after waiting for him to come down the driveway in a trail of dust, he did. Not in a pickup, but in a magnificent little red MG convertible. He parked under the elm trees, then slowly climbed out of his convertible. I watched him from behind a curtain hoping he would not see. In high school he had possessed a kind of gangly, cocky, brash good looks, but now he was drop-dead, brooding-movie-star hand-some. His red-brown hair was thick and shorter than fashionable. His eyes dark chocolate-brown, almost black. His skin suntan bronze. In high school the rumor was that Luke was part Cheyenne. His grand-mother on his father's side, or was it his father's grandmother had been a full-blooded Indian. He denied it vehemently. But I once overheard the track coach say it was his "Injun" blood that made him such a fast runner. He always won state medals in the sprint. As Odyssey High School's star quarterback, once he got the football he was unstoppable. Luke's two sisters were as blond and blue-eyed as our family was. It was as if all the Indian genes—if indeed the rumors were true—had been saved up and funneled into Luke alone. He was wearing a rust-colored silk shirt with long loose, fluttery sleeves, open a couple of buttons down from the collar. It was not a Western Kansas kind of a shirt. In fact, that was the kind of shirt that could get you thrown out of Dodge. When he knocked at the door, I took my sweet time answering.

He looked at me. He said nothing, but with just a hint of a smile, he seemed to appreciate what he was seeing. My hair was long and straight, sort of like Mary's of Peter, Paul and Mary. Blowing in the

Wind. I probably had overly-teased, overly-sprayed helmet hair when last he'd seen me in 1964. Tonight I was wearing a white and peach print silk dress that hit four inches above the knees. It was, after all the early seventies. Sheer stockings, white high-heeled sandals, a little mascara.

We both looked more Los Angeles, California than Odyssey, Kansas. We knew it without saying it and both laughed as we folded ourselves into his vehicle, also not a Western Kansas kind of car. Convertibles don't make sense where the dust is always blowing.

Luke was a man of few but well-chosen words. In that, he was still a man of the High Plains, despite the silk shirt, the pipe hanging from the corner of his mouth and his Ivy League arrogance.

Western Kansas men are creatures of few words. And Western Kansas women are creatures of too many words, words that tumble out unbridled to fill the empty spaces created by the sky and the silent men around them. The mens' words, when said, are blunt, to the point, often funny. Saying only what is needed and no more.

I've tried to mimic that. And often my speech is that of a Western Kansas man. But when I write, I blow it. The words spill out in endless repetitions, scintillating variations, twisting and turning and experimenting with the very sound of themselves. I think it's poetic. My editors think it's crap. They yell at me and sharpen their red pencils. And when they are finished, my stories—at least for the *Chicago Tribune*—are long on content and short on style, just the way the World's Greatest Newspaper wants it. But in my journals and on these pages, my words wander where they wish.

But now, with Luke—the dark-haired, dark-eyed, bronze boy of my daydream years—beside me, I kept my verbiage in check.

"Wonder why I called?" he asked.

"Nope, I know. We're the only two people in our class not married yet. That probably makes me the only single girl in the county."

"That's not why."

"Then why?"

"Cause you're the first girl I ever had a crush on."

"Yeah, sure. That's why you never asked me for a date in four years of high school."

"I was afraid to ask you out."

"You didn't know I was alive. I was the class wallflower. Remember?"

"Wrong again. Everyone noticed you. You were the prettiest girl in school."

I WAS AMAZED AT LUKE'S SMUGNESS, and his ability to lie—not a Western Kansas trait. I remembered what a mutual friend, Matt, had said one night when he was slightly—well, way more than slightly— drunk in a bar just off campus at the University of Kansas.

He looked deep into my eyes and out of the blue said, "Becky, promise me something. Stay away from Luke. He treats women bad."

It was a curious statement since we hadn't been talking about Luke. Plus, he was miles away on the East Coast at some Ivy League school that his father's new oil well made affordable. Matt had been reminiscing about some prank he'd played on our high school Spanish teacher for which he was now saying made him, Matt, somehow to blame for our former teacher's suicide last year.

I didn't respond to Matt's warning about Luke since it was completely irrelevant. Plus, I was busy thinking about how I had to make sure I got Matt's car keys away from him in case he thought he was going to drive home in his present state of beer-soaked regret over our Spanish teacher's untimely death.

"It's as if I killed him, Becky," Matt pounded the table, making the empty beer bottles shudder, and I thought he was going to cry.

We were supposed to be celebrating his Fulbright scholarship— announced just the day before—and here was Matt . . .

See what I mean about Western Kansas women? We fill way too much space with our words.

LUKE STOPPED TO PUT THE TOP down as soon as we reached the paved highway.

"So where are we going?" I asked.

"You'll see."

He turned south. Must be going to Liberal, I thought. Must be a new steak house in Liberal. Out here, all the better restaurants are steak houses. Judging from his speed, perhaps he's even going to Amarillo. That's more than two hours away. They would certainly have good steak houses in Amarillo. Actually, I knew nothing about Amarillo. I'd never been there. That was after all, *south.*

But then when the highway curved east, Luke kept going straight, flying down a gravel road.

"Nothing's as beautiful as sunset from Wagonbed Springs," he said matter-of-factly.

He took it real slow on the trail. I assumed this was a whim, an unscheduled sidetrip, a good one, though. I loved Wagonbed. We got out at the trail's end. He opened the trunk, and lifted out a fully loaded wicker picnic basket.

I began to laugh.

"For this you made me get dressed up?"

"I never said dress up. I merely said fancy dinner."

We walked, me hanging on to him awkwardly, as I negotiated the clumps of buffalo grass and prickly pear in my high-heeled sandals. We picked our way down a cow path leading to the river's edge. He found the least steep way down. It was June and the riverbed was dry, the sand as white as today.

The sunset was minutes away from its peak in color. He opened the basket. Out came a red and white checkered tablecloth. A bottle of Champagne. A second bottle, this one Merlot. French bread, Brie cheese, a cluster of red grapes. Two long-stemmed wine glasses. Small glass plates, a knife and two red-checkered cloth napkins.

"I forgot the blanket for us to sit on," he said, and scrambled up the embankment to go back to the car. With one deft motion after Luke was out of sight, I got rid of the pantyhose and heels. While waiting for him to return, I played around squishing my toes in the sand. I felt almost frightened. I had, after all, been dropped down into the middle of a girlhood fantasy with the object of my earliest adolescent longings. Furthermore, there were few places on earth I loved more than this bend of the Cimarron River. He didn't know that. He couldn't know that. I had never talked with anyone about it, not even my soulmate buddy, Matt.

And how did he know I loved Brie? My cousin didn't even know what Brie was, let alone that I liked it, so she couldn't have told his sister at the bank. And where do you buy Brie in Western Kansas, or French bread, for that matter?

There followed the most romantic meal of my lifetime. We toasted the sunset with Champagne. We spread the Brie on bread, then he added apple slices on top of the Brie. We switched to Merlot, filling our wine glasses far too many times. We rolled around the sand giggling like the teenagers we might once have been. We fed each other grapes with adult sensuousness as dusk fell on the dry river.

When he began to undress me I did not protest or feign surprise. I took off his silk shirt slowly and carefully, button by button. Like in a dream with no words, we made love. And when we finished we looked long into each other's eyes. Still no words. And we made love again.

When we were finally satiated, we lay side by side and covered ourselves with the tablecloth because now the night chill had set in.

The wise cracking between us was forever over.

"You really are the first girl I ever noticed."

He told me about the crush he had on me in seventh grade. We had both attended one-room country schools, located a dozen miles away from each other. Several times a year the country schools got together for track meets, spelling contests, pioneer days, and other events the county superintendent devised in her spare time. Luke told me how he stole glances at me every chance he got. How he was too afraid to say one word to me.

So I confessed too—about my hopeless crush on him, starting in eighth grade.

"I always won the spelling contest," I told Luke. "You were the reason I didn't win in eighth grade. You were seated directly behind me, and I was so aware of you, I couldn't concentrate on the words."

"I didn't place that year either," he told me. It was too dark for me to see his sly grin, but I could hear it in his voice. "That's because all I could think of was how beautiful your hair was, so light and blond and fluffy in that ponytail. I'll never forget your ponytail. So close I could have touched it."

We made love one more time, then gathered the basket, and folded the blanket. Then hand in hand, we made our way in the moonlight back to the car. Shortly before reaching the car, the heel broke off my right shoe. I abandoned the sandals and picked my way barefoot the last few steps. After I stepped on a prickly pear cactus, he lifted me in his arms and carried me to the car. Then he fished a flashlight out of his glove compartment and with a tweezers I found in my purse, pulled the cactus spine out of my heel.

TWO WEEKS LATER, in the Russell Square area of London I was still limping from a piece of cactus spine lodged deep inside my heel. I finally went to the university clinic and a doctor cut deep into my foot to remove a tiny sliver of cactus spine.

"Never did that before. Extract a cactus, that is. From the American West," chirped the twerpy British medical intern who did the honors.

I spent the summer in London studying D. H. Lawrence. Luke spent the summer driving across the West to California. "I want to see the whole country before I ship out to Viet Nam, he had told me." I got a postcard from the Grand Canyon, delivered to my dorm in London.

I desperately hoped he'd come to his senses during his soul-searching odyssey through the West. Maybe he'd meet an old Indian medicine man. Maybe he'd see a lone eagle on a mountaintop, and he would disappear into Mexico or Canada. Simply not show up for his Viet Nam assignment.

After I returned from London, and just two weeks after I started my new job at the *Chicago Tribune,* Luke showed up on my doorstep unannounced. "I'm on my way back to Quantico. I ship out in two weeks. I suppose you're just getting home from some protest march."

He was being mean-spirited right from the start.

It was a Thursday evening. I called in sick the next day, giving myself a long weekend with him. I showed Luke the Great Bear Dunes on the eastern shore of Lake Michigan—the closest thing I could get to the Wagonbed Springs dry sand. We slid down the sand dunes on our butts. Then we drove farther north, and I spread out a picnic meal on a quiet beach on the shores of Lake Michigan in an out-of-the-way place John and I used to stop at on our way up to Silver Bay. After dark Luke and I lay quietly under a blanket on the beach and made love to the sounds of lapping waves.

We talked all night, our little sandy campsite lit only by moonlight and warmed by our campfire. Luke regularly added logs and stoked the fire, sending red sparks ascending into the black night. We lay side by side, not even interested in sleep. "I am at a disadvantage with you," I said stroking his cheek, my face inches from his, my breath mingling with his. "You can look into my pale eyes and see what I am thinking, but when I looked deep into your dark eyes I can see nothing but my own reflection."

"It's my Indian eyes," he smiled. "They hold ancient secrets."

So I asked him. "Are you really part Indian, like Coach Beldon used to say?"

"One-quarter Cheyenne. I'll tell you about it if you promise not to put it in that novel you're writing."

"I'm not writing a novel."

"Well then, the novel you will someday write."

"If I do, I'll disguise it so you'll never recognize it," I teased.

As you know, my grandfather was one of the first ranchers in the area. Had a pretty big spread south of Odyssey—at one time, even bigger than the Houston ranch. An operation his size took a lot of cowpokes and they bunked on the ranch. My grandmother had to feed them when they weren't out on the range. She found a young Indian woman to help her cook, actually they brought the girl down with them from Nebraska where Grandpop ranched with his dad on the North Platte before he moved to the Odyssey area.

"Anyway, turns out my father was the love child of my grandfather and this Indian girl. When the baby was born—the girl had managed to hide her pregnancy from Grandma—Grandma hit the ceiling, went to the bunkhouse demanding to know which of the cowboys had been sleeping with her. They all denied it. Grandma was furious. She was fixing to fire whoever it was. A couple of weeks later, when the baby's black hair fell out and red hair grew in, she realized who the child's father was.

"The Indian girl mysteriously disappeared," continued Luke. "Grandma adopted the baby boy, raised it as her own, even told everyone it was her own. Most of them weren't fooled. Especially since Doc Anderson—who would have been the person to attend to Grandma's pregnancy and delivery—had a big mouth.

"My father says that the rumor, at least among the cowhands, was that Grandma poisoned the Indian woman and buried her in the garden.

They'd noticed a suspicious-looking plot of freshly dug earth in a corner of the garden the next day, and that part of the garden grew up with
a tangle of weeds that could not be tamed. The cowhands feared getting on Grandma's bad side, and after that they always got the youngest,
dumbest cowpokes in the bunkhouse to taste Grandma's food before
they'd eat it."

"Do you think it was true? Do you actually think your grandma
could have killed the Indian woman?"

"Who knows? She was a mean old lady. That's for sure. I was scared
of her even before I heard that story," Luke grinned.

"That's quite a tale," I teased Luke, who obviously had enjoyed
telling it—so much so, that I half believed he was pulling my leg. "That
definitely goes in my novel."

Luke started tickling me. We were rolling over and over in the sand,
laughing so hard we nearly rolled into the campfire.

When we fell quiet again, I asked, "Luke, why did it upset you so
much when you were a teenager and somebody would refer to your
being part Indian? Why wouldn't you acknowledge it?"

"I didn't know it was true then. Everybody in our family denied it,
that is, as long as my grandma was alive. When my father was dying of
cancer in the hospital, he just out and told me the story one day. Dad
didn't really look Indian, not with that red hair, though I can see it now.
But somehow the Cheyenne blood showed up in me. I guess that's why
my grandmother always hated me. She was mean to me, even when I
was a little kid.

"So if it was such a big secret, how did your father know about it?"
I asked.

"Another deathbed confession kind of thing. Dad heard it from my
grandpop shortly before he died—he'd had a stroke. Lost most of his
memory. But all Grandpop could talk about on his deathbed was her."

"The Indian girl?"

"Yeah, I guess he really loved her."

"Do you know what her name was?"

"My father said it was Cheyenne for Burning Fire. That's because as
a girl, she once rescued her baby brother from a burning teepee and was
badly burned. She had scars on her arms and legs. But Grandpop said
despite her scars, she was the most beautiful woman who ever lived."

"That's a lovely story." I was in awe.

We were quiet, contemplating the romance of the story, the romance of the night, our night, our last night.

Luke broke the silence. "It explains a lot."

"About your father?"

"No, about me."

"Your speed," I said, remembering the coach saying it was the Indian blood that made Luke so fast. I was thinking about his track medals and his extraordinary touchdown dashes as quarterback for Odyssey High.

"No, I'm like my grandpop. I can't resist beautiful, mysterious women."

Suddenly, I felt anger rising from my chest.

"No, no, no. It's you," he soothed me. Apparently my eyes were indeed giving me away, and Luke, as no other man before or since, could read my eyes. "It's you," he repeated. "You are the mysterious and beautiful woman that I can't resist."

But my anger did not abate. Inexplicably, I felt the urge to haul off and slap him. Luke seemed oddly pleased that he had stirred something so tempestuous within me. He soothed me with kisses and held me while I cried. I touched his face, and found it wet with tears as well. I don't think either of us understood my anger that night. I was angry and jealous, not of other women, but of a war. How could he leave me to go off and fight a ridiculous war?

When he dropped me at my apartment the next morning, he took from the trunk of his car a cigar box filled with little boyhood treasures: some arrowheads, track medals, class ring, newspaper clipping of football victories, Marine medallions, some old black and white dog-eared photos, a dozen other curious objects whose significance was known only to him.

"Keep this box for me," he said. "If I return, I'll pick it up. If I don't, you can keep it or throw it away. It doesn't matter." He continued to rattle instructions—like the Marine commander he was. "I won't write any letters. And I don't want you to write me any. I need to be totally focused on what I'm doing over there. I'm going to come back a three-star general. The youngest one ever."

We tried to say goodbye. I clung to him. He disengaged me.

"By the way, I *did* touch it."

"What are you talking about?"

"Your ponytail. Eighth grade. Spelling contest. I let my pencil roll off the desk. Then when I leaned over to pick it up, my cheek brushed up against your ponytail."

He didn't say, I love you. He had never said those words. And neither had I.

The very last thing Luke said to me was, "Promise me. The next good man you run across, you'll marry him."

His little red car disappeared down Sheridan Road, swallowed up by Chicago's early morning rush hour. I knew he would not come back. I called in sick for another day. And when I finally returned to my cubicle in the city room, I wore dark glasses. My eyes were still swollen.

FIVE MONTHS LATER. February 19, 1972. I knew the exact moment of his death.

I left work early and drove south in my ladybug—now properly repainted black—down the Dan Ryan Expressway until it ended. Then I drove south on a road going toward Kankakee. I kept going, turning west, then south until I was hopelessly lost in the Illinois countryside as dusk was falling. I parked my car beside a pasture of tall, dried February grass and wandered into the middle of it. Somewhere deep in, I lay down prone in the grass and wailed. Out where no one could hear me, with the tall grass hiding me, I wailed, and ranted and felt sharp stabbing pains in my belly. I writhed on the ground in the dirt and grass.

A group of black and white dairy cows left their grazing and encircled me, softly mooing and shuffling about, joining in my mourning.

Just nine months earlier another group of cattle had paused on their slow march along the banks of the dry Cimarron River on their way to their watering tank and watched our coupling. I know what they're saying I had whispered to Luke. *So that's how humans do it.* This afternoon, on some farm in Illinois heading into an early dusk, the cows were again pondering human behavior.

When the moment was over, I got up and woodenly, absently, picked bunches of dried grass for a flower arrangement to take home as I walked back to my car. That vase still sits on the mantelpiece of the non-working fireplace in my Chicago apartment. And Luke's cigar box of boyish treasures is still tucked away in my Civil War trunk at the foot of my bed. Some day I will bury the box here in Wagonbed Springs.

I didn't seek or receive confirmation of Luke's death for two months. My mother sent a clipping from the *Dodge City Globe* with the terse note: *I think you may have gone to school with the Mahoney boy. P.S. His sister took it real hard.*

The article told how Luke parachuted into enemy territory and caught machine gun fire, landing mortally wounded in a field of tall grass beside a river where a small platoon of Viet Cong were lying low amongst grazing water buffalo.

A week later when I was depositing the envelope with my mom's clipping into the cigar box—that seemed like the logical place to put it—I pulled the clipping out again to see the picture of Luke's face. I noticed a second small clipping, overlooked before, that had apparently stuck to the inside of the envelope. It was Luke's obituary clipped out of the *Odyssey News.*

It was the usual litany of boyhood achievements, awards, honors—not too much to tell when the person is only twenty-five. The last sentence caught my attention. *He is survived by one brother, two sisters*—listing their names—*and his wife Christine Morrison of Santa Monica, California. The couple was married in Santa Monica one month before Luke left for Viet Nam.*

Was I surprised? Did I feel betrayed? Not really. We had never needed to discuss how poorly matched we'd be—how unsuited I would be to the role of a military wife, moving from base to base, or he the husband of a relentlessly liberal reporter.

Even from the first time, on this Cimarron sand, the love affair felt illicit despite our both being properly unmarried. His farewell visit to me, I now knew, had been as a married man. It hardly mattered. Why did he marry one woman, but leave his box of valuables with another?

It's hard to explain your whole life to a California girl when you have only two weeks until you ship out. Maybe it's impossible for anyone else to understand what it's like to deliberately roll your pencil off your desk just so you can brush up against a ponytail—except for the girl with the ponytail.

We were connected but not by compatibility or even love. We were connected like the buffalo grass, runners reaching out along the ground to join one hardy tuft to another. No drought, no blowing dust, no whirling tornadoes, not even a war could sunder that bond. He could love another. And so could I. But we could not deny the passion that bound us fundamentally, intrinsically root to root.

The night I headed for Kankakee to roll around in some cowfield while I shared Luke's painful death, that very evening I was supposed to be picking out wedding rings with Bill—Bill, who remains my friend but was never husband. I had called him up from a pay phone in a gas station somewhere in a southern suburb of Chicago. "I just don't feel good, could we pick out the rings another night?"

The next day, when he came to dinner, I couldn't explain the vase of memorial wild grasses on my mantle to him any more than Luke could have explained his cigar box of loose ends to his new wife. I can't explain any of it to anyone. No one knew about us. No one would have understood about us. Not our mutual friend, Matt. Not Luke's sister or my cousin at the bank. Not even my sister.

Through that gossip line, however, I would eventually hear the rumors and scuttlebutt. How this beautiful but spoiled California brat insisted that he be buried in her family plot in Santa Barbara, while Luke's family wanted him in the family plot in Odyssey. So they'd compromised on a full military burial in Arlington National Cemetery, far away from both families. And I heard how Christine had shown up in Odyssey a couple of months later, demanding her "share" of the Mahoney family oil well, when her own family was many times more wealthy.

I'm the only one who knew Luke's last wishes. Scribbled, signed and dated, a note in the cigar box requested that his body be cremated and his ashes scattered over the dry sand of the Wagonbed Springs bend of the Cimarron River.

IT'S DARK NOW, but I cannot leave. There is just enough moonlight that it makes the white sand of the river bend glow. I feel so alone. But I do not fear the night. I know somehow I am safe—immune from any evil or danger as long as I stay on this sand. I had forgotten how many stars there are. In the outskirts of Chicago, or even in the Illinois countryside, you see a night sky scattered with stars, nearly evenly spaced over the expanse of the sky. Here each section of the sky looks different. The Milky Way is just that—a white band across the sky, so many, many billions of points of light that it becomes a wide, luminescent smear across the heavens. In other parts of the sky, some stars are very bright, others are dim. Some shine steadily. Others blink. Some are red, some are bluish or green. The infinite detail of the universe is visible to the naked eye here at Wagonbed Springs, away from the haze of city light.

I sit here cross-legged on the sand. While gazing at the heavens, I begin allowing the sand to fall through my fingers, like a child in a sandbox, playing . . .

Buried deep inside me, as my fingers play in the sand, a memory rises to the surface.

Oh Luke, I'm so sorry I lost our baby. Not lost, *destroyed*. I destroyed our child.

That same perky London medical intern who'd extracted the cactus spine from my foot, a few weeks later extracted our child from my womb. I did it because I didn't want you to feel tied to me, obligated by our one night of abandon. We were, both of us, careless like teenagers. Careless on this sand. And just as carelessly, I rid myself of the tissue that was your only progeny.

How could I have been so thoughtless? My baby, no, *our* baby, conceived on this sand, lost in the quicksand of my selfish, busy life. Now I have nothing of you, except your box of treasures and the memory of the tears I shed while you lay dying far away from me. If only I had your ashes I would scatter them across this sand, letting the night breeze distribute them evenly, dark flecks amongst the white granules. To mix forever on these Plains that so many people have loved and lost.

You and I both loved this land. It lost us. And we both lost it.

34

The Dig

WHEN I AWOKE, hot-white morning light was pouring through the window. I had forgotten to draw the curtain. I had slept so heavily for so many hours I was disoriented, like an alcoholic who awakens in an unfamiliar bed and doesn't know how he got there.

When I left Wagonbed in the dark, at what hour I do not know, I had driven straight to the motel and without supper, had fallen into bed, not even shedding my dusty jeans. I was barefoot so I had at least removed my cowboy boots. Should I pack up and leave? Was I finished here? Was there nothing more for me here in Western Kansas on this my final visit? While I showered and dressed something gnawed at me. I felt like a person who has made a list then lost it, fixed an agenda and then forgotten it. I had come all this way to see the feedlot up close but I had left without the answers I had come for. Now that the shock of it had washed over me, now that it was a new day, I knew I must go back.

I would finish the tour. I would insist on it. I rehearsed my opening line as I drove into the lot just behind an enormous semi-trailer truck. Running through my mind were random facts from yesterday's tour— 1800 tons of feed are consumed daily, sixty semi-truck loads of commodities come in each day—which truck out of the sixty was this? As I walked from the parking lot to the main building, the hot cement radiated the searing heat through the soles of my shoes all the way into my face. Once in the building, I asked for the manager and wandered around the lobby while waiting, uncomfortably surveying the crude, almost childlike oil paintings of cattle roundup scenes that occupied nearly all the available wall space. My back was turned to him when he walked out of his office.

"Do you like the paintings?" Mr. Moustache asked almost bashfully.

Realizing quickly that they were his, I replied. "They are charming. When do you get the time to paint?"

"Oh, it's something I play around at on vacations. I have a cabin up in the high country outside Delta, Colorado."

Before I could spout my opening line, his demeanor changed dramatically. "If you're here about your brother, you can forget it. I won't drop the charges this time."

"I think you've confused me with somebody else. I'm the person from the tour yesterday who got sick. I'm here to finish the tour, if you would be so kind."

"I know who you are, Rebecca, and I know why you're here," he snapped. "Our surveillance cameras picked you up exiting the property. Seems our security chief went to school with you, says you haven't changed much—I guess that's a compliment."

"You don't need to be so nasty. I came to tour the feedlot because I was genuinely curious about it. I don't deny I've got a history here. But I had no ulterior motives."

"Right. Just like you got locked out of your car at the cemetery so you could get into your old house."

"That was not planned. I really did lock myself out. Okay, I lied a little bit—I locked myself out not because I was visiting a grave, but because I wanted to get a photograph that would show the size of this place, and I closed the damn door with the motor running, which apparently if you are driving an Oldsmobile isn't allowed. It was embarrassing to me, and very uncomfortable. But I never let on I'd once lived there. The woman was very kind. I was very thirsty."

"You could have come here. I'd have even given you a beer. Now, we need to talk some business."

His nastiness suddenly changed to exactly that: business. He ushered me into his office.

"About your brother . . ."

"What does my visit have to do with my brother?"

"He was digging again last week. Far edge, down near the holding pond. Middle of the night. Our cameras caught it."

"Digging? What are you talking about?"

"Your brother, Thomas. It wasn't the first time. Twice before he's done it. We called the sheriff both times. Had him removed for trespassing. Those first two times the sheriff talked us out of pressing charges. Bob claims he's just loony. Always was. But we're getting tired of it. This time I pressed charges. And I'm not dropping them. No matter how much you compliment those piss-ass paintings out there."

He was a Texan all right. Maybe he'd been in Kansas for fifteen years. But he was a Texan. "Are you telling me my brother Thomas has been digging in this feedlot? What the hell are you talking about?"

"He's not digging now. He's sitting in the county jail. Bob says he's got nothing to make bail with. Been there for two weeks. I guess he finally called you, huh?"

"Until this moment I had no idea Thomas was here. This is coming out of the blue. Why would he be digging here?"

"You tell me. But now that you know, I guess you'll go make bail. But I'm telling you, if you do, I'll hold you personally responsible if he comes on this property again."

My head was spinning. Thomas had promised Dad he'd go dig for the buried gold. I assumed he'd been humoring Dad. Even if he wasn't, Dad was dead. Thomas had done his duty by my father. He had granted his dying wish—if not in fact, in Dad's reality. Actual digging wasn't necessary.

The word, schizophrenia, was flitting, no grinding, through my mind again. Maybe the Utah psychiatrist had been right. Maybe Thomas, my poor wandering, homeless little brother was—I hated to give the word a shape—*schizophrenic*.

As if reading my mind, the moustache said. "He's sick, you know. One pathetic, sick son of a bitch. If I were you, I'd get him some help."

"Where was he digging?"

"I told you. Down below the holding pond."

"Show me."

"I'm not going to show you. What the hell? Are you going to go dig too? Your family, I'm told, kept the mineral rights to the land. You're already probably getting a fat check from those two gas wells."

"If you call $27 a month fat. I'm just trying to understand why Thomas was digging. Maybe if I know where, I'll have a clue to his behavior."

"You don't need clues. You need medication. And you also need to leave. I have a lot of work to do. Phone calls backing up," he glanced at the blinking lights on his phone and got up to usher me out.

He walked me to the door, and then, despite his waiting phone calls, out into the parking lot, suddenly, awkwardly, kind again. Outside, I remembered something I had wanted to ask.

"Down below what you call a holding pond, there used to be a creek. It meandered in two big U-shapes. And there was a ridge, a kind of bluff above it, there somewhere." I pointed. "Where is the creek? I don't see anything. It's all bulldozed nearly level. But the water has to go somewhere. I don't see any creek."

"Don't ask me. I've only been here fifteen years. I wasn't here when they were preparing the land. I've never seen anything like a creek."

"But the water, when it rains in Eastern Colorado, has to go somewhere. It used to flood every spring."

"In fifteen years, I've never seen any water, not even any runoff. Certainly no floods."

"But it has to go somewhere. It was the North Fork of the Cimarron. It ran down towards town. In fact, downstream, by Odyssey, just yesterday I saw water in the banks. It would have to come through here first. Was it rechanneled somewhere else?"

"Like I said. I don't know anything about a creek. I'm the wrong person to ask. Maybe they put some culverts in, underground somewhere. But I really don't know." He was actually being kind. He assumed I was making some kind of small talk.

"Thank you. You've got quite an operation here. Good luck to you." I tried to leave on a polite note, kind of an obligatory neighborliness that came naturally from growing up here feeling connected to everyone around you, even the people you don't like. And after all, he didn't own this place. He was not here when the blackmail went down. He just drew a salary like everybody else here.

"No need to be polite, Rebecca. I know how you feel about us. Nothing's the same where I grew up either. Nothing's the same anywhere. You need to get over it."

This guy was getting on my nerves. I unleashed a bit of Chicago on him.

"You don't want polite? Okay. Your paintings stink. You make a cow look like a piece of wood. If you'd give these cattle a little room to move around in instead of having to stand in their own shit all day, you'd find out what a cow looks like when it moves. Maybe you could make them look real in your paintings."

He threw his head back and laughed. "There, doesn't that feel better?"

Condescending son of a bitch. "If you want to see real paintings, check out the first floor hall of the court house next time you're there. You'll see my 'sick' little brother's paintings. His animals are so real they nearly leap off the canvas. Now I'm going to get him out of jail, thank you very much."

"You want to say something about my handlebars too. That'd make you feel good."

"No thanks, that's all right. I kind of like your moustache. It takes real guts to wear something that silly on your face in this part of the country."

He liked that. He was laughing.

I rammed my car back and left, spraying gravel down the drive. I made town in eight minutes and headed straight for the sheriff's office in the new wing of the county court house building. I walked through the corridor, lined with paintings of horses and grazing cattle, wheat fields and old sheds and windmills—Thomas's early work which he had given to the county in a fit of patriotic zeal one Fourth of July, on the day he turned sixteen. I turned left into the new wing. Burst into the sheriff's office.

IN MY HIGH SCHOOL CLASS if we'd voted the person least likely to ever become sheriff, it would have been Bob Jessup. Even at age sixteen, he was regularly landing in the lock-up for public drunkenness or threatening someone with a knife. When he didn't show up for school on Monday, we always knew where he was. So how did he end up becoming sheriff?

Everyone here reads minds. The moment I walked in Bob said. "Hello, Becky. Surprised to see me here, right?"

"Well, you have to admit . . ."

"I just got so used to being here, even though it was behind bars, I just kind of fell in love with the place."

"Hey, somebody's got to do it."

"I'm a damn good sheriff, Becky. When I was twenty-seven years old, the Lord found me. He picked me up, dried me off. And I'm a better lawman for the days I spent in here in my youth. I understand these fellas. Most of them. But I tell you, I don't understand Thomas. He doesn't even seem to mind being here. Never even once asked to use the phone."

"I wish you had called me, Bob."

"Would have, if I'd had your phone number. Heard you were in Chicago. Phone company said you were unlisted. I gave up. I hate keeping him here. I told him just yesterday that if he promised me he wouldn't go out there again, I'd just find a way to let him go. He said he couldn't promise. Do you believe that! So what am I supposed to do?"

"What's his bail?"

"A thousand bucks."

"I'll make the arrangements. Let me talk to him."

Bob ushered me through the hallway, clearly embarrassed by the whole thing. He unlocked the cell. I walked in. Thomas looked at me vacantly.

"Why didn't you call me?" I asked Thomas crossly. "It's only by chance that I'm here in Odyssey. I was getting ready to leave town when I heard about you."

"I figured you'd come."

There was no use scolding Thomas, telling him I could have been in the middle of Africa on assignment, that I had no reason to be in Odyssey—had in fact vowed never to come back here and certainly no reason to have visited the feedlot and learned of his arrest. Thomas believed in fate, that everything worked out the way it was supposed to happen. There was no use telling him how close he came to rotting here for months before anyone knew he was here.

"They feed me good. Huge, home-cooked meals like I'm harvest crew. You should try it, put some meat on your bones," Thomas was grinning. "A hell of a lot better than the gruel they fed me in the Moab lockup."

"Let's get out of here and have a picnic. I know a good place."

We bought some rotisserie chicken, some warm rolls and potato salad, and half a watermelon at Rusty's Deli on the highway, and we headed out for the Springs.

Thomas seemed totally at peace and in control. He didn't look or act like some wild-eyed lunatic.

First we ate. Then I asked him the question, turning my big sister worry into accusatory anger. "Whatever possessed you to go out there and dig? What the hell were you digging for? You have no further obligation to Dad. He's dead, remember? What the hell were you thinking?"

"Becky, I wasn't doing it for Dad. I wasn't looking for gold. I was doing it for the Old Woman and for the children."

I said nothing—for a whole minute. Stunned. Silent. And then out of somewhere my voice was asking, "Did you find them?"

"Yes, one or two of them, there are plenty more skeletons all bunched together, but I didn't have time to get them all out."

A cool dusk wind began rattling the cottonwood leaves above us. "You know about it." He said it more as a statement than a question.

"Yes, but not until yesterday."

"How did you find out?"

"I don't know, Thomas, I don't know. I got this strange feeling while I was there, and then when I drove down the gravel road past our old pasture, I just saw the whole thing happening in front of me. Am I going mad, Thomas? Am I going as mad as you?"

"You're not mad, Becky. The world is. It was not the first or the last time marauders have murdered innocent children to drive a people from their land."

"How did *you* find out?"

"I've known it since I was a teenager. From the eagles."

I didn't argue. I didn't question. Was listening to an eagle any different than seeing visions after staring into the eyes of a muddy white cow? At least Thomas and I can tell each other. When you are bursting with too much joy or too much sorrow, some must spill out. Thomas can tell what he knows through his paintings. I guess I will have to tell what I know through poetry or novels. We can never speak of it in words to anyone else.

"After I found out, I got the buffalo for them. I hoped it would comfort their spirits."

"Why are we digging up the children?" I asked woodenly, realizing I was now part of the mission.

"Because their spirits cannot stay there under that desecration, and sooner or later they're going to bulldoze the landscape differently and their bones will be disturbed. They long to go elsewhere and be with their ancestors."

"How can we find their ancestors?"

"We'll have to look in the other direction."

"The other direction? Is that like Mom's 'other side'?"

Thomas smiled for a split second as we savored our shared last memory of Mom.

"What I'm thinking is, I figure we must find descendants of theirs. They'd be in Oklahoma. That's where they were marched."

"Thomas, that was more than a hundred years ago."

"There must have been brothers and sisters yet unborn who survived. We will find their descendants."

"Thomas, this is impossible."

"We must try. I can't do it without you. With your reporter connections, maybe . . . well, that's why I asked you to come."

"Thomas, we need help. On getting them out, we need permission." I sighed, leaned back against the trunk of the cottonwood whose shade we were borrowing. I closed my eyes and tried to think. I finally said, "Let me work it my way. I have a kind of rapport with ole handlebars. We hate each other. It's somewhere to start."

APRIL 17: I don't have time to put this all on paper right now. Time is short and we have to get on the road. He was awfully surprised to see us show up at his office together. We talked with him behind his closed door. I laid it out very simply. There were children's bones under the feedlot from a massacre that sooner or later were going to be accidentally bulldozed up and cause everybody embarrassment, and it behooved him to let us get them out of there quietly before it became a federal issue. I didn't talk visions or eagles or white cows. We didn't even go into how we knew. And strangely he didn't ask, didn't even doubt it. Then the three of us went out in his pickup, stopping to pick up a couple of shovels from the equipment shed. Then we drove to the spot. When Thomas showed him the first child's skull, shattered in pieces, then another with a large hole ripped in the front, I thought I saw tears rolling down his checks, dripping down into his moustache.

"We need some help," he said. He called his two teenage sons, swearing them to secrecy and they joined the dig, real decent kids. I wish I had time to tell you about that long extraordinary night as we worked side by side through the night, training floodlights on the site, working feverishly until we had the remains of all twelve children. Thomas laid them out carefully on his flatbed. I wrapped them, each one separately, in burlap. In the early morning light, the men went over all the area to make sure we hadn't missed anything. That's when we found the skeletal remains of one grown man, off a few yards from the others.

At sunrise we washed up in the bathroom off the lobby, and we wrapped our stiff, blistered hands around the mugs of hot, bitter coffee he brewed in his office. We didn't talk.

"I need to say goodbye to someone before we leave," I told Mr. Moustache. "That kind, gray-haired young woman with the sick child who lives in our old house. I want to thank her again."

"Rebecca, that house is vacant. It's not fit to live in. We just haven't gotten around to knocking it down."

"I got water from her. You know I did. I told you that."

"No, you got water from the woman in the trailer just in back of that old house."

I'M TIRED OF TRYING TO UNDERSTAND anything. I'm going to sleep now. I have to catch a couple of hours before we head out south to Oklahoma. It will be a tedious trip. We have to take side roads all the way through Oklahoma because the '45 Dodge doesn't move fast. And we don't want to have to explain to some highway patrolman who might want to search the vehicle why we've got thirteen skeletons in back. I'm following along behind him in my rental car. I wish I could ride in the truck with him, but I've got to eventually turn this car back in at the Wichita airport. Along the way, I've got a lot of calls to make from my cell phone to locate the Bureau of Indian Affairs or tribal leaders, anyone who can help us trace where descendants of these plains-dwellers may have ended up. I know one tribal leader—I'm pretty sure he was Kiowa—I interviewed him once in Washington, D.C. He was some sort of government consultant and also a high school principal in

Oklahoma City. If I can find him, if he's even still there, he should be able to help. I'm too tired to think right now. I want to catch a couple of hours of sleep. Thomas is anxious to go, though. He never seems to need any sleep. Never did.

APRIL 18: We're on the way to Oklahoma City. Thomas chose a route that went into the panhandle of Texas, just skirting Amarillo to surprise me with an extraordinary sight. We were just traveling on flat dry land, looked like around Odyssey, when suddenly we were at a precipice. Dropping hundreds of feet down, out of nowhere, is this deep canyon called Palo Duro. Thomas tells me this was one of the last holdouts of the Plains Indians before they were driven into the reservation. Deep inside this canyon, hidden from White Man's view, were a group of Comanche, Cheyenne and Kiowa villages. On that fateful day in November of 1875, Colonel Mackenzie's scouts stumbled on the canyon in the early, dimly-lit dawn hours and saw thousands of horses and hundreds of teepees down inside the canyon. Mackenzie was thrilled. He knew Plains warriors were hiding from him somewhere. He'd been chasing them for months. He realized this must be the base from which Kiowa, Comanche and Cheyenne bands were making their daring raids, then disappearing from sight. This was it. This was the last of the last. Destroy these villages and the job of emptying the Southern Plains of these savages would be finished.

There was no need to kill anybody. Mackenzie just let the Indians flee out the other side of the canyon. Then his men burned every teepee, every store of grain and every shred of dried buffalo meat, every buffalo robe and blanket, every beaded buckskin dress left behind, every ceremonial headdress, every intricately-beaded baby carrier. His men punched holes in the bottom of every cooking pot, confiscated guns and other weapons left behind.

Every trace of the Palo Duro villages was wiped out. Then his men, after picking the best animals for themselves, herded a thousand horses into the next canyon and shot them, leaving their carcasses to the sun and the vultures.

The famous Civil War colonel had done more than stumble onto the last Southern Plains Indian hideout. He had stumbled onto the most effective method of eliminating the Native American presence from the entire West. Not by outright massacre, but by starvation and demoralization. No more would the American army try to kill Indians. Now, from the Southern Plains to the farthest reaches of the Northern Plains, the mountains and the deserts of the West, a new policy would go into effect. A policy that quickly brought every remaining Indian into the reservation: burn their teepees and lodges, exterminate their fresh food supply, destroy their stored foods and supplies. It was the perfect way to finish off the process begun by the great buffalo kills. The great warrior chiefs, their people starving, sick and exhausted, would lead their ragged bands into reservations and forts across the West.

And that's how the American West was finally won.

WE DECIDED TO DESCEND INTO the canyon to make camp for the night. Thomas does not believe in motels or sleeping in real beds. Spring was in full bloom down in the canyon, with exquisite outbursts of a yellow flower I did not recognize. The canyon walls revealed their ancient layers of rock, some layers orange, others a soft purple. Dark green cedars dotted the canyon, and lush cottonwoods bursting with new leaves flanked little streams of clear water meandering along the canyon floor. Wild turkeys strutted about, puffing up their feathers, wary, unwilling to share the campground with us. Though the canyon had become a state park with camping sites, we were the only ones there. It was still too cold for most campers. We chose a secluded spot near a stream. A layer of last fall's cottonwood leaves blanketed the ground, creating a virtual mattress for our bedrolls. I noticed the leaves had a curious iridescent silver-gold sheen, which gave our campsite a kind of magic aura.

It was eerie sleeping down in this canyon. Near these same cedar trees, where our Plains kinsman spent their last few days. Of course, I realize they are not really our "kinsmen," yet deep in my bones, I somehow feel that they are my ancestors. I especially feel it tonight, as we hide from the prying view of authorities down in this canyon—we didn't fill out a permit and we're not camping in a "designated spot." We made a fire and sat around it like we used to as kids. Our hearts had been heavy, our journey solemn. And lonely too, both of us in our separate vehicles. We know instinctively that we are very likely tracing the very trail our Ridge clan was made to march in 1875 on the way to the reservation. Except, on this journey, when we get close to the Indian lands, we will be turning off east to Oklahoma City where we will meet the Kiowa principal—I found him—Bill had taken this magnificent photo of him in his buckskin jacket and long, black braids. *Tribune* photographers always have to secure signed releases from photo subjects. I called Bill, he dug it out of his files and sure enough, he found his name—George Angel, with an address and phone number. I made Bill promise he wouldn't tell anyone he had spoken to me or divulge where I was. He didn't even ask. (That's Bill. Loyal, uncompromising, uncomplicated. Somewhere deep in the recesses of my broken, weary heart I do love that man.) I called George Angel and told him the bare minimum of details. He said he'd set up a meeting in Oklahoma City with officials of the Bureau of Indian Affairs. He told me about NAG-PRO—stands for National American Graves Protection and Repatriation Act, a law passed five years ago that requires federal institutions to return all sacred and funerary objects and human remains to their rightful heirs. So the remains we were bringing have a good chance of ending up in the right place if we were careful about how we proceeded. He will guide us through the process.

Staring into the campfire embers tonight, with the night chill setting in, I can't help but remember my solitary night at Wagonbed Springs. Only two nights ago. Seems like two years ago. It's almost as if centuries of history are spinning out of control in my brain.

"Since you're so good at sneaking into secured areas and digging up bones, I have some bones for you to dig up in Arlington Cemetery," I told Thomas, needing I guess, to let someone else into my reservoir of old pain.

"Arlington National Cemetery? I'm nuts, but not that nuts." It was good to see Thomas grin. He had not lost his sense of humor about himself.

"I made a promise to a friend to scatter his ashes over Wagonbed Springs. But somebody went and buried him before I knew what was happening."

"Luke."

"How do you know?"

"I went to visit you once in Chicago. I got to your apartment in the morning after driving all night. As I pulled up, I saw you and Luke walking out. He gave you a small box, then he left in his convertible."

"I'm surprised you recognized him. You didn't really know him."

"Actually, yes I did. About a year before he left for Viet Nam, he gave me seven head of buffalo. Six cows, one bull."

"Luke had buffalo?"

"Yeah, he kept them on his older brother's place. But he couldn't get his herd going. The calves always died. He heard about mine. While he was at Yale, he didn't get home very often to look after them, and his brother wasn't keen on the whole idea."

Both of them, I thought to myself, true Western Kansas men. Didn't see a need to talk about the very details that defined their souls. You have to be passionate about raising buffalo, or why would you do it. Why had Luke never mentioned it to me? Never mind the cousin at the bank story. That June evening so long ago, Luke knew I was home, probably because he was checking on the buffalo.

"Why didn't you let me know you were in Chicago? You can't imagine how many times I wished you would come visit me," I complained.

"Even from across the street, Becky, I could see how broken up you were. I figured you needed to be alone."

I remembered the day I did the same for him, high up on a cliff above the Colorado River as he communed with his eagle. I didn't mention it. We both stared a long time into the fire, nearly out, smoldering. Now and then a burst of crimson flared, just when all seemed to have become black.

"Funny that we're going to Oklahoma," I mused. "Don't you think it's strange that Grandpa came from Oklahoma, that Dad was born there, that our great-grandparents homesteaded there, yet we know almost nothing about Oklahoma. In all the driving trips we took, Dad never took us to Oklahoma."

"He always said there was nothing worthwhile south."

"I think I finally know why he said that," I told Thomas. "When Aunt Selma died, her stepchildren gave me some of her papers, since they heard I was a writer. I came across a story from their days in Oklahoma."

Then I told Thomas the horrifying tale Aunt Selma's papers revealed, one she remembered from her childhood. Our great-grandparents had settled in an area with other German-Russian immigrants, and they lived much as they'd lived in Southern Russia, clinging to their German customs and language and pretty much keeping to themselves. During the First World War masked locals had burst into their church as they were conducting services in their native German dialect. They accused the congregation of being German collaborators. Masked men grabbed one elder, tarred and feathered him, tied him to a horse, and left him to be dragged to death. And then they vandalized the church but stopped short of burning it down. That elder was our grandpa's older brother.

Not only was no one punished for the violence, but town officials forbade the congregation to conduct any more services in German. So teenage boys—including our uncles who spoke English—had to do the preaching. Singing was more difficult. No one knew any hymns in English, so the old women just hummed the old songs with tears running down their cheeks. It was the Cossacks all over again.

Thomas seemed almost not to be listening to my story. He was, I think, reliving instead the terror that the fleeing Kiowa villagers felt as they ran, trapped in their hiding place while Mackenzie's troops moved in with their buffalo guns, right here in the narrows of the canyon where we now took refuge.

Thomas tossed me a bedroll from the back of the truck and busied himself with putting more wood on the fire. "It might get pretty cold tonight," he warned, "even though we're protected from the wind down here."

It will be a joy to sleep under the stars tonight. Thomas seems to be restless, but I feel strangely safe here in the depths of this canyon, I will sleep well tonight. I must. Tomorrow, we hope to find a resting place for the fragile restless spirits we carry on our backs.

35

Anadarko

JUNE 19: It has been two months since Thomas and I completed our mission to reunite the massacred children with their tribe. I am back in Taos, New Mexico. I have pulled up my existence in Chicago and have come to this part of the world to stay, temporarily living in the same room Willa Cather once inhabited in the Mabel Dodge House on the outskirts of Taos.

But I have once again lost my little brother.

When we were children and Thomas and I would head out to the pasture to play, my mother would call after me, "Becky, take care of your little brother. Don't let him wander off." Always, as we ran along the ridge, poked around in the willows, or waded in the muddy shallows of the creek, no matter how involved I would become in my fantasy adventures, I made sure he remained in eyesight. It became second nature.

When we were adults and he disappeared from my life, I could not shake the feeling that I had become so involved in my own life that I had failed to keep an eye out for him.

I suppose that's why finding him became an obsession. The quest had taken me to the canyons of Utah and the plateaus of New Mexico. And when I had found him, it gave me a sense of ease and safety I had not known since childhood.

But now I have lost him again.

Two months have passed since that day in Anadarko, Oklahoma forever altered my life. It is only now that I can begin to speak—or write—about what occurred. I cannot yet say that I understand it. You will forgive me if I give only dry details. I cannot yet muster the building blocks of my language. Words no longer spill from me. They come slowly and begrudgingly. Like a stroke victim who takes time and great perseverance to move her leaden limbs, so too I use words haltingly, trusting that gradually they will once again begin to flow effortlessly and gracefully from my brain and fingertips. For now, I offer you the events as would a reporter—not a poet.

As we drove from Palo Duro Canyon—Thomas in the truck, me in the rental car—wending our way east to Oklahoma City, we passed from rolling sagebrush-covered hills into rolling farmland. We took a side road north to see the Black Kettle National Grasslands and visit the site of the bloody Washita Massacre, a 1868 army campaign under the command of Lieutenant Colonel George Custer that attacked Black Kettle's Cheyenne winter camp, killing scores of men, women, and children. We crossed the Canadian River several times as it snaked back and forth across our path. Thirty miles outside of Oklahoma City, when we saw a great column of smoke rising from the center of the city, I turned on my car radio. Only then did we discover that the Federal Building had just been demolished by a massive bomb. Until that moment, it had seemed to be an exceptionally beautiful spring day.

We quickly decided not to drive into the city. We did not wish to endanger our mission. What if we were stopped and searched by the FBI? How would we explain the remains of thirteen bodies wrapped in burlap in the back of our truck on a day when paranoia and fear ran deep? So Thomas and I retreated west and south, finding a small state campground at Fort Cobb Lake on the edge of Indian Territory.

Oklahoma has become, in the last decade, very proud that many Native Americans make their home in central Oklahoma, milking it for all it's worth to promote tourism. Auto license plates proclaim Oklahoma as "Native America." Billboards along the highway urge motorists to visit various Indian museums—every tribe seems to have one. And each village in the area seems to be the headquarters of a specific tribe. For instance, the Kiowa tribal headquarters, which locals refer to as a "compound" is in Carnegie, the Apache compound is in Anadarko, the Cheyenne in Concho. We didn't know where we'd find the Nadi-ish-dena—if they'd even retained their identity. Officially called the "Kiowa-Apache," we were not sure whether to search in Carnegie or Anadarko. After a solid night's sleep—we were the only ones in the campground—we attempted to reach George Angel, who had promised to guide our search. We had been scheduled to meet him at an office in the Murrah Federal Building the morning of April 20, a building which no longer stood. We were unable to reach him at either his office or home number. (Two days later I would discover his name was among the missing. His body was pulled from the rubble five days later.) We understood from that first day, amidst the chaos and suffering of Oklahoma, that we were on our own to find the people we were seeking.

So Thomas and I mapped out our strategy. He would remain at the lake, keeping watch over our precious cargo. I would scout the area until I found a tribal leader for the Kiowa Apache, or Plains Apache, whatever they were calling themselves these days. When I located the right person, I would fetch Thomas and we'd meet with the leader to explain what we had found.

First I drove to the Kiowa compound in Carnegie. The sheriff—or at least someone wearing a shield and law enforcement garb—claimed there was no such thing as "Kiowa-Apache." But if there were, they were not part of the Kiowa nation. I sensed the problem was bad blood between them. "Try the Apaches," he said with a look that oozed profound disdain for both Apaches and nosy white women.

Thirty miles and thirty minutes later at the Anadarko Apache headquarters, I encountered the same "don't know who you're talking about," as if Plains Apaches were an invention of my confused mind. I was getting a royal runaround and none of my usual Chicago reporter tactics were working.

It was just dumb luck that I eventually found them. I stopped at the Indian Hall of Fame along the highway out of town on my way to bring Thomas some lunch. The guard was locking the door as I drove up. He apologized for closing early. "With the Oklahoma City thing there are no tourists and most of the staff decided to go in to join the rescue teams," he said.

I asked whether he could tell me where to find the Plains Apache office.

"Oh, sure, turn left at the second traffic light, go about two or three blocks and turn right at the gas station. It's the third building. Red brick, two-story. It ain't marked or nothing. That's the best place to go if you have questions."

I wanted to ask why the building wasn't marked, but I didn't want to push my luck.

"They have a little museum of their own," he added, eager to be helpful. "At the back of the gas station's convenience store on that corner, if you want to see it."

I stopped to buy a bottle of water and walked to the back of the store. Sure enough, in a space no bigger than the dining room of my Chicago apartment I found a makeshift museum of the Plains Apache tribe. A few artifacts—beaded baby carrier, a doeskin dress, arrowheads, a ceremonial headdress—were displayed in glass cases. Handmade posters told the story of the tribe, hand-drawn maps showed their former hunting grounds which I quickly confirmed centered around the Cimarron River, a few fading photos from early reservation days were framed behind glass. Scattered amongst the posters, were hand-lettered placards recording the sayings of the elders—wisdom learned from grandfathers and grandmothers. The sayings were familiar to me, things I'd heard whispered in the wind on Indian Ridge. At the counter, I noticed a CD of wind flute music by a Plains Apache musician. I bought it.

Then, leaving my car parked in front of the convenience store, I walked around the corner to the red brick building third from the corner and entered through two glass double doors. An attractive young woman at a reception desk asked me who I wished to see. I noticed some alarm and concern in her voice and on her face. Clearly she was uncomfortable seeing a person she did not recognize.

"Is this the Plains Apache office?" I asked.

Not answering my question, she looked helplessly around her. "Well, this is kind of a cultural center," she said. "Perhaps you are looking for the Apache compound. That's across the street behind the high fence."

"No, I am looking for the chief of the Plains Apaches."

Becoming flustered she said, "Let me get someone for you." She left her desk and practically ran down a hallway. An elderly man came out and suggested I wait in the room at the end of the hallway while he found the "Cultural Officer." The old man was wearing matching sand-colored khaki pants and shirt that looked like a uniform but I couldn't tell whether it was the uniform of a janitor or a security officer. Despite his official air, he did not introduce himself. He merely directed me to a large room with desks, many with computer stations and then left me there without another word. Several children of different ages were busy with homework or using the computers. One boy—he was perhaps eleven or twelve years old—looked up from his computer when I walked by him and said, "You can sit down here if you want. Are you waiting for someone?"

"Yes, I'm waiting for the chief," I said.

"Oh, that's my grandpa. He's out somewhere. But he'll come back." Then he added, as an afterthought, "But you might have to wait a long time."

"That's okay. I have lots of time," I shrugged.

The boy looked at me, sizing me up. I found it slightly unnerving. He began asked questions: what was my name, had I ever been to Oklahoma before. He was the only talkative person I'd met since entering the building, so I was grateful for the chance at conversation. As a reporter, I've always found my most useful sources to be children. They usually tell the truth, and they see things through fresh, unpoliticized eyes. So slowly, I began asking my own questions. He told me this was a homework room where kids came after school to study, use the computers or get help, but that he mostly played computer games, if his grandpop didn't stop him.

"What do you call your tribe, Kiowa-Apache or Plains Apache?"

"Don't use the word Kiowa around here. People get real sore about that. That's just a mistake. We aren't Kiowa and we aren't Apache. But the government doesn't recognize our tribe, and we have to be something, so we just call ourselves the Apache Tribe of Oklahoma instead of our real name, which is…" He caught himself, embarrassed, as if he had almost given out a secret.

"Does your tribe have its own language?"

"Oh, yeah, A few old people know it. So they teach us the words. We have a class every Friday after school."

"You're a reporter, aren't you?" he said quite suddenly. And I saw a quick, meaningful glance pass between him and the old man in the khaki uniform who had reentered the room and was wandering about, glancing over children's shoulders as if checking on their progress.

"Well, yes, but how did you guess?"

"The way you ask questions. Kind of in circles," he replied matter-of-factly.

"I am a reporter, but I'm not here as a reporter. In fact, I've quit my job. My boss doesn't know it yet. But I've quit."

"Will he be mad?"

"Yeah, but he's always mad at me. See I'm a bit of a wanderer. I just leave without telling anyone where I'm going."

"That sounds cool, but why did you do that?"

"Because sometimes I don't know where I'm going myself. Like now, I didn't intend to end up in Oklahoma. It just happened because of something my brother and I found."

I understood by now that the old man in khaki was the boy's grandpa and therefore the tribal leader. I should have suspected it from the start. At least I had caught on after the reporter question that I was now the *interviewee,* not the interviewer. Clearly, I was talking to the chief through this boy. The boy's questions were direct and skillful.

"You know, you could be a reporter," I told him.

"Naw, I'm no good at spelling."

"Reporters don't need to know how to spell. That's what editors are for."

"Naw, I wouldn't want to be a reporter. I don't want to live someplace else. I like it here."

"Don't you have newspapers here?"

"Yeah, but all they do is stories about shootings and knife fights and elections and stuff like that. That's not cool. What did you and your brother find anyway?"

Good job. Bring it back to the subject. This boy was relentless.

"I used to live on a farm by a small creek that emptied into the Cimarron River up in the southwest corner of Kansas. My brother and I used to find a lot of interesting stuff on the ridge in our pasture—grinding stones, arrowheads and all sorts of treasures. We practically had a museum in our house—not as good as yours at the convenience store, but not too bad. Then someone cheated us out of our farm and it became a feedlot."

The boy's grandfather had stopped circling around and was now listening intently as he stood over a boy at the next table.

"So you have a bunch of that stuff for us, arrowheads and things."

"No, I have something a whole lot more important, and I need to take it where it belongs. I need to know if this is the tribe that used to live on that ridge. I'd like to talk to someone, someone very old who remembers things about the history of your tribe."

"That would be Old Anna," chimed in a young girl seated behind us. Clearly the whole room was involved in our conversation.

"How old is she?" I turned and asked the girl.

"I dunno." She became suddenly shy.

"She's ninety-six," said the old man.

"Is she well enough to talk to me?" The question provoked laughter. Even the small children in the room giggled.

"Well enough? She's a medicine woman, healthy as a horse," retorted my twelve-year-old guardian, reclaiming his rightful role in the conversation.

"What did you say was her name, again?"

"We call her Old Woman or Old Anna, but I think her name, before she got so old, was Running Antelope."

The children found that funny too, I presume because at ninety-six she no longer moved with the speed and grace of an antelope. One young girl volunteered, "Old Anna talks funny and she knows everything."

"Of course she talks funny," reprimanded an older girl. "She's a medicine woman."

I decided not to divulge anything further to the chief and his young spokesman. Thomas and I should pay a visit to the "Old Woman" of the tribe as our first step. But when I asked where to find her, everyone retreated into silence. I was just becoming frustrated when a young man rushed in holding a cell phone.

"There's been a shooting down on Main Street. Two guys got into a knife fight right in the middle of the street. Some white guy with a yellow ponytail tried to stop them, and one of them pulled out a gun. Two guys are dead, maybe three!"

I knew it immediately.

"My brother," I shrieked.

"Come with me," the chief said. I ran with him out a back door and jumped into the passenger side of his pickup. The boy jumped into the back. The chief grabbed a gunbelt from the glove compartment, and while driving, affixed a flashing Mars light to the roof of the cab, switched on a siren, and we sped to the center of the town.

A crowd had gathered around the intersection. Pulling me along with him, the chief—whose name I still did not know—pushed his way through the crowd, and we stepped over the knee-high, yellow crime scene tape.

An old woman sat on the pavement with Thomas' head in her lap, cradling his limp body, chanting a song. Paramedics were attending to a young Indian man a few feet away.

I ran to her and knelt beside her, stroking Thomas' hair and cool face. Dark blood oozed from his chest, soaking through the shirt and pooling on the pavement. Then through my tears I looked pleadingly into the old woman's deeply creased face. "Can you help him?"

"Sunflower," she said to me. "I cannot save your brother. He was born to die this day. He has fulfilled his duty." She continued chanting, then broke for a moment to tell me, "His spirit is now traveling up to reunite with the Golden Eagles. He is happy."

It was so matter of fact. So clear. So final.

We stayed beside Thomas, she chanting, me weeping until the ambulance came to pick up the body.

"No," she rebuked a heavy-set Native American medic who tried to gently move her away. "I must prepare the Golden Shaman for burial."

"You will come with us, then, Old Woman, but we must take him now. You know the White Man's rules. The coroner first."

"You know my rules," she barked. "I must be with him at all times."

To me she said. "Come along, Sunflower. But do not interfere."

I CALLED MARGARET FROM the coroner's office. She called my brothers. They left the details in my hands. I left the details in the Old Woman's hands. My siblings caught their planes. Somehow, I had the presence of mind to call Jensen in Taos and Joe in Moab—I must write all this without the detail. I cannot bear the details. I moved through the next few hours, the next few days, as a sleepwalker in a dream. I don't actually remember much. I only know that I slept in my clothes on the couch in Old Anna's apartment, located on the lower floor of an old red brick building on Main Street, just feet from where Thomas was killed. I slept there because Old Anna said I must. Her granddaughter Sally, who lived with her, described herself to me as "twice-divorced and per-manently between husbands." She was practical, a bit bossy, and took charge of me, just as she had given herself over to caring for the revered Old Woman of the tribe. She reminded me of Jenny. I knew instantly that we would become friends and that she would help me make sense out of the chaos.

I must have called Jenny on that first day, because she showed up two days later. She tracked down Bill, who was an hour's drive away cover-ing the Oklahoma City bombing. Bill found me in Old Anna's apart-ment the day before we buried Thomas. He could not take his eyes off Old Anna's face. I could feel his fingers twitching jammed inside his pockets, missing his camera. Out of the respect, he had left it in the car.

WHEN OUR FAMILY AND SEVERAL of Thomas' friends assembled, we were joined by the local Plains Apache nation for a burial in their cemetery on a hillside above the Washita River. Thomas was laid to rest together with the remains of the twelve children and Chief Two Eagles. The ceremony, no doubt one of ancient origins, presided over by Old Anna, was an outpouring of grief and celebration that I cannot describe in these pages. It is secret. I only know that during the dancing and drumbeats of sacred rhythm, I felt Thomas' spirit ascend into an Oklahoma sky already hazed over in deep sorrow. The *Nadi-ish-dena* tribe sang songs that I had never heard before but somehow knew. A strikingly beautiful native man, whom I recognized from the CD cover, played a wind flute with a plaintive, wavering melody. His long hair lift-ed and flowed in the breeze in time to the music. There was one weep-ing Navajo woman whom I greeted with a hug and no need for an exchange of words.

The day before, Jensen and I had found someone to engrave a few words on a small red boulder that the Old Woman's great-grandson found for us. Under the words, "Thomas Kluger 1952-1995," was chiseled the inscription, "T.S. Eagle." It was our hope that one day some art lover might stumble over the grave and discover the identity of T.S. Eagle.

After the ceremony, as people began to drift away, Old Anna turned to me. "Sunflower, you will stay to sing at my grave." She pronounced this instruction in the same autocratic tone she'd used to explain Thomas' death to me.

There was no question as to whether or not I would.

I said goodbye to my family, to Jensen, to Joe, to Bill, and I dashed off a letter of resignation for Jenny to take back to the *Chicago Tribune.* Despite her willingness to be there to comfort and steady me, Jenny's nose was out of joint because I had never told her that her blond "River Jesus" was my brother. She assumed it was because I was angry that she had been attracted to him. My reasons had more to do with superstition. I had not wanted to share Thomas' existence with anyone. Once I began to talk about him, I feared he would disappear. Furthermore, it would have been hard to keep a lid on the T. S. Eagle secret once I told Jenny. At any rate, in a tearful conversation, as we parted, I told her. "If it hadn't been for you, Jenny, I would never have found him." We left one another with our friendship intact.

And so as everyone left, I stayed behind to continue sleeping on the couch in Old Anna's small apartment which was situated behind a gift shop named "Sally's Trading Post." As Sally explained it, "Indian people learned long ago that tourists would stop anytime they saw a sign saying trading post."

"The only thing that gets traded here," added Sally, pointing her chin toward a group of yakking old Indian women, "is gossip." Indeed, Sally's inventory of tacky Indian dolls, plaster of Paris buffaloes, and feathery dream catchers seemed not to diminish with passing days. However, the fresh bread she baked each morning disappeared off the shelves by noon.

There followed several days of sitting across a kitchen table and listening, yes, even taking notes, at Old Anna's invitation, as she recounted the bare outlines of her ninety-six years. She spoke in her tribal language most of the time and Sally translated.

Old Anna explained that she was the daughter of a Cheyenne woman named Burning Fire, who had been captured and brought to Indian Territory from Palo Duro Canyon. She was among the band that left Oklahoma with Chief Dull Knife in a defiant journey to the north land of the Cheyenne. Burning Fire survived the bloody uprising at Fort Robinson, Nebraska, by running so fast she outdistanced the white soldiers—even though she was pregnant and had taken a bullet in the abdomen. Burning Fire was found unconscious, half-frozen in a blizzard and rescued by a kind white ranch woman who took her in and cared for her. Her baby boy was born dead a few days later. Burning Fire stayed on at the ranch, grateful for the kindness shown her, helping with household chores. One day she jumped bareback onto an unbroken horse and earned the admiration of the ranch hands by showing off her horse-riding skills. She soon became the "cowhand" who broke the difficult horses. When the rancher's eldest son married, his new wife found it impossible to live in the shadow of her husband's parents. And so the son and his wife decided to move south. They asked that Burning Fire come with them to help with the move. Burning Fire did not want to leave the kind older woman to whom she felt a bond for saving her life. But she did as she was asked, journeying south with the rancher's son and his wife to a new home on the Plains that were once the *Nadi-ish-dena's* sacred hunting grounds near the Great Buffalo River. Burning Fire was happy to be on the Plains her adopted mother, Wind Storm, had so lovingly described. But she endured harsh treatment at the hands of the rancher's wife who regarded her as a slave. When some years later she bore a second son—for she had become the rancher's lover—the wife stole the baby and banished Burning Fire, paying a teamster to transport her to Indian Territory. He was a cruel and vulgar man who repeatedly raped Burning Fire during the trip and kept her tied up in the wagon to prevent her from running away. In Oklahoma, Burning Fire was reunited with Wind Storm, daughter of Gentle Wind. Heartbroken at the loss of yet another baby, Burning Fire nearly died of the injuries to her body and spirit during the cruel journey to Oklahoma. Patiently, Wind Storm nursed the beloved daughter, for whom she had stayed alive long after her spirit wished to leave the earth. After recovering, Burning Fire married a *Nadi-ish-dena* medicine man and she bore a third child, a daughter. But even as her baby drew first breath, Burning Fire took her last. The now elderly Wind Storm raised the girl, naming her Running Antelope which had been Burning Fire's name before the dark day in Palo Duro Canyon.

"That is me. Running Antelope," the old woman finished in English, as she folded her arms across her chest.

LATER THAT DAY, WHILE OLD ANNA napped I ventured down the street a few blocks to buy aspirin. I found myself in an old-fashioned drugstore that resembled the one in the Odyssey of my childhood. It had a soda fountain with padded round stools and a red and gray Formica countertop. On a happier day I would have ordered a cherry coke and sipped it slowly. While waiting in line at the cash register, I overheard two white-haired town ladies clucking over the infamous shootout. "It's time someone cleaned these drug dealers out of here. Did you know there was a meth lab up there on the second floor?" one woman whined to her companion. "Why they were selling the stuff openly right on the street. It brings in all kinds of riff-raff. That guy with the ponytail came to buy drugs. I guess he got what he deserved."

I was burning with anger, but restrained myself. Back out on the street, I felt a need to know more. I spotted a teenage girl with hair braided in fashionable cornrows whom I'd seen in the cultural center's homework room. She was loitering outside the drugstore with a group of friends.

"About that shooting," I asked her. "Is it true there was a meth lab up in that apartment?"

"Oh, yeah. These two guys—one of them was Kiowa"—the girl gave me a knowing look—"they'd been brewing drugs up there. They got in a fight."

She took me by the arm and pulled me away from her friends and whispered, "But the truth is, Old Anna put a curse on them." Then, remembering my loss, she suddenly became embarrassed. "I'm sorry about your brother. I guess he just got in the way. In the wrong place at the wrong time, you know."

"My brother was always trying to be the peacemaker," I explained.

"Old Anna says your brother was a prophet."

Back at the apartment I asked Sally about the rumor on the street that Old Anna had put a curse on the drug dealers. She smiled. "Oh, you might say that. A few days ago she climbed those stairs up to the second floor and burst into the apartment. She gave them a talking to, you can be sure of that. I raced up the stairs when I realized where she'd gone. She told them if they didn't stop making and selling White Man's drugs, they'd die by those drugs. The Kiowa one was quite disrespectful. He said, 'Old Hag, I'll bet you took peyote in your day. This ain't no difference.' Old Anna told them that peyote was a sacred gift to the Indian people and the visions it brought were from the spirit world, but that the visions from White Man's drugs would only bring death.

"The Plains Apache guy was incensed that his business partner could talk back to Old Anna. No matter how bad one of our own is, they show respect to Old Anna. That may have been what started the fight between them," Sally explained.

"How did Thomas come to be there?" I finally wondered out loud.

Ignoring my question, Sally continued, "She was looking out this window here. When she saw your brother walking into the intersection, she said, 'The Golden Shaman has arrived.' And she was down the stairs so quickly, as spry as a sixty-five-year-old, that I could barely keep up after her. She was running to him when he was hit."

"Did he die right away?"

"No, for a little bit, Old Anna and Thomas exchanged some words in our language. I couldn't even understand what they were saying. I saw him smile at her—a little boy smile over his whole face, like he had come home to his granny."

WHEN ANNA RETURNED to her chair at the kitchen table after her nap, I asked her the last question on my mind. "Old Anna, when you said Thomas had completed his mission, you meant the return of the children?"

"No," she said, "the return of the buffalo. The return of the children was your mission, Sunflower."

Then she corrected me further. "I said fulfilled, I did not say *completed*. No prophet completes his mission. He merely begins it. It is to others to continue."

THE NEXT DAY, OLD ANNA ORDERED one of her great-grandsons to bring the pickup around to her house. "It is time to go to your great-grandmother's grave," she announced matter-of-factly. After the previous day's discovery of Old Anna's direct bloodline to Luke, I had ceased to wonder at coincidences. Neither the word nor the concept of coincidence appears in Native American language. Nothing is accidental. In a rush of recognition as Aunt Selma's stories came back to me, I had a vision—instantaneous and fleeting, as if I'd seen it in an old photograph—of a young Running Antelope playing in the dust at the feet of two old friends, Wind Storm and Bessie Kluger, who sat on three-legged stools outside a teepee that stood beside the log cabin in which Wind Storm refused to live.

• • •

WITH MUCH HELP, WE HOISTED Old Anna into the passenger seat of the pickup. She had become increasingly weak in the last few days. Sally and I rode in the back of the pickup, enjoying the wind in our faces. Old Anna's great-grandson drove slowly down one dirt road to another until we reached a small graveyard that sat in back of a white clapboard church in the small village with a formerly German-sounding name. We stood beside the gravestone of Bessie Kluger as Old Anna released some white, underdown feathers to flutter in the breeze above the gravesite. I kneeled and cried for my lost mother and generations of grandmothers. I cried for my lost lover. I cried for my lost brother. When my tears subsided I lifted my face to Old Anna.

"I lose everyone I love, Old Anna. Why is it, that I lose everyone that I love?"

With the same impatient tone I heard so long ago from Gentle Wind when I asked about my dead grandfather's appearance, Old Anna replied: "Sunflower, do you not know that it is impossible to lose those you love. You carry them with you forever."

THAT NIGHT, WHEN OLD ANNA got up from her chair to go to her bed, she said. "It is now time for me to go. I am too old. It has been long enough already."

Laboriously, refusing help, she walked to her bedroom. I looked at Sally with alarm. "What did she mean by that?"

"Pay no attention. She says it every night."

Old Anna—Running Antelope, daughter of the beautiful Burning Fire and granddaughter of Wind Storm, the daughter of Gentle Wind—died in her sleep that night. The whole tribe gathered the following day to bury her next to Thomas, the newly entombed Golden Ridge children and many generations whose names are whispered in the wind.

THE FOLLOWING DAY I flew from Oklahoma City to Chicago. I packed my few belongings—my mother's beloved hutch, my Civil War chest, my sunflower pottery, a few books and one suitcase of clothing. Jenny helped me give away the rest and close down my apartment. I loaded my belongings into the back of a used pickup I bought for the trip. I took Diva—no more leaving her with Jenny—my cat was old and we needed one another more than ever. And I set out on my final trip west.

I could not go home. I have no home.

I headed for Taos, New Mexico. Jensen had already secured a room for me at the Mabel Dodge bed and breakfast. For several lazy days I stayed in Taos and Jensen and I sipped coffee at Rosa's Bakery in the morning and sat in the shade of the Plaza's cottonwood trees in the afternoon, swapping stories about Thomas. Jensen told me that he has dozens of Thomas' paintings hidden away in a warehouse. Thomas was a prolific painter, but Jensen had felt that if he released them too quickly, it would fuel the rumor that T.S. Eagle was more than one painter. Jenson had always handled Thomas' financial and legal affairs as well as his artistic management. He explained that Thomas had recently drawn up a will deeding the paintings, the dugout, its surrounding land, and the buffalo herd to me, with the stipulation that any proceeds I did not need continue to be distributed to grassland preservation projects and various bison management schools. I assured Robert that I could make a living off my writing and would not need to touch any of Thomas' funds. Jensen smiled and said, "Thomas said that was what you'd say."

"And what did he tell you to answer?"

"That with ownership came the responsibility to learn to love the buffalo."

I could see Thomas' little boy grin spread across his face when he said that, and I had to turn away for a moment and contemplate the tinkling of the cottonwood leaves above the bench where we sat until the choking feeling in my throat subsided. Then, when I could speak, I recalled for Jensen the times I would complain bitterly about not being able to walk alone in the pasture for fear of Thomas' herd.

JULY 19: There is little I need to do. Buffalo are low maintenance as long as the grass grows and water bubbles from the earth. A local Indian chief and his veterinarian son, Little Jack, have in recent years been in charge of looking after the herd, which mostly involves an occasional slow horseback ride through the herd looking for signs of disease or injury. Little Jack is also in charge of deciding when to sell off some of the stock to a packinghouse whose mission is to reintroduce bison meat to Native Americans. The packing plant, owned by a local food cooperative, believes bison meat could curb the diabetes that plagues Native

American communities who have adopted the high fat habits of white Americans. Little Jack also thins the herd by giving weaned calves to newly organized bison enterprises springing up on reservation lands.

When I was ready, Jensen drove with me out to the dugout, where Little Jack met us to help unload the hutch and the trunk. I ceremoniously carried in the Underwood typewriter that once belonged to my father. Those few items are just enough to make Thomas' one-room dugout ready for a poet to inhabit. This will be my summer home. I don't want electricity lines brought into it—Thomas, like me, didn't want the hum of the twentieth century to impose itself. I will keep the laptop packed away in my little pickup, ready for travel. When here, I will learn to scribble in longhand again, and pound the keys of my father's typewriter when my mind requires speed. I will keep my room paid up at the Dodge House so I can enjoy the company of the Taos artistic community when I tire of solitude. And of course I will travel the Southwest, just as Thomas loved to do. Joe has offered me that back bedroom in his too-empty ranch house any time I wish to come to Moab. Sally will see me when she visits her son who lives in New Mexico. Bill will come to see me frequently—he promises. I know he will love to photograph the buffalo herd just as Thomas loved to paint them.

I have no illusions. I will be alone most of the time. Alone, but not lonely.

A few steps from my dugout, I smell the fresh prairie grass. I inhale a hint of dust in the wind. When the sudden brief rain of a thunderstorm dampens that dust it releases an ancient sensuous aroma that only a plainsdweller can understand. On still mornings, I hear the meadowlark song. On long hot afternoons, I see hawks and golden eagles riding the warm wind currents—a pair of eagles seems to be keeping watch over me. At day's end, I thrill to brilliant sunsets. When night falls, I read and write within the circle of light cast by the very same oil lamp my father kept lit in the center of the round kitchen table on the old home place.

And I realize, yes, I am home.

I am finally home.

Epilogue

A family goes both forward and backward.
With us are the spirits of many generations before us
as well as many generations who will come after us.
They are all part of us. So we are never just one.
We are everyone.

Sunflower, you will never be just one.

—Gentle Wind

Author's Note and Further Reading

WHILE THE CHARACTERS in this novel are fictional, as is the specific Kansas town and county in which the main action takes place, whenever historical references appear, I have tried to present events as accurately as possible. I took particular care to research the Plains Apache Indians who once lived on my fictitious ridge, beginning with the earliest record I could find of their contact with European culture. I was very excited to run across the book *Bourgmont: Explorer of the Missouri,* by Frank Norall which presents Bourgmont's journals as he encountered the Land of the Padoucas (Plains Apache) in what is now Western Kansas. Amazingly, the French explorer returned to France taking with him several Plains Indians to meet King Louis XV. He then returned them to the Plains. The story of this journey is told in Chapter 12—with minimal fictional embellishment. Whether the attack on the hidden Plains Indian villages in Palo Duro Canyon in 1875, or the uprising of Dull Knife's band of Cheyennes at Fort Robinson, Nebraska in 1879—I have attempted to tell the story accurately. It is my hope that reading *Buffalo Spirits* will give the reader the same education that writing it did for me as an author as I researched events and wove them into the lives of my fictional characters.

A further note: much of the story takes place in fictional places such as Odyssey, Kansas, but I used real names for other locales because of their historical significance, whether it was Moab, Utah, Taos, New Mexico or Anadarko, Oklahoma. However, the characters and events portrayed in these towns are wholly fictional creations.

Sadly, the ecological information the novel presents about the Great Plains is not fiction. It is true, for instance, that the Ogallalah Aquifer, currently being drained by irrigation at a rate of twenty-seven billion gallons a day, is estimated to become depleted in about thirty years. This could return the area to a dust bowl of enormous proportions. Not only is the water that once fed the springs and tributaries of the area about to disappear forever, but the land has also been denuded of the vegetation that once thrived on the Plains. Gone—replaced by agriculture— are the native grasses that once held the soil and supported bison herds numbering in the many millions as well as a thriving nomadic population greater than the number of persons now living on the Great Plains.

We are facing a crisis on the Great Plains. What misguided agriculture has wrought on these vast Plains is a disaster every bit as devastating as the destruction of the rain forest in another part of the Americas. But this is a disaster little known at the edges of our continent or our consciences.

If you wish to delve further into both the history and destiny of the Great Plains, I highly recommend the following books, by no means a complete list, but a good start. The following books both informed and inspired me. I cannot praise them enough.

Frank Norall, *Bourgmont: Explorer of the Missouri, 1698-1725,* Lincoln: University of Nebraska Press, 1988.

Elliott West, *The Contested Plains: Indian, Goldseekers, and the Rush to Colorado,* Lawrence: University Press of Kansas, 1998.

Paul H. Carlson, *The Plains Indians,* College Station: Texas A&M University Press, 1998.

Paula Mitchell Marks, *In a Barren Land: American Indian Dispossession and Survival,* New York: William Morrow & Company, 1998.

Ian Frazier, *Great Plains,* New York: Farrar, Straus, Giroux, 1989.

Robert D. Kaplan, *An Empire Wilderness: Travels into America's Future,* New York: Random House, 1998.

Dan O'Brien, *Buffalo for the Broken Heart: Restoring Life in a Black Hills Ranch,* New York: Random House, 2001.

Richard Manning, *Grassland: The History, Biology, Politics, and Promise of the American Prairie,* New York: Penguin Books, 1995.

The last book on the list, *Grassland*, which I read some months after finishing my writing, is a book that should be read—before it is too late—by anyone who cares about the ecological survival of the Great Plains. If you can read only one book, this is it. As I read *Grassland*, I shivered as I recalled the rhetorical question from the wise Old Woman Spirit who visited the pages of my book:

First they came for the buffalo. Then they will come for us. When we are gone, what will they come for? The grass?

Previous Three Oaks Prize Winners

2002
Bridge of Sighs
by Paulette Roeske
Paperback / 1 58654-019-X

2001
Going Away Party
by Laura Pedersen
Hardcover / 1-58654-010-6